UNSTEADY

THE TORQUED TRILOGY

SHEY STAHL

Copy Editing by Becky Johnson, Hot Tree Editing

Cover Image Copyright © Sara Eirew

Cover Design by Tracy Steeg

For Marisa. You know why.

"It seems to me, that love could be labeled poison and we'd drink it anyways."

    ~ Atticus

1

REDDINGTON

AN HYSTERICAL CRY greets me as I unlock my front door. It's nothing new. Our little girl is headstrong and has no problem letting you know when she's not pleased.

My keys fall out of my hand when I open the door. As I lean down to retrieve them, I yell for my wife.

"Nevaeh?" I call out, closing the door with my foot as I set my lunchbox on the floor. "Where are you?" For a second, I listen for her to yell back, but I can't hear anything over Nova's hysterical crying from her bed. She does this at night sometimes, cries until one of us comes and gets her.

Jogging down the hall, I open her bedroom door and find her standing on her bed holding her pink teddy bear by its foot. Tears stream down her red face as she shakes. Immediately I know this is not her normal fit. The look on her face is pure fear. My heart pounds in my rapidly beating chest, and my hands tremble as I hold her close. "Shhhh, darlin'. Calm down."

She doesn't. Instead, she picks up with more hysteria and points toward her door. "Mommy! Mommy!" And she screams that, over and over again, so loud I can't help but think again, this is more than just her nightly thing.

"Okay, okay," I say, kissing her temple, attempting to comfort her by rubbing her back. "Let's go find Mommy." I keep her in my arms as we walk down the dark hallway, a lump rising in my throat with every step.

The moment I notice the light from the kitchen on, my chest tightens. It claws at me knowing something's very wrong. The walls are closing in, suffocating me, and demanding I see what's wrong.

As I come around the corner, her bare feet are the first thing I see, and then her legs. She's lying on her back, eyes closed, looking like she's sleeping. Only she's not. The sight punches my chest.

Nova's screaming hasn't stopped ringing in my ears as she struggles to get free. Nevaeh doesn't move amidst the devastating cries from our daughter. She's so still, undeterred by the noise.

I notice the blood next, a small amount pooled under her head. Everything seems to move in slow motion once I see that. Me setting Nova down, her screaming for Mommy, me scrambling for the phone. It's just like the movies, caught in the middle of a nightmare as I try to shake her awake.

She's not waking up. Her lips have a bluish tint to them, and her face seems to have faded to gray. "Nevaeh, honey... wake up." I shake her again. Nothing. No movement at all.

Oh God. No. This can't be happening. What do I do?

"Hold on baby, please." I'm trying to keep my cool with Nova in the room but I know I'm scaring her. "Hold on!"

I know she's hurt. Badly. Gently, I cup my hand under her head as blood wets my hand and I hold the phone with my other hand. "911, what's your emergency?"

"It's my wife." My voice shakes around those three words. "She's bleeding. She won't wake up."

"What's your address, sir?"

"Uh, 877 Kees St." Beside me, Nova lets out a hysterical cry as she runs down the hall, and I can't help but think I've subjected her to something she shouldn't have seen.

Fuck!

"Is she breathing?" the dispatcher asks.

I check, my fingers pressed to her neck as I hold the phone against my shoulder and ear. Nothing. No pulse. "No, she's not."

"Okay, sir, I've dispatched paramedics to the scene. They're about a minute away."

A minute? I don't have a minute. I don't have seconds.

Twisting my head to bury my face into my shoulder, I let my hand fall away from her neck. I know in my heart she's gone already, and there's no bringing her back. It's clear looking at her.

This can't fucking be happening. *No.* I want to vomit. It's rising up as the dispatcher rattles off things for me to check, but I don't. I stare at my wife, the mother of my child, wondering what the fuck could have happened. "Breathe, baby. Please just fucking breathe for me. Take a breath," I sob, clutching her hand to my chest. "Open your eyes!"

"Daddy!"

Nova's screams are like a knife in my body, over and over again. "Daddy, wake up!"

I blink at the screams, trying to focus on Nevaeh and how I can save her. Only I know there's no hope. She's gone.

"DADDY! OPEN YOUR EYES!"

"DADDY!"

I startle awake with a jolt and gasp, sitting up in the bed. My chest heaves with memories racing through my head. Swallowing back tears stinging my eyes, I look at the side of my bed that's now empty. The place where Nevaeh used to sleep.

"Daddy?" I jump at the sound of Nova's voice as she touches my forearm. "Did you have a nightmare again?"

Blinking rapidly, I make out my daughter's face beside me, dressed in her princess pajamas with her hair a wild mess. Her eyes hurt me, so badly, because they're Nevaeh's eyes.

I nod, still trying to control my breathing as she pushes her teddy bear in my face next. "Hold Teddy. He might help you." He's always a peace offering for her, so she must think I need him too.

I take the bear and then wrap my arms around Nova, bringing her up on the bed with me. "I'd rather hold you," I tell her, pulling the blankets back and yanking them over our heads.

It's not the first nightmare I've had about the night Nevaeh died, and certainly not the last.

Nevaeh had an ex-boyfriend, Viktor, who I never cared for. He was one of those guys you just didn't trust, and I *never* did. I wouldn't say he gave me a reason not to. I mean, I didn't get the vibe from him he was mentally unstable. I wish I would have, at least then I would have seen it coming.

Nevaeh and I were together about a month when I met him for the first time at a party. He got in my face and immediately regretted it. About three years later, he got his payback when I was working late one night, and he came into my home and killed her. I'm not sure he intended on killing her, but she hit her head on the counter in the process and ended up dying from that.

Two days later, they found him in his car, dead. He'd blown his own head off. Then I understood he was mentally unstable and later learned it was something he had been struggling with his whole life. Did it make it any better?

Nope. He took my wife from me and now I'm raising our daughter by myself. Nothing makes that okay.

Nova giggles as my breathing tickles the side of her neck, snuggling up against my chest with the bear in between us. "What are we doing today?"

I know she thinks it's weird I haven't gotten up to go to work yet today. I guess she's more perceptive to change than I realize. "We have to go to the church today."

Nova considers that and pushes her hair from her face as she stares up at me. I love how wild it is in the morning. She doesn't say anything for a minute, and then she wiggles. "You're squishing me, Daddy." And then she rips the covers off us and moves to sit up, watching me. "Why do we have to go to the church?"

"We just do."

MY UNCLE HENDRIX shakes his head, drawing in a deep breath. "Damn, Red. I don't even know what to say right now. Whatever I can do to help with the shop, let me know. "

Since my father passed away, his shop, our family business, is now mine and today, the shop is the last thing on my mind.

Even though I know my uncle cares, there isn't anything he can do that's going to make this any easier on me or the little girl at my feet wondering why life is changing once again. She's only five, and I can't bring myself to look at her knowing the look I'll see. The one of loss.

Her tiny hand slips into mine, her cheek pressing against the back of my hand as she grips it. Looking toward the sky, I draw in a heavy breath and struggle to calm my racing heart. Though this loss is different, the pain is equally crippling.

Before me, my father's being laid to rest and about fifty feet away, fresh flowers surround my wife's grave, the bright yellow and pink lilies almost blinding against the cloudy sky above us.

Once again, I am holding our little girl's hand as she wonders why someone she loves was taken from her so suddenly.

It breaks my heart that she looks to me—her daddy—the one person who is supposed to have all the answers, because honestly, I certainly can't explain this. I don't even understand it myself. One minute he's standing in front of me, drinking a beer on Monday night and winding down after another long day at the garage and the next, I'm on the ground performing CPR on him. It didn't matter what I did. Not the CPR, not my begging him to hold on and not to leave us. Nothing changed. He still died that night of a heart attack. Healthy man, worked hard, maybe drank a few too many beers but dropped dead at fifty.

"Daddy, why is Papa gone?"

Dropping to a knee next to her, I take her precious face in the palms of my hands to brush locks of brown curls from her cheek. Innocent blue eyes, a beautiful reminder of her mother, blink away tears. "Papa's heart was sick, and he had to go too," I say, choking back tears. "It was his time to go."

"Go where?"

"To heaven."

What else would I say? She doesn't have a concept of time let alone what happens when you die, or where we go.

Nova considers my words, her eyes dropping to the ground and then raising back up. "With Mommy?"

It's like a knife is plunged into my chest when she says that. Though it's been two years since Nevaeh was laid to rest, it never gets any easier. I doubt it ever will. She was my true love, the one, and she was taken from me, brutally.

"Yes, in heaven," I finally answer, blinking back tears. "Like Mommy."

I'm hoping that's where her questions will end because I'm not sure I believe in heaven anymore. The more questions my daughter asks me about why her mommy and grandpa were taken from her too soon, the more I doubt that I believe in religion for that matter, but I won't push my beliefs on my daughter.

"But they're going to put dirt on him." Nova stares at the grave, her brow furrowed. "He can't breathe with it on him."

"I know."

She lets go of my hand. "Tell them to stop."

Pushing her curls from her face, I draw in a deep breath. "They're only doing their job. Papa doesn't need to breathe anymore."

Oh God, did I really just say that?

I probably shouldn't have said that but what else was I going to say? There's certainly no manual on explaining death to a child.

Thankfully, I hear footsteps. Turning my head, I see my mother. She places her hand on my shoulder. "Red, honey, can you go find Rawley for me? I haven't seen him today, and I'm getting really worried."

If I know my younger brother at all, he's fucking out his sorrows in the bathroom with some chick. No way am I telling my mother that.

He didn't come to the gravesite, and I don't blame him. It's a tough day for a lot of us.

You wouldn't think it looking at her today, but my mother is the strongest and most selfless woman I've ever met. On a day like today where she's saying good-bye to her husband of the last thirty years, she is putting aside her own grief and is focused on finding my troublesome younger brother and making sure he is okay.

I nod, standing and reach for Nova's hand again. "Wanna help me find Uncle Rawley?"

Nova nods, but doesn't say anything as she squeezes my hand.

"Where do you think we should look for him?" I ask, looking down as she walks beside me. I love the way she walks, so confident even at her young age with her head up and sassy demeanor. You'll never tell my little girl she's wrong or what to do. Even as a parent, I can't tell her what to do. I have to give her options and let her decide. I don't care what anyone says about that either. I parent her the way she wants to be parented, the way that works for her. In turn, it works for me.

"I think he in there." Nova points at the church.

Walking up the stone path, I take the first step and then look back when I notice Nova's let go of my hand. "What's the matter?"

"You go." She doesn't look at me. "I gonna stay here." And then she sits on the steps; her arms crossed over her chest.

See? No convincing her otherwise.

The corners of my lips lift. "Okay, darlin'."

Turning, I hesitate to step foot inside the church, one I haven't been in since Nevaeh's funeral. I actually told myself I'd never step foot in this place again. Looking back at Nova, I bet that's why she won't come in here. Yeah, she was barely three years old when her mother died, but part of me still thinks she remembers being inside the church. I pray that's the only thing she remembers about her mother's death.

As I enter, I glance to my left and can't help a small smile that comes to my lips realizing that once again, Nova was right. Rawley's in here, seated in the last pew with his feet up and arms behind his head staring at the ceiling. I can tell he's been crying, but I'd never say anything. Not my place. We are all dealing with this loss in our own way, and I've shed quite a few tears today myself. If you knew my father, you'd understand why.

Silently I take a seat next to him, slouching. There's an eight year age difference between Rawley and me, so sometimes it's hard to know how to talk to him.

Rawley lets out a heavy breath but doesn't move. "What are you doing in here? You hate churches."

I shrug. "Ma sent me lookin' for ya. She was worried when she didn't see you at the funeral."

"Yeah, well, I stayed in the back." Leaning forward to rest his elbows on his knees, he clears his throat. "She needs to stop worrying about me so much. She acts like I'm a baby."

"You'll always be my baby brother." I reach forward, ruffling his hair with a soft smile, though it feels forced.

He snorts. "And nobody in this family will let me forget it." I know what he's referring to. The last time Rawley spoke to our dad was an argument where dad told him it was time to grow up and get his shit together. Start acting like an adult.

Rawley's nineteen. I remember being nineteen and what it was like starting out, thinking you're untouchable, and then quickly realizing you're not. Only with Rawley, he hasn't quite reached the "you're not" stage.

Mine didn't come until Nova was born and I knew then I had to grow up for her. Even more so now that Nevaeh wasn't around.

"Don't be so hard on yourself," I tell him before standing, giving a nod outside. "Come on, man. Ma's waiting for us."

Drawing in another deep breath, he gives the church one last look and stands beside me.

Rawley doesn't talk much, unless he's been drinking and then you can't get him to shut up. He's more of a recluse compared to the other men in our family. Maybe that's why he's such a great musician. He's got that brooding personality that's perfect for it.

"Hey, princess," Rawley says, messing with Nova's curls on top of her head.

She doesn't look up at him. Instead, she glares in the distance. She's upset today, and I know it's gonna take a while for her to come out of this, just like it will everyone.

My father, Lyric Walker, was someone special. Even the name was badass and he, well, I've never met anyone like him. He was the hardest working man I knew. Owning his own garage and working his ass off so he could provide us with a good life. He built his business from nothing and earned a trusted reputation through hard work. When it came down to it, there was no better mechanic than my dad. He could fix anything with a set of tools. But the truth is that as great a mechanic as Lyric Walker was, he was an even better father. Not a day has gone by as long as I can remember that I didn't know my dad had my back. When I told him I wanted to be a mechanic just like him, he never hesitated to teach me. Probably because I kept taking the engine in his truck apart, desperate to learn, and he wanted me to know how to put it back together.

Whatever my siblings and I wanted in life, my dad was right beside us encouraging us. The only thing he ever asked in return was for us to take responsibility for our lives. No excuses, just hard work. Rawley and Raven are still kinda working on that last one.

"I want cake." Nova stands, her hands on her hips. "Grammy said we having cake."

I smile, picking her up off the steps. "Grammy said that, huh?"

Rawley reaches up and tugs on her hair, just to annoy her. She swats his hand away and stares at me, intently. "I *need* it."

I give Rawley a sideways glance. "She's workin' me, isn't she?"

He nods, smiling but doesn't say anything.

Just as we're beginning to walk toward the cars parked near the grave, Raven, my younger sister finds us. Nova immediately reaches for her. I'm so grateful Nova has my mom and sister in her life. With losing her mom so young, I constantly worry that I'm not enough. But knowing my mom and sister will always be there for her, guiding her through the things I can't, brings me some relief.

As much as I'm grateful for Raven being in Nova's life, I have to keep a close eye because while I love my sister, she can find trouble like no one else. Like Rawley, Raven hasn't reached her "you're not" stage in life. She's a bit of a troublemaker, and if Nova turns out like her, I'm gonna need a gun strapped to me at all times. Don't think I haven't thought about it.

"Jesus, Red, did you brush her damn hair today?" Raven asks, trying to tame Nova's hair down by running her fingers through it.

All that did was annoy Nova, who whipped her head around. She hates people touching her curls.

I glare toward Raven. "I did brush it." I'm actually not sure if I did, or not. I might have just ran my fingers through it to get the knots out. Apparently, I didn't do a very good job because I see a knot in it now.

Raven rolls her eyes and reaches to take Nova from my arms. "Sure you did."

As we're gathered by the cars now, arguing about whether or not I brushed my daughter's hair, Mom approaches us. "Are we all ready?"

Raven smacks my shoulder as she pushes past me. "Yeah, Ma. We're coming."

The five of us pile inside my other baby, an old Chevy Nova that's definitely a work in progress and head up the street to my parents' house. Though our family isn't all that large, my father was well respected and widely loved, so the small house seems crowded when we get there. On any other day, this wouldn't bother me, but because today's a day where I want to be alone, even the smallest gathering seems like so much.

NOVA and I keep to ourselves, seated on the couch with a small plate of food. She stays on my lap, her head resting on my shoulder while she plays with the collar of my shirt and nibbles on a carrot. She has this habit of taking a piece of material between her thumb and index finger when she's tired and rubbing it back and forth. I find it incredibly adorable and hope she never grows out of it.

"Do you want to take a nap?" I ask, kissing her forehead.

She shakes her head, adamantly refusing. I don't think Nova's willingly taken a nap in her life. Even as a baby, I would have to trick her into sleep, or take her for a drive.

Raven's watching us from the kitchen. I can see her from my place on the couch with a slice of cake in hand, her legs dangling off the counter. "You want some cake, darlin'?"

Nova perks up, her head bumping my jaw when she sits up straight. "Yes."

Laughing and rubbing my jaw, I stand with her on my hip and make my way into the kitchen. Sliding off the counter, Raven immediately holds her hands out for Nova, who willingly goes to her. She sways to the music softly playing in the background, holding her close.

I take that moment to get her a piece of cake. Just as I'm cutting into it, someone bumps my shoulder.

Turning, I nearly roll my eyes. It's my young neighbor. And I say young because she's seventeen. "Hey, Red," she says, sticking a fork in her mouth to lick frosting off it. I know she thinks this is a seductive way to get me to look at her mouth but honestly, all it does is make me cringe.

I keep my eyes on her eyes as always. Sam's a nice girl, but shit she's young. She watches Nova for me sometimes but even then, I try to keep those instances to a last-resort situation only. "I'm sorry about Lyric."

"Thanks, Sam."

When I have the cake on the paper plate, I begin to walk away when she says, "If there's anything you need, let me know."

Is she serious?

She bats her eyes.

Yep. Serious.

I know what she means. She's never been shy about letting it out there she's interested in me. I don't understand it. Honestly, there's a ten-year difference between us, and I know there are plenty of guys her own age who would be happy to take her up on her offer. I find it uninteresting. And illegal. There's one thing I've noticed since my wife died. Women, especially the younger ones, they have a soft spot for a single dad. And when I say soft spot, I mean they spread their fucking legs easily.

I'm sure some would wonder why I don't sleep with any of them, but I just can't. Hell, it took me a fucking year to remove my wedding ring and even now, I carry it around on my key chain. If that doesn't scream widower with issues, I don't know what would.

Tyler gives Sam a smile as he approaches, and then bumps my shoulder. "A few of us are gonna head down to the shop to you know, honor Lyric the right way."

Sam walks away, watching me as she passes by.

I kind of chuckle because I know what Tyler means by that. This is nice, all of this my mom and aunt set up, but it's not my dad. He'd want us to be at the shop. The same place we had his fiftieth birthday party a few months back where he and Hendrix did shots of Jägermeister off the table when the bottle spilled.

That memory of them laughing and holding each other up.... Fuck, it hurts he's gone now.

"Hang on, let me see if my mom can keep an eye on Nova for a bit." I leave Tyler in the dining room and find mom in the kitchen with Raven.

"Hey, Ma?" She turns and looks over her shoulder at me. "Can you watch Nova for just a bit? I'm gonna run to the shop with Tyler for a while."

She gives me a tender smile, the one she always gives me. It's the same smile that tells me she'd do anything to make my life easier. She just lost her husband, yet she's worried about her kids. I remember when Nevaeh died, I locked myself in our room for a week. I didn't eat, or shower or God forbid take care of my kid. I couldn't even function. I'd never experienced true devastation until that moment. I could barely breathe. The thought of continuing my life without Nevaeh seemed impossible.

But here Ma is, making food for everyone and forcing a smile six days later. Raven props herself up on the counter next to the plate of cheese, which Nova has taken a bite out of every piece and put it back. "Try not to get shitfaced."

Nova comes running through the kitchen, her brown curls all over the place. She stops in front of me and pushes them out of her face, eyeing the keys in my hand. "Where you going? Can I come?"

I kneel to her level. "I'll be back before bed. I just need to check on the guys at the shop. I won't be long." I want to promise her I'll be back later, but I don't promise anything anymore. The last one I made was never granted.

"I promise I'll be home in an hour and make it up to you."

Well, that hour turned into three hours, and when I came home, Nevaeh was dead. Had I been home when I was supposed to, maybe it wouldn't have happened. At least that's what I've been telling myself.

Nova does that thing where her brow scrunches together, and her hands go to her hips. "You promised to read *Pete the Cat*!"

I hate seeing this face. She does it a lot because she always wants to keep me in her eyesight. Nova won't talk about that night, and I don't ask what she remembers from the night her mom died, but she remembers being alone for hours before I came home to find her. They tried to get me to take her to counseling afterward; hell, they tried to get me to go, but it wasn't for me and I couldn't see forcing her to go either. We needed to heal on our own.

"I will, darlin'. I just have to do a few things, and I'll be back."

My mom rescues me, wrapping her arms around Nova and picking her up. "Come on, now, little lady. Let's let Daddy get going so he can get back quicker and read you that book. You can hang out with me and your auntie."

Naturally that distracts Nova enough I'm able to sneak away.

TYLER and I pull up to the shop, the gravel crunching under the tires as we bring the car to a stop. It's weird being back in here again without my dad and even more so hearing his favorite song without him playing it.

As Bruce Springsteen's "Devils & Dust" moves through the steel building, my eyes immediately go to the spot on the floor where he collapsed, and my chest hurts. My mouth is unusually dry and a knot that hasn't gone away for days lodges in my throat as though it's a permanent reminder that no day from here on out will ever be the same.

All the guys are there, Colt, Uncle Hendrix, my cousins Jude and Eldon... everyone who keeps this shop together. We closed the shop down for a week on Tuesday, the morning after his heart attack, but Monday we'll be opening back up with me as the new owner of Walker Automotive.

Colt Davis, one of the mechanics in the shop, hands me a beer. "Hey, Red."

I take it, running my free hand through my dark hair. The moment we're standing in a circle, tossing back beers, I want to laugh at the irony of this. We did this very same thing the night my Grandpa Carson passed away.

"Hell," Colt breathes in deeply. "I still remember the day he hired me. We were just two kids who didn't know a goddamn thing about making a business work, but somehow did it."

Clearing my throat, I shift my stance slightly, my hand shaking as I bring the beer in my hand to my lips, but don't take a drink. "I know this isn't going to be easy on any of us, but I'll do my best to make it work."

As I finally do take a drink, silence spreads over us, and I should say something more to these guys as they share stories about ways my father made them feel like their presence here was needed. Each and every one of them understood they were family to him. And they were. His theory on running a business was you take care of your employees and they'll in turn take care of your business. He was right on that.

"Fuck I don't even know what to say. I can't make this any different," I tell them, my gaze on the concrete floor where I tried to revive him. "If I could, I would." My voice cracks, shaking with each breath I take. Squeezing my eyes shut, I nod a few times and swallow back the emotion building. I'm at a loss for words as I struggle to say more.

"We're gonna be all right here, man." Tyler bumps his beer to mine, the sound making a ping through the air. "We're gonna make this place work for him."

I'm not sure we can, but I'm damn sure going to try.

When someone dies, there's nothing you can do about it. You can't change it no matter how much you try. And once the angers gone, you accept it because you have no choice. Eventually you'll be forced to. Reality's a bitch like that.

2

REDDINGTON

HOW DO you know when you're in over your head?

It's actually pretty simple.

If anyone were to look at the line of cars out the door and the mound of paperwork on my toolbox, they'd see exactly what I'm talking about. It's also not helping that I have a brother not showing up for work on time because he's fucking out late again, or my sister riding my ass because the guys in the shop suddenly forgot how to fill out time cards.

See? Pretty simple.

The afternoon sun blares through the open shop doors, blinding me as it hits the top of my toolbox. Sweat trickles down my back from my black shirt attracting the sun. It's only June and already in the nineties. I can just imagine what July and August are going to be like.

I stare at the sheet in my hand wishing we had air conditioning in the shop. "Where's this car at?" I ask, holding up a repair order for a Camry that's supposed to be in my stall right now and hoping someone answers me.

Colt, whose stall is right beside mine, gives me a blank stare, scratching the back of his head. "I don't know, man."

Colt and I don't always get along. He once said to me, "You're controlling, dictating, callous, and have expectations we can't meet."

It was last week.

And then I thought, that's ridiculous. Absurd. But I have to agree, it's a totally accurate assessment of who I've become in the last month.

Days like this, everywhere I look I'm reminded of my father's presence in this shop and the hard work he put in day after day to keep it running. I'm also reminded I'm doing a fairly shitty job of keeping it going.

Every bay has a car in it. Some have been here for days as we wait for parts or whatever else we need to finish them up. I don't know how the hell he managed to keep everything running smoothly for so long.

Around noon, fucking noon, when his shift starts at eight, Rawley comes walking in with his guitar around his back and last nights wrinkled shirt on. "Nice of you to show up, asshole," I mutter when he walks by me.

I almost envy Rawley's ability to not care.

He squints his eyes, making them look black under his dark brows. Widening his arms, he smirks. "Hey, I showed up, didn't I? Why you gotta take everything so serious all the time."

Yeah, I know, I'm an asshole. Believe me, I know this. And if I didn't, I'd be reminded. Daily.

"Is this a fucking joke to you?" I grab him by his arm before he can escape me. "Don't fucking walk away from me. Everyone else can get here on time. You start at eight. Be here at eight. If you can't handle playing in your so-called garage band and getting here on time for your shift, then don't waste my time."

Rawley's icy brown eyes scan the shop and then land on me. "Fuck you." He rips his arm from mine. "You're not my father."

I laugh, once, and keep my eyes level with his. "You didn't listen to him either. It's time for you to grow up. This place is falling to shit, and we need help. It's a family business, and we're all pulling our weight for a business *our* father created. I know you pulled this shit on dad, but it's not going to work with me. You either get here on time, or you find someplace else to work."

Rawley shakes his head, rolling his eyes. "God forbid anybody pisses off *Red*. I thought you were difficult before dad died, but since then, you've become impossible. You think you're the only one that has stress."

"What stress do you have?" I practically yell, causing all the guys to stop and stare at us. "You fucking wash cars and change oil. You don't have anything to worry about but getting here on time. But you can't. You show up when you want, you live at home. It's really not that hard, is it?"

Rawley's certainly never been one to back down to me. He's actually incapable of it. Growing up in the same house, he purposely used to piss me off for his own entertainment. "It's not my fault you're doing this shit on your own. It's not my fault your wife died. Quit blaming everyone else for your shit." He throws his arms up and then lets them fall dramatically. "I'm so tired of you thinking you're better than everyone. You're an arrogant dickhead who walks around here barking orders and expecting everyone and everything to fall into place. You're not the only one who lost Dad. We lost him too. Stop thinking the weight of the world is on you only."

All right, there's certainly some truth to what he's saying, but I'm not going to agree with him.

What I am going to do is teach this little fucker a lesson, right here and now. Not because he called me a dickhead. That's daily. But the fact that he brings up my wife is what has me living up to my nickname.

Rawley's jaw clenches and for a minute, I think he's gonna take a swing at me, wouldn't be the first time, but something distracts him, and he looks over my shoulder, his eyes unfocused. "Whatever." And then he begins to walk away.

I reach for him, fisting my hands in his shirt. That's when mom screams for me to let go of him. "Red, that's enough. Rawley, get to work. Red, knock it off."

Turning around, I notice she's glaring at me too. I'll never understand it, but she babies that asshole like he can do nothing wrong.

"You wanna know why I don't go to church?" Colt asks as my mom retreats back to the office.

Rolling my eyes, I draw in a deep breath and stare at Colt. "Because they won't allow you to?"

"Sorta," he muses, and then eyes me carefully. "I don't believe in being a hypocrite. Most people who go to church and preach God to me, they're some of the biggest hypocrites I've ever met." Our eyes meet. Maybe he might be talking about me. What the fuck? I'm no hypocrite. "They go through their week, fucking people over, lying... cheating, just dirty shit. And then they go to church on Sunday, beg for forgiveness and think that'll make it better. It don't fuckin' work like that."

"Is there a point to this?" I ask, picking up another repair order on my toolbox.

"Uh, yeah. Don't judge someone just because they sin differently than you."

"I'm not the one showing up late for work every morning. He is. What does this have to do with me?"

"What are we going to do?" Colt asks, tipping his beer back as if his sinning church comment was never made. It's the middle of the goddamn day, and he's drinking, which is no surprise to anyone. Pushing fifty, Colt's set in his ways and he claims having a beer midday helps take the edge off the work day. I also tend to think it's the only way he can go home at night. Half shitfaced to deal with his crazy-ass wife.

Colt rubs the side of his head. "There's no way we can keep this place running if things keep going like they're going. Without Lyric around, this place is going to shit."

"Thanks for the pep talk, man," I grumble, tossing the repair order on my toolbox.

Colt's been working here for as long as the shop's been open since the early 90s, so I listen to what he's saying, even when I don't want to. If anything, he knows what's best for it too. And my dad trusted him.

There's some truth to what Colt is saying, but I also know my dad had faith we would keep the shop running. Since I was just a kid, about Nova's age, this shop has been the only repair shop in Lebanon. I'll be damn sure it's kept that way.

As I'm standing near the doors scanning the parking lot for a white Camry, Tyler walks up to stand beside me, waiting for me to talk to him. It's his simple way of knowing when I need to vent, and I do a lot of it these days. I never thought I'd be put in this position. Though I did know if something ever happened to my dad, his intentions were to leave this all to me because I was the oldest and showed the most interest in the shop.

Also, with Rawley and Raven only being nineteen, they just weren't ready for something like this. Hell, I didn't even think I was ready but I'm the only one with his shit together.

"I think it's time I hire someone to help us out. We're drowning," I tell Tyler. Walker Automotive would be here long after my father's presence in this world was gone. I would make sure of it; even if I didn't know how that was going to happen. I gesture toward a Ford truck parked in my dad's bay, the last thing he worked on. "We need to get the fuel pump in Dan's truck. He knows what happened, but I don't want him waiting any longer."

"I know someone," Tyler says, leaning against his lift beside us, his tattooed arms crossed over his chest. "A mechanic that is."

Tyler's been my best friend since we were smart-ass kids racing cars through the streets and getting thrown in jail when we landed one in the sheriff's front yard. He's two years younger than me and I wouldn't be lying if I said I'm probably the one who corrupted him and his need for speed.

I think for a moment, but then I know he wouldn't steer me wrong on this one.

"Yeah? Who?"

"Lennon Reeves. Been working at a shop in Oklahoma for the last few years."

Lennon? I'd never heard him mention that guy before. Like I said, Tyler and I have known each other a long time, and we mostly know the same people.

"Any good?"

"*Really* good. Fuck, man, better than me even." He shifts his weight from one foot to the other. "Grew up working on cars. Dad was a mechanic too."

"Okay, well, send 'em by Monday. If he's as good as you say, he has the job already. I don't have time to interview anyone."

Tyler's brow pulls together, and he looks over his shoulder at the office, smiling. "Yeah, will do."

I want to ask him why the hell he's smiling, but the truth is I don't give a shit. I assume he's probably waiting on Daniel, our lube guy, to come back with the parts for the race car in his stall. "What do you have going on over there?"

Tyler groans and shakes his head. "Fuckin' Daniel smashed the shit out of that thing over the weekend. Gotta replace the rear axle and then it'll be out of here." And then he smiles. "Help me out tonight?"

"Sure." Walker Automotive has been sponsoring Daniel's car for about a year. We do all the work on the car in exchange for free advertising. I'm starting to think Daniel has the better end of the deal considering how he drives his fucking car like it's a pinball bouncing off walls and shit.

"Red!" Mom yells out the door from the office. "I need you for a sec, honey."

"Yeah, Ma! Give me a minute." I turn to Tyler, only he's gone, heading toward the race car.

Mom smiles the moment I'm in the office with her and Raven. My whole family works for Walker Automotive. It's been a family effort since day one. It's the same next door at my Uncle Hendrix's body shop where my cousins work the business with their father. If you didn't like family, you had no choice here. It was a good thing we liked each other most days.

"Hey, Red," Raven says, standing with a pile of papers and then tosses them at me. "Tell Tyler I'm looking for him. He didn't call that customer with the blazer back, and he wants to know where his damn car is."

I wave her off as usual and knock her stapler off the counter. "You go tell him. He's in there."

She pushes against my chest, her nose scrunching just like she does when she's about to tell me off. But first, she picks the stapler up and puts it back in the exact spot it was, even adjusts it a few times to be sure. She's fucking OCD as hell. Everything has a place, and she's insistent it stay this way.

"Not my job. You're the boss man." She smacks my arm. "You tell him."

She's impossible.

I nod and look toward my mother when Raven's out the door. "What am I doing wrong here? How did Dad do all this?"

Mom shakes her head, tenderly smiling and moves the stapler about an inch, just to fuck with Raven too. "It's not that you're doing anything wrong. It's just that your dad was a business man. He knew how to run a business. You're still learning."

I cross my arms over my chest. "So if I were *Lyric Walker*... what would I do?"

Her cheeks warm as if hearing his name sends her heart racing. I know the feeling. "Before he passed, he talked about hiring another mechanic. Maybe it's time we do that?"

"Yeah, Tyler and I were just talking about that. He said he was gonna send somebody by and see if they might work out."

Mom nods and hands me an application she dug out of the cabinet. "Tell him to give this to him and have it filled out before he comes by."

I take the application from her. "Always prepared."

My mom smiles then winks at me. "It's why I run the books, son." She then hands me my phone. I must have left it in here earlier when I was grabbing a cup of coffee. "Elle called. Nova apparently punched a kid. She wants you to go pick her up." My mouth gapes open, though I'm not at all surprised she hit someone. My little scrapper is notorious for landing some mean right hooks. I've been behind a few. "Want me to go get her?"

Drawing in a heavy breath, I shake my head. "No, I'll go. I've apparently lost a Camry anyway."

"Oh." She holds up a receipt. "That car left this morning. Colt finished it."

That bastard. I specifically asked him where it was.

Outside the office, I push Colt and throw the repair order from the Camry at him. "Finish the paperwork."

He laughs. "Whoops. There's that car."

Grabbing my keys from my toolbox, I pass by Tyler's stall. Clasping my hand over his back, he smiles, knowing what I'm about to say as I hand him the application. "Give this to Lennon. And... my sister is pissed at you, so bad news for you."

Tyler gives me a blank stare as he takes the application, his eyes wandering around the shop looking for my sister, and then landing on mine. "You leavin'?"

"Gotta go get Nova. I'll be back in an hour."

NOVA TURNED FIVE IN MARCH, so she wasn't ready for school just yet, but I just enrolled her to start in September. I can honestly say I'm not prepared for her to start kindergarten. I have enough troubles trying to keep her in daycare. It seems every other day I'm getting called to come get her early or for fighting and her foul language.

That's my fault. I'm a bad influence and fuck flies out of my mouth more than civilized conversation does. She's also been raised around a bunch of mechanics. Kid has a mouth on her for sure.

"Hey, darlin'," I say when she's walking toward the car. She doesn't wait for me to come inside Elle's house. Instead, she's on the front steps with her arms crossed over her chest, scowling at the driveway. "How was your day?"

I don't like that she's waiting outside either with no adult supervision. I mean, Christ, she could have run off. Just as I'm about to say something, Elle's waving at me through the front window. At least she'd been watching her.

Nova climbs into the car, jumping over the seat and into the back. "Not awesome," she huffs, crossing her arms over her chest again as she gestures to the straps on her car seat. "And Dad, I'm five. Can I please get out of this thing?"

"No. You can't." Twisting around in my seat, I buckle her in and then turn back to look out the windshield. "Why did you hit Kale?"

"I didn't hit him."

Our eyes meet in the review mirror. "Don't lie to me."

"I'm not." Her eyes meet mine, her little brow scrunching.

"Then why did Elle call and have me come pick you up?"

Nova keeps her eyes trained straight ahead as if she knows she can't look at me now. "She must have seen me punch him."

"You said you *didn't* hit him."

"I didn't. I punched him," she clarifies. "There's a difference."

I lay my arm over the front seat and look at her. "In what world, Nova?"

"In most worlds, *Red*." Her eyes never break contact with mine.

"So now I'm Red?"

"When you're mean to me, you are."

"I can't wait for you to be a teenager," I say with sarcasm.

"Me too. Maybe then I can get out of this stupid car seat!"

"Maybe."

It's only around three, but I know Nova is going to be hungry so I should probably feed her before I take her back to the shop. We're halfway to McDonald's because I know that's the only thing she ever wants to eat when Nova asks, "Can I have ice cream?"

"Tell me why you punched Kale and then I'll decide."

"He kissed me."

That little fucking brat. How dare he?

"Yep. You can have all the ice cream you want."

Nova looks around when we're at a stoplight, seeing we're heading the opposite way from our house. "Where are we going after McDonald's?"

"I gotta head back to work for a little bit." I'm actually not sure why she asked. It's not like this is much different from any other night. Poor kid has spent most of her time inside a shop keeping herself busy while her daddy works all night. It's certainly no life for a little girl, but then again, I was raised that way and so were Raven and Rawley. Let's just hope she doesn't turn out like them.

Nova's eyes light up, and she leans forward a little in her chair, her hands on the back of my seat. Our eyes meet in the mirror again, her smile damn near radiating through me. It's nice to see her this happy, considering when I picked her up moments ago she was ready to punch even me. "Can I play cards with Uncle Colt tonight?"

"Colt is *not* your uncle." I don't even know how that term got started with him but knowing Colt, he probably taught her it.

"He might as well be."

"No."

I chuckle, rolling down my window as we approach the drive-thru to McDonald's. "Daddy?"

"Yes, darlin'?"

"When are you going to date? Auntie said you need to get a girl in your life."

This conversation has been coming up monthly for the past year. My sister is hell-bent on finding me a date, and now she's using my own daughter against me. Next thing you know my mom's gonna jump on board too. "I have a girl. You."

"Oh, right." She looks at the McDonald's menu out the window. "I want a toy. See if they have a My Little Pony."

"You can't choose the toy. You get what they have."

Groaning, she face palms her forehead when she sees the menu. "I don't even like Barbie."

"Welcome to McDonald's, would you like to try our new Carmel Frappuccino?"

"Yes!" Nova yells from the backseat. "With whip cream!"

"No, we wouldn't," I say, waving my hand for Nova to be quiet.

Nova crosses her arms over her chest, curls falling on her face. "Fine. Get me nuggets."

Our eyes meet and I glare at her.

"*Please* get me nuggets," she revises.

After we get her chicken nuggets, Nova and I head back to the shop. The sun is now peeking over the tips of the trees, just about swallowed by the night. We sit in the car for a moment, Nova crunching eating and me watching the parking lot as I eat a hamburger knowing it's probably bad for me.

"Ready?" I ask when I'm finished with my burger.

Nova's out of her seat immediately and reaching for her root beer next to her. "Yep."

"Nova!" Colt yells the moment she walks into the shop. "I've been waitin' on you, princess."

Naturally, she runs to the crazy bastard. I'll never understand why she likes that man so much. Then again, he may seem perfectly normal to her.

Tyler's over in the corner of the shop, arguing with Daniel. "Bring it here. I don't give a fuck." Their voice carries through the shop as I walk toward them. I turn to watch Nova for a second, making sure she doesn't trip over anything, her white sandals clicking against the concrete floor.

"Uncle Colt!" she squeals, wrapping her arms around his neck.

I'm screwed at trying to get her to stop calling him uncle.

The image sends a quick pain to my chest. She used to run to my dad's arms like that. Nova's the only grandchild and the only child that's ever in this shop. Naturally, since I work so much, she's always here and holds a special bond with everyone who works here.

Except for Daniel. She doesn't seem to like him much. Probably because she's smarter than him.

As I reach Tyler, he and Daniel must finish whatever discussion they were having because Daniel is walking toward the office and Tyler starts to gather what we need to replace the rear axle in Daniel's modified. I just hope he stays in the office for a while. I'll never understand why my dad hired that little greasy-haired shit.

I help Tyler get started on replacing the axle, only Daniel's constantly trying to help us in the process. The kid knows how to drive a car but working on them, not so much.

"You heard from Berkley lately?" I ask Tyler as we work. They broke up a few months back after dating for nearly two years. After she'd had a miscarriage, she'd called him up one morning and broke up with him. By the time he got home from work, she had his things packed and told him to get out. Since then, he's been living above the office in the apartment my dad had built there for grandpa when he retired.

"Haven't heard from her in a while." Tyler digs through his tool cart looking for the right socket he needs. "Saw her at the bar the other night hanging on your brother though."

I look over at him. "Figures." I'm not at all surprised she's messing around with Rawley. Or that Rawley would even consider her. Fucker has no morals anymore.

He shakes his head. "I don't know what her fucking deal is, but I'm not gonna keep putting up with it."

"She ever give you a reason?"

"Not one I understood." He takes an impact gun in his hand and lets it hang at his side. "Said something about needing to find herself after losing the baby."

"Wasn't she only like a month along?" Don't get me wrong, a loss is a loss, but she literally missed her period, found out and miscarried like two weeks later.

Tyler laughs, just once. "Exactly my point. I mean, I get it, she was upset by it, but to throw away two years with me over it seems a bit drastic."

Daniel leans over me and points at the brake. "Do you think that's the right way?"

Daniel's all for giving advice, but I'm not entirely sure what he's referring to because it's not like there's more than one way to replace an axle. I don't pay any attention to him. That is until he grabs the brake from me. Or tries to.

"Fuck, man," I bark, dropping the brake caliper on the concrete. "Shut up."

His head snaps up at my harshness, clearly offended. "I'm only trying to help."

"Well, you're not. You drive and change the oil. Leave the rest to us."

I've got five cars I need to be working on right now. But I also know my dad had a soft spot for Daniel and would want us to help him. Still pisses me off, though.

Ten minutes later, we're examining the old axle. Tyler and I are discussing it when Daniel feels the need to try to help again.

Tyler and I work well together. Daniel and I don't.

There's just some people you don't get along with, and everything they do seems to set you off. I suppose that's Daniel for me. I try. I do, but it's not easy.

Nights like tonight where I'm already struggling with working late seem to be the ones when he gets in my face. It's like he can tell I'm on the edge and his mission is to just push me over it.

"What if you do it this way?" he suggests, and then proceeds to do it the wrong way.

Tyler steps back, smiling, as if to say, I can't wait to see where this goes.

I look at Tyler, no doubt my face turning a little red as my blood rushes in anger. "Fuck, Daniel, you come here so *we* can fix your car. Why don't you shut up and let us do it?"

"Hell, Red,"—he wisely backs up a step—"I'm only trying to help."

"You're not." I point to the left rear quarter panel that's been pushed in. "What happened here?"

"Oh, well... you know just racin' hard."

I nod. "Uh huh." There wasn't a lot on the track Daniel didn't hit on any given night. I'm amazed he won races.

Tyler gives Daniel another smile. "Why don't you go grab Red here another beer."

"I don't need one," I say, standing up and running my hands down my pants. "Where'd you put the new axle?"

I calm down for about ten minutes, maybe twenty, when Daniel starts in again. This time talking about how he thinks we damaged the axle seal. "Are you sure? I think you damaged it."

The wrench in my hand goes flying and hits the concrete ten feet away. "Shut the fuck up!"

"Daddy!" Nova yells at me. "Don't yell."

"Dude." Daniel backs up, holding his palms up. "You need to get laid."

Why does everyone assume I'm cranky because I need pussy?

I get right in his face. "No, what I need is for you to keep your damn mouth shut for five minutes so we can finish fixing your fucking car. And my sex life is none of your business."

"Or lack of," Tyler adds.

I point the wrench in his face. "You stay out of it."

"What? All I'm saying is maybe if you found a way to release some of your tension you may see things with a different perspective."

Daniel laughs. "Yeah, Red, you should come to the track with me. Maybe you can bag yourself a pit lizard looking for a good fuck."

Did they really think me meeting some chick for a random fuck was going to make my life easier? I hadn't been with anyone since my wife and I didn't think there was a need to be. She was it for me and when she died, the need did too. Or so I thought. And the notion that I just needed to fuck out my stress pissed me off.

"Fix it yourself then. I got better things to do than listen to this shit." Turning, I walk over to my toolbox and clean up.

By the time I'm ready to leave, Nova's asleep on the couch in the office, but I know it's only temporary. She always seems to wake up whenever I move her.

"Where we goin', Daddy?"

I kiss her temple when she lays her head against my chest as we walk outside. "Home, darlin'."

When I have Nova inside and in bed, she looks up at me, those pretty brown curls falling hopelessly in her blue eyes. "Daddy, do you need anger management?"

Huh. If my five-year-old says that maybe I overreacted tonight....

Nah.

I set her glass of water on the nightstand. "No... who said that?"

"Uncle Colt."

I groan, scrubbing my hands over my face before letting them fall on my thighs. "He's *not* your uncle."

She sits up, reaching for her glass of water. "He's nice enough to be."

Taking her glass from her, I set it on the nightstand. "Okay, Darlin', it's time for bed."

"Daddy?"

The questions never end with her. I wonder if this is the case for all parents, or do I just have a curious kid? "Yes?"

"What's getting laid mean?"

Fuck. I should have known she would overhear us. Sadly, it's not the first time. I once had to explain what jacking off was thanks to Tyler. I told her it was jacking up a car and then letting it down. In some ways, there's some truth to it... just not a car.

I stand up and shake my head, smiling down at her. "You're not allowed in the shop anymore."

"Whatever." She rolls her eyes, reaching for her teddy next to her and tucks him in beside her. "Just tell me what it means."

What the fuck was I going to tell her? She knew when I was bullshitting her; she always did. Try convincing her Santa Claus is real. She flat out told me I was smoking crack that a man could fit down our chimney. Considering we didn't have one.

"It means going to bed." Believe it or not, I say it with some confidence and I think she might actually believe me this time.

"So you're tired?"

"Yep." I pull her blankets up and tuck them in around her. Leaning in, I kiss her forehead. "Night, darlin'."

"Night, Daddy." And then she sits up. "Wait... can I have a play date with Ollie soon?"

"Who's Ollie?"

"The boy down the street." I try to recall the boy down the street and then I remember he's the same one who had her on a skateboard last week trying to see if she'd test out his ramp. It was innocent enough, but no way.

"Nope."

She groans and flops back in bed. "You're so unreasonable."

As I leave her room, my skin feels hot. This parenting shit keeps getting harder, and I have no idea how I'm going to handle her being a teenager.

Making my way into my room, I take out a pair of shorts and shed my work clothes on the floor.

My house is fairly modest. Actually, it's tiny, so I wouldn't use the word modest. It's a thirteen hundred square foot rambler but perfect for Nova and me. I bought the house with Nevaeh right before Nova was born and chose to stay after she died. Not only did I not have the money to move, but this house held the only memories Nova had of her mother. I couldn't take that away too.

I did however rip out the kitchen flooring about a month after she died and put in hardwood floors. I couldn't look at that white tile with pink-stained grout.

On my back patio, I have some gym equipment. Basic stuff like a bench, some weights and a few bars. On the weekends, I take Nova to ride her bike and run beside her. Anything to get some exercise and relieve some stress.

I enjoy working out after I put her to bed. Mostly because it's quiet in the backyard and the sun sets just on the other side of the fence. Though it's dark, it's still nice to be out there.

I turn on some music, grab a glass of water and head out there. It's quiet tonight, not even a breeze to keep me company. I prefer it this way.

After four sets of bench press, push-ups and flies, I sit on the end of the bench and look up at the sky drinking my water.

I come out here most nights, and usually have Nova running around between my feet. Her cars from last night are still lined up on the edge of the concrete patio.

It makes me laugh, seeing her presence everywhere I look; it holds comfort. Since Nevaeh died, and now my father, I'm so thankful I have Nova. Her smiles, the shine in her eyes, her magic, are unlike anything I've ever experienced.

I never saw myself being a father and certainly not so suddenly. Nevaeh got pregnant after what I thought was a one night stand. I can honestly say never once did I think, "Fuck, what am I going to do?" Now I can't imagine my life without her.

As I push the weights up, my chest muscles burning with each movement, I think back to what Daniel said that prompted Nova's question. Unfortunately, the asshole was right. I did need to get laid. That much was evident every morning I woke up with a hard-on.

I definitely wasn't looking for a relationship but at this point, sex could help my mood for sure. After Nevaeh had died, it took me a good six months before sex was even on my mind. Then a year went by, and my body was doing a good job at reminding my head I missed it. Now two years later, I certainly wasn't looking for love but someone to relieve some stress with, sure, I could go for that.

Tyler hired a hooker for my birthday a couple months ago. Only problem with that was he sent her to my damn house, and Nova answered the door.

I lied and said the lady was there selling cookies. Naturally Nova wanted to know where the cookies were, and surprisingly, the chick had two boxes of Girl Scout cookies in her car. At least she came prepared. Needless to say, the only person who got any that night was Nova scoring two boxes of thin mints.

And yeah, I would have fucked her given the chance. She gave me her number and sometimes I even think about calling her.

Standing up, I'm ready to head inside and shower. I check on Nova to find she's sound asleep, and then I sneak inside the bathroom and lock the door. With one bathroom, I have to be careful.

Leaving my clothes in an untidy heap on the floor, I stand in front of the shower waiting for it to warm up. Once it is, I step inside and let the hot water wash away the sweat and grime from the day. As I'm letting the water run over me, my thoughts shift back to getting laid. I suppose since it's been two years, some needs just don't go away.

Naturally my dick is erect, forcing my attention there and making my hand unthinkingly find its way to palm my erection. It throbs against my palm, urging me to continue.

My hand slides along my length, and I reach out to rest my left hand on the tile wall in front of me letting the spray of water slide down my back. Taking a small amount of soap in my hand, I grip myself harder, imagining my dick inside of Nevaeh, the way it used to feel. I'm so hard I ache.

It's not the first time I've done this. The need, unfortunately, doesn't go away, even when your wife dies.

I'm tempted to stop myself from this, fantasies about her and what we did together, but I don't. Instead, I picture myself pounding into her, over and over again, working my hand firmer and faster. Eyelids heavy and muscles taunt, I picture her with her head thrown back, a spray of water cascading down the valley of her breasts, writhing under me as she comes, her mouth parting as she gasps my name in my ear. I close my eyes, picture her screaming out, her nails clawing at my chest and back, begging me for more as her sweet naked body clings to mine.

With the heat of the water, it's easy to imagine being inside of her. I groan quietly as my hand moves faster, urgent and desperate, visualizing my wife's pussy and what it used to be like sliding in and out of it, simulating me fucking her in the shower like we used to late at night.

I grit my teeth. My frantic rhythm on my dick increases, and my orgasm begins to surface, building pressure. The sensation began in my thighs, warmth crawling its way through my groin. With an involuntary jerk of my hips, I rest my head against the shower wall, my knees buckling just a touch. With my eyelids squeezed shut, my orgasm spills over my hand as I pump my dick slowly, drawing out the sensations.

Drawing in a heavy breath, I try to regain some composure and catch my breath.

Tilting my head under the water, I close my eyes because this is when it hits me. The overwhelming confusion settling over me as to why I'm still jerking off to images of my dead wife. If that doesn't scream rock bottom, I don't know what does. Every time I get to this stage, I'm reminded she's gone and never coming back.

"Fuck." I shake my head, breathing out slowly.

A sensation, a heaviness, collects in my chest. No matter how many times I fantasize about Nevaeh and how it felt to be with her, the truth is she's gone, and I'm alone. Nothing will ever change that, and I'm reminded I'm the one who didn't protect her that night.

3

LENNON

I HATE MY HUSBAND.

I hate that I was young and dumb and married because he told me he loved me and I believed him. Not that I was in love with him. At the time, I was in love with the idea that someone could love me. The take back child no one ever wanted for very long.

I get it, people change over time and not always for the better. And that brings me back to my previous point. I. Hate. My. Husband.

I know, strong choice of words, but anyone who says I shouldn't use the word hate, I'd gladly invite them to find out for themselves what Ben Snider is really like. Actually, I fucking dare them to spend a night with him after he's been drinking and smoking all day.

I know he's going to be pissed. He always is when I get home late. The story behind Ben and me is simple. I met him at a bar, went home with him, got married two months later. All's good, right? Nope. He turned into the biggest piece of steaming shit after about six months.

Here's some advice. Don't marry someone you meet in a bar and let bang you doggie style outside said bar. It just has bad news written all over it.

And that brings me to now, the present, as I rush through the door, my lunch box in one hand and a bag of groceries in the other, I push the door to our trailer open and step inside. Our trailer is another steaming shit heap and reeks of weed and stale beer. It's also in the middle of nowhere. No really, we literally live in the middle of nowhere. Every day I wish for a tornado to suck me into the sky and land my ass in another city far away.

Some might dare to ask, if I hate my life so much, why stay? Well here's another instance where I would say spend a night in my house. I dream of running away, I do. But this is reality and dreaming and actually doing are entirely different. I can dream I'll be rich someday but the reality of this is unlikely. I'm a mechanic. Not exactly a career that's going to get me rich.

My point is, leaving someone is harder than it looks, especially once you're married. And when you have no friends and no family around, it's even harder because you have no support. No one to fall back on when the plan doesn't work.

Ben is inside, sitting in his chair and staring blankly at the beer in his hand, tearing at the paper label wrapped around the outside of it. The television's on, though he's not watching it. No, he's obsessing. I don't even have to look at him to know.

"Hey," I say, testing out his mood and easing into conversation.

He doesn't say anything.

Nothing.

Great. So it's going to be one of those nights. Awesome.

And when he does speak, I wish he wouldn't. "Why were you working late?" His voice is throaty as if he just woke up, but I know that's not true.

Here's the thing about living in the middle of nowhere on a dead-end street. You generally know everyone that comes down your street, or leaves for that matter. That rusty black 80's Camaro that was creeping down the road when I came home didn't belong down here. But you know, if she wants to fuck my husband while I'm at work, go for it. I don't give a rat's ass at this point.

I roll my neck, the muscles sore from lying under a car all day. "Eric needed me to finish up an alignment for a customer who was waiting." I place the carton of milk on the counter next to the two boxes of cigarettes for him and the case of Coors Light. "Sorry I was so late."

I'm not sorry. I'm never sorry anymore.

He's silent for a moment. "No, you're not." He stands, coming closer to me so his breath pelts the side of my neck, his fists tightening at his side, making the veins stand out on his tattooed forearm as he sets his beer on the counter.

Breathing in deeply, I study him, taking in the stiffness to his shoulders and the hard set of his jaw.

Great. Tonight is going to go badly.

Ben leans into the counter with his arms crossed over his chest and his jaw set. "Got off work early today. Thought I would come by the shop and surprise you. Guess I was the one who was in for a surprise." And by surprise, he means check up on me.

"What are you talking about Ben?" I sigh, not wanting to hear the answer. There's a heaviness in my stomach, a chill crawling up my spine that tells me to stop now.

"I saw you. Why were you flirting with him?"

"I wasn't. I don't want to go through this with you again. I *work* with Eric. There's nothing to it. And in case you've forgotten, Eric is your step-brother. Why would I cheat on you with your brother?" And then, I laugh because I can't seem to help myself tonight. Especially not after seeing Val leaving just as I was pulling in.

That sets him off. "Why are you laughing? You think it's funny to disrespect me?"

I take a step away. "It's funny that you're accusing me of flirting when we both know *you've* done more than flirt."

He sighs and adjusts is stance, his legs wide apart. He's trying to be intimidating. Ben doesn't react much, doesn't get emotional, but when he does, it's not pretty. It's actually terrifying. He's like a tornado. No warning at all, just bam, deal with this side.

His eyes narrow. "Well, maybe I wouldn't have to step out if you'd give it up sometime."

It's *always* my fault in some way. It's how guys like him work. Accuse to avoid being accused.

Drawing in a deep breath, I try to keep myself from reacting too much. "Whatever, Ben." I blow off his words just for the hell of it. It helps me in some way. Pretend I have the upper hand in a situation that I *never* will. My whole life has been a fight for some kind of control when I know I might never have it. "Don't blame me for *you* being a two-timing piece of shit."

He snorts, wetting his lips. "Tell me, though...." He waits for me to look at him and then smiles. It's not that he thinks this is funny. He's vindictive. There's a difference. "How long have you been fucking him?" The question's asked in his low, labored voice, the one that demands my attention.

I scrunch my face in incredulity that he thinks I *would* do that. I consider the possibility of saying nothing, turn the words over in my head before I say anything, but my mouth has a way of remaining quiet at times when I need it the most. The selfish bitch.

"Keep in mind *you* live in my house," he reminds me, as if I would have forgotten. "*You* sleep in my bed. It's because of me that *you* have anything. Be careful how you talk to me right now. Show me some fucking respect in my home."

Breathing deeply through my nose, I push him back, needing the distance. "Screw you, Ben. You don't know what you're talking about. I'm tired of this crap. I can't live like this anymore. This isn't a life. It's a fucking prison sentence."

He reacts, smiling and takes a step back, his arms widening as if he's inviting me in. "There's the door, sweetheart. Go for it. Just remember when you come crawling back, you're gonna be doin' it on your goddamn knees." He reaches for me, a fist full of my hair in his grasp. "Matter of fact, maybe you need to be reminded of how that feels."

This is why I hate my husband. One of many reasons.

Instinctively, I stand my ground, despite him moving his hands to my shoulders and struggle against him. He's stronger than I am, my defensive stance absolutely no match for his bulging muscles. With as much strength as I can muster, I push against his chest only to crash back against the wall, my head connecting with the wood paneling.

Next thing I know, his hand draws back, and he hits me across the face with an open palm. It stings, but I show no reaction other than raising my hand to my cheek. Both his hands raise and he wraps them around my throat, constricting my breathing. "Don't you *ever* walk away from me when I'm talking to you. Do you hear me, Lennon? I'm your fucking husband. I will tell you when we are done!"

Does he think I'm going to apologize?

Hell no. Everything he just said only fuels my hatred for him and who he's become.

His breathing falters, the muscles in his shoulders tensing as he bends down to look me in the eyes, one hand on my neck, the other on the wall behind me. "Did you fuck him in my bed?"

"I've *never* had sex with Eric," I answer truthfully, reluctantly making eye contact with a monster.

"What about the other guys in the shop?" He speaks in a dark tone with words that roll off his tongue easily, ones laced with a bitterness that I chose to work late, as opposed to being here acting like the perfect wife. But what he's forgetting is he is the one who has been fucking other women in our bed. He's not thinking about how *he's* chosen to betray me.

My stomach churns at the thoughts of him thinking I would do that. With quick short breaths, I swallow my irritation, but I'm sure he can hear it in my voice. "Stop being an asshole, Ben."

"I'm the asshole?" He walks away, in the living room and straight to the liquor cabinet, reaching inside for the bottle of tequila and taking a drink straight from the bottle, squinting at the burn. Guaranteed, he's already drank half that bottle today. The beer in his hand when I came inside was probably a cover. "Yeah and you're a fucking bitch who can't keep her goddamn legs closed."

"I should have known when I picked you up in a fucking bar you'd eventually turn into this... *this*... I don't even know what the fuck you are beside a cunt who fucks anything with a dick." I will never forget the look on his face when he says that to me. It's one of disgust, and the meaning behind them, the blazing eyes, all of it makes me flinch back at his tone because it's not me. This person he's portrayed me to be in his mind is nowhere close to who I actually am. Sure, I slept around before him, but I didn't once we were married.

The glass in his hand crashes against the wall, and curse words are muttered under unforgiving breaths. The fury inside him is blinding as he stalks toward me.

Timidly, I stay rooted in place, my arms flat at my sides, afraid to move, afraid to even breathe as my mind scrambles for how this might end.

"I'm not going to hit you, again." He snorts, bringing the bottle to his lips and then back down at his side. It's a lie. There's an eerie calm about the way he's acting so suddenly. Something seems off. Remember that tornado theory? This is it. This is when the sky turns black and the wind picks up. "But I am going to fuck you. I think you need reminding who you belong to." He pushes himself on me, pinning me against the wall. "Have you forgotten you're still mine? People are starting to talk around town, *Lenny*." Trying to create space between us, my hands jet out against his chest. He pushes against me, leaning in to spit the words in my face. "People are wondering what you could be doing at the garage so late. They think you're fucking around on me. You're embarrassing yourself. You've embarrassed me!"

"Screw what people are saying." I shove him back away from me. "I haven't done anything wrong, Ben."

He catches himself against the wall, rage racing through his veins by the heavy breath he takes. "Oh, honey, you've done *everything* wrong since the day you were born. You're so worthless. Even your crack whore mom didn't want you."

The sound of my hand connecting with his cheek echo's through the

though I know her name was Tess, that's about all I know about her, other than she was a crack whore and died about a year after she gave me up.

I never quite found my place in life. In many ways, I was invisible to everyone around me. I *was* invisible. Nobody even knew my name half the time.

By the time I was ten, I was living with a couple in Kennewick Washington, a set of foster parents that took me in. It was the longest I had ever lived in one house and at times; it even sort of resembled a home. Maggie was kind to me, and Wes mostly kept to himself, which was fine by me.

They had family close by, so in the summers, we would spend our time in someone's backyard enjoying a BBQ and hanging out. I even started to make friends with her nephew, Tyler.

Everything was going well until Maggie died of pancreatic cancer when I was fourteen. The thing was, I liked Maggie too and when she died, it was as if I'd lost the one person who cared about me.

After Maggie died, Wes moved me to Fairview Oklahoma where his family was from. The thought of Wes sends shivers down my spine. Though he never touched me, I wouldn't have put it past him that he wanted to. He was a dirty, vile old man who moved me away from the closest thing to family I had ever known to a small town in Oklahoma where the rest of my life was destroyed. Wes didn't give a flying fuck what happened to me. I was a paycheck for him. When I turned eighteen, I moved out.

Unfortunately from that point on, he was the only family I kinda had until I met Ben. Seeing how I didn't exactly have a good understanding of how a woman was supposed to be treated, I had developed a thing for bad boys and the ones who basically treated the girl like shit.

That was Ben Snider. And the sad part was I thought that type of behavior was completely normal.

KNOWING I need a plan and gas, I stop my bronco sometime after I cross the state line into Colorado. The only person outside of Oklahoma I know is Tyler, Maggie's nephew, my kinda sort of cousin who lives in Lebanon Oregon. I don't want to call him, but I know I need to. As much as I would like to do this on my own, I need help. Tyler is a good guy, and I'm grateful that we have kept in touch over the years. He's the only person I trust.

I hold the phone against my shoulder and ear, closing the door to the phone booth and dial his phone number. I don't use my cell phone because if Ben has any brains, once he figures out I'm gone, he's going to track it. I've watched enough television to know I need to dump it and get one of those prepaid phones, but it's just something else I'll take care of once I figure out where I'm going. "Tyler... is that you?"

"Yeah, it's me." His voice sounds distant, cracking with the poor connection. "Who's this?"

"Lennon."

"What?" he asks, again, our connection fading with the sound of the rain.

"Lenny! It's Lenny, remember me?"

"No shit? Wow! How the hell are you, girl?"

That heaviness in my stomach returns, the one reminding me just how stupid I might be to think I can get away with this. "Not good." I stumble over the words, drawing in quick breath to blurt out what I'm saying. "That's kinda why I'm calling. I need your help."

"Anything you need. Talk to me."

I tell him what happened with Ben and everything I haven't told him in the past six months since I talked to him last. He takes it all in, breathing out slowly like a whoosh of breath he's been holding in. "Did you tell anyone where you were going?"

"No." My voice shakes around the words because I'm so damn nervous that this isn't going to work. Right now it's still all in my head that my plan to actually leave might actually work. "I didn't even tell my boss. I mean, I left him a voice mail but I left in the middle of the night. I have a bag of clothes and a few tools. I left everything else behind."

"Okay," Tyler finally says. "Come to me in Lebanon and I'll do what I can for you."

It's not that I wanted to put any burden on Tyler, but I also have nowhere else to go. What choice do I have?

I PROMISED Tyler I'd call him once I got into Oregon, so I stop off at a diner outside Boise Saturday night. It has a gas station next door, so I purchase a prepaid phone to make the call.

"Hey," Tyler answers, his voice somewhat cheery given it's nearing eleven at night. "I got a job for you."

"Really?" After paying for my coffee, I shove what's left of my money in my wallet. "Please tell me it's not stripping."

"No." He laughs and I can almost remember what he looks like. Tall, brown hair with bright green eyes and a boyish grin.

I remember when I was twelve I had the biggest crush on him because he was an older boy and paid attention to me. It was the little things back then. That was until I realized I was technically related to him. He just had this adorable look to him, like you didn't know if you wanted to kiss or hug him, maybe both.

"Not stripping," he finally says. "At the shop I work at."

Stirring my coffee, I'm silent because I'm not prepared for that. It's perfect. The only thing I'm any damn good at is working on cars. "Dude, please tell me you're not joking with me."

"Nope. Not joking. My buddy owns the shop. He said you basically have the job. Can you be here by Monday morning?"

"Holy shit... okay." I draw in a deep breath sitting up straighter in the booth. "Yes. I'll be there Sunday night probably."

I can barely contain my excitement. "What's the address and I'll meet you there first thing."

Tyler rattles off the address, and I write it down on a napkin and shove that in my bag as we hang up.

In a rush to get back on the road, I drive straight through until I reach Lebanon around midnight Sunday night. Pulling off the highway and into a truck stop, I try to catch a few hours of sleep.

As I lay in the back of my bronco, I think about Tyler's friend giving me a chance without even knowing who I am. I'm almost afraid to think it, but my mind keeps pointing to the fact that for once in my life, things may actually be heading in a good direction. It's a foreign thought. One that hasn't crossed my mind in a long time.

LEBANON IS a small town tucked in between the trees off the interstate in Oregon. Everywhere I look are small privately owned shops, it's the type of town people come to and never leave. Not because they're stuck here, but because they want to stay. Hell, I've been here all of four hours, and I don't want to leave.

As I pull up to the shop, I take in the surroundings. It's early, maybe around seven, but the sun is peeking over the metal roof glistening like diamonds from the rain that peppered the ground. It's a large gray building with red and white trim, two oversized doors and then two smaller ones beside it. To the right of the shop appears to be an office with windows facing the parking lot and a covered walkway around the side.

In front is a stone sign that reads Walker Automotive in stainless steel letters. Immediately I can tell whoever owns this place takes pride in keeping it looking nice.

I spot Tyler sitting on the tailgate of his Ford truck drinking coffee. I haven't seen him since I was what, like fourteen? The gravel shifts under my feet as I make my way toward him, nerves rising inside me.

By the look on his face, I'm a sight he wants to see. "Damn girl...." He slides off the tailgate with ease, standing toe to toe with my five-foot-nine frame. "You've grown up."

I shrug, burying my hands in the pocket of my jeans shorts, my eyes on my worn-out Converse sneakers. "It happens."

Stepping closer, he touches my cheek gently. "Care to tell me what that's about?"

Instinctively, I shy away from his touch. "Dropped a wrench when I was doing an oil change."

He nods, waiting for me to make eye contact with him. "Uh-huh."

He's waiting for an explanation, and the only reason I give him one is because he got me a job. "Listen, I got into some deep shit back in Oklahoma with Ben, and I couldn't stay there any longer."

Eyeing me carefully, he waits. When I don't give him anymore, he says, "Okay, so what do you need?"

"I just need a job. I don't want anything from you but a job. Not special treatment. Just a way to make some money."

"You got it. Like I said, I got you the job. He said it's yours." And then he pauses, still staring at the bruise, unwilling to let it go. "Did this Ben guy do this?"

"Don't worry about it."

Tyler nods, dropping his head forward as he rubs the back of his neck. "You know, it's been my experience, and those around me, a guy who is willing to leave a mark on a girl doesn't take lightly to her leaving."

"No, probably not." I know what he's implying.

"Is this going to follow you?"

"It could."

Unfortunately, I know it's going to follow me. As much as I would love Ben to just give up and let me go, it's not in his nature.

"Okay, well, we'll deal with that later. Red will be here shortly. Let's go inside for now."

With a deep breath, I follow him inside hoping I'm not making a mistake.

There's a smirk on his face as he looks back over his shoulder before we enter the shop, scratching the side of his face. "You don't have any jeans you can wear?"

"None that are clean," I tell him.

"Well." He chuckles lightly. "You're going into the lion's den here. Just be prepared for them to stare at your legs."

I'm suddenly regretting not grabbing different clothes in my rush.

4

REDDINGTON

WATCHING A CHILD SLEEP FASCINATES ME, though watching Nova sleep is sometimes scary. The fact that she's still alive and hasn't dislocated anything with how violently she sleeps is one of life's mysteries. And sleeping next to her is like sleeping next to a fucking boxing kangaroo. I can't count how many times I've been drop kicked right in the junk. It'll be a miracle if I can still father children.

"It's time to get up," I say, opening her blinds and letting the early morning sun in. It's the middle of June, and the sun rises around six in the morning, which makes it nice for getting Nova up. If it's still dark, it's a risk going in her room because it's like waking a bear from hibernation.

Nova groans at the sound of my voice and the light streaming inside. "But I got up yesterday." She rolls to the right bringing her pillow over her head. "Why do I have to do it today?"

"Because you need to go to daycare." Sitting down on the edge of her bed that's home to about a dozen stuffed animals, I take her favorite pink teddy from her and hold it to my chest. "Daddy has to work today." When she doesn't say anything, I remove the pillow from her head and turn her over.

She frowns. "I *hate* daycare. Why can't I hang out with you all day?"

"Because I can't have you corrupted by the guys."

She rolls her eyes and rips the bear from my hands. "Can I have a donut for breakfast?"

I scratch the short layer of hair on my chin as if I'm thinking. Nova will do just about anything for a chocolate donut. "If you get out of bed."

Her face is cute, even with her stubborn scowl. I can see her considering her options, donut or no donut, before she lets out a sigh. The breath blows the curls that fell in her face out. "You're being ridiculous. I'm corrupted by you."

Very true.

"Which is why you need daycare." A smirk plays on my lips. I love mornings like this where we're teasing each other. "Cleanse you of all the bad."

After five minutes of arguing, I manage to get her in the bathtub, cleaned up from the shop last night, and I'm brushing her hair, trying to make sense of the madness.

With a smirk on her face, she looks at me in the mirror. "Daddy, did you get laid last night?"

I nearly choke on my coffee I've just taken a drink of and set the cup on the counter as I reach for a hair tie.

I'm stalling. I honestly don't know how to answer her question. I can't for the life of me figure out why the hell she would ask me that.

It's only when Nova looks up at me and asks, "What? Didn't you have a good laid last night?" that I remember our conversation from last night.

I smile, despite my attempt to keep a straight face. "Uh, yeah. Slept great."

I MANAGE to get Nova ready, and her hair and teeth brushed before we stop by the coffee shop down the road. The girls at the coffee shop adore Nova and give her basically anything she wants.

"Hey, Red," Jessie greets me as I roll down my window to order my second coffee of the morning and Nova's donut. This Jessie girl is another one who's always giving me openings to ask her out. Only she's a kid too. Graduating high school this year I think. I honestly don't know what's with these girls. They are all around eighteen and nineteen years old and have a thing for older men. Sure they're legal, but I'm twenty-seven for Christ's sakes. In my mind, there is way too much wrong with that scenario.

"Mornin' hon." I wink at her, knowing damn well that's probably a bad idea. The early morning rain finally stopped but still drips inside the car off the door frame and onto my arm. Her eyes immediately go to my forearm and the tattoos on it. All women stare at my tattoos. Probably trying to decipher what they are and their meaning. "Can I get an Americano and a chocolate donut for the little one?" I gesture in the backseat with a nod to Nova, who's fully engrossed in my cell phone and the game she's playing.

Jessie leans out the window. "Hey, Nova."

Nova gives a nod, but doesn't even say hi, or look up from my phone. Little shit. Laying my right hand over the back of the seat, I nudge her foot. "Don't be a brat. At least say hi."

Nova raises her eyes to Jessie. "Hi." And then drops her stare back to the phone.

Jessie laughs it off, but I still feel bad. Nova has a tendency to be standoffish with women. I don't know if this is because for the most part, the only ones she's around are my mom and Raven. Or because she has a good bullshit detector and can tell a lot of the women she meets are trying to get to her daddy.

When I turn back to Jessie to hand her money, she's still hanging out the window with my coffee and Nova's donut reaching out to me; her breasts pushed up to the point her cleavage is all I see. Can't look anywhere else at that point.

I'm not sure what to say, or do, but it's pretty fucking obvious she did that on purpose to get me to look, and it worked.

I grab my coffee and donut and hold the twenty up. Her fingers brush mine as she takes it. "Thanks... I'll be right back with your change," she says, and winks back at me.

When she returns with my money, I eye her chest once more and then look out the windshield after tipping her.

I know I'm a good-looking man, and it seems being a single dad just adds to the appeal. Which I guess is the reason I have half the girls under twenty-five in Lebanon chasing me around. The thing is, I'm not overly nice or flirty to any of them. Why is it they take that as an invitation to show me their breasts?

"Daddy?"

"Yes, darlin'?" My eyes raise to the rearview mirror to Nova seated in the backseat, only she doesn't look up.

"Do you like that girl?"

She asks me this a lot. "No, why would you ask that?"

Nova shrugs. "She seems to like you."

"Who doesn't like me?" I tease.

My kid doesn't think I'm funny. "I don't like you sometimes."

"Like when?"

"Like when you make me go to daycare."

And we're back to that. Every day it's a struggle to get Nova to daycare. She wants to spend the day at the shop with my mom and sister, and while I allow it on Fridays, we can't do it every day because it's a place of business and needs to stay that way. If I start letting Nova come to work with me every day, I'd never get anything done. She has a tendency to come out of the office and watch us work, which isn't watching. It's playing with our tools and hiding them in places that takes us days to find.

"DON'T HIT or punch anyone today," I tell Nova when we're in the car outside Elle's house. My eyes are on the house when I turn off the ignition and look at Nova standing up in the backseat as she grabs her backpack she insists on taking with her.

Her lips part in surprise as she hands me back my cell phone, her hands placed belligerently on her tiny hips. "You're putting too much pressure on me. What if he hits me first?"

"Well then deck the little jerk."

I probably shouldn't be provoking her because I know what's gonna happen. She's going to pretend he threw the first punch. She's sneaky like that.

Knowing it's nearing eight, I need to get to the shop, but I also need to talk to Elle about yesterday and what the heck is going on with Nova and Kale.

Once we're in the house, Nova jets in the direction of the Littlest Pet Shop toys she always plays with as I approach Elle, who is attempting to clean strawberry jam off a toddler's face. "Hey, Red," she says, standing from her kneeling position to greet me.

With long black hair, she seems to always have perfectly curled, Elle is an attractive woman. I'll give her that much, but she screams clinger. I know if I were ever to take her up on her countless attempts to get me in her bed, it'd be a disaster.

Smiling at her politely, she pushes out her chest, attempting to draw my stare there. I don't budge and cross my arms over my chest, nodding to Nova in the corner, now laying on the ground talking to Elle's son who's crawled over to her. Another fun fact, Elle's married. I've never met her husband, and I don't think he's home all that much, considering how she's been trying to get on my dick for the last year.

"What happened yesterday with Nova and Kale?" I ask her, still watching my daughter play.

"Oh, that." I can't tell, but I think she was hoping I came over to her to just say hello. "Well, apparently Kale stole a pony from her, and Nova decked him."

I want to laugh, but I don't. It's probably not wise to support this behavior, but I love that Nova defends herself. What father wouldn't?

"Listen, Red." Elle gets closer, like right in my face. "Nova's a bit of a bully around here."

Bully? Nova? No way. Okay, well maybe a little but wouldn't I rather she stand up for herself?

Yes! I don't want to raise a daughter who's gonna take shit from anyone.

"I'll work on it," I tell her. Maybe she forgot the fact that this kid took something from her.

I leave Elle and walk toward Nova, kneeling next to her. "Hey, South Paw," she won't look at me, so I have to physically turn her around so she's staring at me. "Control yourself today."

She rolls her eyes and turns away from me. Ruffling her hair, I kiss the top of her head and then leave. I already have two text messages on my phone from Tyler asking if I'll be in soon.

"I'll be back around six if that's okay?" I ask, passing by Elle.

"Yeah, no problem at all."

Leaving my little hoodlum in prison as she calls it, I head to the shop. The drive from Elle's to Walker Automotive is fairly short, and thankfully in the small town of Lebanon, Oregon, there's not much traffic, so I make it to work well before we open.

MOST OF THE guys are already at the shop, standing around outside either smoking cigarettes or drinking their morning coffee.

I take a deep breath and give myself a little internal pep talk about how today is gonna be a good day. The new guy Tyler recommended is starting today, and I can't help but put a lot of faith that the addition of a new mechanic is exactly what we need to keep our heads above the shit storm that seems to be a constant since my dad died.

"Let me guess, there's more Kahlua than coffee in that?" I ask, gesturing toward Colt's stainless steel mug he's holding as I approach the open shop doors.

He grumbles something at me, staring off into the parking lot as he leans into the metal siding of the building, but I don't know exactly what he said. You need Colt Code to decipher most of what he says unless of course you understand grumbles and cursing.

When I walk inside, there's a woman standing in front of a car; her head's under the hood. She's wearing cut-off shorts and a loose black tank top with a black bra that leaves little to the imagination. All I saw was a hot-as-hell tight ass that leads to two long, tan legs that I want wrapped around my waist instantly.

With her back to me, I find amusement in her shirt that reads Get Off My Dick on the back of it. Classy and my kind of girl.

My first thought is how to get rid of the instant hard-on without anyone noticing. Directly followed by who the fuck is she?

The coffee girl did nothing for me this morning but *this* woman, Jesus Christ. My dick twitches again at the sight of her tanned, smooth skin, remembering how fucking long it's been. My first instinct is to tell everyone to go the fuck home so that I can run my hands up her legs and then throw her on the hood of that car.

Jesus, I really do need to get some.

She stops whatever it is she was doing and turns as I walk toward her, her perky breasts drawing my stare as she nods to Tyler who had brought this car in last night because a check engine light kept coming on.

Shit, I didn't even see him there.

"Looks to me like it's the sensor and not the circuit," she tells him, taking a step back.

As I discretely adjust myself, I wonder why the hell she's in here talking to Tyler and messing with that car. The guys, especially Tyler, know my policy on allowing customers in the shop. The only one who doesn't listen is Rawley. Not surprising since he thinks he doesn't have to listen to anyone.

I glance over my shoulder when I hear the guys laughing as they enter the shop. Everyone is heading to their stalls to get the day started and when I turn back to the mystery woman, I notice Tyler is gone. I walk toward his stall to find out what the hell is going on.

"What are you doing in here?" I ask once I'm close enough and come to a stop next to her. She's slender with blonde hair cascading down the middle of her back that she sweeps over her shoulder when she turns. The smell of her sweet but light perfume invades my senses with the motion.

She looks at me like I'm some sort of devil, brushing her hair from her face with the swipe of her hand. "What the fuck does it look like?" While her tone is confident, her body language says something else entirely. Her eyes are guarded, her gaze on my feet.

Is she serious? She shifts her gaze to my face, drawing my reluctant eyes to hers. Yep. She's serious.

"It looks to me like you're messing with shit you don't know anything about," I deadpan, glaring at her. "Shouldn't you be in the waiting area?"

She points the wrench in my face, her fiery stare on mine. "Who the fuck do you think you are?"

A slow, derisive smile spreads across my face. "I'm the goddamn owner of this place," I bark at her, crossing my arms over my chest. "Who are you?"

Her eyes widen, maybe shocked, maybe appalled, or both. "Lennon."

I'm confused. Lennon... why do I know that name? Wait... she's Lennon? Like the mechanic Tyler was bragging about?

My mouth falls open. Christ, Lennon is supposed to be a fucking dude. Goddamn you Tyler!

My eyes snap from hers and scan the shop for Tyler, wherever that motherfucker went. Suddenly he's nowhere to be found. Fucking figures.

The two of us stare at one another, and it's pretty fucking evident she's not one to back down, which I appreciate, but I'm not happy that I was led to believe Lennon was a man.

When I look at her—really look at her—my head spins. Shit, she's... well, beautiful and I know it's a bad idea for her to be working here. I don't like how in just five minutes she has me thinking of all the ways I want to make her moan my name. No, this is definitely not a good idea.

She's wearing very little makeup. She has a natural beauty and doesn't need to. Her clothes are wrinkled like she's been sleeping in them for days. Freckles dot her nose and cheeks giving her an almost innocent look, but I can tell by the glare I'm receiving, this girl is far from innocent. I bet she talks dirty too.

Fuck. The idea of her talking dirty does nothing but make the tightness in my jeans more apparent.

Nope. This is a recipe for disaster, and I need to find Tyler so he can get her out of here. I frown because this is not what I needed right now.

"What are you looking at?" she asks, placing her right hand on her hip in annoyance, yet her eyes darting around the shop nervously shows her bravado.

"I'm still trying to figure that out."

Lennon purses her lips and shakes her head, her mouth curling into a disdainful smile. I know then there's a tough side to this girl. She can probably dish out as much shit as she gets for being a woman in a man's world. "Oh yeah? And why is that?"

"I'm just wondering what the hell you're doing in here. Tyler told me he had some guy who was a great mechanic. Said he grew up working on cars."

Her face flushes with anger at my implication, her shoulders rise and fall with her labored breaths. "I *am* a great mechanic."

"Doubtful. You're a chick," I state smugly without apology.

Ah, yes, I've hit a nerve. Her reactions when mad make me want to piss her off all the time. I'd gladly do so if she'll keep looking at me like this.

She takes a small step back, and her eyes go wide in surprise. My comment takes her off guard, but she quickly recovers, twisting her mouth to one side and raising a cynical brow. "So what, you don't have women mechanics around here?"

"Not in this shop." The corners of my mouth raise. "We're a bunch of assholes."

"I'm assuming you're the king of the assholes around here," she says with a sardonic laugh

Jesus Christ, she's beautiful.

Before I can say anything else to her, Tyler claps me on the shoulder. "Oh, hey, great, you two met."

My distaste for him returns. I point at Lennon when she reaches for the hood of the car. "Don't touch that. As a matter of fact, don't touch anything. Let me have a word with Tyler." I grab Tyler by the arm, pushing him aside forcefully in front of my toolbox. "The fuck, Tyler! Explain yourself."

"Whoa, dude. Listen, she needed a job," he says immediately, raising his hands up.

I want to punch him in the fucking throat for misleading me. He knew exactly what he was doing when he conveniently left out the fact that Lennon was a smoking-hot piece of ass. Bringing her here was a huge mistake on his part. There is no way I am going to be able to focus on what has to be done if she's here. And it's not just me that I'm worried about. I wasn't joking when I said that we're a bunch of assholes here and the thought of one of these guys feeling the way I do about her only makes me more pissed off.

I exhale a resigning breath. "You purposely mislead me, asshole."

"Not exactly." He snorts a little chuckle. "I never said Lennon was a man."

He's right. He didn't. But still....

"What the fuck? I trusted you. Shit, man, you know what we are dealing with right now. I don't have time to fuck around with some girl wanna-be mechanic. We are sinking, and I need someone in here that can handle their shit. Fuck! I don't know what the hell you were thinking!"

He shifts his feet and twists his head slightly looking up at me. "Listen, Red, I know I should have told you from the start Lenny was a chick, but I wanted you to give her a chance and if I would have said she was a woman, you wouldn't have hired her. I know you. She knows what she's doing. She's been working on cars her whole life, and Wes, her foster dad was a wrencher." He looks defeated, like he's struggling with something more than this right now. "Just... man... she really needs this, and we need a mechanic. Give her a chance to show you what she's got."

I wasn't budging. No, I was fucking thinking about her legs even now. I'd love to see what she's got under those tiny shorts too. Out of the corner of my eye, I catch sight of her and the shorts, well, damn. They're short enough I don't have to do much imagining. Fuck... stop.

"Come on, Red, you know me. I'd never lead you in the wrong direction. You and this shop mean everything to me and I wouldn't jeopardize that."

He has a point. I've known Ty for years, and I know he would never do that to me. "She better be as good as you say Tyler or it's your ass I'm gonna beat," I snarl, pushing past him and heading for the office. I pass by Lennon as I walk, but I don't make eye contact. That's the last thing I need to do right now.

All I keep thinking about is there's no way this is going to work. Taking a look around, I look at the guys, and I can't figure out how this can possibly go over well. There's Daniel in the corner, opening an oil filter and watching Lennon out of the corner of his eye as she stands near the door with her arms defiantly crossed over her chest.

Then there's Colt, who's flat out staring, along with Rawley, who's doing the same. No sense in hiding it, guys. Jesus.

Drawing in a deep breath, I look back over my shoulder toward Tyler. "Don't make me regret this."

I don't look at anyone as I make my way to the office. I can't because if I look up, I know my eyes are going to find her and drag slowly up those long legs.

"Hey, baby, how's your morning going?" Mom asks the moment I'm inside the office. She doesn't look up as she hands me a hand written sticky note with a phone number on it. "Harry wants you to call him.

He's got the billboard done for Willamette Speedway. Wants you to approve it."

I nod, tucking the note in my pocket and take a seat on the couch in the office underneath the window. "Did you know Lennon was a chick?"

"No." She giggles, fucking giggles like this is entertaining and then quickly covers her mouth. "Why is that a big deal?"

"Well for one, she's a chick," I point out.

Raven chooses then to come in, leaning casually against the counter and looking out the window that overlooks the shop above my head. "So you hired a hottie. Who gives a shit?"

I ignore Raven altogether and stare at my mother seated in front of me. "She's not going to work."

"Says who?" Raven asks, still staring out the window, and I assume she's watching her. "Damn, she's got some long-ass legs." And then her eyes drop to mine. "I'd do her if I was into girls."

Mom kinda looks at her like she's crazy, which let's face it, Raven is, and then regards me. "Red, honey, give her a chance. I raised you better than to be some kind of male chauvinistic jerk who thinks women can't do what men do."

That pisses me off, and I stand. "I'm not saying she can't work on cars. I'm just saying here, with this group, it's a bad idea."

Raven turns her head to mom and takes a slow drink of her coffee. "He makes an arguable point there."

Colt comes into the office to fill up his mixer for his flask. "This chick,"—he gestures with a nod to the shop—"she didn't make eye contact with me. Should we trust people who don't make eye contact?"

I stare at him. "You didn't make eye contact either. You were staring at her tits, old man."

He snorts and sets the coffee pot down. "I'm just saying you can tell a lot about someone who doesn't make eye contact."

"Clearly you're talking about yourself," Raven remarks, shaking her head.

"Well, yeah."

Groaning, I push away from the counter when mom waves me off. "Go show her around and act like a damn gentleman to her or I'll personally kick your ass."

My mom threatens me with violence at least once a day. Every threat has gone unanswered so far.

Digging through the repair orders on the counter, I glance out the front window to see a car being towed in. I meet the tow-truck driver outside and nod to the car. "What's wrong with this one?"

He shrugs, handing me an invoice. "No idea. She said it just died alongside the freeway."

I look over the newer silver Nissan and then wave him to drop it off near the front doors. As I'm walking into the shop, Tyler asks, "Want me to look at that one."

"No," I bark over my shoulder, stalking toward Lennon, who hasn't moved from in front of my toolbox. I motion for her with a simple flick of my hand for her to follow me. Surprisingly, she does. "Looks like I'm your boss. My name is Reddington. Everyone calls me Red. I own the place. What do you go by, Lennon?" I don't bother looking over my shoulder at her. I can't.

"Most people call me Lenny." She keeps step with me, never faltering.

We stop walking and stand in front of my brother's toolbox, the first at the opposite end of the shop from me. "Rawley... this is Lenny. She's our new mechanic." I look to Lenny. "Lenny, this is Rawley. That guy over there is Daniel. You know Tyler, and the old guy over there drinking a beer in the morning is Colt."

I give her a quick rundown of the shop from where the bathrooms are, the office, the lunch room, our specialty tools we share, the brake lathe, tire machine, oil drain, places to drain the oil, smoke testers, alignment machine and our computer with manuals on them.

Finally, and though she keeps up with everything I'm saying to her, I have to be honest with her if she thinks she's going to get any sort of special treatment from me. "I go by the same rules my father went by. If you want to work here, great, do your job." I shrug. "If not, there's the door."

"I'm ready to work," she remarks, not the least bit phased by my harshness.

I'll work you out. Fuck! Stop it.

Fuck! Why does everything she say sound dirty? Shit. Stop it.

I swallow, forcing myself to look away before I answer. I need a minute to calm my thoughts before I tell her what's really on my mind, which is, I want to fuck this woman and her attitude.

I point to the Nissan that was just delivered in the parking lot "Okay, well, if you're as good as Tyler thinks, and you're ready to work, tell me what's wrong with that car."

"Is it running?" she asks, her eyes following my hand.

"Nope. Customer said it died on the freeway."

Rawley calls my name from the opposite end of the shop, holding up an oil filter in his hand. "Red, we need you!"

I leave Lenny with the Nissan outside and approach Rawley and Daniel, who work together most days as our lube techs.

From the corner of my eye, I watch Lenny walk over to the Nissan and pop the hood. She then bends forward to reach underneath. Fuck it. At this point, I physically turn to watch, gawking like a teenager. Fucking sue me. I can't help myself.

As she bends over the engine, her shorts ride up just enough to see the beginning of the swell of her perfect ass. She's definitely *not* allowed to wear those shorts. Ever again.

After I get Rawley and Daniel on track for the morning, I walk back to my toolbox and go through the repair orders for the day and who can do what. It's my job to hand out the jobs to the mechanics, as well as do work on them myself. By nine, I have everyone going on a job, but my eyes keep drifting back to Lenny in the parking lot.

I half expected her to just start putting in parts, but she surprises me with doing some diagnostic instead. She checks for spark, fuel pressure, compression, and then finally comes over to me wiping her hands on a shop rag. "There's no fuel pressure."

I smirk, nodding to the car. "So I suppose you want to put a fuel pump in it?"

She's not angry with me or surprised I'm acting this way. Maybe she's used to it, but she's somewhere between jaded and indifferent, and I kinda like that she can take shit when it's handed out.

Lenny raises her gaze from the car to mine and shakes her head. "Wow. You really don't think I know what I'm doing at all, do you?"

"Well... until you prove me otherwise, I'm inclined to think your looks have gotten you every job you've ever wanted." I push off the wall to stand directly in front of her. "If you're in over your head, just say so, *princess*."

"I could say the same about you," she says, her voice laces with a mixture of annoyance and amusement.

I'm not sure if she's saying I'm hot or what that comment is about but I like her attitude. Our heated gazes collide before I slide my eyes down her body but then I snap back to reality before my behavior can be misconstrued as inappropriate as my thoughts are.

"Honey, you don't know a damn thing about me," I say brusquely, trying to ignore the anger rising inside of me. Though I'm pretty fucking quick to judge her, I don't like her judging me.

She's undeterred by me completely, which sparks my irritation. "I need to check to see if the pump is getting power first."

She's gone for maybe ten minutes and returns.

I raise an eyebrow. "Fuel pump?"

She barks out a forced laugh and looks away toward the car, her platinum blonde hair with black streaks throughout it brushing her bare shoulders. "No. It needs a relay, not a fuel pump."

Goddamn it, she knows her shit. Fuck, this is gonna suck.

I take a step back, a frown pinching my forehead. "Well then, get to it. You're wasting time standing here with me."

She turns to me, eyes painted in angst. "Are you sure you don't want to hover over me and watch. Tell me everything I'm doing wrong so you can be a dick all day long?"

Stepping forward, she's trapped between me and my toolbox as I reach around her for the tools she needs to replace the replay. The calloused pads of my fingers lightly graze her forearm in the process, and the touch sends a jolt through my body. She shivers under my touch, her breathing increasing.

I move in closer, letting my chest mold to her as I reach around her to grasp the hose.

Stupid fucking move, Red. Stupid move.

She shudders for just a second before seeming to melt into the contours of my chest. Either that or she feels my erection, and I'm not even sure if I would be disappointed by that. I'm barely able to keep myself from unzipping my jeans and thrusting up into her right here. Hell, look at her shorts. I bet all I'd have to do is push them aside a little. "You tell me, can you handle it?"

Am I referring to my dick?

Her gaze never falters, not even the slightest. "I'm sure I can take care of it."

And I hope like hell she's referring to my dick.

I nod. "Yeah. I'm pretty sure you can handle a lot of pressures just fine."

What. The. Fuck. Is. Wrong. With. Me?

She says absolutely nothing.

With a chuckle, I step back creating space.

Fuck, Red, really? I want to punch myself. What the fuck am I thinking doing this shit?

Clearly, I'm not. Not only is my self-control on the line but my body is having an insanely unprecedented response to her.

I know what I need to do.

I need to send this woman *away*, tell her this just isn't going to work and to find work somewhere else, hell, maybe even send her over to my uncle's shop. But then, fuck that. I don't want my cousins looking at her this way.

So I don't do anything, because right now, all I can think about is helping myself.

I turn to Tyler, who's glaring at me. "I fucking hate you."

Note to self: Be more of an asshole so she wants to leave. If not, I'm screwed.

And just like that, I have to adjust myself again.

5

LENNON

STANDING in the bathroom that is clearly only used by men, I look into the mirror hoping to find some sort of answer to the one question I have been asking myself for the last two hours. What in the hell was Tyler thinking?

It's obvious that Red had no idea *who* he was hiring, and while I should feel bad about that, all I'm left with is disgust at what an asshole he is. I've been here for less than a half a day, and the only thing I can think of that would make this day any better is punching the hot son of a bitch in the face.

Wait. What? Hot? No, not hot. Definitely not hot. Okay, maybe a little hot.

Being a woman in a job that is deemed a man's domain, I've had to deal with my share of assholes over the years. In fact, I've become so accustomed to this type of behavior that I don't expect anything else. The difference here is usually once I show that I'm not some dumb blonde trying to play garage, and actually know my shit, things get better. That does not seem to be the case with Red. Nope. The more I show him I know what I'm doing, the more he seems to get pissed.

How is it that I can go from one shit situation to another?

Easy. Story of my life.

When I was five, I lived with this family in Seattle. They had two older daughters who insisted on treating me like their slave. Sounds familiar, doesn't it? That shit was straight up Cinderella's nightmare. My point? I was so glad to leave that house that the group home I was stuck after that where this girl Nora bitch slapped me at least once a week seemed like paradise.

I guess in some ways this was similar. Anything was better than living with Ben.

With a heavy sigh, I walk back into the shop.

In the few hours I've been here, Red has given me every shit job that comes in. I wasted a good hour trying to find a non-existent rattle in a woman's Lexus only to then be given the bullshit task of removing a dead fucking rat from a heater vent.

It's not more than five minutes later, and the lady is standing outside the shop doors waiting for someone to talk to her.

"I thought you were finished with the Lexus," Red says, dragging in a heavy breath. I'm clearly annoying the hell out of him being here. The feeling is certainly mutual.

I'm confused and look around the shop. "I did."

He gives me a dismissive nod outside. "Well, she's still here. Go see what she wants."

In my head, I'm grumbling the entire way outside. All twenty feet. It's not like I haven't done this sort of thing before.

The woman's older, maybe in her early forties so not that old, just older than me. With a look of complete disdain, she looks at my jacket, and then my shorts, and then finally my face. I'll admit, I didn't choose the best clothes for my first day of work, but I did drive three days to get here, and when you only pack what you can toss in a suitcase, you're limited.

"I have a rattle in my car. I can hear it," she tells me, sweeping her perfectly straightened golden brown hair over her shoulder with her perfectly manicured nails.

"I heard the rattle. It was a dead rat in your heater vent."

The woman stares at the shop, and I know immediately what's going on here. Eric, my old boss, was pretty good-looking, and he constantly had chicks coming in to work on their cars. It was more about them wanting to watch him than anything actually being wrong with their cars.

"I think Red should check it out." She looks past me; her eyes focused on him as he continues to work. "He's in there, right?"

"He is, but I'm capable of finding the rattle."

She gives me a once over, her stare lingering on my legs. I know, bad choice of attire for your first day. "You're a woman."

Congratulations, you know your genders. "I'm telling you, the noise is a rat." I'll admit, my tone is somewhat harsh and not one I should be using with a customer, but come on. She's basically implying I can't do my job. "It's in my trash can."

Her perfectly tan and toned arms cross over her chest, and she purses her lips. "I want him to look at it. I don't trust you. He's been my mechanic for years."

I feel bad for her, I really do. Mostly for putting up with him for years. "Fine." I turn on my heel and head back in the shop as Red is smiling. Who knew he could.

"What?" He looks up as soon as I'm in front of him.

I place my hands on my hips. "She wants *you*."

Our gazes lock in a stare down for a moment. "Okay," he tells me, suddenly serious, staring down at my lips as he speaks.

My tongue darts out to wet my bottom lip, suddenly dry under his stare. "She doesn't believe me."

So Red goes out there, I watch his ass the entire time, and talks to the lady and I can see she's working him over by flaunting her chest in his face, laughing and literally acting like she's brain dead. After fifteen minutes, she leaves, and he returns to the shop.

"She's full of shit. There's nothing wrong with her car," I point out.

"Yeah, I know." He chuckles, flipping a wrench around in his hand before tossing it inside a drawer and closing it with his hip. Immediately,

I imagine the power behind his hips. It's a pleasant thought. "She's a nice lady," he goes on to say, "and if she wants me to look at a rattle that's not there, I look at it."

"It was a rat."

"Well." He takes a carburetor off his toolbox. "Last week it was a bird. I'm pretty sure she sticks dead animals in her car, or she loses a lot of pets. She's been a customer for years, and she pays us. So if she wants us to fish out dead animals...."

I find it entertaining he actually spoke to me, but then I remember the jobs I've been getting this morning.

I get it. I do. It's the drill when you're the low man in the shop. You get the jobs no one wants to do, and you don't complain. The thing with Red is it's like he's waiting for me to fail. Like if he keeps shoveling shit my way, I'll jump in my truck and head for the hills. Ironically, all this does is make me want to shovel shit right back at him. I'm not a quitter, and I'm definitely not gonna let some asshole chauvinistic jerk take away my chance at a new start. For so many years, I've sat in silence while it seemed people would go out of their way to make me feel worthless and insignificant in order to make themselves stronger. No more. I refuse to bite my tongue this time. I'm nobody's princess.

"You know, I'm capable of doing the harder jobs," I tell Red, tossing a rag over the dead rat. I don't want to look at it anymore. It's certainly not the first time I've fished a dead animal from a car. I nod to the row of cars in the parking lot. "It looks like you could use the help."

I take a closer look at him as we stand there. Not that I need to take a closer look. My brain seems to be in overdrive reminding me exactly how hot my new boss is. But I stand there anyway taking in his profile and appreciating how his gray T-shirt with the words Walker Automotive across the right pec, clings so perfectly to his muscular chest. The arms fit just snug enough to showcase his well-defined biceps. His black jeans look as though they were created for the sole purpose of highlighting his muscular legs and gorgeous ass. Oh, and did I mention the bastard has tattoos. Perfectly displayed hot-as-hell tattoos. Damn. I've had to remind myself to stop drooling over them more than once today. I've also been tempted to handcuff myself to his toolbox and eat the key. Maybe then he'd be nice to me, or do something else. All options I'm willing to explore.

To top it all off, he's got a stubble across his jaw, and I have to stop myself from wanting to reach out and run my hand over it. Mostly because I have a thing for the 5 o'clock shadow look on dirty mechanics. Asshole makes a tempting-as-hell package.

Shaking myself out of my blissful admiration, I'm reminded that this man, in the short time I've known him, has made me experience more crazy-ass emotions than I thought I was capable of. The strongest of these emotions being the irrational need to pull his hair. It's shaved close on the sides and long on the top to the point when he looks down, it falls on his face, and he has to constantly push it out of his eyes.

Yep, I've got the scenario all figured out. I want to pull it while he sets me on the hood of the car he's working on, and I wrap my legs around him.

Damn, Lenny. Calm the fuck down.

Another one of the crazy-ass emotions I was referring to... confusion. I'm totally confused about what he's doing to me. Just days ago I was running from my husband because he thought it was his right to beat the crap out of me and now I'm ready to straddle this guy like a hormonal teenager.

Way to be strong, Lenny. I am woman, hear me moan!

To Red's credit, he hasn't done anything wrong except displaying a total douche bag mentality while demanding I do these stupid little jobs. But, and I'm not proud of saying this, if he walked up to me and demanded I suck his dick right now, I'd sadly consider it.

He makes a noise that sounds like a grunt as I continue to admire his chiseled arms and broad shoulders. He turns toward me, and I can't help but think how powerful he looks, like he can lift any of these cars if he wanted. "Look, I'll let you know when I need your help. I know what I'm doing," Red mutters, tossing another repair order at me. "In the meantime, take care of this."

Great. It's another rattle. "It seems to me that if you knew what you were doing, you wouldn't have at least two-days' worth of cars backed up outside."

I should keep my mouth shut.

Red's weight shifts to one side, standing as though he's completely relaxed and unfazed by me being a bitch to him. Unfortunately for him, his eyes tell another story, which I'm assuming is why he doesn't look at me directly. In just the quick glimpse that I did get, I can see in his eyes he's fazed by this. And most certainly attracted to me. "Well, *Lenny,* you better hope I know what I'm doing, or you're gonna end up living in your car."

Too late, I think to myself, and then he turns to face me completely.

His voice is low but filled with enough heat I have to look away. "And I'd watch what you're saying to me. I'm the one who signs your paychecks."

"I wasn't trying to insult you."

Red stares at me, fire in his eyes. He hangs his head; a slow shake reveals his aggravation. "Just get back to work. As you've pointed out, I don't have time to stand here talking to you."

Why does he have to look so damn hot when he's angry?

Shake it off Lenny. Right now.

Tyler, the cheery motherfucker that he is today, comes walking by me as Red stomps away toward the office. "How's it going?"

"He hates me. And that's putting it lightly." I take a deep breath and place my hands on my hips. "I can't do this."

"Lenny, I get that you're upset, and that's my fault."

"Upset? That's putting it lightly. How can you work for that douche and not want to kill him?"

The older guy I was introduced to this morning, Colt, stares at us smiling. "It takes a lot of practice, honey."

Tyler grabs my arm and pulls me aside into their lunch room out of earshot from the crazy old man with the flask in his hand. At least I think it's a lunch room. It's not like Reddington took the time to actually show me around. He mostly gestured to shit and ordered me around this morning. "Seriously, Lenny. This is on me. I didn't explain the situation to him."

I cross my arms defiantly over my chest. "I don't care whose fault it is. That guy is a fucking asshole."

Tyler holds up his hand. "All right, hold up. You need to stop right there. Red's under a lot of pressure, and he's been through hell these last two years so don't stand here and start judging him. You have no idea who he is. He's a great guy, one of the best people I know. I'll admit he can come off as an asshole, but he's got a lot on his plate, and he's passionate about keeping this shop running."

I stare at him, still not completely convinced I'm coming back tomorrow.

"I know it doesn't seem like it at the moment but this is the best place for you. Trust me on this. You're safe here, and we're a great bunch of jerks to work with."

"I don't know."

"Okay, truth." Tyler shifts his stance, and his arms cross over his chest. "You need a job, don't you?"

I nod.

"You got anybody else offering you a position?"

I shake my head.

"Well, we need a mechanic. And I'm thinking you need us as much as we need you."

He has a point. I need this job.

LUNCH TIME ROLLS around and most of the guys head out leaving me alone with Red. I'm still trying to figure out where the damn rattle is coming from on the car Red wanted me to look at when Tyler walks out with the promise that he'll grab me some tacos on his way back.

As I'm looking over the car, I catch Red staring at me. His eyes are dark and disbelieving for a moment. "For someone who not so long ago was telling me how she was capable of helping out with the bigger repairs, you sure do seem to be taking your time on fixing this one." He shakes his head, his jaw clenching as he bolts parts on the engine in front of him. "I mean wasn't it you who said I must not know what I'm doin' if we're so backed up, but yet here you are still working on a simple rattle. So I guess I have to ask, how's that rattle coming?" he asks just as I have the car on the lift.

"I'm still looking," I tell him, trying to keep my voice even, not wanting to give him the satisfaction of knowing he's getting to me. "She said it makes a noise when she goes around a corner, so I'm thinking it's a stabilizer or a bearing."

Come over here so I can let this lift down on your head.

His brow pulls into an affronted frown. Maybe he heard me. "Is that so?"

What the hell does that mean? I swear he's decided his only job today is to piss me off. What ticks me off even more is that he says it just above a whisper, and I hate it because his voice is so distant, yet it's enough that it's going to echo in my head all night. It's the kind of voice you want to utter your name in the midst of an orgasm. "Did you check the wheel bearings?"

"I will." I can't wait to wipe that smug look right off his face.

Red shrugs, tossing a shop towel on his toolbox and walks into the bathroom.

"God, he's such an asshole," I mumble, looking up at the car on the rack. Reaching up under the Explorer, I take the stabilizer in my hand and attempt to move it. Sure enough, it wiggles and makes a popping sound.

"So you're the new girl?" a voice asks from behind me.

I turn my head to a pair of familiar brown eyes. Only they're not

Red's. It's obvious they are related, though. She's young, maybe eighteen or nineteen with long wavy brown hair that's kissed with subtle golden-blonde highlights.

"Hi. Yeah, I'm Lenny." I hold out my grease-stained hand to shake hers. I really should have put on a pair of gloves and there's a reason why my nails are painted black.

She takes my hand despite it being dirty, smiling widely, and I can definitely tell—though I'm positive Red never actually smiles—they have to be brother and sister.

"Nice to meet you. I'm Raven, the asshole's sister."

"Sorry, you heard that."

"No need to apologize. I get it. He's an asshole. But he's also a really good guy. Our family just has a lot going on, and Red's taking the brunt of it."

I'm not sure what to make of her, but I can already tell Red takes on more than his share. Probably because he can't let go of anything.

Raven waves her hand around, a cup of coffee in the other hand as she focuses her eyes over my shoulder. "So listen, the reason I came over here is I was wondering if you want to hang out sometime? It's a small town, so it's obvious you're new, and I have to admit I find that very attractive. Oh, wait... not like in a 'hey, you want to make-out on Snapchat kind of way,' although that could be fun because you're hot, but in a 'it would be nice to hang out with someone who doesn't remember what I looked like when I had braces and made the mistake of perming my hair.'"

After she says this, Raven stares off into space pinching her brows so that her face looks like she is remembering something very painful. I'm beginning to think something might be wrong with her and my eyes go wide. "You okay?"

Suddenly she snaps out of it and shakes her head. "Let me tell you, back then the struggle to be normal was real. Anyway,"—she waves her hand around again—"like I was saying, I thought it would be cool to spend some time and get to know each other. Maybe go down to the river and hang out. There's usually some kind of party going on any given day."

I can't help but smile. Raven is obviously *nothing* like her brother. Thank fuck. I can only take one of him. She's open and friendly, and I honestly can't help but hope for the first time since I got here that maybe things could work out.

And then she leans in. "By the way, I *love* your shirt."

Yeah. We are going to get along just fine. I tug on the front of it looking down at the Beastie Boy symbol. "It's the only clean shirt I had. I know it's inappropriate but..."

"Nope. You'll fit in great with these crazy bastards. Even my dad would have laughed at it."

Raven is talking my ear off about some mystery guy that she's been "kinda" seeing, though she says his name is not important, and she can't figure out if the relationship is headed anywhere when I notice a young guy with a smirk on his face that can only lead to problems approaching us.

Raven reacts before he can speak and shoves her hand in his face. "Go away, shitballs."

The guy acts like he didn't even hear her when he looks at me and takes his time looking me over from head to toe. I guess I pass inspection because when his eyes reach mine again, he gives me an appreciative wink. "You must be Lenny."

I stand there staring at him. He looks like Red, just shorter, about Raven's height. "Yeah, and who must you be?"

He extends his hand for me to shake. "I'm Rawley."

As I take Rawley's hand, I can see out of the corner of my eye that Red comes back, his attention on us. And since I've had tons of experience with this today, I can say with complete confidence that he is pissed. The question is why?

A quick thought that maybe he is angry that Rawley is outwardly flirting with me jumps into my head. I quickly shrug away the thought.

He made it pretty obvious from his behavior so far today that he could give two shits who flirts with me.

I glance back to Rawley, and it's pretty obvious he is aware of Red's reaction also as he decides to hold onto my hand a little longer than necessary while giving me what I'm guessing is his best panty-dropping smile.

I guess it could work for some. Not me, but some.

When Rawley finally decides to let me have my hand back, he folds his arms across his chest and shoots Red a quick smirk.

"Since you're new in town, maybe I could show you around." He's flirting for sure. Look at that smirk, totally flirting. "My band is playing tonight at Torque. You can come by to listen and then we can grab a beer afterward."

Is this guy for real? I look toward Raven, and she grabs Rawley by the arm pulling him away from me.

Raven eyes him disapprovingly. "Seriously, Rawley. Cut the shit. She doesn't want chlamydia and you're gonna piss him off, and you know what happens when he gets pissed off. We'll all be miserable."

He smirks while backing away, holding his hands up in defense. "Yeah, well it's too late. I piss him off just by breathing."

I can hear Raven let out a deep breath and then turn to me. "I don't get it. I spent nine months with my legs wrapped around his torso and we couldn't be more different."

I raise an eyebrow. "You two dated?"

"Oh hell no!" She mock gags. "Rawley is my twin. And as you can see I'm clearly the more attractive of the two."

She then leans in like she is going to tell me a secret. "Don't let these guys corrupt you. They're fuckers."

I smile. Red's sister is cool. I wonder what went wrong with the other two.

With a heavy breath, I make my way over to Red wondering if this day will ever end. I watch him for a moment, admiring the way his tatted-up arms flex as he unbolts an intake manifold. There's a sheen of sweat covering him, as I swear it's a hundred degrees in this shop.

There's a brief second where I envision the two of us fucking against the wall and the way his forearms would make that same flexing motion as he holds me still.

Stop. It. Right. Now.

"Did you find that rattle on the Explorer?" Red's left eyebrow rises a fraction. The very way he stands there tells me he's an asshole and has me burying any "wall fucking" thoughts I have. I've got a very distinct asshole radar these days, and it's definitely going off. Not unlike his brother his eyes move up and down my body but very unlike when Rawley did it, Red's actions get me to shift uncomfortably under his heated gaze.

I straighten my stance. "Yeah. Looks like it needs new stabilizer end links."

"Make sure you replace both sides, so she doesn't have to come back a month from now for the same thing."

"Yeah well, thanks for the advice, but like I said earlier, I know what I'm doing." Jesus, I'm being a jerk too.

Amused, Red gives me a nod from his position against his toolbox and moves to stand over an engine block that was open in his stall. Below him, various parts are scattered around the hoist it's perched on, and I can see he's in the middle of a big job. "Sure you do, princess." And then he winks because he thinks it's funny. I wonder if he'd think it's funny if he had a screwdriver shoved up his ass.

Ha! Now that would be funny.

I look back at Raven. "Your brother is great."

She knows I'm being sarcastic and stifles a laugh with her hand. "Oh yeah. He's a real gem."

I FINISH THE RATTLE JOB, my shoulders so tight with agitation I feel a headache is coming on. I'm counting down the minutes until this day is over.

I pull the Explorer into the parking lot and start walking back inside when I see Red again.

"Finish filling this out." Red all but throws my tax form at me that I quickly filled out this morning.

Hey, Lenny would you mind finishing filling this out?

Sure, Red, not a problem.

How fucking hard is that?

But I'm learning there's no asking with Red. Only demands.

I glance down at the paper. My fingertips brushing over the white paper leaves smears from the grease on my hands. And then I look up at him. "I did fill it out."

He steps toward me, his voice lowering. "You left the marital status blank."

"Does it matter?" I interrupt, confused and annoyed.

His eyes run over my face, and I wonder if he's looking for something. "Yeah, it matters. Look, if it's on the form, it needs to be filled out. You got a problem with that, take it up with the IRS," he rattles off.

Standing this close, much closer than I need to be, I can see for the first time not only how dark his brown eyes are, but that they have gold in them, around the outside as if to highlight their beauty. I find myself getting lost in the liquid depths, wondering what secrets he has because I know they're in there. Nobody as crass and arrogant as him gets away clean without having some sort of demons in his closet. I wonder what past pain is hidden behind those long lashes, and if it's as fucked-up as mine.

After getting a good look, I do have one assessment.

I don't like his eyes. Don't get me wrong, they're beautiful. But that's the problem. And they're inquisitive, like he knows I've got a story of my own to tell and he's trying to figure it out. I also can't help but wonder when he's looking at me, if he's judging me. Like he's certain I can't do this job and that inside, I'm weak.

Both are wrong.

I break his gaze and look at the tax form in my hand. What I don't like is that marital status question. Is it any of their business if I have a husband? A soon to be ex-husband.

Red walks away from me, so I take the tax form into the office and quickly mark the box that says separated.

"Red said you needed this," I tell the lady I assume is Red's mom, who is sitting at the desk, only to turn quickly and head back to the shop. Tyler had said his mom was the bookkeeper, and the last thing I want right now is to deal with his mom. Mostly because I'm afraid I'll ask her if she dropped him on his head as a child.

Thinking back to the tax form, I wonder what this guy's deal is. Do I go around asking his marital status? Automatically my eyes wander to his left hand in search of a ring.

Nothing. Although, he's a mechanic and they rarely wear rings.

So single... Maybe. Unless he has a girlfriend. I doubt it. Doesn't matter how hot he is. No one would put up with this attitude.

When I approach his stall, Red's spine stiffens slightly, so I know he senses I'm behind him but his head never lifts as he thoroughly studies every part he removes from the engine.

I've spent my life around mechanics and right away I can tell Red is very different. One thing was glaringly evident. Red is probably good at anything that has to do with his hands. They're beautiful; long fingers that are obviously strong, and I immediately imagine them gripping my hips and him making me scream his name. I'd scream it all right.

Lock it down, Lenny. Lock. It. Down.

I'm standing near his toolbox like an idiot, watching him work on the engine. His sleeves are snug, showcasing his tattooed arms and the muscles defining them. "Are you waiting for something?"

His voice startles me, and I look up to see he's turned toward me, a look of impatience on his face. I can't meet his eyes for some strange reason. His eyes scare me because of my own naughty thoughts about him when I look into them. Unfortunately, I'm a sucker for guys like him, the ones who hardly give you the time of day, and I hate myself for it.

"Anything else you need?"

He tosses a repair order at me. "Can you handle this?"

Standing tall, I answer without even looking at the order. "Yes."

"Show me then." His lips twist in amusement, his eyes lingering on mine for several intense moments. I try to convince myself that his stare is annoying, but my body betrays me as a warm shiver races through my body.

Is he for real?

AN HOUR LATER, everyone in the shop has gone home for the day, and I'm closing the hood to the celica in my stall getting ready to pull it out to the parking lot.

"I finished replacing that gasket," I tell Red, wiping my hands clean on a shop rag. I'm covered head-to-toe in dirt and grease and am probably a laughable site. "Anything else?"

He raises his head, looks at me and then turns away, his eyes focused on his quick hands in front of him. "Nope. See you tomorrow. We open at eight. Don't be late."

I'm just about to thank him for giving me a chance when he walks away from me.

"You're welcome," I utter just as he's walking away.

I watch his footsteps falter, and the muscles in his shoulders tighten. I hit a nerve. He stops but doesn't turn around. "And Lenny, don't wear those shorts tomorrow."

As I stand there watching him walk away from me, I huff out the breath I'm holding and remind myself I know what the fuck I'm doing. I'm not that girl who sits in silence and takes crap. I wasted a year doing that, and I'm done with it.

But even with my new resolve I can't help but think maybe this is too much. Maybe I should just find something else. This dude hates me.

No. Don't think that way.

To hell with maybe. I've spent my life working on cars, and there's not a chance in hell I'll let some male chauvinistic pig run me off now. Fuck him.

Well, a girl can dream.

LUCKILY FOR ME Lebanon has a pretty nice travel stop not too far from the shop. I'm starving. Those tacos didn't cut it, but before I head out in search of something to eat, I *need* to wash this day off of me.

I park my bronco outside the women's restroom and head straight for the shower. Setting the water to scalding, despite the heat outside I get goose bumps waiting for it to heat up. Once under the spray, my shoulders relax. I take my time washing my hair enjoying the sensation of washing away not only the grime from today, but also all the tension throughout the day.

Unfortunately, my time alone is interrupted by some chick standing outside my shower stall, intently watching me, and hacking up her goddamn lung. Who coughs that much and doesn't need to be on a ventilator?

"What are you doing?"

She eyes me up and down. "I'm waiting for the shower."

I can see why she needs to shower. She has more dirt on her than me, and her urine-colored hair is matted to the side of her head in what appears to be a poor or natural attempt at dreadlocks. "Well then, wait." I rip the small curtain closed, though I know for sure she can see me through it. Creepy old hag. "Don't spy on me."

"Can I join you?"

"Why?"

"I could wash your—"

Before she can finish her words, I rip the flimsy excuse for a curtain back open, completely this time so she sees me naked, which is a *horrible* idea. "No, you can't fucking join me. Give me five minutes and you can have the shower to yourself."

The thing is, she doesn't leave. She fucking stands there watching me even after I close the curtain.

I open it again. "Seriously, what are you waiting for?"

"The shower." And then she eyes my tattoo down my side. "I like your ink."

"I'll be done in a minute."

Butch lady looks down at my clothes on the bench beside her. "Can I have your shorts?"

I eye her curvy figure under her oversized Mickey T-shirt. "I don't think they would fit you."

She holds up my black lace thong panties. My fucking underwear. "Can I have these?"

I sigh, the shower spray hitting my face as I wipe away the water. "Again, I don't think they'd fit you."

She smiles, and I wish she wouldn't. It's scary, and I'm pretty positive she's never ever brushed her teeth. "I wasn't planning on wearing them."

"Okay." I rip the curtain closed and resume my shower. "Get the fuck out!"

Amazingly enough, she does but waits outside the bathroom. When I'm finished, I put the same clothes back on.

As I'm leaving, I toss my panties at Butch Lady eating fried chicken straight from the bone. I really do not want to know where the chicken came from. No way she had time to go and get that from somewhere and bring it back.

"Here, creepo. Enjoy."

6

REDDINGTON

AFTER LENNY LEAVES for the night, I flop down on the couch in the office trying to figure out what the fuck I'm going to do. I want to stand up and watch her walk away, just so I have one more visual of her and those shorts for later. I don't because my mom is in the office and I've spent the entire day with either an erection, or a semi. I need a break.

"How did everything go?" Mom asks, shuffling through paperwork. "Is she going to work out?"

"Shit... I don't know." I throw my arms up and let them flop back down on my knees. "If you're asking if she can do it, yes. If you're asking me if I want her here, I don't know that either."

"So what's the problem?"

I raise an eyebrow. "You know damn well what the problem is."

"Look, Red, I know what you went through with Nevaeh. She was taken from you in a way that was sudden and awful but sometimes it's okay to be a man. You've done nothing but be a dad for the past two years. And you're twenty-seven. Allow yourself to be a man. There's nothing wrong with satisfying some needs."

"Okay." I stand, ready to run out of the office and dig out my cell phone to check the time. "I'm not talking about this with you."

"I remember this one time with your dad."

"Nope. I'm leaving. Stop talking to me."

Mom laughs, reaching for her purse. "If it weren't for your dad and I getting it on, you wouldn't be here, son."

She has a point.

One I refuse to acknowledge.

We leave together, Mom's laughter still ringing out as she heads to her car.

AS I PULL my 1974 Nova SS to a stop in front of Elle's place to pick up Nova, I can't help but find it funny that it's literally the end of the goddamn day, yet Elle is always wearing fresh makeup. My mind automatically drifts to Lenny and the way she looked with very little makeup on.

Elle's standing at the door with a pair of jean shorts and her bikini top. "Hey, Red."

"Hey." I step forward but remain on the pebble stone pathway as opposed to their front porch. "Just came to get Nova."

"Okay, come in and I'll grab her." She motions over her shoulder to the back. "They were playing on the slip n' slide."

"I'm kinda in a hurry. Can you just send her out?"

"Uh, sure." Elle looks disappointed, but the last thing I need is to spend the next fifteen minutes inside while she tries to shove her tits in my face. I'm so wound up today I'd probably say something I shouldn't, like, "Where's your husband?" which would certainly be a justifiable question, but I also know I might upset her, and Nova's already been kicked out of two other daycares for her attitude.

Wonder where she gets it from?

It takes Nova five minutes to change out of her bathing suit, and she comes around the corner with her long brown wet curls perched on top of her head in a bun. Her cheeks are splattered with fresh freckles, her eyes glimmering blue against the light pink shirt she's wearing.

I smile at her, kneeling to her level when she runs to me. "Daddy!"

I love that sound. "Hey, darlin'. How was your day?"

"It was good. I went swimming!" Everything she says is exaggerated as I pick her up and carry her. Breathing in deeply, sunscreen and grass fill my senses.

Elle hands me a plastic bag with Nova's wet bathing suit in it. "Here you go."

Nova turns in my arms to look at Elle. "Why are you wearing lipstick?"

Elle laughs nervously, twirling a strand of her wet hair around her finger. "I wear it all the time." Her eyes land on mine. "Keeps my lip moist."

She should never use the word moist. Placing my hand over Nova's mouth, I turn her before she can say anything else and mumble, "See you tomorrow."

When we're in the car, Nova jumps over the seat and into the back. "She's so desperate."

"No more hanging out with Raven," I say, chuckling as I start the car.

"Uncle Rawley actually taught me that one."

I meet her eyes in the mirror as she buckles her car seat. "Do you even know what desperate means?"

She shrugs. "I think it means putting on lipstick right when my daddy arrives."

She's too smart for her own good.

"Where do you want to go for dinner?" There's no way I want to cook tonight. Though I don't cook much anyway and when I do, it's easy stuff like steaks or chicken. Shit you can't fuck up on the grill.

"McDonald's."

"No."

She pushes out her bottom lip. "We never do anything I want."

"Really?"

"Yes."

The only other thing Nova will willingly eat besides chicken nuggets is pizza. "How about pizza?"

"Okay!"

There's a small pizza shop down the street from our house. When Nevaeh was pregnant with Nova, I made frequent trips here, which is probably why Nova likes pizza so much. The moment we're inside, Nova wants quarters for the games, though she has no clue how to play any of them.

I dig four quarters out of my pocket and hand them to her as I approach the counter. She heads in the other direction leaving me alone with the kid behind the counter. "What'll it be tonight, Red?"

I stare up at the black chalkboard with the combinations written in white chalk. "Can I get a large cheese pizza with pepperoni and pineapple on one side and just cheese on the other?"

The kid writes down the order and rings it in. "Want a pitcher of Bud, too?"

I nod and reach for my wallet in my back pocket. "Yeah, sounds good."

Taking the red plastic number sign they give me, I head to a table in the corner near where Nova is yelling at the Pac-Man game to give her quarter back to her.

"Did you put the money in to play?"

"Yeah," she replies, crossing her arms over her chest and kicking the side of the machine.

"Well, did you play?"

"Yeah, but it took my money."

"If you play the game, it takes your money."

She scowls at the game, and then me. "That's dumb."

"You do this every time we come here. You know it's not going to give your money back so why are you mad?

Nova looks at the game and then shakes her head. "I guess I was just hoping this time would be different."

See what I mean? No idea how to play video games.

Shaking my head, I chuckle to myself as a pitcher of beer is placed on the table. I don't look up, but I thank whoever sets it down and pull out my cell phone. There's a message from Tyler... two actually. Both of which he's apologizing and the other asking what I thought of Lenny.

With the text, my thoughts shift to that ass again. What the fuck am I going to do? I gotta figure this shit out because all I'm thinking about is her ass and those fucking legs wrapped around me.

I've got too much on my plate as it is, and the last thing I need is a distraction at work. Though, if I fucked her, she wouldn't be a distraction anymore, would she?

No. Don't even go there, Red. She's off limits.

And that's one of the reasons why I want her.

Jesus, what the hell is wrong with me.

You haven't had pussy in two years. That's what's wrong.

"Daddy, are you listening to me?"

Fuck... I hadn't even realized Nova was talking to me.

"Uh... yes."

She looks up at me with a glare. "Then what did I say?"

I stare blankly at her and hear a familiar voice. "Can I get a small pepperoni and sausage?"

My head whips around to the cash register to see those same legs that've haunted me all day. Goddamn it. Though she's clearly showered, she's still wearing the shorts. I hate those tiny denim dick-teasing shorts so much that I glare at her without knowing it.

"Who's that?" Nova asks, following my stare. "She's pretty. I like her shorts. Can I have some like that?"

Fuck no. Never.

I let my head flip to the back of the booth and stare at the ceiling. "She's nobody. And you'll never be allowed to own a pair of shorts like that."

"She's alone. She should come sit with us." Nova hates seeing people eating alone. Doesn't matter if they prefer that or not, she'll invite them to dinner. You don't know how many times I've had dinner with the bum on the corner. The funny thing is she never invites women over. She won't even acknowledge most women, let alone a younger one like Lenny.

I don't say anything because I really do not want Lenny coming over here. I want distance from her. Miles and miles of distance.

"What does 'Get off my dick' mean?"

My head flies up from the booth. "What did you say?"

Nova just sighs and points toward Lenny. "I said, what does 'Get off my dick' mean?"

Realizing she is talking about Lenny's shirt, I ask, "When did you learn to read?"

"Uncle Colt's been teaching me to read." She shrugs. "What does it mean?"

Fucking Colt. What the hell is he reading to her that she knows how to spell dick?

Here's the thing. I never taught my kid the proper anatomy. I just didn't. When she was little and learning she had private parts, she called it her potty. So I went with it. I'm not sure how, but she understood I had something different and called it a tinkle. I wasn't exactly okay with my kid walking around saying penis and vagina. Don't ask me why. It just sounded too grown up. So I let it go, and we continued with the potty and tinkle.

I *never* want the word dick coming out of her mouth again. That's for sure.

"I don't know what it means," I mumble.

Nova shrugs, buying my bullshit excuse.

Just as our pizza arrives, Lenny turns and looks right at me. Probably because she can feel my stare on her ass. I shift further down in the booth away from Nova because of my reaction to the legs. *Goddamn, this is awful.*

Lenny stares at me and then looks to Nova, who is smiling at her and returns the smile. "What are you doing here?"

"What does it look like?" I gesture to the pizza and beer with a flick of my wrist. I know I'm being mean but damn it, I'm trying to get away from this chick, not spend more time with her. It's only Monday. Imagine what the rest of the week is going to be like for me.

"Daddy, be nice!" Nova drives her sneaker-covered foot right into my shin.

My glare snaps to hers, and Nova looks pretty fucking pleased with herself. Little shit. She stares up at Lenny and then me. "Who is she?"

"Sorry, this is my daughter, Nova." I lean forward, rubbing my shin. "Nova, this is Lennon. She works with me now."

Nova perks up and stands on the seat. "You're a mechanic? I want to be one but Daddy says no."

I sigh and turn my head to face her. "You're five."

"So what." Nova raises an eyebrow and stares at me. "That don't mean I can't be one. I wanna go to the shop every day, but Daddy says I'm too little, but Uncle Colt says Daddy is just an egotistical jerk."

Lenny snorts with laughter.

Figures Colt would say that. "It's egotistical… and for the last time, Nova, that man is not your uncle."

She rolls her eyes and turns her body toward Lenny. "Can you sit with us?"

With the way Lenny looks at me, and then Nova, I can tell she's completely fucking amused that a five-year-old rules my life.

"Sit with us," Nova says again, patting the seat.

Lenny's eyes snap to mine as if she thinks I'm going to tell her to get lost. Though I want to, I can't because Nova will more than likely start freaking crying if I do.

"No, that's okay. It looks like you and your daddy are having a nice dinner together," she says, and then the kid behind the counter calls out her order number.

Nova turns to me giving me a look that says fix this.

I shift to signal the cashier to drop her pizza at our table then turn back to Lenny. "Come on now, don't piss off the child," I tell her, scooting Nova toward me so Lenny has a place to sit. "Just sit down."

She ruffles Nova's soft curls. "Since you asked so nicely, pretty girl." And then she glares at me. Fucking glares at me.

"I like your nails. Your hair is so pretty!"

"Your hair is pretty. I love the curls." Lenny looks at me, eyes wide, probably unsure what question to answer first, or if she should.

"She's a lot to take in." I keep my eyes on the beer and pizza, only because I can't make eye contact with her and not get hard. It's not ideal with my kid sitting here. Thank God I'm sitting down.

Lenny's lips press against the glass as she takes a drink, her tongue darting out to lick her bottom lip when she pulls the glass away. I shake my head, mentally telling myself to stop thinking about her this way. Especially with my kid sitting beside me.

Nova's face rumples with confusion as she picks at the slice of pizza in front of her. "Why is it called pizza?"

"No idea," I tell her, watching Lenny's reaction when Nova takes a bite too large for her mouth and tries to chew it.

"Lenny?" Nova looks over at her, wiping pizza sauce from her face with the swipe of her forearm. "Do you like working for my daddy?"

You can clearly read the answer on Lenny's face. Lucky for me, Nova isn't so good at reading emotions just yet. Give her a year or two. "Um, well, I've only been there a day and everyone was very... *welcoming*." Her voice drips sarcasm with each word. Also something Nova hasn't picked up on... yet.

For twenty minutes, Nova asks her questions, all fairly juvenile in a sense, but then she asks, "Do you have a boyfriend?"

Suddenly I'm all ears, like it fucking matters if she has one or not. Lenny's face goes blank as she finishes her beer. "No boyfriend, sweetie." She stands from her seat ruffling Nova's hair. "Thanks for letting me sit with you. I have to go now."

To my complete surprise, Nova hugs her good-bye. It's been a long time since I've seen her do that to anybody but family, or Colt.

As I'm watching this, Lenny's eyes drift to mine. "See you tomorrow."
I nod, offer a half smile and she's gone.

And I'm watching her ass as she walks away.

"DADDY, WHAT DOES THAT TATTOO SAY?" Nova asks when I take
my shirt off after being soaked by her splashing in the tub.

I point to my bare chest to the tattoo over my heart. "This one?"

"Yeah."

She can read the words "Get off my dick" but she can't read heaven?

"It says heaven. Mommy's name spelled backward is heaven." I reach
for the cup on the floor to rinse the soap from her hair. "It was for her."

She takes two horses and sets them on the edge of the tub galloping
them across the tile as the soap comes out of her hair. "When did you
get it?"

"Not long after we got married. She always thought it was stupid to
tattoo someone's name on your body, so I did that."

"Did she like it?"

I smile, remembering her crying when she saw it for the first time. "I
think so."

"Did Mommy have tattoos?"

"She had birds on her collarbone."

"Is Mommy in heaven?"

"Yeah, she is."

"With Papa, right?"

"Yep."

"Do you think Mommy misses me?"

Nova's smile and the weight of her words hit me like a ton of bricks,
bringing me back to reality. "I'm sure she does. She's always with you,
though. Mommy's an angel now."

Her eyes light up. "I wonder if she knows the tooth fairy." Crazy kid
believes in the tooth fairy, just not Santa Clause apparently.

"I bet she does."

"How did you come up with my name?"

Because you were conceived in the backseat of my car on a backroad. "Mommy liked it."

"Kale said it's a weird name."

"Yeah, well, he's named after a weed. Don't let him tease you."

7

LENNON

THERE'S a problem with sleeping in your truck with an open back.

Bugs.

I have some many mosquito bites and spend most of the night itching them. It's like I've been eaten alive. I've been sleeping in my truck for the last week or so since I left Oklahoma, and I'll admit, it's not so bad. Minus the bugs.

Tap. Tap. Tap.

"Ma'am?" someone asks.

Fuck.

Groaning, I peel my coat from my face, the pale blue painted sky a little too bright. I knew I couldn't stay in my car forever.

"Howdy, Sheriff."

The sheriff scratches the side of his dark hair that's graying at the temples. "You can't stay here, Ms. Reeves."

I sit silently, my impending sense of loss in this life I have now revealed by my blank stare, and then say, "Okay."

He shifts his stance and puts his night stick away. "I didn't mean to scare you, but you can't sleep here."

"I'm sorry," I say, beginning to get nervous. "I'll move."

"You know, you're not allowed to sleep in your car." Though he is basically telling me to get lost, his tone is patient. "Doesn't matter where you park it. Do you need a place to stay?"

I know you can sleep in your car. I've done it on and off for twenty-three years. "I'm sorry. I'm staying with a friend."

He looks at me and knows I'm lying. He stares at me, and I wonder, when our eyes meet if he knows the reason I'm out here, sleeping in a parking lot and showering at a truck stop with a butch woman. "You've been in this parking lot for two nights."

I don't say anything. I probably shouldn't lie to the police. The last thing I need is trouble here.

"You're working for Red, right?"

More like I'm a prisoner to him. Believe me, the thought of being tied to a bed for him is real. Especially after seeing him with his daughter.

I swallow back the dryness in my mouth, wishing I had a bottle of water in here. "Yeah, just started there about a week ago. How did you know?"

"It's a small town, honey. People talk."

My eyes go wide. If people are talking, what does that mean? I know they're curious about me. I get a constant stare wherever I go.

"Listen, if you need a place to stay, my wife and I have an extra room above our garage... or I'm sure the church could set you up with something."

Living with the police? Nope. Not a good idea.

I reach forward and put my keys in the ignition, waving him off with my other hand. "Thank you, but that's all right. I really do have a place to stay."

I breathe a sigh of relief when he leaves, his patrol car passing by as he nods to me. It's then I realize I'm running late this morning, and I know Red will have my ass if I'm late.

I'd gladly give him my ass.

Oh, stop.

And then I think of Red, all manly beastly smoking hot Red, and I want to punch myself for thinking of my boss like that. He hasn't been nice to me once since I started at Walker Automotive. The most civilized conversation I had was with his daughter.

I didn't quit my job, surprisingly. I went back to work and made it an entire week there and hadn't been fired yet. I tend to think it's only because he wants someone to do all the jobs he doesn't want to do.

I wonder why I don't quit, and then I'm quickly reminded that I *need* money. I also have no place to live, and the last thing I want is to go back to Oklahoma.

There's no way that I want Red to see me as some chick trying to hang with the boys. I want him to see me as something more. Strangely, I want him to know me and not the person I pretend to be. The person I am deep down. The person no one but Tyler has ever seen.

As I pull into work, about twenty minutes late, Red's in the parking lot talking to a customer. He doesn't even look my way.

When I'm inside the shop, Daniel, the lube tech, nods to me. For the past week, he's been awfully flirty. If I didn't know any better, he was looking for a one-night stand. He's not bad looking, but he's got this greasy hair that just looks gross. And he's shorter than me, and that's a no go in my book.

"How'd you get the name Lennon?" he asks, sipping what I think is coffee from a stainless steel mug.

"Mom was a stripper," I tell him, shrugging and keeping one eye on Red in the parking lot. I'm teasing him because my mom gave me up. I don't know a damn thing about her, other than she's dead. "Apparently she couldn't come up with anything better... like Danielle."

Daniel's face goes blank, as though he's trying to decide what I meant by that remark.

"Why are you late?" Red asks the moment he enters the shop. He's wearing a black shirt today, and I don't like it when he wears the black one because it makes his eyes look even darker.

"Sorry, it won't happen again."

"I didn't ask for an apology. I asked why."

I inhale a deep breath, trying to summon the courage to deal with him today. "I'm just late." I want to sound indignant and hostile, but my voice cracks, and I have to clear my throat to regain my composure around him. It's none of his business that I had to fight for the shower with the butch lady again and kick her out twice.

His brown eyes search mine intently. "Why?" he presses.

"I'm *just* late," I say again.

He reaches into his pocket, digs out a piece of paper and hands it to me.

Glancing down, I look at it, and it's a donut and coffee order. "What's this?"

"What does it look like?"

"It looks like a food order."

Turning his head in my direction, he eyes me up and down. "Congratulation, you can read, so I suggest you go get it."

"So now I run errands?"

"You do when you show up late."

I stare at the order and my determination begins to wilt under his quick dismissal. "Where's this place at?"

He flips his hand at the door. "Down the street about a mile. Turn left at the stop light. It's on your right."

Easy enough.

Not exactly. After two wrong turns, I finally find it and hand the girl at the window my list. I'm not sure, but maybe she can tell by the writing when she smiles at me.

"You work for Red? I'm Jessie. You must be the new girl, right?"

Is there nothing else to talk about in this town besides the new girl in town?

"I guess I must. I'm Lenny."

She gets this dreamy look about her. I've seen it before. Usually in teenage girls which this girl probably isn't far from. "How do you like working for Red?"

"Yeah." I snort. "It's great if you like working for an asshole." And then my eyes snap to hers, and I realize what I just did. I called him an asshole out loud.

"I would take working for that asshole anytime."

"He's not bad to look at, but believe me. That's where it ends."

"If you've ever seen him with Nova, you'd understand. He knows how to work the single father thing." She makes a clicking sound with her tongue. "Sexy."

What is with this chick? "Yeah, well, I'm not really interested in that. His personal life is none of my business."

"Sure, Lenny." And then she rolls her damn eyes at me.

"IT'S ABOUT TIME." That's how I'm greeted after going to get him coffee and donuts. You'd think he'd be nicer considering it's a very real possibility that I've spit in his cup. I've thought about it. I even thought about licking the lid. I may, or may not have done that last part.

"Sorry it took so long... I met one of your admirers."

Red doesn't look at me, he only squints and keeps his attention on the coffee I hand him that says Red on the cup with a heart. "Jessie?"

"Yeah. The chick that decorated your cup so pretty."

Don't worry, I licked the lid. She didn't.

"She's a nice kid."

I point to the parking lot and the lady with the Lexus pulling in, leaning against his toolbox. "You know, you're a popular guy in this town. You have quite the harem, don't you?"

He laughs cynically and crosses his arms across his broad chest. "You don't know a damn thing about me." And then he walks outside to meet the lady, coffee in hand.

I still have five more coffees on my tray, and I set mine on Red's toolbox because I don't have a toolbox and nowhere to put anything. Hell, my keys are tucked inside my bra.

I give the coffee marked C-man to Colt, assuming that's him, and he immediately takes the lid off and pours whatever it is in his flask, into the coffee. "Thanks, sweetheart. I needed a good mixer."

Shaking my head, I smile at him and keep walking down to the other end of the shop

Balancing the cardboard tray of coffee, I hand Tyler his coffee. "Hey." He smiles, taking it from me. "Why were you late?"

"I had a battle with the butch lady at the truck stop for the shower. She already has my panties. Greedy bitch."

He stares at me, and then shakes his head. "Are you living in your bronco?"

"I know I said I had a place to stay... but I don't."

"Lenny," he sighs. "Damn it. Where have you been staying?"

"In my car."

He shakes his head and dips his brows in concern. "That's not okay. You're staying with me from now on."

"Do you have a washing machine?"

"Yeah...."

I pat his shoulder. "Good, because I gave my panties to a hobo the other night and I'm running out of clean clothes."

His smile turns up a notch. "You fit in perfectly around here."

"IT'S RUNNING LIKE SHIT, and I can't find anything wrong with it." I'm standing beside Red, my skin heated from being this close as he and Tyler contemplate why a Chevy Blazer was brought in for an oil change yesterday and then came back today.

Red stares at the car, twisting a wrench around in his hand like it's a nervous habit he has. "And you checked the oil?"

Tyler shakes his head. "No, I will."

Everyone comes to Red with questions, and he doesn't seem to get much of anything done during the day. As Tyler stands in his stall, the two of them going over a car neither can figure out, Daniel walks up to him and tells him a customer is waiting.

"He's just going to have to wait," he snarls back, never even making eye contact with him as he tosses a crowbar in his tool cart.

"It's *over-filled* with oil," Tyler tells him a minute later, looking over his shoulder at Daniel.

Red shoots his glare at Daniel, who had originally changed the oil. More than likely he didn't drain the oil and just filled it with more.

"Fuck, man." Red groans. "Pay attention."

Daniel raises his hands. "Sorry!"

I don't think Red likes people apologizing. In fact, it seems to only make him angry. And let's face it, that's not entirely hard to do.

I'm just getting to know the dynamics of the shop, but you can already tell who does what, and who Red likes and doesn't.

Guess what? I'm his least favorite person.

Red walks up to me, his eyes on a repair order.

I raise an eyebrow, thoroughly annoyed now. We went from rattles to oil changes today. "An oil change? Really?"

"Well, Daniel doesn't seem to be able to handle them today, and Rawley seems to think his shift starts at noon. Someones gotta do them."

"But an oil change?" I don't even know why I'm making a big deal out of it, probably because I want the jobs where I can show him I know what I'm doing, not this basic shit.

"You know..." Red lets a wrench slide out of his hand, slowly, and I watch intently as it happens, my stare fixated on the motion. "I thought a lube job would be easy for you, princess."

There he goes with the fucking princess shit again.

I take the wrench from his hand. "I don't know. I'd say I'm better at checking the bore and stroke of an engine."

Red smirks at my comment, which makes me want to punch him in the face. Especially when he winks at me and lets the wrench slide slowly out of his right hand to his left.

I take the wrench from his hand and slide it in the back pocket of my jeans and turn to walk away. Leaning over the car in my stall, I remove the dipstick and check the oil when Red comes up behind me. His left hand rests on the car, his chest pressed to my back as he slowly brings his right hand to cup my ass. My breathing stops immediately. I'm pretty sure my heart did too as he reaches in my back pocket for the wrench, long, strong fingers caressing as he pulls. "I believe this belongs to me."

I'm pretty sure I have an oil leak now, thanks to him. But you know, judging by the hardness against my ass, he's having the same reaction to me and you know, I wouldn't mind checking the bore and stroke of his piston inside my cylinder.

All right, maybe working here wouldn't be so bad?

8

REDDINGTON

I'M CONSTANTLY HAVING to find new and inventive ways of waking Nova up and getting her in a good mood first thing in the morning. She's a lot like me in that way. I hate getting out of bed in the morning and if I could sleep until noon, I probably would. Much like my brother. That asshole hasn't gotten in before noon in weeks.

Nova fell asleep on the couch last night, and I didn't have the heart to move her to her bed. She has a thing about sleeping on the couch, which is better than her sleeping in my bed because that's never an enjoyable experience. So I let her sleep out there at least once a week.

Dressed in a pair of shorts and no shirt, I crawl on all fours toward my sleeping daughter and rest my chin on the edge of the couch. She's curled to the side; her tiny hands slipped underneath her cheek in an adorably prone position. I could sit here and watch her sleep forever but since we don't have that kind of time, I decide to rip the Band-Aid off. She's gonna be pissed one way or the other so I might as well have a laugh at the same time.

Taking my socks off, I put one on my right hand, one on my left and lay down on the floor and talk to her in a chipmunk voice.

After ten minutes, she peeks her head over the side of the couch and smiles. "You sound like Alvin." And then she rolls landing on my chest with an umph. Ripping the socks off my hands, I tickle her sides as she squeals and tries to slap my ear.

I'm cackling so hard that I'm coughing, nearly brought to my knees by my daughter's own laughter.

Suddenly serious, she straightens up and places her tiny fist on her hip, her cheeks pink from sleep and the touch of sunburn she has. "I have to pee. That wasn't fair."

I flop back against the hardwood floor in the living room as she scampers down the hall and to the bathroom. "Get dressed too!"

"I don't want to."

I roll over to press my face to the floor and notice I should vacuum soon. "You don't have a choice."

"DO I get to come to work with you on Friday?"

I nod, turning onto Elle's street. "Yeah, but it's only Thursday so tomorrow."

Nova huffs out a breath. "Ugh! I hate Thursdays." And then she's quiet, looking out the window as we pass by the coffee stand. "Can I get a donut?"

"No, not today. I'll get some tomorrow for the office, okay?"

She huffs out another long breath. "Fine."

Guaranteed I piss this kid off at least ten times a day.

When we walk through the door, Elle literally has her left tit hanging out with her kid attached to it. I'm all for what's best for the baby, but come on, the kid is nearly two and I'm positive she knows exactly what time I drop Nova off every day. It's sadly obvious that she's leaving her tit out on purpose.

Turning to leave, I shake my head. Some things you can't un-see.

"Oh, hey, wait..." Elle stands up and straightens out her top before rushing toward me as she practically drops the kid she was holding. "I was wondering if you had plans this weekend. Maybe we could get the kids together for dinner?"

Nova shoots me a glare. She does not like Elle's kids but it's a small town and the only daycare around. The last thing she'll want is to have dinner with them. "Can't. Nova is spending the weekend with her grandma."

"Well then, if you're gonna be on your own then maybe you and I could just grab some food on Saturday. Have some adult conversation."

I don't know why she's constantly asking me this. She's fucking married.

"Are you forgetting you're married?" My eyes drop to her wedding ring. "Why would you ask me that?"

She stutters around words, her mouth opening and closing before she smiles softly. "We're separated." Her voice is hushed, like she doesn't want the kids to know. "I thought you knew that seeing how he's never here."

No, I just figured he didn't want to come home to you.

I look down at my feet and let out a sigh as I shake my head. When I look over to Nova, she's staring at me with a look of disgust on her face. I can't help but think back to the other night and how excited she was around Lenny, and then now how she's reacting when Elle is close to me.

Maybe my kid is trying to tell me something.

I back up, reaching for the door. "I'm real busy this weekend. We've got a lot going on right now, and I don't have a lot of time for going out. But thanks for asking."

I turn to leave, hoping that answer will keep her off my back for a while.

Once I'm back in the car, my windshield wipers sweeping away the first sprinkles of rain, my thoughts immediately focus on work... and Lenny.

I think of those damn shorts again and have to sit in my car for a few minutes before I walk into the shop.

"WHY IS THIS SHIT PLAYING?" I ask when I hear rap music blaring through the shop. It's barely nine in the morning, and this is the last thing I want to be listening to.

Rawley smirks, running his hand through his dark hair and then watching over my shoulder at where I know she's standing. "Daniel put it on."

Yeah, I bet he did.

"And what are you doing here? It's before noon."

He points behind me. "Thought I'd make an early appearance for the show."

I turn my head, and I wish I hadn't. Lenny is dancing. Luckily, she's wearing jeans today. Unluckily, they're so fucking tight I can see the outline of her thong underwear and all I can imagine is walking up to her and slapping that ass while I pull on that G-string with my teeth.

And here's to another day with a constant hard-on.

I'm tempted to tell her that she has to wear baggy overalls and outlaw music playing in the shop if this shit continues. I mean, fuck, look at those hips. After that little wrench incident the other day, believe me, those hips haunt me.

Behind Lenny, Daniel has an oil hose reel in hand positioned between his legs. As Lenny's dancing around, he's stroking the hose with a smile. I stand there, glaring at him, but he doesn't stop what he's doing.

When she bends over, still swaying her hips as she pops the hood of a Honda in her stall, Daniel hits the button on the oil as if he's coming and throws his head back.

Completely inappropriate but I have to bite back a smile because it's kinda funny. Colt slaps him on the shoulder just as Lenny catches on to what happened behind her. "Looks like you got a problem with premature ejaculation, kid," Colt says, walking past him.

Daniel's lame attempts at flirting with Lenny are really starting to get on my nerves. Mostly because I want her and if I can't have her, well, no one will.

Psycho much, Red?

Fuckin' right I am. Despite my behavior toward her, there's one thing I've noticed about Lenny. She can handle her own, that's for sure, but she's so guarded, and that makes me think she's running from something. For that reason, I don't want these guys fuckin' around with her.

Just to test her ability, I've thrown everything I can at her that I didn't think she could handle from valve jobs, timing belts, fuel pump replacements, water pumps, hell, even a head gasket. And to my surprise, she had me eating my words because not only could she do all of it, she did it fucking quicker than most of the guys here.

Colt grins, bumping my shoulder with his and watching Lenny sway to the music. "Ah, don't be mad. Kids just trying to bury his bone."

"Don't you have work to do? Stop talking to me."

To my right, Daniel arches his eyebrow at Lenny when he walks by her again with a hint of a smile playing at the corner of his mouth.

I don't like it, not one bit, especially when she smiles and winks at him.

Truth is, I want it to be me. I want to be the one sparking a smile. All I've managed to do is spark the scowl, and I guess that's for the better.

So I hang back and let them joke around with her.

For now.

Colt bounces on his heels, shaking his head in amusement. "Today just keeps getting better and better. I'm just waiting for you to take your pent-up anger out on the poor kid."

Daniel, having heard that, looks at me like I've lost my mind, and he really has no idea how true that is. I can see the look of confusion on his face.

Colt nods to Daniel, leaning into my toolbox. "How'd that granny work out for you the other night?"

Lenny looks up, smiling at Colt and then Daniel, curious as to where this is going. "What are you talking about?"

"Well the way I see it, you're trying to change her oil but ain't she a little young for you? Last time I heard you were baggin' grannies."

We're all lost now because Colt doesn't make a lot of fucking sense, ever, and in the mornings, it's worse. I think his brain is still shifting into gear until at least one. And then it's a downhill slope after that. He's got one good peak hour of the day. Usually lunch time.

Colt turns to me as if I'm paying attention. I'm staring at repair orders. When I don't look up, he hits my shoulder. "I saw him last Saturday night practically titty fucking this old broad in his pit."

"She wasn't that old," Daniel points out.

Colt levels me a serious look, his brow pinching together. "She could have been a grandma."

"I don't care how old she was as long as her mouth is still working."

Yep. He said that.

Lenny's expression turns from amusement to disgust. "Seriously Daniel? There is something seriously wrong with your logic."

"Whatever. She wasn't that old, just experienced," Daniel barks, walking off into the parts room.

"Get back to work. All of you."

"Your Lexus is back," Lenny says with a smile, nodding to the parking lot and leaning back against my toolbox.

Fuck, not again. I rub my hands over my face trying to refocus my attention away from Lenny and back to where it should be, work. Shaking my head, I reach for my hat since it's raining steadily now and I draw in a breath. Stepping outside the shop, Amber, the chick with the Lexus is huddled under a black umbrella with bright red lipstick on.

I know that lipstick is for me. I'm not trying to be a dick or anything, but I know that Amber is a married stay-at-home mom who has no reason to wear red lipstick around town unless she's trying to put out an invitation.

First thing she asks after I remove a nail from her tire?

"So, Red..." She looks at my hand on her door just before I'm about to close it. "What are you doing later tonight?"

Jesus... what's with this woman?

"Sorry, Amber," I tell her, even though I'm the farthest from sorry. "Aside from the fact that I don't think your husband would appreciate me hanging out with his wife tonight, I gotta date with a pretty girl."

Her cheeks flush. "Oh no. I wasn't implying that you and I should go out alone. No, I was thinking maybe we could get the girls together, and we could all have a playdate." She lets out a nervous laugh, her eyes searching my face for the denial she knows is coming. "I thought I could pick up a DVD for the girls and a bottle of wine for us. And while the girls are having fun, we could talk."

I'm getting really tired of women using a playdate as an excuse to get time with me. I mean what do they think is going to happen? Our kids are in the other room, and I'm going to bend them over the kitchen table and fuck them into orgasm?

That's probably exactly what they're thinking.

I step back. "I appreciate the offer, but I promised Nova that it would just be us tonight."

The disappointment on her face is obvious. "Oh, okay then. Maybe some other time." And then she reaches in the front seat of her car and pulls out a box of donuts. "Here." She pushes the box toward me. "I picked these up for you guys."

Maybe she thinks the old adage is true. The best way to a man's heart is through his stomach. Not so much with me, but I take the donuts.

"Thank you, that was nice of you."

As I turn to walk away from Amber, I notice Lenny staring at us taking in the conversation with a look of amusement on her face.

"What are you smiling about?" I ask, stopping in front of her, opening the box of donuts for her to have one. "Want a donut?"

Her wide brown eyes shine brightly as she stares at my mouth, and then my chest before meeting my eyes. I'm close enough I can feel her warmth and the only thing separating me from making contact with her body is a box of donuts. I want her to pick one so I can watch her lick the frosting off it. "Well, I just get the feeling that Amber there would love for you to do more than just remove a nail from her tire." As she says this, her smile gets wider and more mischievous, selecting her donut. "She would probably like you to, oh, I don't know..." She shrugs, one hand on her hip, the other with the donut in hand as she brings the pastry to her lips. "Check her oil pressure."

Taking a slow bite, she chews even slower, and I can't help but watch the way her lips move. She did that shit on purpose.

When she senses my inability to focus on anything but her mouth, she shifts her eyes to the side of us, and I can sense that this little show is not just for her amusement but for everyone in the shop.

I shift, uncomfortably.

Not because what she is saying is making me uncomfortable but because what she's saying is turning me the fuck on. And the way her lips look with the chocolate on them, I'm struggling to keep control.

I knew from the moment I met Lenny, she had a dirty side. No way a girl who looks like her, and enjoys getting her hands as grimy as she does, doesn't enjoy a little dirty talking between the sheets as well. You can see it on her face as she watches me, if not in her snide comments.

The girl has snarky and sexy down.

"Yeah, well." My voice lowers and I know I have an effect on her. It's the flush of her cheeks and the eyes that lower to my lips. "I do have the skill of making sure there is just the right amount of pressure down to an art." I toss her a wink, and I'm rewarded with a small blush and Lenny biting her bottom lip like she's picturing something she likes.

"Why don't you meet me in the parts room and show me how it's done then."

What in the ass? Well, I'd like to see that ass for sure but fuck me she knows how to lay it on.

I clear my throat and decide I had better change the subject before I bend her over one of these cars and show her just how good I am at applying just the right pressure. "Did you figure out what's wrong with that Honda?"

"Yeah, they said it felt like it was hopping when it went around corners."

I don't look at her as I say, "I know what the repair order said, Lenny. I read it. I'm asking if you figured it out."

A sardonic snort grabs my attention, and my eyes reflexively seek out Lenny again. She picks up the shock she took out of the right rear. "Yeah." And then she takes the shock in her hands and compresses it. Usually, a shock will take some effort to compress, and this one glides freely in an up and down motion. "It's lost its stroke."

I really should sit down, but apparently, I'm into fucking torturing myself with blue balls.

I step in as close as possible. Close enough where I feel her heartbeat against my chest.

"And we all know it's about the stroke, right?" I'm only teasing, trying to get a rise out of her because seeing her flustered makes me weak, and it seems I like being that way lately.

Lenny's reaction is guarded, and I think maybe I've offended her. Until she laughs. Then I realize offending her is pretty much impossible to do. She's just about to say something when Daniel interrupts her. "You baggin' married women now?" he asks, walking toward me when he sees donuts. "Fuck off," I grumble, turning around to my toolbox to hide my erection. "She had a nail in her tire."

"Would you ever—" Daniel's eyes go wide, and he can't finish what he was about to say. He knows he said the wrong thing.

"Don't fucking ask that." I shove Daniel back against the welder near my toolbox and my eyes dart to Lenny's for a reason unbeknownst to me. "She's married."

"You can't be sticking your dipstick in customers," my fucking sister points out, looking through the box of donuts.

"I never made a move on her."

"Yeah... I know. I just like giving you shit." She gives me a sarcastic nod and starts to walk away toward the office. As she's just about to me, I turn and knock the donut out of her hand and onto the floor.

She smiles, and picks the donut up off the ground and takes a bite of it. "You're an asshole."

"Stop your fucking bitching," Rawley says to Tyler as they both walk out of the parts room. "You're starting to sound like my brother now and believe me, we only need *one* in this shop."

When Rawley is outside looking for the car he needs to change the oil in, Colt smiles at Lenny, who's watching all this with a smile. "How many times do you think 'asshole' is said in the shop on any given day?"

"Probably a lot," Lenny replies, smiling at me now.

"I once counted." Colt approaches my toolbox and takes a donut. "Red was called an asshole thirty-six times in an eight-hour period."

"By who?" I ask, never looking up.

Colt chuckles. "Your sister..."

"Though it's strangely accurate,"—Tyler walks by, reaching inside the box as well and side-eyeing Colt and his cup of bourbon—"we should be worried that *you* counted, not that it was said."

"Honestly, I'm impressed your old ass can still count that high," Lenny adds, smiling.

"I also counted how many times Daniel here scratches his balls during the day." Colt leans back into his toolbox and takes a large bite of his donut. "You're a dirty motherfucker, man, if you're constantly scratching the shit out of your nuts."

Rawley walks by and tosses a repair order on my toolbox. Slowly looking through the other twelve I have here for the morning, I don't look up. "I can't fucking find this car. Give me something else."

"Just because you can't find it, doesn't mean it doesn't need to be done. Go find it."

"I said I can't find it. I looked." I can tell immediately Rawley isn't letting up, his ink-covered arms crossing defiantly over his chest.

"Listen, you little fucker." I turn around to face him, getting in his face. "I don't have time for your bullshit this morning. Get your ass out there and find it."

Rawley lets out a bitter laugh. "Make me."

I'm going to. For sure. Just as I have his shirt fisted in my hands and him back against my toolbox, metal clattering as tools crash to the ground, Mom comes out of the office to separate us. "You two, I swear to God I'm going to call Hendrix up here to knock some sense into the both of you!"

"Oh, just let them fight," Colt says, unable to keep the grin off his face. "I'm tired of their shit."

"Stop fucking around." I shove Rawley away from me and toss a pair of keys at him. "Car's in your stall already, dumb shit."

A few minutes later, I shake my head when Hendrix, my uncle, comes walking up the street, that slow walk he has where he limps. He was in a bad wreck when he was nineteen that left him with a broken hip. Since then, he's never walked right.

He takes one look in the shop and smiles. "Who's that?"

Figures my mom called him anyway. She's always sending him lately when Rawley and I get in each other's faces.

"You know damn well who that is old man," I mumble, unbolting the power steering pump on a Chevy truck in my stall.

Uncle Hendrix leans into the car, his burly arms resting on the fender as he examines the engine. "Seems like trouble."

He's not talking about the engine by any means.

I don't say anything because he's right. She is trouble. Hot blonde wearing skin-tight jeans in a shop full of men, it's trouble for sure.

"How's everything else going?"

Of course he would ask that. I get the notion he wants to help out, but there's not a lot he can do.

"It sucks right now," I say, tightening the intake manifold onto the engine. I glance up at him from the corner of my eye. "How's it going down there?"

He shrugs and runs his calloused paint-splattered hand over his jaw. "We're not all that busy. You want Jude to come down and help you out?"

I think about that for all of two seconds. I know Jude, and I also know my cousin's taste in women. He'd be all over Lenny, and that's not an option.

"That's okay. We can handle it. I've got Tyler and Lenny's hanging in there."

Hendrix looks over his shoulder and then back at me. "I can see you're hiring for eye candy now."

He's teasing me, but I don't like it and glare. "She knows what she's doing."

"That's good." He gives me this look, similar to the one he gave me when he caught me stealing spray paint from his shop when I was sixteen and told him I was painting emblems to match my car. I wasn't. I was spray painting "Rachel Clayton can suck my dick" on the wall in the women's bathroom in gym class. She actually did suck my dick, and twenty other guys in school, but that's beside the point. I got caught stealing from my uncle and never did it again.

He crosses his arms over his chest, watching me. "But I can't help but wonder if you know what you're doing?"

We stand there just staring at each other for a minute. Maybe he's thinking about the spray painting incident. Maybe not. Either way, he's waiting for an answer.

"Yeah. Everything is under control." That's bullshit. Nothing's under control and my uncle senses it. He knows when I'm lying.

He laughs, stepping back. "Okay." And then he walks toward the office to probably harass my sister a little. She's the only girl in our family, aside from the mothers, and of course, Nova now.

Hendrix is in the office about ten minutes when Sheldon pulls up to the shop in his 1969 Plymouth GTX 426 Hemi I've been drooling over since I was eight. Here's the thing about a small privately owned shop. People show up during the day just to bullshit. And while that's fine as you want to build relationships and trust in the community, it sucks when you're busy.

You can't miss the throaty hum of the hemi as he stops it in front of the shop. For a car guy like myself, driving this car would be a dream come true, owning it would be fucking heaven.

"Reddington." Sheldon greets me with his wide Ed McMann smile. Sheldon's a salesman. Always has been and he's got the demeanor to go along with it. Looking around the shop, he notices the row of cars. "Wow, you guys are staying busy, aren't you?"

I lean back against the wall. "Yeah, pretty busy. We just hired a new mechanic so it's coming around."

Sheldon's been around this shop as a customer for as long as I can remember. He knows my dad left me a legacy and the last thing I want him to see is that I'm failing.

He puts his hand on my shoulder. "You know your dad had faith in you. He knew you could handle it." And then he nods outside. "Why don't you take a little break? I brought your baby by. Wanna take her for a spin?"

He's never asked me if I wanted to drive it before. "Why would you let me drive it now?"

"Why not? You can handle it, right?"

He'll bring it by a few times a year. Mostly to tease me. I tried to buy it from him not long after I got my license, and again when I turned twenty-one but he never sells it... and *never* lets me drive.

I stand up straight, smiling at him. "Seriously?"

Lenny approaches the car, along with Tyler and Rawley, all looking over her sleek black lines and flawless leather interior. I watch Lenny as Sheldon and I walk toward the car, her gaze faltering as I approach. She does that thing where she looks at me, and then the car, and then me again, unable to keep her stare focused.

Sheldon hands me the keys. "Go ahead."

Tyler glares at me. "I totally fucking hate you right now."

I'm about to offer him to come with me when Lenny's eyes light up at the sound of the 426 with open headers rumbling. Our eyes catch in the window and I give a small nod to her to get in. I know I'll be torturing myself, but I can't help it when her eyes shine like that.

Lenny doesn't move. Instead she stands there open mouthed and looks to Sheldon. "Can I go with him?"

He laughs, adjusting his hat. "Yeah, hon, go ahead," Sheldon tells her, winking at me and watching Lenny slide into the passenger seat.

This is a horrible idea.

Lenny glances over at me buckling her seatbelt. "I know he said yes but are you sure I can come? I've always loved these cars."

"Seriously, he won't mind." I eye Sheldon one last time. "I've always wanted to drive one of these with a hemi."

"I've never seen one before, let alone been in one." She breathes the words out slowly and it sends a jolt right to my dick. Mostly because of the *way* she says it. "It's rumbling my chest!"

I swallow and say nothing, the throaty idle shaking the two of us in the seats.

"Who is that guy that he lets you just take his car out? I mean, hell...." She runs her hands over the black leather seats. "This thing has to be worth a hundred grand."

Exactly why I can never afford it.

I struggle to remain focused at the thought of her running her hands over something else. "That's Dan Sheldon but we call him Sheldon. He's a long-time friend of my dad's and I think he just likes to fuckin' tease me with this car." I eye Lenny's legs and then toss her a smirk shifting into gear. "I'd hold on if I were you."

Those are the last words either of us say as I ease out of the parking lot, careful on the gravel.

When we hit the pavement, the tires squeal as I take off around the corner and onto the main highway. It's a good fucking thing I know the sheriff in town because going one twenty usually draws some attention.

Had I been pulled over, I would have drained my bank account for the ticket just to see the smile on Lenny's face that afternoon, all smiles and laughing.

Or maybe it was when she grabs my arm as I spun the car around into a 360-degree turn, smoke billowing into the car from the tires against the pavement, and all the while, she laughs.

Maybe it's the rumbling in my chest or the adrenaline in my veins, that makes me want to fucking kiss her so bad as we sit at a stop light in front of the shop and she's cackling with excitement.

For a moment, in the middle of the day when I have so much else going on, I'm free from all my obligations and back to being sixteen when nothing else matters but speed and the girl next to me.

In front of the shop, I glance over at Lenny, my heart pounding with the adrenaline. "Enjoy yourself?"

Gasping, she sits there breathing heavy and smiles so wide it hurts my chest. "Can we go again?"

I clearly can't help myself when I say, "Ready for round two already?"

She shifts in the seat, drawing my attention to her legs again. "Well, you know what they say about a mechanic, right?"

"No, what's that?"

Leaning in, she whispers in my ear. "They're who you come to when you need lubricating."

I don't know what to make of that. Mostly because she stares at me wide eyed, waiting on my reaction and I want so baldy to kiss her.

When I don't say anything, she pats my shoulder. "Thanks for the ride."

I've met my fucking match, haven't I? She actually managed to leave me speechless.

I REALLY DON'T KNOW how I made it through the rest of that day.

Between Lenny wearing those jeans and that joy ride around Lebanon, I'm a walking hard-on. I'm so fucking tempted to call that stripper tonight and have her take care of some pent-up aggression. Tempted being the key word, but I won't. Besides, with Nova in the house, the only relief I'm gonna have is me and my right hand.

At the end of the day I swing by Elle's to grab Nova. After this morning, pickup goes nice and quick and as I'm starting the car, I can tell Nova has something on her mind. "What's going on?"

"Don't be mad, Daddy."

"Why?" I stare at her in the mirror.

She blinks slowly, pretty blue eyes beginning to work me over. "Just stay calm."

"Tell me what you did and I'll decide which one it will be."

"No." She crosses her arms over her chest, her bottom lip out like she's going to start crying. "Now I'm not telling you."

"Nova," I warn in my deepest dad voice, and she cracks.

"Gosh, fine. I told Kale to get off my dick. I don't think it means what I thought it meant."

I want to laugh. I really do because it's just like the time she called another kid a stack of cock rings after hearing Rawley call Daniel that.

"Where did you hear that?"

"It was on Lenny's shirt. Just *tell me* what it means already!"

"Not gonna happen and don't say it again." I refuse to tell her what it means because my thoughts can't seem to leave Lenny and her getting *on* my dick. "Did Elle hear you?"

"Well, no, but I think he... I don't know. I think he might tell his mommy on me."

"Why do you say that?"

"Because he said, I'm telling my mommy."

I shake my head and turn back to drive away. We're about a mile down the road when Nova starts in with her questions. It happens every night when I pick her up. She's a talker.

"How was your day?" she asks, staring at the road at the passing cars and I think she's counting them, one by one.

"It was okay." Thankfully, she can't tell by my tone that it wasn't. The last thing I need to do is burden my child with the pressures of my life too.

"Was Lenny at the shop today?"

"Yes." My eyes snap to hers in the rearview mirror, wondering where she's going with this.

"So..." She's dancing around something, and while I have an idea of what she's going to say, it surprises me when she asks, "Do you like having Lenny at the shop?"

"I guess so."

"I really liked Lenny." Her eyes light up, and I want to smile too because it's the first time she's ever said she liked a woman. Other than her mother. "She seems like someone I could hang with."

"Oh, really." I turn the corner at the gas station and start thinking about what the hell I should make her for dinner. "Well, I'm sure she would really like to hang with you also."

"Great! Set it up. We can all have a playdate."

Now that's the kind of playdate I can be on board with.

"Well, Lenny is really busy with work and all, but I'm sure we can work something out." And maybe I can take her in my room and show her my piston.

"You should bring Lenny coffee in the morning. Uncle Colt says you're being a prick to her."

I turn around when we're at the stop light. "Uncle Colt told you that?"

She shrugs, a hint of a smile playing at the corner of her mouth. "Is it true?"

"No, it's not true." I turn back around as the cars begin to move. "And he's not your damn uncle."

9

LENNON

AFTER WORK, I follow Tyler upstairs to his apartment.

He smiles when I get out my one duffle bag from my Bronco. "That's all you got?"

I shrug, looking at the small apartment above the office. "I travel light."

"Or you left in a hurry."

I change my voice into a lowness that sounds dramatic. "Well, there's that."

Tyler laughs at me as we enter through a door on the side of the office, and then up a set of carpeted steps and into an apartment. "I'm just renting this place from Mia, but it works out pretty good for me since it's so close to the shop." He laughs at his joke, and then motions around the place. "It's not much, a one-bedroom, one-bath but it serves the purpose. You can have my room if you want. I can sleep on the couch."

"No." I place my bag on the couch. "I'd be happy with the floor or the couch."

Nodding, he laughs, and then sits on the couch, and I do the same. You can certainly tell a man lives here. It's fairly bare, aside from a black rug in the middle of the living room and a coffee table made from two truck tires and a piece of plywood on top of that. "Classy, Tyler." I smile over at him and pat my hands on the black leather couch. "Do I need to put a sheet on the couch?"

He rolls his eyes. "Whatever. I'm a gentleman. I fuck 'em in a bed."

"Sure you are." I shove his shoulder lightly, sending him rocking to the side with a grin. "Seriously though, I can't tell you how much I appreciate you helping me out."

"You don't have to keep thanking me. This is what family does."

Breathing in slowly, I contemplate how foreign that is to me. "I really don't know how that feels. I've never had family that cares."

Tyler's expression is pained, his brow pulling together. I stare at his blue eyes waiting to see what he might say. "I know you've had a hard time, and I hope it gets better for you. I'm sure work hasn't been the way you thought it would go but hang in there. The guys like you."

"Sure they do," I snort.

"They do. Red just takes a little bit to get used to." He turns his head toward the television and points the remote at it. "Since Lyric died, he hasn't been himself. I think he always knew the shop would be his. I don't think he expected it to happen this soon. He was basically just thrown into it a month ago."

I can understand what Tyler is saying. It's obvious what Red's going through in a sense that it doesn't appear to be easy on him. I mean, I try to remember the guy lost his father a month ago, but then again, does that give him the right to be a douche to everyone?

I'm not sure how long Tyler and I sit on the couch, but I eventually fall asleep and wake up in the morning with a slice of pizza in my hand I don't remember taking from the box of pizza I don't remember ordering on the coffee table. I must have been really tired last night.

TG-FUCKING-FRIDAY! I thought Friday would never arrive. I really did.

I lay on the couch for ten minutes before I notice that Tyler's bedroom door is closed, and I should probably take a shower before he needs to. The most important lesson I learned while living with a man at all, it's that they take a really long time to take a dump and hog all the water.

I make my shower quick, not wanting to use all the hot water on him, and I'm rummaging through my bag on the floor only to realize I forgot my damn shirt.

Cracking the door open, I see Tyler's door is still closed, and it should be safe to grab my shirt.

Tiptoeing across the hardwood floor of the living room, I reach for my shirt that fell out of my bag and suddenly stop when I hear the faint sounds of crunching.

Just when I think Tyler is about to see me half-naked, it's Raven I see, sitting on the counter eating a bowl of cereal, her mascara smeared on her cheek and hair all over the place.

Our eyes lock in a moment of sheer panic on both parts.

Holy shit!

I jump at first, startled to find her there. "What are you doing here?"

With wide-eyes and a mouthful of coco-puffs, Raven points her spoon at me, pieces of cereal falling out of her mouth. "You tell Red, and I will kill you. I mean it, Lenny. I will chop your dick off."

I'm really not sure what to say right then, and all I can do is stare at her sitting on the counter, her legs propped up on the sink wearing Tyler's shirt from last night. "Where the hell are your pants?"

"Um…" She looks down at her legs and shovels another spoonful of cereal in her mouth. When she's finished chewing, she stares at me. "I'm not really sure. Things got a bit out of hand, but I do remember Tyler undoing my buttons with his teeth while we were on the bedroom floor, so that is probably my best bet."

"Wait." I shake my head trying to clear it, and then I realize what must be going on here, and I'm not all that surprised. "You and Tyler are dating?"

"Well, I wouldn't say we are dating, but I would definitely say we're fucking." Her eyes take on a dreamy look, like she's thinking of last night. "A lot."

"Okay." I pull my shirt over my head before Tyler comes out. The last thing I want is for him to see me without a shirt on. "And how long has this been going on?"

Raven shrugs. "Couple of months now."

"And you don't want Red to know about this why?"

She gives me that look that says, *Really, you have to ask?*

"Because Red would *not* approve. I'm sure you've noticed this, but Red is a little controlling. He sees certain things in black and white and has the attitude of my way or the highway. He thinks Tyler is too old for me. And of course, there is the obvious reason. Red's an asshole, and it's none of his damn business." Raven hops down from the counter and puts the bowl in the sink. "I have to go. I need to sneak back into the house so it looks like I slept there all night." She's at the door digging through her bag. Pulling out a hair tie, she swoops her hair up in a bun and points at me, her purse on her shoulder. "Oh, and by the way, don't make any plans for tomorrow. A group of us are heading to the river and you, my dear, are coming."

I'm not entirely sure if she realizes this, but she still doesn't have any pants on when the door closes behind her.

Less than thirty seconds later, she opens the door and sighs. "I should find my pants."

I laugh reaching for the cereal box. "Might be a good idea."

"SO YOU'RE FUCKING Red's little sister?"

Tyler gasps as we're walking downstairs. "Jesus, Lenny!" He stops and points at my face. "Warn a guy when you're about to give him a damn heart attack. And don't you dare say anything to Red."

They really want to keep this under wraps. Can't say I blame them. Red can certainly be intimidating.

"Hey,"—I hold my hands up—"Not my place to say. And if you

haven't noticed, he doesn't allow me to speak. It's just, here, can you handle this?" I attempt a pretty lousy version of Red's voice.

Tyler laughs, taking a few more steps but his voice is hushed. "But still... you can't say anything."

"Are you ever going to tell him?"

"Maybe... eventually. I don't know. We don't even know what we're doing yet. It's not like we're dating. I've never even taken her anywhere but my bed."

"How did it happen? I mean, you've worked together for a long time, right?"

"Yeah... I've known her since I was fourteen, and she was eight, and that seems all kinds of wrong. She's always been Red's little sister to me until one day, she wasn't, and she caught my eye. It wasn't long after Berkley broke up with me. Raven had a really bad break up with some loser she had been dating and we were at a party together, and I listened to her that night. One thing led to another, and she was using me to fuck her sorrows away. Or maybe I was using her... Not sure. It just sorta started like that."

I hesitate when we're at the door. It's Friday and then two days off. I can do this, right?

Tyler notices and puts his arm around me. "Take a deep breath. It's all good. You've already proven yourself."

"Since when did you start giving pep talks? "

"I've gotten introspective in my old age. I'm like the fucking Buddha of Lebanon."

"Right," I draw out slowly, taking another step outside. "A Buddha who's fucking his best friend's sister."

He shoves me away from him. "Shut up."

Inside the shop, Tyler and I go separate directions, and I head over to Red's toolbox to find out what he wants me to do today. With any luck, I'll steer clear of running errands and finding dead rats in heater vents.

As I'm standing at his toolbox clocking in, Red sets two cups of coffee on the stainless steel top and slides one my direction, our shoulders brushing one another.

"What's that?"

He doesn't look at me; his head is bent forward staring at his wallet in his hand as he sets it in the top drawer of his toolbox. "Well, that is what we call coffee."

I scan his face and the dark stubble that seems longer in the last few days. I love a man with the smallest traces of a beard. Immediately, I have thoughts of that beard and his scruffy face between my thighs. "I know it's a coffee smartass. Why are you giving it to me?"

"Because my daughter said I need to be nicer, and that girls like it when you bring them coffee."

"So your five-year-old daughter told you that you need to be nicer and suggested you bring me coffee?"

"You could just take the goddamn coffee that my kid ordered you," he barks, reaching for the repair orders stacked next to the coffee and sits on his stool. "And say thank you. She's in the office so don't piss her off already."

I inhale sharply, that same pulsing frustration I always have around him settling deep within my bones. He's annoying, selfish, arrogant, and extremely hot. Goddamn him.

I reach for the cup in frustration only to have it spill a little on him. Right on his crotch.

Without thinking, I grab a shop towel next to me. "Shit, I'm sorry."

I dab at his crotch with the towel. Yep. Dabbed his crotch. I should have just licked it up.

Red jerks the rag from my hand, and I realize why he does this. I'm basically rubbing his dick.

"I've got it." He scowls, standing up and turns to leave.

Just as Red turns, he slips on a small patch of oil spilled on the ground from where Daniel had been moving the oil cart this morning. He tries to catch himself but ends up falling right on his ass on the ground.

I'm not sure, but I don't think I've ever laughed that hard in my life.

My cackles ring through the shop and soon Colt starts in, and the whole shop is laughing at Red on his ass.

Daniel, who's across the shop, holds up his hands. "My bad."

"Clean this shit up!" Red yells and disappears around the corner into the bathroom.

Colt walks over to me as I pick up a repair order and sip my coffee. It's freaking delicious, but when you've been drinking truck stop coffee for the past week, anything's better than that.

"That's one way to start the morning," Colt says, digging his flask from the front pocket of his overalls. "Would you like something for your coffee?

I stare at him in confusion. "Like creamer? I think it's a mocha... so probably not."

He gives me a look of disgust. "Why the hell would you put creamer in your coffee?"

"Are you offering me alcohol?" I look at the clock on the wall. "It's only eight thirty."

"Honey, it's five o'clock somewhere." Colt leans against the same stool Red had been sitting on and watches Daniel take a pile of shop rags, throw them on the oil spill and walk away. That's one way of cleaning it up.

"How have you survived this long with how much you drink?" I ask, flipping the page to the repair order where the customer is complaining about having an oil leak for the last three months. People are idiots when it comes to cars. There's just some things that should be common sense. Like oil leaks. If you have one, get the damn thing looked at before it destroys your engine.

I set down the paperwork and give Colt my full attention.

"Some families have born athletes and some families have born geniuses, but my family was born with the gift of drink. We can drink large quantities of alcohol day in and day out without any real consequences. It's like our superpower." Colt smiles. "So, where did you come from?"

I'm not sure how much I want to say, so I keep it easy. "Oklahoma."

"That's unfortunate."

I laugh. "I'd have to agree with you."

"You don't see many girl mechanics. You seem to have a lot of knowledge for your age."

"I suppose I do. I paid attention anytime engines were involved."

"So what made you decide to be one? A mechanic I mean, not a girl."

"Wes was a mechanic, and I was raised around cars. I guess it just stuck."

"Who's Wes?"

I shrug. "Foster dad."

Red walks by and hands me that same repair order I had been looking at, his crotch still damp from the coffee. I take it, and Red stares at Colt. "Get back to work, old man."

"Don't be so bossy," Colt grumbles, taking himself and his flask back to his corner. I'm beginning to understand Colt doesn't do a lot of work, but he's like a fixture in the shop. You can't get rid of him because it was basically built around him. There seems to be one in every shop I've worked in, and I usually find them the most entertaining to be around. Colt is definitely no exception.

WHEN I'M FINISHED with the oil leak that basically destroyed this woman's 2011 Honda Civic, I look around the shop and see Red. He bites his bottom lip when he works. I've always found biting the lip sexy. It gets me thinking, what else makes him bite his lip like that? I bet he does when he's fucking.

Oh fuck, the images of him alone, his hand dipping south to grasp his hard cock, yep, I'm lightheaded and breathing heavily so I go sit on a stool.

So far today, Red seems to be doing his best to ignore me, refusing to look in my direction. He's pretty good at it too. But what he fails to realize is that I'm a woman and so much better at making sure he can't ignore me. It's easy to do too.

"Whatcha doin' for lunch?" Raven asks, kicking my stool.

I jerk to attention and drop the wrench in my hand on the floor. Red hears the commotion and looks over his shoulder at me, his eyes on my chest and then my face. He's so obvious. But so am I.

I look at Raven. "I don't know, why?"

"There's a burger place up the street we're ordering from today. Want some?"

"Oh... uh... sure."

"Red's buying," Raven remarks, walking toward him. He simply shakes his head that she volunteered him to buy.

When Raven returns with the burgers, the guys stand around eating and teasing one another. I stay back away from them with Raven near the bench I've been using as my makeshift toolbox.

"So... tomorrow we're going to the river. You got a bathing suit?"

"No," I say with a mouthful of burger.

"Well, get one. I think we're gonna take the tubes and just hang out."

"Okay." I don't even know where to get one, so I ask, "Is there like a Target around here?"

"Yeah, I'll show you after work and then give you a ride back to Tyler's." Raven's voice is hushed and then she stuffs a French fry in her mouth, quickly.

"Sounds good."

Daniel approaches just as Raven heads back into the office. She doesn't spend a lot of time in the shop, for obvious reasons.

"Do you eat meat?" Daniel asks, taking an overly large bite of his own burger. Pieces of it fall onto the floor, next to the pile of shop rags he tossed on the ground earlier today. I know one thing, this kid is a slob.

"Yeah, I like meat," I tell him, wondering where he's going with this, especially since I'm still gnawing on my own burger. "Why?"

By the look on his face, I'm assuming he's wanting to know if I will eat his meat. Which is a flat out fucking no.

"Just wondering." He looks down at the glob of ketchup now on his shirt and then back at me. "Do you like racing?"

"Sure...."

"I race," he says as if I'm supposed to be impressed.

"Good for you." Lifting my milkshake to my lips, I take a slow drink as Daniel's eyes focus on my lips.

Red walks by, his own milkshake in hand. Fuck, look at the way his lips wrap around that straw! Kiss me, damn it!

Ugh, what the hell is wrong with me?

Red tosses a repair order in Daniel's direction, and it lands on the floor. "There's a waiter here. Get your ass to work."

He scratches the side of his sandy blond hair. "But it's lunch time."

Red shrugs as he sets his milkshake on his toolbox and glances at me. "I don't give a fuck."

Reluctantly, Daniel rolls his eyes and walks away.

Just as I'm finishing my burger and milkshake, Red walks up to me and hands me another repair order. "Can you handle a clutch replacement?"

I nod, tossing my trash in the garbage next to me but I keep my milkshake. Maybe I can tease him a little. Automatically his eyes go to my mouth, and I suck in my last drink of my chocolate shake. "I can handle it."

Yes, I'm referring to you.

He gives me a once over, an emotion I can't decipher passing over his face and then he shrugs. "It's the Toyota outside."

And then he turns abruptly and walks away, and disappears inside the parts room. A minute later, he returns with a handful of parts.

I can see he has a big job he's working on, another engine replacement, but I also can't help myself from watching him work. I'm completely in awe of his abilities.

His focus is on the engine as he practically lifts the entire thing before turning it on the hoist for a better angle, his arms and every muscle in his chest flexing with exertion.

I can't see his face very well; his head is bent forward, his attention on his hands as they work inside the engine and I'm pretty much staring. Obviously staring.

I move my gaze to across the shop. Daniel's working under the hood of that car checking the oil by pulling out the dipstick. I smile when I notice what's really going on.

Rawley—who sneaks around the side of the car—honks its horn and Daniel jumps back, smacking his head on the underside of the hood.

Sliding out of the car, Rawley lets out a burst of laughter that rings through the shop. "I do this at least once a week... and it's funny every single time."

With a wrench in his hand, Daniel bolts around the other side of the car to hit Rawley for doing that when he slips on oil Colt sprayed on the floor.

Even I laugh at that one. Serves the kid right.

Red shakes his head, looks over at them and sees the mess on the floor. "Get back to work. We have ten fucking cars waiting on us! This place is a goddamn business and you three need to stop acting like a bunch of fucking dickheads."

Other than taking a ride in the Plymouth the other day, I'd think this guy has no fun in his life.

"Lighten up!" Rawley yells back at him, making his way to collect a pig mat to clean up the oil. "You used to be fun in here, and now you're just a fucking dick."

Red laughs and stands up straight. Dropping the tool in his hand, he shoves him back. "That's funny. You're trying to tell me how to behave now, and you can't even get your shit together long enough to make it here on time in the morning."

And just like that, they're in each other's faces again. I'm beginning to see there's quite the feud between these two that dates back a ways. Before any swings are taken, Mia must sense it and comes out of the office again.

"Stop it, you two!" She places her hands on their chests, separating them. "Walk away and cool down!"

They do. Rawley walks outside, and Red goes into the parts room leaving me standing there staring at Mia walking toward me.

"I'm surprised they haven't killed each other yet this week."

Yeah, me too.

As all this is happening, Colt continues to spray Daniel's ass with the soap and water mixture we use to find holes in tires until he finally turns around and realizes he's soaked.

Daniel brushes off his pants. "You fucking asshole, knock it off."

Colt raises his palms, dropping the water bottle to the floor. "Ain't nobody doin' nothin'."

I'm not sure if I'm crazy, or just looking for some more verbal abuse, but I go into the parts room. Crazy, huh?

"It doesn't hurt to have a little fun every once in a while," I say to him, pretending to look for parts I don't need, and then think maybe that wasn't the smartest of ideas. I should have stayed out of here. I think back to the ride in the car and the way he kinda sorta smiled at me. That's my only reasoning for stepping foot in here.

Red looks up, anger flashing in his eyes. Yep. Horrible idea. "And that means?"

"It means relax. Don't take everything so seriously." I want to scowl at him, but I don't because he's already in a bad mood and I don't want to be the errands bitch again. I also don't because he raises his hand to reach for a box on the shelf and his T-shirt rides up. With one glance at his stomach, all thoughts leave my head. I can't see much, but what I can see is just like I pictured it would be. Tan and hard.

I bet there is more of his body that is tan and hard.

Dammit, Lenny. Grow the fuck up!

What is this man doing to me?

Red turns to face me, his hands raised in the air. "Relax, huh? Well, Lenny, you see I can't relax. You want to know why? Because less than two months ago my father died leaving me to run his business. A business he busted his ass to build. A business that people rely on day in and day out. On top of that, I have a five-year-old daughter who I am raising alone. Every day I have to leave her in daycare knowing all she wants is to be with me. And it fucking kills me to leave her, but I have to do it." He raises an eyebrow, and my breathing falters, coming out in a quick breath at his proximity. He's close enough his eyes shift from mine, to my lips, and then back up again. What I wouldn't give to grab him by the shirt right now, slam him against the wall and kiss the shit out of him. "Why do I have to do it, Lenny? Well, I have to do it so that you can have a paycheck and so that the people of this town know that even though my dad is gone, his legacy is still alive." I stare, dumbfounded at him and a little pissed at myself for making the situation worse. But he continues, steps back and reaches for a bottle of brake cleaner on the top shelf. "I've got five guys in the shop. One's an idiot. One can't drag his ass in here before noon on most days, and one is drunk from the moment he clocks into the moment he leaves. That leaves me with one mechanic who knows what he's doing and *you*." Red raises his arms in the air spread out wide. "So you tell me, Lenny. When do I have time to relax?"

I'll help you relax all right.

"Wait." I swallow over my nerves. "What do you mean me?"

"Fuck if I know...." And then he walks away leaving me to think about that.

I should have stayed outside.

With a deep sigh, I step out of the parts room and into the shop. The next hour is completely silent in the shop, and you can detect hostility in the air.

At the end of the day, Red's standing at his toolbox staring at some paperwork. I don't want to bother him because I can tell he's had a long week, but I say, "Thanks for giving me a chance."

He doesn't look at me. "Yeah... uh, see you Monday."

Just as I'm heading to Raven's car, Colt is outside smoking a cigarette and says, "It's a pretty cool place to work, huh?"

I laugh, walking backwards in the parking lot to look at him. "Entertaining to say the least."

He snorts, tossing his cigarette on the ground and putting it out with his boot. "Honey, you ain't seen nothing yet."

I don't doubt for one second there's some truth to that.

IT'S BEEN A while since I left Ben and though I haven't thought about him once, the next morning, I do. Some people are just mean. They don't have good in them.

Then there are the people who become jaded over time because of the things done to them.

I've been over this, but Ben is just mean. There's no reason for it; he's just that way. His parents are nice people, and he didn't suffer through some awful experience that would leave him jaded and angry. But something isn't right with Ben. There's a meanness buried deep within him. And though I saw it from the beginning, I didn't realize how bad it was. I let it go for the sake that I was away from Wes. Why I thought one bad situation was better than the last, I might never know. Sometimes it's like I'm just living my life through a series of mistakes and hoping not to make the same one twice.

The thing with Ben is he had a way of making you think you meant the world to him, as do all con artists. They'll toss bullshit at you all day long to get you to believe them.

I need a drink. A really strong drink. And you know, I wouldn't mind if I passed out with the bottle in hand.

I haven't let myself take the time to obsess over everything that went down. I know the reason for it is Red. That man has the ability to make me forget anything else exists at any given moment. The problem is he also has the ability to piss me off more than any other person I've ever met. Strangely enough, both of these traits only make me want him more.

"Morning," Tyler says, coming out of his room with no shirt and just a pair of basketball shorts on.

I sit up, placing my pillow over my lap and smile at him. "Morning."

Moving around the kitchen, he reaches in the cupboard and draws a bag of coffee out to start a pot.

"You ready for the river?"

I yawn. "Yeah, as long as I can have a cup of that first."

Tyler laughs and digs out two cups. "Sure. I think Raven's on her way over. I'd go get ready if I were you."

I hop up and head for the shower. I need to shave my legs and other bits because God knows I haven't all week and the bathing suit I picked out yesterday is a little revealing.

THERE'S ONE THING I'm aware of when we arrive at the river. This is where the party is at on Saturdays. I drove us considering Tyler and Raven both wanted to ride in my Bronco with the top off. As soon as we're at the lake, Tyler leaves right away, never lingering by us for very long. I can tell they're desperately trying to keep whatever this is between them a secret.

Breathing in deeply, I enjoy the smells and sounds of the river. Back in Oklahoma, they didn't have places like this. And if they did, I didn't know about it. Most of my time was spent at the shop I worked at or with Ben doing what Ben wanted to do.

"Jesus girl," Raven remarks once I take off my shorts and tank top. "I wish I had your body."

I look over at her as she peels her sundress off. She certainly has nothing to complain about if you ask me. Sure, she's a tad bigger than me but hey, curves are sexy.

She cups her large breasts with both hands. "I took the whole Freshman 15 to a new level when I went away to college," she teases with a laugh, reaching for her sunscreen beside her.

"You look great." I take the bottle from her when she offers it to me. "So you're in college?"

"Yeah, just home for summer break. I attend University of Oregon. Trying to get a degree in accounting. Numbers are my thing."

With commotion around the river, girls half-naked, guys running around shirtless and drinking, I people watch for a few minutes.

Raven takes the bottle I hand back to her, then places it inside her bag and angles the bag so it's nice and neat. "I love your tattoos," she then says, noticing the one I have down my left side that goes from my ribcage under my breast down to my upper thigh. "When did you get them?"

"Oh, uh, couple of years ago. I knew a tattoo artist back in Oklahoma." It was more like I fucked a tattoo artist for six months while he used my body as a canvas. Again, I've never made good decisions.

"Wow, that's cool. I really want a tattoo, but I haven't gotten one yet. I think between Rawley and Red they have enough."

I nod, but I don't say anything more. I love my tattoos, but I also regret a few.

"It's been a week and I don't even know where you came from. Tyler said you're his cousin?" And then she thinks for a second and quirks an eyebrow at me. "Do you have a boyfriend?"

"I guess in a sense I was am his cousin. I grew up in foster care and the lady that was taking care of me was Tyler's Aunt."

"His Aunt Maggie?"

"Yeah. Tyler spent the summers up at their apartment complex in Kennewick. I got to know him that way."

"Oh, right. I really liked her. I met her on spring break once. I think she gave me twenty bucks to clean bugs out of their pool."

I laugh. That sounds like Maggie. I made a lot of money from cleaning out the pool at the apartments we lived at, which Maggie and Wes managed. Funny I never met Raven then, or maybe I had seen her and never knew it.

Squinting at the sun, I look over at Raven applying sunscreen to her skin. She's staring at Rawley standing with a group of guys not too far from us. They all look a little similar in a sense, same height, same build as Rawley, who's next to them. Must be related.

One of the guys, the tallest one of the bunch that kinda reminds me of Red, turns and raises his hands at Raven. "Hey, Raven! Aren't you going to introduce us to your new friend?"

Raven flips him off. "Mind your business, Jude." And then she whispers to me, "He's inappropriate, sorry."

He throws his head back taking a drink of his beer in hand. "Aw, come on now. Don't be like that." He elbows Rawley. "We were always raised to share."

I look at Raven dumbfounded. She shakes her head. "Those guys are my asshole cousins, Jude and Eldon. You'll get used to seeing them at the shop. They work next door at my Uncle Hendrix's body shop."

Our conversations drift, mostly just random things as she tells me about the people gathered around the river. I'm not sure what I'm thinking, but I ask, "So what's with the feud between Rawley and Red?"

"They've always been at each other's throats. I'm not even sure why." Raven sighs. "Red's just been especially," she pauses trying to think of the right word, "angry for two years. He was married before. To Nevaeh... Nova's mother. She died two years ago. Murdered by her ex-boyfriend and Red found her in the kitchen with Nova in her room screaming." Her words are rushed, pained, as though she doesn't want to tell me this so she's saying it as fast as she can.

"Oh my God!" I gasp, covering my mouth with my hand. My heart pounds painfully in my chest. "Jesus... does Nova remember it?"

"Not that we can tell. She never talks about it, and if she does, she just says remember Mommy laying on the floor or that she remembers daddy holding Mommy. It's all just... so sad."

Well, fuck, no wonder the guy is so mean!

"So the guy... did they find him?"

"Viktor... he was gone by the time Red got home from work. Apparently, she and Viktor had just broke up a week earlier when she got together with Red. I think she and Red were like a one-night thing after a concert, and she wound up pregnant. I don't know for sure, but I imagine Viktor wanted her back maybe."

My heart's in my throat. "So what happened after that?"

"They found Viktor a few days later. Shot himself in the head. Dude was mentally unstable. Red went into depression, like locked himself in his room for a week, didn't eat, didn't talk, nothing. He came out one day and started going through the motions for Nova's sake."

I look up at the sky. Jesus, even with all the shit that's gone on in my life, I could never imagine the shock of finding your wife, or husband, dead. And how horrendous of a situation for Nova to be in having lost her mother so young. My mother abandoned me when I was young and I don't have all that many memories of her. I always chalked it up to you can't miss what you never had, but Nova, Nova had her mother for three years and to lose her so suddenly and brutally, my heart breaks for her and Red.

We're laying out in the sun for an hour, my skin a little crispy, when a shirtless Rawley heads over, sits down beside me and rests his arms on top of his bent knees. "What are you doing later?"

I look to Raven. "What am I doing later?"

"You playing tonight?" Raven asks, sitting up to reach for her water bottle.

"Yeah."

Raven shrugs. "We'll come."

Rawley stands and winks at me. "See you tonight."

"Where are we going?" I ask, watching Rawley walk back over to his cousins again.

"Murphy's. Rawley plays there about three times a week. Our Grandpa Carson was in a band, and Rawley really took to music."

"Does Red play?"

There I go with my curiosity into him again.

"No, he's never had the interest that I know of."

"Why does Rawley work at the shop then?"

"Well, he didn't at first. He had a scholarship for engineering. Believe it or not, he's like a super genius or something. Anyway, he turned it down and started working at the shop. When Dad died, Red took over as the owner because Dad left everything to him knowing he'd take care of it. Rawley's more focused on his music, which is why he turned down the scholarship. He wants to be a rock star."

"So we're going to watch him tonight, right?"

"Yep."

Okay, so a bar tonight. That can't be all bad, right?

And then I remember, Raven's nineteen. "How can you get into a bar? You're nineteen."

"Eh, we know the owner." Raven stands and reaches for her bag. "And I'll be twenty in two weeks. We should get going if we're gonna head out tonight."

My nerves jump as I reach for my own bag. "I don't really have anything to wear to a club."

Raven just waves her hand in the air. "No worries. I think I have some things that will fit you." She turns to walk away and yells over her shoulder. "I'm gonna catch a ride with Jude back to my house. Go home and shower then meet me there in like an hour."

"Okay," I reply, even though she doesn't wait for a reply.

What am I getting myself into? The idea of having friends like this is different.

AN HOUR LATER, I pull up to the modest white home with gray trim. I notice immediately Red's Nova parked in the driveway.

Fuck! He's here? Why? Damn it. This sucks.

I'm sitting in the driveway, my hands shaking and I'm half tempted to just leave. I'm not sure I can be around him today without wanting to hug him after knowing his wife died.

Raven hangs out the door and yells, "Get your skinny ass in here!"

Rolling my eyes, I open the door to my Bronco and slide out. As soon as I get to the porch, Nova pushes the door open. "Lenny!" she screams and all but jumps into my arms. "Auntie says we're doing a make-over on you. I'm spending the night with Grandma tonight, and I get to help."

I glare at Raven. "She did, did she?"

Raven grabs my hand and pulls me inside, kicking the door closed behind her and I'm standing in the entry way of the Walker family home. "You spend ten hours a day covered in grease. It's time to embrace your hot feminine side."

In the kitchen, Red steps around the corner, his arms crossed over his chest as he looks curiously at Raven, and then me. He doesn't say anything as our eyes meet. He doesn't look mad that I'm here... just confused maybe.

But then he looks at my shorts and then turns to walk away.

He's so strange with these shorts.

As I'm being pulled along, Nova bouncing around beside me, wild curls all over the place, I think maybe this won't be so bad.

"Plus," Raven adds when I'm sitting in her bathroom on a stool, "you never know who you'll run into tonight. God knows there's more out there than the guys at Walker Automotive."

I nod, unsure where she's going with that considering she's fucking one of them herself.

"It's nice to have someone to hang out with," Raven remarks, digging through her makeup bag and then the drawers below the sink in search of something. "Most of my friends either left for college or got knocked up."

I know exactly what she's referring to, not that I was ever close to anyone.

Nova comes back into the bathroom and sits on the edge of the tub, a Popsicle in her hand with drops of cherry red sugar trickling down her tiny hands. She looks at me, bright red lips pulling into the cutest smile. Seeing her smile like this she reminds me of Red.

She looks up at Raven. "Auntie, can you straighten my hair?"

Raven snorts. "No, we tried that once, remember?"

"I know." Nova shrugs, biting into her Popsicle and then talking with a mouthful. "But I want my hair like Lenny's."

"Well..." Raven finally finds the curling iron she was looking for. "You're in luck. I was going to curl Lenny's hair. You two can match tonight."

Nova's eyes go wide. "Cool!" She hops down from the tub and then disappears into Raven's bedroom.

"I know she's going to drop that damn Popsicle in my room again," Raven groans, reaching forward to plug in the iron next to me.

Ten minutes into this, I have makeup already being applied, and Nova has literally shown me twenty pairs of shoes. They all sit at my feet too waiting for me to try them on, should I want to. And I've also been shown five different dresses. Apparently, Nova thinks I'm going to wear a dress. I hate to break it to the little squirt, but no way in hell I'm wearing a dress. Ever.

Nova returns, standing in front of me as Raven applies eyeshadow to the crease of my brow, the faint sounds of country music flowing through the room. "Do you think my daddy is handsome?"

My eyes go wide, about the same time Raven laughs. "What?"

Nova, annoyed with me, sighs. Wow, she really is like Red. "I said, do you think my daddy is handsome?"

I'm not sure how to answer that. Especially considering what I found out about her mother today... and the fact that she's his kid.

Raven stops and stares at me, a mascara wand in hand. "Yea, Lenny, do you think her daddy is handsome?"

Bastards. They're ganging up on me now.

"I've never really thought about it," I say, glancing down to those huge blues of her blinking up at me with total innocence.

Bullshit. You think about him every hour.

Nova puts her hands on her hips dropping the second pair of red heels she's been trying to coax me into. "That's okay. You can think about it. I can wait."

And by wait, she means standing in front of me staring at me until I answer the question. Persistent little thing. You have to understand how adorable Nova is. Picture this short little version of Merida but with wild brown curls and big blue eyes and cheeks to match. I want to pinch her cheeks so badly and kiss them.

So I do. I lean forward and cup her puffy little cheek between my palms. She smiles, and I ask, "Why do you care if I think your daddy is handsome?"

Sighing dramatically when I let her cheeks go, she reaches for Raven's makeup bag and takes out the red lipstick. Raven immediately grabs it from her and hands her the pink instead.

"Well,"—Nova begins taking the cap off the lipstick and looking at herself in the full-length mirror behind the door—"Elle thinks my daddy is handsome. And Jesse, she does too. They are always asking my dad to go out or come over for a playdate. So I thought if you thought he was handsome, maybe you could tell him and you can come over for a playdate."

A playdate for her... or her daddy? With all the thoughts running through my head, I'm really hoping this playdate might include me being bent over the hood of his car.

My cheeks flush, and Raven lets out a burst of laughter. "You mean playdate with you, right, Nova?" She's curling my hair. Platinum-blonde curls with black ends fall over my shoulders naturally.

Nova makes a popping sound with her lips. "No, Daddy."

"There...." Raven interrupts with a smile, her hands on my shoulders. "Look." She then makes a twirling motion with her finger for me to turn around.

Holy shit. I look like a girl again.

"If you don't think my daddy is handsome, he's gonna think you're pretty," Nova says, standing beside me with a beaming smile.

There's no way I can lie to this kid and whisper, "I think your daddy is handsome."

Nova's smile gets wider if that's possible. "I knew it!" And then she takes off running. More than likely to fucking tell him.

Raven hands me a pair of holey jeans, high-heel sandals with beads and gems on them, a white tank top and a handful of bracelets. "Here, get dressed. I'm gonna go change."

I take a look at my hair, makeup, pink cheeks from the sun, and clothes once I'm dressed. "Wow...." Taking the corner of the tank top, I tie it in a knot to make it a little more form fitting. I seem to be a size smaller than Raven, but the jeans actually fit me pretty well. Leaning forward, I roll them up around the ankles to give them that new-age look. "I look... *hot*."

"Yes, you do." Raven knocks on the door. "Now unlock this so I can see."

I hadn't even realized I locked her out.

"Come on." She waves me forward. "We're running late hot stuff."

Raven looks hot herself in a pair of similar jeans and a black top that was ripped up the side revealing her tanned skin in ways I was sure Tyler was gonna enjoy.

As we step outside, Red's kissing Nova good-bye and getting in his car.

What gets me thinking there's more to the night is the way he looks at me. I'm standing near my Bronco, keys in hand while his eyes drag over the length of my body, then to my face. They linger momentarily before he sighs and slides into the seat.

Raven wraps her arm around my shoulder, kissing my cheek. "I think he likes you."

My face heats, and I want to tell her no, she's just imagining it. But then I think, even for the smallest moment, he might. He's just trying to act like he doesn't. Like the boy in school who constantly chases you just to pull your hair. He's not doing it because he wants to hurt you. He's doing it because he can't possibly leave you alone.

Closing my eyes, I reach for my door handle, my hands shaking at the reality that his demeanor might just be an act.

10

LENNON

I WATCH Red backing out of the driveway. "Where is he going?"

Raven grins tucking her lip gloss she'd just applied in her bag. "I don't know, Lenny. Do you want to know because you think he's *sooooo* handsome?"

Now she sounds like her niece.

Shaking my head, I shove her shoulder. "Shut up. What was I supposed to say? The kid put me on the spot."

"You know... inquiring minds want to know what you really think of my brother?"

I don't answer her. Mostly because my cheeks are red and I can't. So I switch the focus from me to her when she's staring down at her phone. "Is Tyler going to be there?"

This time, her cheeks flush. "Oh, uh... I'm not sure. He might be."

I raise an eyebrow. "You guys don't talk out of the bedroom?"

She shrugs, tucking her phone in her bag too. "Not really. Occasionally, but if I don't want anyone knowing, I can't be seen with him anywhere."

"So no one knows?"

"Nobody but you. *He* sure as shit hasn't said anything." And then she looks a little sad about that last part. "I doubt he ever will. It's pretty clear it's just fucking."

"And you're okay with that?"

A few things pass over Raven's face, and I can tell she's confused. I also have to remind myself she's nineteen, and I remember that age. You're still trying to figure out what you're supposed to do once you're not in school anymore let alone making sense of a relationship that's new.

At nineteen, I was living out of my car, dating a tattoo artist and working at a garage just to make ends meet. I had no sense of belonging, let alone direction in my life at the time.

Raven's smarter than me. She has a good family to back her up, and Tyler would never hurt her. Even if it doesn't work out between them, I doubt he'd ever be mean about it.

The bar is just as crowded as the river was today, country music blaring from a jukebox tucked away near the stage. Raven grabs my hand and leads me to a high top in the corner surrounded by five guys. I recognize Rawley and his cousins, but not the other two guys.

"Holy shit, Lenny... you clean up nice," Rawley remarks, winking at me as he brings a beer to his lips.

Raven punches him in the gut and tells him to be nice.

He frowns at his twin sister. "I am being nice. Fuck." He snorts. "I literally fucking said the word nice when talking to her."

Raven waves him off. "You're a pig."

"Whatever." Rawley rolls his eyes and then points to the guys I don't recognize. "This is Linc. He's my drummer, and this is Beck. He's our bass guitarist."

I smile politely, shaking their hands. Both of them, I mean both of them, openly check me out from head to toe and settle on my chest. "Nice to meet you, Lenny," Beck says, moving closer and waggling his eyebrows.

"Stop it," Rawley tells them, pushing them forward. "It's time to go."

The guys excuse themselves for their set that's starting up, all taking one last look at me.

I stare at Raven, chuckling nervously. "It's like they've never seen a girl."

She gives me a once over. "They've never seen a girl like you before."

I wave her off. "Oh, please...."

Raven nods to the bartender and he brings over a pitcher of beer, and then hugs Raven to his side. "Hey there, stranger," he says, kissing her temple. "Long time since you've been in here."

Raven looks at him like he's crazy. "I was literally here last Wednesday."

"Oh, right." He laughs, shaking off his confusion before drifting his eyes to mine. "Who's your friend?"

"This is Lenny. She's the new mechanic at our shop. Lenny, this is Zack. He's the owner of the bar."

I shake his hand, and for the most part, his eyes don't linger, and I see the ring on his finger.

Jude and Eldon approach the table and immediately pour themselves beer from a handle of glasses in the center of the table.

Just as I'm taking a drink of my own beer, Eldon bumps my shoulder. He reminds me more of Rawley, a little more clean-cut than Red with a white baseball cap hiding his dark brown wavy hair. They all have those same brown eyes, though. Red has his own look, like his own brand of ruggedness that can't be duplicated by anyone. And shouldn't be for that matter.

"How do you like working for Red?"

I've been asked this question so many times it's like I'm forming a standard answer by now. "It's okay. Challenging at times."

Jude laughs beside Eldon, giving me a nod. "It's probably challenging because Red's an asshole and the shop is full of horny bastards."

I laugh. There's really no denying that statement. "Yeah, something like that."

"Ah, hang in there." Jude winks. "It'll get better. Red comes off as a dick, but once you get to know him, you'll see he's a good guy."

The band starts up, and I'm floored at Rawley's ability. Literally fucking floored when he starts out singing a cover of Nickelback's "Burn it to the Ground."

Raven rips my beer from my hand and forces me to dance around with her by the stage. In a passing glance, I notice Jude watching me from his place at the table, his eyes on my body, mostly. I kinda don't even care at that moment because the bass and the way the music pulses in my chest and the beer give me a confidence I rarely have while dancing.

I'm awestruck staring up at Rawley as he rocks the mic, dancing around like a lively version of the smartass kid who has a chip on his shoulder at the shop. It's fucking amazing. Without a doubt, Rawley has talent, and I'll admit, I'm crushing on the kid a little too.

"Holy shit, he's amazing," I scream into Raven's ear when the music lowers and Rawley's gravelly voice belts through the bar.

She jumps around, her hands over her head, her long brown hair flying everywhere. "I know!"

Jude makes his way over to me when Rawley switches immediately into "Little Miss Dangerous."

I mean, Jesus... I had no idea Rawley was capable of *this*. No wonder the dude gave up his scholarship. He definitely has what it takes to make the rock-star career work.

I let Jude dance behind me, about the time some guy comes up to Raven. I'm careful because the last thing I want is to lead him on.

Halfway through the song, I see *him*. Him as in, the only him, really. It's like the air is sucked from my lungs the moment I spot him. My body reacts, a shiver, a fast beating heart, all indications this guy is someone I can't ignore.

Red.

His name is becoming burned into my brain; something I can't get out of my head no matter how hard I try. My mind buzzes and I breathe out slowly, trying to catch my breath. My nerves spark the instant his tall, lean frame comes into view.

Damn it, why does he have to be here?

Jude moves closer, his hips in line with my ass, his hands gripping my hips tightly as my back presses to his chest.

Red scans the bar when he enters with Tyler, his eyes dancing around to Rawley, and then the dance floor. When they land on me, I'm not sure what to make of it. Mostly because he's, well, not looking happy when he sees who's standing behind me. He scowls at his cousin and immediately stares at Jude's hands on my hips. The intensity in which he watches me dance with his cousin is a look I can't shake easily.

He turns, without another look and takes a seat at the bar with Tyler.

"Everything okay?" Jude asks when he notices my movements have stopped.

"Yeah," I mumble, twisting around to face him.

We dance for another song, a slower one this time when Jude's breath hits my ear. "Thanks for the dance."

I nod, turning to walk back to the table when I spot Red near the pool tables.

He's leaning back in his chair, slouched slightly to one side. His head is down, lashes shadowing his cheeks as he shifts casually and drapes his arm over the back of the chair next to him. One leg is kicked out in front of him, the other bent, a resting point for the drink in his hand as he studies my every move.

I want to tell Jude I can't dance with him anymore, ever, but I don't because I wonder what Red's thinking now. Am I trying to make him jealous?

When I get back to the table, the pitcher is already empty. "I'll go refill this."

With hesitating steps and my head down, I approach the bar. Though I don't want to look up, my eyes fucking betray me like the bastards they are and seek him out. There's a tall redhead at his table, sitting next to him now. They're relaxed, and hell if he isn't beautiful when he smiles. It's the first smile I've seen, first genuine one at least.

He needs to smile more. That's for sure. Mostly because I'm ready to give him a lap dance at a smile not even directed at me. Imagine if he smiled for me!

My breathing spikes, a twinge of jealousy burning a hole in my stomach when the redhead reaches out and touches his hand, smiling tenderly at him. Raven didn't mention him dating anyone, but that really looks intimate.

"Need another, Lenny?" Zack asks, drawing me from my stare.

"Yes!" I whip around to face him. "Please."

Fuck, could I be more obvious?

Taking the pitcher of beer filled to the brim, I head back to the table but not before taking one last look at Red. He chooses then to look my way, his brow arching as if to ask, what the hell are you staring at?

Believe me, dude, I'm wondering that same thing.

Raven notices my flushed appearance immediately when I set the beer on the table. "You okay?"

"Yep." Dismissively, I wave my head around. "Sun and beer are getting to me."

Bullshit. Red's getting to you. He gets under my skin and ignites desires and thoughts I was sure were hidden forever behind a girl who didn't know how to love or fall for someone. Not that I was either of those with him.

He gets to me so much that I can't even decipher thoughts and feelings.

For an hour, I pretend I'm drinking and not watching Red with the girl. I don't do a good job at it, but thankfully everyone around me is drunk and pays me no mind.

Rawley returns after his set is done, a group of girls following him. It's suddenly crowded around the table, and I want to find a way to excuse myself. Big crowds like this make me nervous.

"You having a good time?" Raven asks. She's pink-cheeked and talking so loudly it hurts my ears.

"Yes!" I yell back, wrapping my arm around her shoulder. "Thanks for inviting me."

My eyes, the betraying bastards they are tonight, scan the bar again when I've turned Raven's direction. He's gone.

Suddenly, I panic and start searching the rest of the bar for him only to see he's sitting in a booth off in the corner, the same redhead beside him. She's laughing at something he said and for the first time, his laughter rings through the room. It's distinct and captures my attention despite the crowd and noise.

I hate that I've been working right beside him and couldn't make that sound come out. What was it about me that he didn't like and she had?

"Who are you looking at?" Raven asks, bumping her hip into mine and leaning across the table to see where I'm looking.

Crap.

"I see where your brother went." I point with my thumb in their direction. "Hot date apparently."

Raven stares at them and then bursts out laughing, covering her mouth with her hand. "He's certainly not on a date with her. They're friends. That's Crystal. She married Red's friend from high school. Her husband Lane is in the military and deployed right now. Red checks in on her and her two boys from time to time. Red watches their boys sometimes for her too. I think she watches Nova on occasions." And then she levels me a serious look, waits a beat and then smiles. "Nothing to *worry* about."

I'm so transparent. My cheeks sting with heat.

"I'm not worried. I'm not into him like that," I tell her, avoiding eye contact like any guilty person would. Lying has never been my strong suit.

"Well, he hasn't dated anyone since Nevaeh, and from what Tyler says, hasn't gotten laid either."

My eyes widen. "He hasn't had sex since his wife died?"

"Nope. I'm pretty sure that's why he's such an ass all the time."

She's probably right.

"Hey, listen," I say to Raven, pulling her close. "I'm tired. Can we head out soon?"

She nods, drinks the rest of her beer and then points to the door. "I'm ready."

We say our good-byes. Jude hugs me a little longer than needed and we're heading for the door. I do well. I don't glance at Red even once. I keep my head down and walk straight to my Bronco on the street before I actually even look up. It's not without effort, though. It's like trying to keep your eyes open when you really want to blink. Nearly impossible.

"You'll have to give me directions," I tell Raven, not remembering where she lives. "I'm horrible with remembering streets."

"Just take me back to Tyler's place. I'm gonna lay in his bed naked until he comes home."

I laugh just to tease her a little, and then ask, "What if he brings a girl home?"

"The fucker better not. All this beer made me horny and I'm gonna take Ty for a ride tonight."

"Ewww, Raven. There are certain things you should keep to yourself."

"Hey, I'm just letting you know. It could get loud tonight."

My mouth drops open. "There's something wrong with you. You literally have no filter."

"You wouldn't either if Red and Rawley were your brothers."

She has a point there.

And she was right. For the next three fucking hours after Tyler got home, they went at it and I heard things like, "Fuck me harder! Just like that, ahhh, yes! More!" and then, "You like my cock, don't you? Nobody fucks you as good as I do. Remember that, baby. Your pussy has my name on it!"

Really, it was all just too much. Those are things I never wanted to hear from Tyler or Raven, and now they're burned into my head forever. I might never be able to look at either one of them without laughing now.

And also, if I'm being honest, I'm a bit jealous.

11

REDDINGTON

I STOP by my mom's house, my head still pounding from last night at the bar. As soon as I pull into the driveway, I see Lenny's truck parked there.

Damn it, why is she here? I thought I would have had a little time to get my head straight before work tomorrow. I'm half tempted to text my mom to have her send Nova out, but then she'd kick my ass if I did that. And then I remember we're going to dinner tonight so that won't work either.

Just pretend you're in a hurry.

Sighing, I think about the way she watched me last night at the bar and the way she looked in those jeans. I don't know how many times I had to stop myself from grabbing her last night, dragging her to the bathroom and fucking her right out of them.

Classy, Red. Fuck her in the bathroom of a dingy bar.

What the fuck is wrong with me? Why can't I stop thinking about her this way? I've been doing fine for two goddamn years, and now her. There's plenty of hot women around town. Why am I suddenly having this reaction to her?

I'm not even sure I had this physical obsession with Nevaeh. Before her, girls were more of a want than a necessity. This girl... it's like she's a necessity. A need I can't seem to stop.

She's off limits.

With a heavy sigh, I open the door and walk up to the house. As soon as I open the door, Nova lunges herself in my arms. "Daddy! I missed you *so* much last night!"

Instinctively, I pull her close. Now that I'm with her so much, it's hard leaving her with other people, even if it is my mom. I always miss her come morning. "I missed you, too, Darlin'."

Immediately, I see those fucking legs and shorts. It's like my eyes seek the temptation out. She's handing Raven her clothes and then turns around.

Internally, I groan. "What are you doing here?" I'm not trying to be a dick, but as always, it comes off that way.

Raven speaks up before Lenny can reply. "She's here to drop off my stuff and what the hell is it any business of yours what she's doing here?"

I stare at Lenny, my eyes intent on hers. She can't take me looking at her. Every time I do, she flushes and turns away.

Nova takes my hand and swings it back and forth. "I helped Auntie give Lenny a makeover. Did you see how pretty she looked?"

I nod, refusing to say just how fucking pretty she looked. Believe me, the image of her dancing is one I can't seem to forget.

"Guess what, Daddy?" Nova yanks my arm down making me look at her.

"What?"

"Lenny thinks you're handsome!"

Lenny, who'd just taken a drink of her iced tea Mom handed her, spits it all over the front of Raven.

Raven's laughing so hard, she doesn't even care that she's now covered in tea. Pulling at her shirt, she shakes her head and moves past Lenny down the hall to change. "Nova, you're awesome."

You know, I have to say I'm completely entertained by this myself.

"Nova," Lenny gasps. "I didn't say that."

"Yes, you did." Nova glances up, her brow creased in confusion. "I asked you if you thought my daddy was handsome. You said yes."

I roll that information around, and I want to say something, but I don't in front of my kid.

Lenny flushes an even brighter shade of red. "Well, yeah... I guess I did say that but then...." She pauses and draws in a shaky breath. "Crap. I need to go. It's late."

It's not. It's only four in the afternoon. Clearly, she's freaking out, but hell, if she thinks I'm handsome, I wonder what she'd think if she knew the attraction I had for her.

Nova runs over to her before she gets to the door. "No, please don't go. You should come to dinner with us. Grandma is going too. It'll be fun. We're going to Daddy's favorite restaurant, Valentino's, because Daddy loves spaghetti. I don't like it that much, but the breadsticks are really good."

Lenny blinks a few times, her eyes wide like she doesn't know what to make of that. I can also see sadness in her eyes, and I don't like it. "Well, I wouldn't want to intrude on your family."

Mom walks into the room with her purse and overhears Lenny saying that. "Nonsense, the more the merrier. Right, Red?"

No!

Everyone turns to me as I glare at my mother in disbelief. She glares right back. "Yeah. Sure. The more the merrier."

Nova jumps up into my arms again and throws her arms around my neck. "Thanks, Daddy."

I tap the freckled bridge of her nose. "Anything for you, darlin'."

She wiggles back out of my arms, grabs Lenny's hand and drags her to the car. "You can sit by me at the restaurant."

Fine by me. I'll be the one in the corner with a napkin protecting my pants with the raging hard-on all night. I know this for sure because the moment I see those legs walking down the driveway in front of me, my dick twitches to life.

"I'll drive myself," Lenny says, attempting to let go of Nova's hand.

Nova pouts. "No, you can't. I wanted to sit next to you in the car."

No one can ignore Nova and her pouting. Believe me, I try, and I still haven't mastered the "no" word with her.

"Okay," Lenny finally agrees, sighing, as if she needs to prepare herself to get inside of my car. Mom flips the seat forward for her, offers to sit in the back with Nova, but that doesn't last long before Nova breaks down in tears.

"No, I want her to sit next to me." She's in her seat now, big tears rolling down her cheeks and Lenny is a sucker.

"I'll sit by you."

My biggest problem is when I catch sight of her perfectly round ass cheeks peeking out of her shorts. I'm staring. Blatantly fucking staring.

What the shit? Why can't I stop myself?

Mom notices and elbows me. "Red," she whispers, smiling. "Don't stare."

Rock meet bottom. My mother fucking caught me.

Like a child told to stay out of the cookie jar, my eyes drift back tempting myself. Fuck me. I want Lenny.

And there's the hard-on.

When I hunch forward awkwardly, Nova notices. "What's wrong, Daddy?"

I reach to start the car. "Nothing."

Just as we're pulling out of the driveway, Nova starts in with her questions. I don't think Lenny knew what she was getting into by agreeing to this. "Did you know that Daddy's car and me have the same name?"

"Nova, let up a little," I warn, eyeing my overly talkative daughter.

She doesn't even look at me and says, "I was made in here. That's how I got my name."

I gasp. "Who told you that?"

Nova shrugs. "Uncle Colt."

I'm gonna fucking punch him tomorrow.

Lenny and mom both start laughing as I toss a dirty look at Nova again and grip the steering wheel a little tighter.

"Do you go to school?" Lenny asks Nova.

"No. Daddy forces me to go to Elle's house, but I start kindergarten soon. I'm five now." She groans, putting her hands on her face and shaking her head dramatically. "It's a big waste of my time because everyone there is a dumbass."

"Nova," I warn. "Watch your mouth."

"Daddy, on Friday, Kale ate paste for lunch."

Well, she has a point.

WHEN WE'RE at the restaurant, I'm not sure how much more of this I can take. I know this is going to be bad taking her here. I've never brought anyone here but family, and it feels wrong. Feels like I'm cheating on my wife.

Valentino's is a small family-owned Italian restaurant that's the heart of Lebanon and has the best spaghetti around, aside for Nevaeh's recipe. The building is small, basically an old house converted into a restaurant back in the early 90s when they moved from Italy. Literally couldn't get more Italian than the Valentino family, which was why they were the best in town.

Most of the time just to get in here, you needed reservations months in advance; only we never did because we were family.

I stand back as we step inside, and Lenny and my mom follow Nova in. She spots him right away and runs directly to him. "Papa!

Tony picks Nova up in his burly arms and spins her around. "Ah, there's my grandbaby." It hurts watching him hold her like that, mostly because you can see it on his face. He's reminded of his daughter at that age.

Mom must sense it and looks back at me. This is why I didn't want Lenny coming here. It's hard enough being in this restaurant let alone seeing Tony, my wife's dad.

"That's Tony, the owner," Mom tells Lenny. "This is Nevaeh's dad's restaurant."

I stay back, lingering near the door and half tempted to excuse myself and sit in the damn car. I have these empty spaces in my heart, and places like this are empty reminders of what I once had. Empty memories, empty experiences for Nova. There is and always will be a void space in every life my wife touched, and time doesn't make that go away.

Here, I'm reminded of it, more than anywhere else I shared with her. I can't explain why, but it is. And now here I am, with another girl I can't stop thinking about sexually, with a knot the size of a bolder in my chest. It pisses me off more than anything.

With Nova on his hip, Tony approaches us. "Well, look who finally came by." He reaches for my hand. "Good to see you, son." And then his gaze shifts to Lenny, probably wondering who she is.

I step forward. "Tony, this is Lenny. She works for Walker Automotive now." My fucking words shake like I'm a scared teenage boy asking his daughter out. "Nova wanted her to come."

And I sound like an asshole. At least I'm keeping up with my persona.

Mom glares at me smacking my shoulder. "Knock it off," she mouths back.

Burying my hands in my pockets, I drop my head forward as Tony shows us to a table. The restaurant is fairly busy, but Tony always keeps our table free, back in the corner near the kitchen.

Nova makes Lenny sit next to her like they're best friends all of a sudden. It's not lost on me that I really need to get this kid a friend her own age.

Not that he needs to, but Tony brings out menus and hands Nova a stack of white paper and crayons. "I need some more artwork for the wall, honey."

Lenny's eyes drift over my shoulder to the wall where Tony kept the drawings of all the kids that came here. Along the top are framed ones.

Her smile falters and I know why. There's a picture of Nevaeh, me and Nova up there. It's one of me holding a baby Nova in one arm, the other wrapped around Nevaeh's shoulders smiling at the camera while my wife is looking at Nova and me like we're her favorite people in the world.

Lenny's eyes snap to mine, and I hate the empty sadness. Empty. There's that word again.

Clearing my throat, I look to Tony when he hands me a menu. "Why are you handing me that? I'll have my usual."

I don't know what makes Lenny laugh right then, but she does. I stare at her and her cheeks flush as she proceeds to bite her lower lip. I shift in my seat, turning to look out the window. Reaching for my napkin, I drop it in my lap and hunch forward over the table.

This is exactly the reaction I didn't want to have here. All over her biting her lip.

"Are you okay?" Mom asks, looking at me like I've lost my mind tonight.

I nod but don't look at her.

"Your waitress will be around soon," Tony says. "I gotta get back in the kitchen."

The table is quiet, aside from Nova talking to Lenny when our waitress approaches to fill drinks. "Oh, hey, fancy meeting you here," Jesse, the girl from the coffee stand, says with a little too much excitement as she touches my shoulder.

Great. The hits just keep on coming tonight, don't they?

"What are you doing here, Jesse?"

"Oh well, my hours at the coffee shop weren't paying the bills, so I needed another part-time job and it worked out that Valentino's was hiring, so here I am. Isn't it great?" Jesse then turns to glare at Lenny, and Nova notices immediately.

She glares at Jesse giving her a look of disgust and shakes her head. "No. Not great."

I nudge Nova's chair with my foot under the table, and she looks up at me innocently. "What?"

"Be nice."

She just rolls her damn eyes at me, handing Lenny a green crayon. "Can you draw the grass for me?"

Jesse glances at Nova with a furrowed brow and then brushes it off. "What do you want to drink?"

We order drinks, and eventually, I find myself completely enthralled with watching Nova and Lenny interacting together. Especially when Lenny ties Nova's hair back before dinner so her curls won't get in her pasta.

There's an odd stab in my chest watching them. It's something like sadness and anger all rolled into one in the hollow parts of my heart I thought died two years ago. It's intense, just like that emptiness inside, and harder to avoid when I shift away from the two of them giggling.

Tony returns half way through the meal to check on us, sitting next to me with a chair he pulled up and a bottle of wine. After refilling our glasses, he drinks straight from the bottle.

"This is the best lasagna I've ever had," Lenny tells him, smiling at him.

"Thank you. I appreciate that," Tony says, refilling her wine once more. "It's my wife's recipe. Sadly she passed away before we built this place, but her memory is here. Along with Nevaeh's."

My heart aches hearing her name, it's a sudden drop in my stomach, a knot forming and Tony notices. He's careful to mention her around me, usually because even after two years, I don't deal with it well. I'm not sure I ever will.

"What brought you to Lebanon?" Tony asks Lenny.

Lenny begins to fidget, almost immediately. "Oh, uh... just looking for a change." Her chest pricks with pink blotches and I can tell the last thing she wants is to be talking about herself. It seems to make her uncomfortable with the slightest twist into why she moved here.

"Aren't you related to Tyler?" Mom asks and then takes a sip of her own wine before placing her napkin on the table over her spaghetti.

Lenny's face goes blank for a beat, and then she slowly lifts her eyes to my mom. "Yes." Lenny sets her fork down. "Tyler's Aunt Maggie was my foster mom. Tyler used to come every summer and hang out with me."

Tony nods and then smiles at me, and then Lenny. "So how do you like working with the big guy here?"

He had to ask that.

"I'm grateful for the job." Lenny's eyes meet mine. "They seem like a great group of guys."

She's *not* talking about me.

"Lenny's a great mechanic," Mom remarks.

I have to agree, though I haven't told her yet.

When we're finished with dinner, I reach for my wallet. "How much do I owe, Tony?"

Tony picks up Nova and kisses her cheeks. "Family doesn't pay here." With Nova still in his arms, he winks at Lenny. "It was a pleasure meeting you. Come back anytime and I'll have some more of that lasagna ready for you."

Lenny smiles wide. "I'll definitely be back."

Tony then reaches for my hand. "Thanks for bringing Nova in."

"Don't fool yourself, old man. I come for the spaghetti."

Tony throws his head back and belts out a loud laugh. "Oh, I know, but it's still nice."

THE DRIVE back to mom's house is quiet as Nova begins to fall asleep. I can't stop thinking about how flustered Lenny got when she was asked about her past. What could have happened that would spark a reaction like that? I have this overwhelming urge to protect her and find out what she's running from. I want to keep her safe and if that means working with me, torturing me, well then, I guess it's gonna have to be that way.

Our eyes catch in the rearview mirror a few times, and I can see it. She feels bad for me. The widower. The man who was left behind to take care of his daughter after his wife was murdered. It's the same look I've gotten from everyone since she died and I fucking hate it. I don't want to see it on her.

I watch her on the drive back, inquisitively examining her every movement. It's as if my mind is trying to find ways to not like her and I can't seem to find one anymore.

No sooner do we pull into the driveway and Lenny kisses Nova on her temple, says thank you for bringing her along, and she's out the door and getting into her Bronco.

Mom looks at me with a puzzled expression. "What did you say to her?"

"Me?" I point at myself. "You were sitting right next to me. If I said something, you would have heard it."

"You weren't very nice to her," Mom notes with raised eyebrows as she gets out and then looks to Nova.

"Uncle Colt says Daddy's a prick."

Mom glares back at me. "See... told you." And then slams the car door on me.

I turn to Nova. "He's not your uncle."

She shrugs. "Can I have ice cream?" It seems she's fully awake now.

"No."

Backing out of the driveway, I'm half tempted to follow Lenny to Tyler's house and ask her what her problem is. The thing is I know what her problem is. I'm a jerk to her.

When Nova and I get home, she runs directly to the television to turn it on.

"Nope," I say, turning it back off and dropping the remote on the coffee table. "Bath time."

"I took a bath yesterday." She huffs, flopping back on the couch.

"And you need one today too." I fan my nose. "You kinda stink."

She lifts her armpits to smell them, smiling. "I guess you're right."

Once I have her in the bath, it's not more than two minutes into it, and she's soaked me.

"Why can't you keep the water in the tub?" I ask, trying not to get angry with a five-year-old. It's just water, but she does this every time she takes one.

"I don't know." She takes the cup she has in the water and goes to dump it on me.

"Don't you dare!" I jerk back away from the tub. Not because I don't want to get wet but because I don't want the bathroom to flood again. Damn kid has done that twice already.

When I stand up, my hands on my hips, Nova stares at me. "Daddy, why do you have a tinkle and I have a potty?"

I nearly laugh, but I don't.

"Can a boy have a potty and a girl have a tinkle?"

"I think it's time you start taking showers instead of baths," I tell her, reaching for the faucet.

She freaks out and jumps up, bubbles flying everywhere. "No! I don't want to take a shower." She points to the showerhead bursting into tears. "It's gonna make noise, and I don't like it."

"Too bad." Reaching down, I pull the drain and hit the knob to the shower. "Kids going into kindergarten take showers."

Nova thinks anyone in kindergarten is something special. If I ever need her to do anything, I just lie and say kindergarteners do it. Bad parenting probably, but I don't care. I'm doing this shit on my own and sometimes we have to lie as parents.

"I don't understand why you make me do things I don't like to do. It's not fair." Her tears slow once the spray hits her tummy and then she giggles and dances around in it.

"A lot of things in life aren't fair." Shaking my head, I step back and close the shower curtain. "I'll be back in a minute."

Just as I'm reaching for the towels in the closet to mop up the water, I hear a crash in the bathroom.

Rushing back into the bathroom, I drop the towels on the floor and nearly laugh at the scene before me. Nova's sitting in the tub, the spray hitting the top of her head, shower curtain on the floor and she's vigorously scrubbing her hands.

She looks up at me when she notices me standing there. "I fell."

"Are you okay? Did you hurt yourself?"

She stares blankly at me, then her hands. "I fell in the shower...." I go to say something to her, and she holds her hands up, silencing me. "And when I tried to catch myself, my hand went in the toilet."

Pursing my lips, I try not to laugh. Nova has a fear of toilets and more importantly, toilet water. Potty training was a real bitch.

Kneeling down, I kick the wet towels out of the way and pick the shower curtain up. "I'm sorry, darlin'. But at least you're not hurt."

Nova looks me dead in the eyes, her soapy wet hands cupping my cheeks. "I fell in the shower, and my hand went in the toilet, Daddy! The toilet!"

I can't help it any longer and break out in laughter as I turn the shower off. "I know, and I'm sorry but let's get you dried off and ready for bed."

She's certainly okay with that and hops out of the tub reaching for a clean towel on the counter. "I told you taking a shower was a bad idea."

Just as she's leaving the bathroom, she gives the offensive toilet one last look and shivers.

I'm getting her dressed when she asks, "Can I sleep with you tonight? The toilet will give me nightmares."

"No, you can sleep in your own room tonight." I nod to her room. "Go pick out a book and I'll be in shortly."

After I change into a new shirt and shorts, I go back into Nova's room across the hall, and she's in bed with the blankets pulled up and book in hand. "I picked this one."

Looking at the book, I smile. She picked *If I Could Keep You Little*.

"Do you remember this book?"

She looks at the cover curiously, then up at me. "No, why?"

"Mommy used to read it to you every night."

As I settle in to read to her, she reaches toward her nightstand and grabs the photograph of her, Nevaeh, and me. It's the one where Nova's sleeping on my chest, and my head is in Nevaeh's lap. She's looking lovingly down at the two of us with her hands in my hair. "Do I look like Mommy?"

A knot forms in my chest, squeezing my heart. "What do you think?"

She stares down at the picture again. "We have the same curly hair and blue eyes."

I pull her closer, kissing her temple. "You're exactly like her, darlin'."

"Can you tell me about how you met?"

That hurts even more. I still remember the moment I locked eyes with her at the Dave Matthews Band concert at the Gorge. She was swaying to the beats of "Jimi Thing" and she smiled. Cheesy as it is, that's all it took for me to make my way over to her. I think back to that concert, and I can't say that I fell in love with Nevaeh that night, but I certainly knew she was something special. It was that night Nova was conceived. About a month later, Nevaeh had walked into the shop crying and telling me she understood if I wanted nothing to do with her, but that she was pregnant. Of course, I owned up to my responsibilities, and we made it work. It was the best decision I've ever made.

"Mommy would like Lenny," Nova says, smiling.

I know exactly what Nova's hinting at. "I'm sure she would." Bending forward, I kiss her forehead and then move off the bed to stand. "Time for bed."

"But I really want to sleep with you."

I pat her head. "No, you need to sleep in your own bed tonight. We'll have a sleepover on Tuesday night since I don't work on Wednesday."

"What's Wednesday?"

"Fourth of July."

She raises her hand above her head and then pulls it back down in a fist. "Yes! Finally a day off."

"Good night, I love you."

Just as I'm at the door, she pipes up with, "One more thing...."

I pause. "Yes?"

"Can I sleep naked?"

"What? Why? And you just wanted to sleep in my bed. No way."

"I want to feel the sheets on my butt."

I can't even look at her without wanting to laugh. "No. Put clothes on."

She folds her arms defiantly over her chest. "Why?"

"Because I said so."

As I close her door, I don't want to think about Nova ever sleeping naked again so I think about what she said, about Lenny. She's right. Nevaeh would have liked Lenny.

12

LENNON

JUST A FEW DAYS of living at Tyler's apartment, it's clear he and Raven are some kind of sex demons. I'm literally amazed the girl can walk normally during the day. Seriously, don't they realize I can't un-hear that shit? Maybe someone should have a talk with them about using their damn inside voices.

Not to mention how they haven't been caught by anyone but me.

As I lay here, trying to ignore yet another round of earsplitting escapades courtesy of the deviant sex duo, I'm staring out the window as the sun peeks up over the trees. I know eventually, I'm gonna need to get my own place rather than sleeping on Tyler's couch. It's crazy comfortable, but I want something of my own besides a Bronco.

My whole life I've lived in someone else's house or slept in someone else's bed. For the first time in my life, I want something that's mine.

When I was little, I used to imagine myself digging out a map, pointing to a small town on the coast and living there. I imagined I'd show up with nothing and start fresh where no one knew me, or my past.

I guess in some ways, I've kinda done that.

Tyler opens his door and sneaks into the bathroom with Raven.

Sighing, I think about that picture of Nevaeh and the look on Red's face. Sitting up, I bring my hands to my face and run my palms over my cheeks. What the fuck am I going to do? I'm infatuated with a man that's completely off limits in so many ways.

Flopping back against the leather couch, my feet knock my purse off the coffee table and my papers go flying. With the help of Tyler and his lawyer friend, Karl, I was able to get an attorney in Oklahoma who was willing to take my case pro bono. I filed for divorce on Thursday morning because Karl was nice enough to come in early and meet with me before work last week. I don't want anything getting in the way of this job and that includes getting there late and being asked why. There is no way I want anyone else knowing about Ben. It's bad enough that Tyler knows what a dumbass I am.

Along with filing the divorce papers, Tyler pushed me to immediately file a restraining order against Ben. He was supposedly served with both Tuesday morning, and I'm really fucking curious as to what will happen next. I'm hoping he'll do the right thing and let me go. Hope is the key word here.

I wait twenty minutes for them to get out of the shower, only they don't, and I know I'm going to be late if I don't shower soon. I can't listen to those slapping sounds anymore. You know, I mean, you *fucking know* when people are having sex in a shower. It's not something you can hide very well. No way do I want to go in there after they have.

And then I remember there's a shower in the shop. I could potentially sneak down there before the guys arrive and shower. I'll smell like oranges from the soap down there, but at least I'll be clean.

Gathering my bag up and a towel, I head down to the shop, flipping on lights as I go. I shower quickly, kinda like I did at the truck stop in fear someone would walk in. Yeah, well, just as I'm drying off, wrapping the towel around my back, Red opens the goddamn door.

Damn it. Fuck. Shit.... And he's staring.

Red, meet my very naked self. Enjoy the view.

He eyes me, from my toes all the way up my wet, very naked body to my eyes. A smile twists his lips as he leans into the door frame, but he keeps it at bay and crosses his arms over his chest. "Well, good morning to me."

I let my eyes drift to his crotch just to see if he's really turned on by this. And looking closely, his pants seem a little tighter in that general region.

Rolling my eyes, mostly at myself, I wrap the towel around my front, ignoring the heavy beat of my heart and my burning face. "What are you doing in here?"

"I work here." He snorts, like I should know. "Why are you taking a shower down here? Is the shower not working upstairs?"

"No, it is." I'm pretty sure my cheeks resemble his name. Reaching for my bag in a rush, I slip on my flip flops. "Tyler's taking too long."

His brow furrows as I step past him and into the shop. Thankfully, it's just him here and not *all* the guys. "Must have someone in there with him," Red notes, watching my every move.

Shit. Fuck. He can't find out. The last thing I need is for Tyler and Raven not to trust me.

I panic and begin to hurry out of the shop and leave him standing at his toolbox, more than likely watching me walk away in only a towel.

When I'm going up the stairs, Raven's opening the door, fully dressed now with cherry red lips. "Oh, hey." She smiles.

"Careful, your brother is down there."

Her eyes widen, hands on the rails to stop her. "Shit." She backtracks back up two steps. "Now I'm gonna have to sneak out." She then motions me away. "Go distract him."

I glare. "He already saw me naked. Let's not get carried away."

Raven bursts out laughing as we walk through the door to the apartment. I don't think it's funny at all.

Apparently, Raven's done this before because she climbs out the window in the bedroom and jumps off the roof like a spider monkey.

Girl's got skills for sure. Hopefully, she's good at lying too when Red catches her.

I inhale a deep breath once I'm back upstairs and dressed. What a fucking way to start the day, but damn, he did take a long lingering glance at my lady bits, didn't he?

Internal fist bump happening right now.

"ARE YOU A LESBIAN?" Daniel asks that afternoon. The kid is really weird, and I do mean super weird like I'm sure he's been in too many crashes at the track. Random shit spews from his mouth constantly.

I have half a mind to deck the little shit. "No... why?"

"Just wondering what my chances are."

Um. Never.

Red walks up behind him and shoves him forward, smiling. "Don't you have oil to change?"

Daniel looks over at me and smiles. "Yeah, hers."

I turn to walk away but look over my shoulder to Daniel. "I don't know, Daniel, from what I hear you don't even know what to do with a dipstick."

Red lets out a loud laugh and shoves Daniel again. "Stop messing around. Get back to work." As he passes by, Red hands me a repair order without saying anything when suddenly my phone rings.

I jump because I nearly forgot I had a cell phone since nobody calls me. Scrambling through my bag on the bench, I reach inside and pull out my cell phone.

"Ms. Reeves?"

"Yes, that's me."

"This is Karl Karson.... Tyler's friend who helped you out with the divorce proceedings and restraining order."

I breathe out a sigh of relief but then my heart starts pounding as I know *why* he's calling. Ben got the papers yesterday. Wanting some privacy, I quickly walk around the corner and into the parts room and shut the door behind me.

"The attorney in Oklahoma that is helping us with the divorce called me this morning and let me know that Ben was served with the papers and this morning they were taped to the attorney's door with the word 'Never' written across them."

Sounds exactly like something Ben would do. Letting out another deep breath, I shake my head. What a fucker. "I knew he was going to be a dick about this. Now what do I do?"

"It's not all that uncommon in cases where one of the spouses doesn't want the divorce," he assures me. "The next step is to wait out the mandatory twenty days the court allows for Ben to respond. If he doesn't respond within those twenty days, then we file for a Motion for Default. This will allow you to be granted the divorce even without his consent. Now with this filing, you may be required to attend the proceedings but we'll cross that bridge when we come to it. He's abusive, right?"

"He hit me, yes," I whisper.

"Just that one time?"

"That was the first time he struck, yes. But he's thrown things at me and forced me to do things I didn't want to... to him." That wasn't even the half of what Ben has done, but it's all I'm willing to tell him about right now.

Karl clears his throat. "Okay...."

I can hear the scrape of his pen against a notepad when I ask, "Could Ben stall the proceedings if he gets an attorney himself?"

"Yes, the usual time for divorce proceedings that are uncontested in Oklahoma are ten to ninety days depending on assets and custody. Since you don't have any kids and you're not asking for any splitting of assets or spousal support, this should go rather quickly, but *could be* strung out for months if he chooses to file papers contesting."

I lean against the wall, my adrenaline spiking. "Crap. Okay, thanks."

"Everything will be fine, Ms. Reeves. I'm here if you have any questions."

What the fuck was I thinking when I came here? Did I really think he would just let me go?

Blood rushes to my cheeks, my stomach twisting as my mind goes over what Ben might do next.

Taking in deep breaths, I need fresh air. My hands tremble as I rush past Red standing at his toolbox. "Are you okay?" he asks as I walk by.

I shake my head no and keep walking outside, tears that refuse to listen fall over my cheeks.

I'm not out there but five minutes, sitting in the gravel with my back against the metal siding when Tyler approaches, his head bent forward and hands in his pockets. Of course he would come looking for me. "What's up?"

I spit out my thumbnail I chewed off. "Ben refuses to sign the divorce papers."

Tyler kneels down to my level, his eyes intent on mine. "That motherfucker..." he curses, and then shakes his head, sitting back against the building.

"I'm not surprised. At all. I just can't believe I thought this was going to go smoothly. I mean, *if* he finds me here... there's no telling what he'll do. He's crazy, Tyler. Batshit fucking crazy. I didn't stay with him because I was afraid he would beat the crap out of me. He only hit me once. I stayed because he was mentally unstable. The hitting me was just the last straw. Jesus Christ, why is it that I attract all the assholes? Ones that only want to hurt me."

Tyler moves to sit beside me and bumps his knee to mine. "There are still some good guys out there."

Gravel crunches in front of us and I lean forward to see Raven walking up to us. She puts her hands on her hips and stares down at me brushing tears away. "Did my asshole brother yell at you again?"

"No." I laugh, smiling now.

Her eyes stay on mine, never shifting to Tyler. They play this game well. "Well, be at our house at two tomorrow for our Walker family fourth-of-July party."

"I don't think that's a good idea. It's family and it should stay family."

Tyler rolls his eyes and stands up, then reaches for my hand. "It's hardly family. Even Daniel goes to the damn thing and he's barely an employee."

There's nothing I want more than to hang out with the Walker family. And Red... shit... but maybe this isn't the right time for me. Maybe I just need to lay off everything until all this blows over with Ben.

Raven can sense my refusal coming and kicks my foot once I'm standing. "There's no option. It's mandatory. Mom said so."

I stall for what seems like an entire minute before saying, "Fine. What can I bring?"

Raven seems satisfied and turns away from us, never once looking at Tyler. "Nothing. Just your hot little self."

"Tyler..." I all but whine, thinking maybe he can break it to them that I shouldn't be there tomorrow.

"No." He holds his hand up and begins to walk away. "You're coming whether you want to or not." And then, he mimics Red's deep voice. "Get back to work, Lennon."

I PULL up to their house, the driveway and streets filled with cars, I begin to panic. Tyler left early to pick up a keg with Red and that left me showing up alone. There's nothing worse, as far as I'm concerned, than showing up at a party after everyone else. I'd rather not go at all when that happens.

I'm also nervous because after the conversation with my attorney yesterday, Red noticed something was wrong. And get this. He was nice to me. Threw me for a fucking loop. I didn't say much yesterday because I didn't want Red finding out about my divorce, or that my soon to be ex-husband was a total fucking nut job. I couldn't even tell you why I didn't want him to know. Probably because of what happened to his wife, and what I came from. I thought for sure everyone saw me as weak for staying with Ben despite his behavior. The last thing I wanted was for Red to see me *that* way.

I sit in my Bronco doing everything I can to talk myself into getting out of the truck. I think the only reason I do is because it's hot out and I could use something to drink.

As I'm walking up to the house, I'm fidgeting with my tank top, and my hair that I've actually curled today. It looked so good the night Raven curled it I decided to give it a try. The only thing I'm not fidgeting with is my jean shorts because I know Red likes those. Look at me, dressing to impress my boss now.

Once I'm on the front porch, I realize the party's around back and follow the smell of charcoal burning and country music flowing.

The moment I open the gate, Nova spots me and runs toward me. "Lenny!"

Everyone turns when she screams, and looks right at me. I avoid their eye contact and stare down at Nova. "Hey, pretty girl!" She wraps herself around me so I pick her up and carry her with me. Breathing in deeply, she smells like a hot summer day, sunscreen, sugar and dirt. "I missed you and it's only been three days."

"I was just thinking the same thing," she says with a beaming smile that lights up her face, a giggle falling from her. "Now I have someone to play with."

Glancing around the yard, I can see there are a couple other kids, two or three boys, but it's pretty much just adults.

"What about me?" Raven asks, tickling Nova's sides, a beer in one of her hands, another tucked under her arm.

Nova rolls her eyes as I set her down in the grass. I notice then she's barefoot and covered from head-to-toe in dirt and what looks to be something that's stained her lips bright red. "You don't count, Auntie."

Raven hands me the beer under her arm and glances down at Nova. "In what world do I not count? I should be your favorite person."

"Raven!" Mia yells from the deck carrying out two platters of what looks to be condiments for burgers in her arms. "Can you help me bring out the rest?"

Raven grabs my hand yanking me with her. It's then, just as I'm stepping onto the porch, that I see *him*. It's like the bar... only this time he's not looking at me. He's in a pretty intense conversation with his uncle and Tyler, standing near the keg with plastic cups in hand.

He's wearing black board shorts and a white T-shirt with his black hat. He looks fucking amazing and I want to go over there and lick him from head to toe.

My heart beats fast when I notice him because he's here and I can't ignore him like I know I should.

I know one thing, I want to get drunk, immediately, like totally shit-faced to be able to deal with him, but I also know if I'm drunk in front of him I'll either tell him off and lose my job, or try to hump his leg. Both are equally bad given his daughter is with him.

Raven and I help Mia bring out the rest of the food for the barbeque and I'm starving once I see it all. They really know how to put on a spread from hamburgers to hot dogs, ribs, corn on the cob, potato salad. Everywhere I look, there's food.

Taking a sip of my beer, I smile at Mia. "Thank you so much for inviting me."

She hugs me to her side, her shoulder-length hair pulled back neatly under a bandana in a country-mom look she pulls off so well. Raven looks just like her in so many ways from the brown eyes to the full lips. "I'm so happy you decided to come. We love having you here." She looks around the yard at everyone enjoying themselves, laughing and listening to music. "I wasn't sure I wanted to do it this year, what with Lyric passing, but I knew I needed to. Now I'm glad I did."

"Sounds like Lyric was an amazing man. I'm sorry for your loss," I tell her, knowing my words won't comfort her, but thinking I need to say them anyway.

"Oh, honey, it's fine. He was a great man, but I have a loving family who's here for me. I see him so much in the kids, too. Raven's got his balls-to-the-wall outlook. Rawley's got his love for music, and Red's got his loyalty and love for anything with an engine." And then she shakes her head, watching Red next to his uncle who now has his arm around him near the barbeque. "He was seven years old and hanging out in the shop changing oil before he knew how to do subtraction."

I smile, thinking about what Red would have been like as a child. I think about him walking around confidently, brown eyes shining bright as he sweeps his dark hair from his face. And when I look at Nova, I can tell she's a spitting image of her father in that regard. They both have that same confidence.

Nova finds me again when I'm outside, tugging on my arm. "My daddy is over there. Do you want to talk to him?" She gazes up at me with what I can only gather is her begging face. It has to be because it's hard to say no to Nova. I'd rather make a puppy sleep in the pouring rain than tell Nova no, and puppies are my downfall. I'll pick one up every single time and talk nonsense in a voice even I don't recognize.

My gaze falters, finds his in the distance. He's talking with his uncle still, girls around him, laughing and smiling at everything he says. Why is he smiling to them yet I never see the hint of one? Does he sense I can't make a good decision to save my ass?

It's like he senses that I only know how to make the *wrong* choices. It's not like I've given him any idea as to just how badly I've fucked-up in the past, but when Red looks at me—I mean really looks—it's like he can see straight through me and into my soul. Like whether I like it or not, Red will always know the real me, not the Lenny I'm trying to be.

Nova pulls my arm in the direction of the barbeque, and toward Red and that's the last place I want to go so I excuse myself and find Mia. "Can I use your restroom?"

"Definitely." She motions inside. "It's down the hall from the kitchen next to the laundry room. You can't miss it."

Their house is so cute, a country-chic style with lots of white and navy blues around. I saw most of it last weekend. It's so open and airy with nice light colors keeping the room fresh and up-to-date.

Inside the bathroom, I splash water over my face and try to calm my nerves. My cheeks sting from my sunburn I got on Saturday at the lake. When I look closer, I can see my nose is also peeling. Awesome. Flaky skin for a night when I wanted to look hot for Red.

Ugh, what's wrong with me? Why am I constantly trying to make myself look good for him? He's my freaking boss.

My very hot boss.

Stop worrying so much. Have a good time. Who gives a shit whether or not he likes you? The last thing you need is another moody son of a bitch in your life.

That's certainly easier said than done, but I'll start with that. Maybe I just need another beer.

Outside the bathroom on the wall are more framed photographs. It's then I finally see Red as a child and he's exactly like I imagined. Nova resembles him a lot, but when I see the photograph of Nevaeh and Nova together, she's a spitting image of her mother but with Red's chin and smile. Not that I've seen his smile up close, but from what it looks like in the photos, it's the same.

"You lost?" My heart sails into my throat and I grasp my chest with my hand and turn to see Red watching me.

"It's rude to sneak up on people."

He shrugs one shoulder and casually leans against the wall, his eyes on the floor. "It's rude to nose around in other people's homes."

Pressing my lips together, I try to tamp down the embarrassment clawing at me. I poke at his chest with my index finger. His very hard, muscular chest. I want to lick up and down. "You don't always have to be a dick to me. I was only using the bathroom and the pictures caught my eye."

Looking down at my finger pressed to his chest, it's then I realize I'm touching him. By the quick intake of his breath, he notices too. You know in the romance novels when people touch and they claim they tingle? Well, I tingled all right. Between my thighs.

Red focuses on his hand that's not holding the beer and begins to peel at the label as I withdraw my own hand.

Jesus, he makes leaning and acting casual sexy too.

There's a slight flush to his cheeks and I can tell he's probably got a pretty good buzz going. It's freaking adorable. A thrill shoots through me wondering what a drunk Red is like. Hopefully, he's a nice drunk and not like Ben.

I can see it shining in his eyes. He's nothing like Ben.

Tilting his head, he looks up at me with those ridiculously long eyelashes that are such a waste on a boy. Though confident and alluring, his eyes soften when he speaks in a nonchalant grace only he can master. "Relax, Lennon." Oh fuck, panties melting, he called me by my name. Goddamn him. "I was only kidding."

I'm speechless. Is he... *no*... he can't be being playful.

I offer him a smile, trying to keep myself under control. It's *hard*. Look at him, it's about as hard as his fucking muscles.

Pushing himself off the wall, he looks back at me over his shoulder. "Come back out here. The party's just getting started."

Red walks in front of me, and I stare at his ass the entire time and the way he looks relaxed in a pair of black board shorts. He's got on this white T-shirt with some black logo on the back, but all I see is the way his tattoos stand out against the brightness of his shirt. I hate that he looks so good tonight.

Outside the house, the moderate-sized, fenced backyard is crowded with people. Along the cherry-stained deck are tiny twinkle lights along the white rails that lead down into the well-manicured lawn. It's beautiful and should be on the cover of Pottery Barn.

Country music pulses through the air but it's not too loud, enough that you can still hold a conversation.

Raven finds me, looping her arm in mine. "Sounds good, huh?"

"The music?" Raven nods. "Yeah, it does."

"Berkley always sets us up. She's a bartender at Murphy's." And then her face scrunches. "She's *also* Tyler's ex-girlfriend."

Whoa. That face tells me she has feelings for Tyler, more than she cares to lead on.

Glancing around the yard, I wonder who she is. Probably one of the hot babes hanging around Red, or even Rawley. "Which one is Berkley?"

"The one standing next to Rawley and Linc." Raven points near the back fence. "Short girl with shoulder-length black hair."

My eyes follow to where they're standing and it's clear this Berkley girl is into Rawley by the way she's staring at him with that stare. You know the stare, the one where she's looking like she's going to walk up and drop to her knees to suck his dick any second. I know the look because I'm secretly giving it to Red. I'm seriously *that* obvious.

I wonder if Red knows the look?

"Are they dating?" I ask, and then notice three other girls beside him. "Who are all those girls beside him?"

"The ones around Rawley?" Raven smirks, bringing her beer to her lips and nodding to an empty pair of chairs near where Nova is playing with some kids.

I follow her over there and we take a seat. "Yeah, those ones."

"His harem. The dude's a fucking whore. So Berkley broke up with Tyler about... I don't know, like a few months back, and she's been hanging on Rawley ever since."

"No shit?" I knew about Tyler and Berkley, but Rawley... I try to imagine him as a player and I can't. But I also never thought Ben was a nut job until after we were married. Guess you never can tell with people.

"Yep. Small town. I figure eventually, everyone will have slept with someone in their family."

I laugh. "That's disgusting."

Nova takes off chasing one of the little boys only to have Rawley grab her by the waist and swing her around. They run back near us and Raven nods to her brother. "Hey, Rawley, look, Sophie's here... and look, Jesse too and Sam... and Berkley. What are you going to do since they're all here at once? Do you schedule in ten minute increments for them to blow you?"

He tosses a glare over his shoulder at her covering Nova's ears. "Shut up, Raven."

She looks back at me. "See, told you he's a slut."

"Are any of them actually his girlfriend?" I ask once Rawley leaves, chasing Nova around the backyard.

"Well, Sophie was his first girlfriend in high school," she explains. "But they broke up shortly after spring break senior year. Then he started getting blow jobs from Sam. It's just one after another but he still hangs onto Jesse."

And here I thought my life was complicated. "Lots of drama."

She nods. "Pretty much."

Fidgeting with the label on my beer, I'm reminded of Red, mostly because he's staring at me from across the lawn. "Doesn't Jesse have a thing for Red though?"

"Yup." Raven crosses her legs, leaning toward me. "Which is why Rawley only gets blow jobs from her. I don't know... I think there's more but she only uses him to get to Red."

"I bet that pisses him off?"

"Yeah, Red and Rawley have always had their differences. Maybe it's because he's eight years older than us, but deep down, Rawley looks up to him. Only he doesn't want to follow in his footsteps if that makes sense."

"It totally does," I agree, trying to understand how Rawley must feel living in Red's shadow. "He doesn't want to be Red's little brother forever."

"Exactly. He's a good guy, just confused... and slutty."

"What happened with his girlfriend? Why'd they break up?"

"She cheated on him over spring break. Claims she doesn't know how it happened but whatever. Anyway, Rawley was into her. I swear they were gonna get married and she begged him to forgive her, but he wouldn't. He lost his shit over it shortly before graduation, almost got himself killed drinking and driving one night. It was all fucked-up for a while. He's still not the same guy since her."

"That's kinda sad."

Raven levels me a serious look. I half expect her to bitch slap me. "Do not feel bad for him. He and Sophie started talking again about three months ago and he fucked that up by sleeping around on her." She gestures to the girls and they're all hanging out together like they're friends. "I'm waiting for the day they find out about one another. I mean, really, I can't fucking stand people who cheat. Holden, my boyfriend of four years cheated on me... and it *sucked*." She looks down at her beer. "Shit, I'm out."

We both stand to get another one, and then end up eating with Nova. It's something like an hour later and someone yells, "Seriously? *Seriously*, Rawley?"

The majority of the heads surrounding the house look over to see Rawley exiting the house with Jesse right behind him adjusting her dress and Rawley buckling his belt. I've never understood why people don't adjust themselves in the bathroom before opening the door. I mean, so you fucked around. Way to make it more obvious by remaining half put together as you exit the bathroom. That's just asking to get caught.

Rawley appears shocked, shaking his head maybe at his own disappointment, or his dick's, and follows Sophie as she storms around the side of the house away from him. "Sophie!" he yells after her, like it will make a difference. "It's not what it looked like!"

Raven takes it upon herself to yell, "Run, Sophie. It's exactly what it looks like."

Rawley pauses at the gate, scowling. "Shut the hell up, Raven."

"Why is she mad at Uncle Rawley? Did he pull her hair?" Nova asks, trying to swipe a drink of Raven's beer.

"Hey." She yanks it up out of reach. "I told you beer is off limits. That was a one-time thing when I let you try that hard apple cider."

Nova backs up a step and takes the Capri Sun next to her. "Fine." She then stomps off.

Red walks toward us, shaking his head in laughter. "Stupid fucker. Deserves whatever shit Sophie throws at him. I can't believe he thought he would never get caught."

Standing beside him, Raven hugs Red with one arm around his waist, their height difference apparent. "See, Lenny. This is a *real* man. My big brother knows how to treat a lady."

"No, I wouldn't." Red smiles, winking at me, and then hugs Raven to him. "Are you wanting a raise or something?"

Mia then walks up shaking her head as well. "I honestly don't know where we went wrong with Rawley."

"You dropped him too many times," Raven adds.

"I kinda want to blame your father," Mia snorts, rolling her eyes at Raven. "He allowed Colt to watch him too many times."

Colt, having heard that, yells, "Hey! I'm standing right here."

Mia turns to him, grinning and holding up her wine glass. "I know. But you know it's true."

Everybody laughs and Raven and Mia walk away to check on Nova who is playing with Crystal's two boys leaving me alone with Red.

Red takes a swig of his beer and looks at me, giving a head nod. "Are you having a good time?"

I notice then we're drinking the same beer. As I stand there, amped and nervous, afraid to move even an inch because I never want that smile to fade, I reply with, "I am. It's been a long time since I've had fun."

He eyes my choice of attire, the jean shorts and tank top. Bringing his lips close to my ear, he murmurs, "You look nice."

I shiver at his breath on my skin. "Yeah, well I thought about wearing the 'Get off my dick' shirt but Raven stole it from me."

Damn it, the smile's fading. Shit. Say something funny. Make it come back!

I stare at him, waiting for what he might say next and then maybe I can reply with something witty.

Only his eyes darken with the night and he studies me for a reaction. When I don't say anything, his smile fades as if he's seen something he didn't want to, or heard something he didn't want to hear. He looks away, his jaw tight as he exhales and raises his beer to his lips.

Fuck, say something else so he doesn't leave. "You're really lucky to have a family like this."

He nods, though I can sense apprehension in his face. He's sad by what I just said. "This was always the place to hang out when I was younger. Seemed like the whole town was here most of the time." He glances up at the driveway where Rawley and Sophie are arguing. "We don't always get along, but we always have each other's backs." And then his eyes, those fucking eyes I can't resist, drift my way and I openly sigh... openly fucking sigh. "You feeling better?"

My brow pinches together. "Huh?"

"I mean after yesterday." His brow pinches. "You seemed upset when you got off the phone." Our eyes lock and he knows I'm hiding something from him. "Whatever it was affected you all day."

My posture stiffens, my eyes dropping from his because I can't hold them as the lie slips past my lips. "Sorry about that. It won't happen again."

He shrugs. "I'm not mad. I'm just hoping you're doing better."

We're close now, closer than before and the loud music causes me to glance away, the lingering light around us obliterated by the rapidly falling night. The music catches my attention, and I look around. Purple and pink paint the sky as the sun sets and I take in a deep breath, inhaling the smells of heated coals and barbeque sauce.

Mia and Red's Uncle Hendrix are dancing, everyone's clapping for them. Red leans into my shoulder. "My parents used to belong to the Eagles. They'd go out dancing with Hendrix and his wife, Sherrie." He points her out by lifting his beer and leaning into my side. I can smell him now, the faint smell of his beer on his breath, his warmth and the sounds of his steady breathing. "That's my aunt."

Our eyes drift together again, and he smiles. For the first time, he smiles, at me.

"What?" he asks when I don't look away.

"You're smiling."

"It's natural."

"I've just... never seen you do it. At least not directed at me."

He's about to reply, his mouth opening when an older woman touches his forearm. "Red, honey, dance with me?"

He winks at her. "Sorry, Linda, I'm really not much of a dancer to this." He gestures to the line dancing.

She shrugs and then settles on her husband, Colt. I laugh. "Wow, you seem to attract all ages."

Red doesn't answer because he can't; he's being asked by Sam to dance now.

Chuckling, his feet shift and he casually lifts his beer to his lips. I think maybe he does this on purpose because it not only draws my attention to his lips, but Sam's as well. "Sorry, Sam, but I don't dance."

Sam's cheeks flush and she blinks rapidly, taking offense to Red's refusal. "Someday you're going to regret saying no to me all the time."

Red snorts, leaning into me and I nearly hyperventilate, my heart trying to jump out of my chest and fist bump his. "That's a chance I'm willing to take. You're seventeen, honey, find someone else."

Ah, yes, there's the Red I know.

Once Sam's out of earshot, I glance at Red again.

"You're a popular guy around here. You really should dance with one of these girls."

Red snorts. "Nah, I like sitting here."

Oh shit, really?

He bumps into my shoulder. "Thanks a lot. I could have used your help there."

"Oh no, you're not dragging me into your teenage drama."

"What teenage drama?" Raven asks, wrapping her arms around our shoulders and worming herself between the two of us.

I'm about to say Red's when he clears his throat. "No one," he grumbles and looks to Nova at his feet. "Are you having a good time, darlin'?"

She's crawling around on the ground like a dog. "Ollie asked me to be his girlfriend."

"And why are you crawling around on the ground then?"

"I'm his servant."

Raven and I burst out laughing.

Red steps sideways, grabs Nova by the waist and hauls her to her feet. "The fuck you are," Red snaps. "Get up. Where's that little shit Ollie?" And then he takes off in the other direction.

He crooks a finger at the rebel child after his daughter. "Ollie, get over here."

Ollie's eyes widen and he shakes his head. I think Ollie knows what's good for him and takes off running.

Raven shakes her head, handing me yet another beer when she notices mine is empty. "I feel bad for little Ollie."

A new song comes on Nova seems to love. "Daddy, dance with me!"

Red smiles. "Whatever you want, darlin'."

I love that he doesn't deny her a dance.

Red carries Nova over to the makeshift dance floor on the deck, hoisting her up on his shoulders so he can spin her around to the music. Watching Red with his daughter, his attention on her 100 percent is something. Being a good dad has nothing to do with just being present in the child's life. It has to do with the dad's passion to show her she means the world to him.

It's obvious from the moment you see Red and Nova together that Red certainly knows how to do that.

Almost everyone is dancing now, the twinkle lights basking the deck in an illuminated glow. I want so badly to be a part of this, a big family, one who loves unconditionally and doesn't love for evil, or to make you do or be what you're not. I don't know the feeling. I only know love that's forced or made to believe you should love if and because.

My gaze dances around and then lands on Red as he looks at me, his eyes sparking and then I drop mine to his mouth as he sets Nova on her feet. Holy shit. Red is smiling at me.

As if the scene is playing out perfectly, one that leaves us alone again, Nova runs off the other direction, into Colt's arms.

I stand there, completely awed that one of his gorgeous smiles is finally directed toward me. The smile should be framed. It's easy, contagious, and comes so easily now I'm confused why he doesn't do it more often. Maybe it's times like these. When he's surrounded by the people he loves and a few beers in him that he finally lets go of his worries and enjoys himself.

I've seen him smirk, but it's nothing like this.

My stomach twists at the sight.

With cheeks still flushed, Red approaches me, his smile ready to bring me to my knees. "Did you miss me?" he asks, finishing off the beer in his hand.

As I stand this close again, amped and nervous, I remain rooted in place. "Maybe. Did you miss me?"

Smooth, Lenny.

"Maybe." He gives me a fucking head nod. Why am I turned on by a goddamn head nod?

"You better be careful, Red," I say, bumping into his shoulder as we stand together, twinkling lights illuminating his smile to my attention. "You're being so nice to me, I just might start liking you."

Red answers as he lifts a new beer to his lips. "Well we wouldn't want that now, would we?" He winks. Oh God, there's something worse than the head nod and a wink, and he knows exactly how to deliver it and lean in at the same time. He's a fucking pro at seduction.

"No, I guess not. Quick. Do something to piss me off so the feeling passes."

Red reaches over and tugs at my hair. Not just any tug, I can literally feel his knuckles turn white and wraps around the tiny sensitive hairs around the base of my neck, and he pulls, gently.

My teeth sink into my lower lip drawing his eyes there. His lips part, a tender sound passing by his wet lips. "I said piss me off not turn me on."

He smiles, again, and cocks his head back, tilting it to the side just a little. Bringing his beer to his lips, Red pauses, keeping the bottle at bay. His beer bumps to mine, the glass pinging through the night. "In that case... need another beer?"

Snorting, I nod. What the fuck was I thinking?

I watch him at the table, digging into the cooler for two longnecks and Nova runs up to him, wiping the chocolate off her face. She throws her arms around his neck when he kneels to her level, his face between her hands as they talk.

Watching them, I know these feelings I have for him suddenly aren't just for him; they're for her too.

It scares me because I can't hurt either of them and me being close to them is dangerous. I only cause harm.

I need to go. He's distracted right now. I need to leave.

With a sigh, I give the party one last look and turn to leave.

Turning to do so, I run right into Raven in the driveway. "Holy shit." I startle, grabbing onto her shoulders and then see Tyler walking around the other side of the house. They must have been talking, or other things.

"So..." Raven begins before taking a large gulp of her beer, raising an eyebrow. "Are you into Red?"

"What? No," I reply immediately in mock offense. "Why would you ask that?"

Because she can see right through your lying ass.

"Because I was watching you two standing there smiling at each other like a couple of teenagers. I haven't seen my brother even look in another woman's direction, let alone smile at one since Nevaeh died. Oh, and he's staring at your ass."

"I'm sorry, what?"

"He's staring at your ass."

A thrill shoots through me. "He's looking at his daughter."

She looks past me, to him I suspect. "Nope, he's been staring at your ass all night."

I want to say something to her but then we see Sophie and Rawley standing in the driveway near his truck, appearing to be still fighting from over an hour ago. "How can you act like this?" she asks him, brushing tears away. "I gave you another fucking chance and you're still getting your dick sucked by that little whore."

Rawley shifts his feet, his head hanging as he stares at the ground. "Why do you care?"

Sophie shoves his shoulder. "Why do I care? How can you even ask me that?"

"No really, I'm curious." His eyes find hers at about the time Raven groans beside me and we duck down behind a car to listen. "You fucked around on me first," Rawley points out. "I was ready to fucking marry you and that's how you repay me. Think about how I feel."

Sophie snorts. "So that's it, you can justify this because I made one mistake?"

"Yep. Brutal ain't it, sweetheart?"

Jesus, now I know being an asshole runs in their family. Sophie raises her hand as if she's about to hit him across the face, and he smiles condescendingly at her. "You fucking hit me again and be ready for what comes next."

"Screw you!" she shouts, walking away from him.

Raven breathes in deeply when they're gone, standing up. "They'll be back together before morning."

I fidget with my keys. "Shit, this is like a soap opera."

"I know." She sighs. "I loved this shit when we were younger. You should see my diary. I wrote down all these fights."

I laugh, wishing I'd always had a friend like her. "Is it weird I kinda want to read it?"

"Nope." She smiles, too. "I even named it. It's called *The Young and the Stupid*. I'm gonna pitch it to Lifetime someday."

"You know, I bet they'll pick it up someday."

"That's what I'm saying."

There's a moment of silence between us, and I shrug. "I'm just gonna head out."

Raven frowns. "I get it. You're not comfortable with us yet, but I hope someday you're gonna see that even though we're a bunch of assholes, we're a good family with an open-door policy. You're always welcome here."

She's right. They are a good family, which is exactly why I need to leave. I shouldn't drag them into my shit storm.

Inside my Bronco, I stare up at the sky, a canopy of luminous stars materializing in the darkness. It's a perfect imaginary significance of the moment here. One where there's dullness met by shimmering stars.

13

LENNON

MORNING COMES WAY TOO FAST. Everyone at the shop is dragging their feet and Red seems to be focused on a truck that was towed in first thing, barely looking up when I come in ten minutes to eight. I pride myself that I didn't get to bed until two this morning, because of Tyler and Raven, but still made it to work on time.

Can't say the same for Rawley.

Watching Red out of the corner of my eye, chewing on his thumb as he talks on the phone and jots down notes, I think to myself how nice it was to see him relaxed last night. He's so tense at the shop, as if the world's on his shoulders, and I guess in many ways, it is.

A blush creeps over my face when he grips his phone and sets it down on his toolbox and I'm reminded of when he pulled my hair.

Twisting, he walks toward me, a clipboard in hand, his focus on it and then he looks up and sees me standing next to the bench. "Oh, hey." And then he nods over his shoulder. "This one was towed in. Customer said it died while they were on the freeway so they towed it here. I took a look at it this morning."

I take the clipboard from Red to look over his notes.

He immediately grabs it back. "Didn't anyone ever teach you it's not nice to grab other people's things?"

I snort. "Says the guy who pulled my hair last night."

Oh my God, I'm an idiot. I look up at the ceiling, wondering why I can't act normal around him and he laughs. "Don't go playing the victim with me now, Lenny. We both know you loved it."

My response is to roll my eyes. Because I can't breathe, or talk.

"There was an oil leak and it damaged the bearings," he then says. "They're in a hurry to get back on the road so we need to see what we can do for them."

"So you're getting an engine somewhere then?"

Red nods, leaning back against the bench. "Yeah. It'll be here by two at the latest. She's a single mom who just lost her husband. They're on their way up to Seattle so I wanted to get them back on the road tomorrow if I can. Got a refreshed engine from Portland."

"Do you need some help with it?" I ask, hoping he says yes. I love engine replacements. Everyone usually hates them but there's just something about removing an old engine and putting a new one in that gives me a sense of pride I can't get anywhere else. Maybe because most think I can't do it, or wouldn't want to. Or maybe it has a more metaphorical outlook on my own life.

I'm more inclined to think metaphorically. "I'll help you get it done if you want."

He winks at me, smirking and then tilts his head as his eyes travel south. "Well, it's always nice to have two people to run the hoist and guide the new engine in."

Oh, my fuck... he's hinting at something sexual with me!

"It can get a little tricky getting them in with ease," I say.

"So you'll help me out?" He looks at me intently, his head cocked to one side, waiting for my answer. It makes me nervous. Really nervous, so I tear my eyes from his and stare at the carburetor.

A night with him... alone... in the shop?

Fuck yeah. Okay, shit. Calm yourself down a notch. Don't seem too eager or he'll think you're crazy.

"Sure, I mean, if you think you could use the help." I shrug before surveying the shop at who's within ear shot of this conversation. No one. Everyone's too tired to pay any attention to me.

"You sure? I'm not keeping you from anything?"

Only from dreaming of you.

"Nope." My gaze falls to his hands folded over his chest. The black ink on his arms catches my attention and the detailed patterns. I want hours to inspect the meaning behind each one. He doesn't seem to be the type of guy who would tattoo just anything on himself.

"Okay, so we'll get started when the engine gets here," Red says, intruding on my thoughts of his hands sliding up my thighs as he sets me on the fender.

"Uh, yeah... yes. Sounds great," I sputter, looking doe-eyed and praying he can't read my thoughts.

He's just about to leave when he stops and then gets closer, his shoulder touching mine sending my heart racing. "Where'd you go last night?"

"What?"

"You snuck out early... why?"

Last night, the look in his eyes when I told him I was starting to like him. The way he smiled when he was dancing with Nova. All of it played on repeat in my mind.

"Tired?" Yep, I say it in the form of a fucking question.

Shaking his head, I can tell he doesn't believe me. Thankfully, his mom calls his name and he brushes past me without another word. My heartbeat evens out and then I think, how the hell am I going to make it the rest of the night with him, alone for the first time?

THE ENGINE ARRIVES AROUND two thirty and Red calls me over to help. He lets me tear down the new one as he finishes another job he's working on. I drain the oil and coolant out, remove the belts and power steering pump, air conditioning compressor, radiator... and then take a quick break.

When I look up, the shop's empty and Red's at his toolbox making notes. He looks over at me. "I'll help you out in a minute."

I shrug, wiping my hands on a shop towel. "I got it. No rush."

Leaning over the fender, I take out the heater hose, fuel line and air box as Red leans into the fender of the truck. "I'm curious... what made you want to work on cars?"

I get this question a lot, mostly because it's rare to see women mechanics around. Usually I give a smartass comment but this time, I try some truth. "My foster dad, Wes, he worked on cars. I... never had much of a father figure around and I was ten by the time I had one. So I'd sneak out to his shop and watch him work. He started teaching me one day and I was fascinated with how you could take a vehicle that was broken down and needing repaired, and giving it another chance at running. It's a lot like being a doctor, only these patients can't tell you what's wrong. You have to figure it out for yourself."

He nods, seeming to agree with me.

Red and I work well together. We talk on occasion but even the silence as we work isn't awkward. I keep my attention on the engine, but my head is swimming. I wish things would have ended up differently for me. I wish I would have stepped into this shop, and not that motorcycle shop where I met Ben for the first time.

The reality is, girls like me don't end up with guys like Red. We end up with guys like Ben and dream about guys like Red sweeping us off our feet someday.

"Are you getting hungry?" Red asks, holding up his phone. "I was gonna order a pizza."

"Yeah, actually I am. That sounds great."

Red turns, looking through a phone book on his toolbox and orders the pizza. I'm in the middle of trying to unbolt the transmission when I hear him talking to Raven on the phone and asking her what Nova had for dinner.

There's practically sweat pouring down my face at this point so I strip my flannel off leaving me in just a midriff camisole tank top. When I set my flannel on the bench behind me so I don't get any grease on it, I notice Red isn't talking anymore.

He's staring at me. Only his eyes are nowhere near my face. He scans the small peek of my tattoo on my side, and then my breasts that are on display for him. More than likely, my nipples are hard.

Damn it.

When I see the heated hunger in his, I'm excited to see he's attracted to me. I always knew he liked what he saw. I felt his erection against me that first damn day. But now we're alone and there's certainly more here than just attraction.

Shaking his head, I can tell he's attempting to focus on his sister talking, and not me.

Turning around, my heart pounds as he comes up behind me, his breath near my ear. "You know this isn't a strip club, right?"

I keep my eyes on the engine and then run my fingers through my hair and gather it up to put it in a ponytail so it's off my neck. "What can I say, engines make me hot."

"If that's the case, I got one you could look at," he teases.

My voice dips lower. "Is that the best line you've got? I bet you got ladies lined up around the block with moves like that."

"Lenny." His words are low and raspy as he watches the movements of my neck when I swallow. He knows I'm nervous around him. "I don't need moves to pick up women."

"You're right." I look up at him. An uninvited sensation of lust snakes up my thighs. "You don't."

He gives me that relaxed grin and hands me a beer. "Want one?"

I know what happens when I start drinking with him, but I take it anyway.

"Pizza will be here in like ten minutes. They're just down the street."

Stepping back from the engine, I take the beer from his hand, our fingertips grazing in the process. A jolt of excitement shoots through me when we touch and I know he feels it too, because he backs up a step and creates a little more space between us.

I'm about to say something, probably inappropriate when someone knocks at the door and Red casually steps back.

As soon as his back is turned, I want to wash my mouth out for the dumb shit I keep saying. Jumping up and down, I shake out my hands and try to clear my head. "Get yourself together," I whisper, reminding myself his innocent flirting means nothing.

There's silence between us, the sounds of air tools filling the shop. When the pizza arrives, Red opens the shop door to pay for it.

He returns a moment later, a white pizza box in hand and sets it on his toolbox. He tosses his wallet next to it. Gesturing to the stool, he grabs Tyler's and moves it closer. "Take a break."

It's about a minute into my break when I let my vagina talk for me. "This is the best pizza I've ever had. Nice and greasy," I say, with a mouthful. Very lady like.

Red chuckles, his chest shaking as he takes his second slice from the box and then closes it. "You like greasy pizza, huh?"

I love his chuckles. I want to make him laugh. Too bad I'm hardly funny.

Licking sauce off my thumb, I reach for another, giving him a view of my cleavage. Not that my cleavage is all that presentable, but I'm a solid B cup for sure. "Red, I'm a girl who works on cars. I'm pretty sure you know I'm not afraid of a little grease." I wink, sitting down on my stool. "A little dirt never hurt anyone."

"I guess not." Red smiles, adjusting his position on the stool. He relaxes, leaning slightly to the right as he reaches for a napkin. "So where'd you come from?"

"Oklahoma." I cover my mouth as I chew, attempting to be ladylike and not talk with my mouth full. "Though I was actually born in Boise."

"You were adopted though, weren't you?"

It's hard to give him any background on me because that's the last thing I want to do, for him to get to know me and care. "No, actually, Maggie and Wes never adopted me. I was just placed with them when I was ten. My mom gave me up shortly before my third birthday. I don't remember anything about her or why she gave me up."

Red clears his throat, reaching for yet another slice of pizza but there's an emotion on his face, one I didn't want to see. Regret for asking. Sadness maybe. "What made you come here?"

My soon to be ex-husband is a dirt bag.

I shrug, trying to keep from letting my emotions surface. "Needed a job and a fresh start."

"And you left behind?" I don't dare look at him when he asks that. I can't because I know my answer is going to be a lie. And I don't want to look at him when I do it.

Of course he'd ask this. "Nothing."

He nods and then reaches for a napkin to wipe his hands off. "I have a confession to make."

My heart races. Shit... what could he possibly confess? That he has feelings for me? That he wants to kiss me? That he wants to fuck me on his toolbox? Honestly, all those are things I'd agree with, but shouldn't happen.

"Um, Red, listen—"

"I called your old boss, Eric."

I stop immediately, as does my breathing. He did what? "I'm sorry, you what?" I'm pretty sure my mouth is hanging open.

"Last week when you started, I pulled your paperwork and called your old boss." Fucking shit, what if he saw that tax form and knows I'm married?

"Why would you do that, Red?" I scowl at him, knowing he had every right to call him, but still. "I've proven myself to you over and over again this past week. Why would go behind my back and call Eric?"

"Look, Lenny." He drops his eyes to the floor, crossing his arms over his chest. "You may have a pretty face and a great ass, but no one is working in this garage without some kind of professional reference. I had to know you were as good as you say you are. It's no big deal."

No big deal? Is he crazy? Well, I mean I get why he called, but still.

I look at him expectantly for a moment, and then huff out a breath. "And? What did he say?"

"He spoke very highly of you. Said you were one of his best and he was pissed when you left town and called him from a payphone to say you weren't coming in. Although he was glad to hear that you were okay."

"Oh. Well, he was a good guy. Always looking out for everyone." I stare down at the pizza in my hand, half eaten, and I'm suddenly not hungry anymore. I wanted so badly to leave Oklahoma behind and never think about it again. Why can't I have that?

"So, did you tell him where you were calling from?"

Red stares at me for a moment as if contemplating how he wants to answer the question. Rubbing his thumb across his lower lip, he shakes his head. "No. I didn't really think about it at the time, but he was happy to know you were okay. He didn't even ask where you were."

That sounds like Eric. He probably didn't ask because he didn't want to have to lie to Ben, should he come looking for me. And I know he probably did come looking for me.

"Tell me about Nevaeh," I blurt out, wanting to change the focus from me to him as I reach for my beer.

Red shrugs and places his hands on the edge of the stool in front of him. The action causes the muscles in his forearms to flex and pop. "Not much to tell. We met at a concert and she took advantage of me in the backseat of my car." I shake my head when he winks. No way she took advantage of him, more like he probably winked at her and he was able to get her to do anything he wanted. "She got pregnant and it went from there."

"Were you married when Nova was born?"

"I asked her to marry me when she was seven-months pregnant. We tied the knot in Vegas three weeks later."

"Do you miss her?"

Seriously, Lenny? Do you miss her?

Red snorts. "That's a dumb question."

"Sorry."

Just when I think he's not going to answer me, he says, "Yes, I miss her. She was an amazing woman and mother." And then he opens up with, "I try to take Nova to her grave every Sunday. We take her flowers and Nova likes to leave a drawing for her. I just want to make sure that she remembers her."

I can't fathom what it would be like to lose your wife, that unimaginable, unbearable pain that must eat at him when he looks at Nova knowing her mommy is gone. I can see he struggles with it a lot.

Standing, I nod to the truck. "Ready to get the engine out?"

He nods himself, and reaches for the stereo and turns on the radio. He's probably done with me talking and asking stupid shit. Can't say I blame him on that one.

It's freaking midnight when we finish getting the new engine inside the truck and I'm stretching out my arms from trying to hold the engine steady while we were lowering it in. The action causes Red to look right at my chest when he's putting away tools.

"See something you like?"

Red smirks. "Well, I wouldn't be much of a man if I didn't." His eyes have a hunger in them and I can tell he's turned-on by watching me. Internally, I'm gleaming because I honestly didn't think I could turn a guy like Red on. I mean, he's all hard and rugged. I was beginning to think he can never crack.

Laughing nervously, I shove his shoulder and reach for my bag on the bench. We both walk toward the door after he locks up, me walking in front of him when I stop. I need to thank him for giving me a chance to do this with him. "Red, I wa—"

Red's staring at his phone in his hand and runs right into the back of me and the two of us knock into the door. He automatically reaches out and grabs my shoulders to steady me from falling.

And then he touches my neck. As he drags each fingertip over my skin, my body ignites at his touch. It's been so long since I've experienced a rush of sensations like I do now, or if I ever have.

He grazes my jaw with the tips of his fingers, stroking my chin to my ear. I instinctively lean into his touch, soaking up the warmth like I've been starving for attention of this kind.

In my fucked-up reality, I have been. I've been starving for attention, love and sincerity.

I want to believe I can have this, but it would be a total contradiction to what I should be doing. Good thing I hardly listen to my head and my heart rules my actions.

He's watching me again and I can tell he wants to kiss me by the way his eyes roam over my lips, but he doesn't just yet. Instead, he bends down and wraps his hands around my ass.

He takes a fist full of my denim shorts. "Do you have any idea what these shorts have been doing to me this last week?" The way he looks at me, the craving I've created in him with his steady stare, well, it does things to me.

"No," I say, my insides coiling. Closing my eyes as he brings his mouth to mine, it's only when I part my lips that I remember *this* is how a kiss should feel.

He hoists me up, never breaking the contact of our mouths and sets me on the bench by his toolbox. His left hand goes to my hair, the other, firm and powerful, on my hip to keep me in place. With an anguished moan, I angle my head to deepen the kiss. He catches the moan I let out with a growl, exploring my mouth eagerly with his tongue. My breasts crush against his rock-hard chest and I can tell his excitement matches my own. And if I didn't, his erection when he slides my hips against his confirms he wants so much more than my mouth on him.

My hands dip underneath his T-shirt, hoping he takes the hint and removes it. He does, and then immediately finds my mouth again. But not before I notice the tattoo on his chest over his heart, the one that makes me think twice about what's happening here, and what it could mean if I keep kissing him.

My heart does a somersault. Over his heart is a tattoo. The word Heaven in a fancy script with three sparrows flying over it. A strange pressure in my gut gathers, tightening into a massive knot.

In a sense, being with Red, right now, is like heaven. Something I don't deserve.

Something happens to me when I see that tattoo. I know it's for *her*.

With my hand on his chest, I know what I have to do. I have to stop this. He was right to be an asshole to me in the beginning. I wish it would have stayed that way.

14

REDDINGTON

OUR MOUTHS BREAK APART, gasping for a much-needed breath. I stare at her slightly swollen lips and the grease smudges from my thumbs on her neck.

Thinking about what I want becomes more than thinking. It's lingering on the edges of my conscience, demanding some sort of attention.

I close my eyes, her hands on my chest. "What the fuck are you doing to me?" I don't expect an answer, but I get one.

"I could ask the same of you." Slowly, she slides her delicate hands up my shoulders and around my neck.

She looks at me and a sad smile touches her lips. I'm not sure what to say so I look away like a coward.

What the fuck am I going to say?

She flutters those dark lashes and her eyes grow large at what just happened. "I can't do this," she whispers, her lips red and swollen.

My answer to that is grinding my rock-hard length into her, wanting to fuck her through her damn jeans that have been haunting me all day.

I *need* her.

I need to hear her moan from my dick buried deep inside her. Pawing at her clothes, wanting them off, I need the gratification of my skin touching hers.

Apparently, I need a lot of fucking things.

I kiss her again trying to make her see there's nothing wrong with this.

"Wait," she whispers

I don't part my mouth from her, not right away. I can't. She stops, her lips barely moving.

I groan in response, stepping back and looking at her intently. "Are you stopping because you want to, or you think you have to?" I know she can sense the hunger in my words. My need is made even more obvious as the adrenaline coursing through my body causes my hand to shake when I lift it to brush the hair off her shoulder. Yet she says nothing.

Instead, she watches me, sucking her bottom lip in her mouth, coaxing me forward.

My thumb drags over her bottom lip. "That's kind of your answer, you know," I say, stepping closer. Close enough for her to feel my erection. I'm certainly not afraid of my body's reaction to her, but I'm thinking she is.

She inhales before sucking her bottom lip into her mouth seductively. "Because you have to stop. I can't. You're my boss."

All right. I've got two options here.

Option one is to stop. Walk away and continue as if this never happened and that I don't want her.

Second choice is to kiss her into submission so I can fuck her right now in this shop to satisfy my need.

Yeah, right. Like the first option makes any goddamn sense at all. Screw that. Here I go again, complicating this based on my own need, or the tightness in my pants.

But I'm a noble guy and I let her slide off the bench and leave me hanging.

Truth is she scares me a little. There's undeniable attraction between the two of us and my obsession with her is growing. She's unlike anyone

I've ever met, including Nevaeh. But there's something about her, so genuine and unexpected that I have to find out why that is.

Closing my eyes, I blink slowly and exhale my frustration, trying to will my breathing into control. It's a tall order for someone who hasn't been with a woman in two years.

Lenny walks away toward her bag and puts her shirt back over the camisole. The flannel was once covering her shoulders, open to the shirt underneath. Frustration clenches my chest. She's covering herself like a curtain blocking the morning light, afraid to let me see an inch of skin. Disappointment washes over me that she's covering herself from my view. She's hiding.

Lenny's back is to me when she says, "Oh my God," she whispers. "What did we do?"

We didn't do anything. That's the problem but thinking like that is me thinking with my dick, and she needs better than that.

"Lenny..." I step toward her with my hand outstretched, wanting to ease her worries. "It's okay."

"No." She shakes her head adamantly. "I told myself I wasn't going to do this. You're my boss, Reddington. I'm not this girl who goes around sleeping with her boss."

She's right. She's not that kind of girl and I never thought she was. Okay, in the beginning, I might have, but then I got to know her and realized that couldn't be further from the truth.

Nodding, I retract my hand. I certainly never thought she was sleeping around. And I definitely don't give a fuck if I am her boss. I still want her.

With a quick intake of breath, her trembling hand covers her mouth in horror, an apologetic expression thrown my way.

Then she walks out.

And I don't follow her. Not because I don't want to, but because I'm confused as to what happened and it takes me a moment to react.

I don't know where this girl came from, or what she's running from, but I don't want her running from me.

By the time I get outside, Lenny's pulling out of the parking lot.

"Damn it," I curse, kicking at the gravel.

It's nearing one in the morning by the time I get to the house and thankfully, my adrenaline and hard-on is gone. Only problem is I'm exhausted. I wish it was Friday already.

As I enter the house, I'm careful to deactivate the alarm so it doesn't wake Nova or Raven, who's probably sleeping on the couch. After Nevaeh was murdered, I installed an alarm in the house and motion detectors around the perimeter of house. Most of the time the motion detectors are set off by animals but other than that, I hadn't had any problems since then.

I'm surprised to see Raven on the couch and Nova on the floor curled up on the rug with my blanket off my bed.

Raven drops her phone in her lap and looks up at me. "Jesus dude, I thought you'd be home a while ago."

"Sorry, thanks for staying. I thought you'd be asleep."

"I was... but Rawley was texting me."

"And where was he today?"

"Drunk... where else."

Careful not to wake Nova, I sit next to Raven. "Fucker."

She adjusts her pillow on the couch like she's getting ready to sleep and stares at the television. I groan quietly when I realize what she's watching. "Why the hell would anyone willingly want to be on a show where you're naked and scared?"

Raven gets me and says, "Right? These people are like attention whores. It's like a bad car accident. I can't look away from it." And then she's reminded of why I was so late. "Did you get the engine in for that lady? I felt so bad for her and her kids to have that happen right after her husband died."

I run my fingers through my hair. "Yeah, we got it done. I'm not charging her for labor. She's been through enough."

Raven fluffs her pillow and pulls her blanket over her shoulders.

"Careful there, word on the street is gonna get out that you're actually a nice guy."

I snort, leaning forward to rest my elbows on my knees and stare down at my sleeping daughter. Fuck, she looks so damn innocent with her wild curls everywhere.

"Everything okay?" Raven asks, sensing there's something wrong.

"Yeah."

She slaps my shoulder. "Don't lie to me. I'm not a little girl anymore. I'll be twenty in eight fucking days. Talk to me."

I don't know why, but I do. I fucking spill my guts because who else do I have to talk to right now? Nova's sleeping and the last thing I want to tell her is that I kissed Lenny. She'd want me to go pick out rings tomorrow if that were the case. "I kissed Lenny."

"What?" she yells, causing Nova to jump in her sleep and then roll over. Raven slaps her hand to her mouth, and then mouths sorry to me.

Both of us remain frozen for a minute to see if Nova's gonna wake up.

"Holy shit," Raven whispers. "You really kissed her?"

I nod, unable to keep the smirk from forming.

Raven grabs the remote and throws it at me, smacking me in the ear. "Oww! What the fuck did you do that for?"

"When did you kiss her?"

"Tonight."

She picks the fucking remote up again and nails me with it. I grab it and toss in onto the other couch across the room. "Stop that."

"Why did you kiss her?"

I shrug. "I don't know. Seemed like the thing to do. We were leaving and then I bumped into her and it went from there."

She giggles quietly covering her mouth with her hand. "And you didn't finish?"

"No... she stopped us. Said I was her boss and it was a bad idea."

Raven sighs and I glance over my shoulder at her. "I can see why she'd say that."

"Why?"

"Because, Red." She moves, tucking her legs up under her and moving to face me completely. "Look at the position she's in now. She needs a job, for reasons we don't really know, and she's a woman in a male-dominated business. The last thing she needs is the reputation she sleeps with her boss to get ahead."

Well, I initially thought that when I first saw her. I guess I'm no different, and I understand *why* she would think that. But I don't see her that way anymore. "That's ridiculous. She's a great mechanic. One of the best I've ever seen and I love that she doesn't give a shit what people think."

Raven reaches for her water on the end table beside the couch, takes a slow drink and then looks back at me. "I think she cares more than she lets on. There's more to her than she leads us to believe, a sadness almost. Like at the party the other night. She left because she thought it was a family thing. I can't convince her we're here for her. She's a great person. I just think she might be in over her head with something she's not willing to share with us."

I nod. "I get that feeling too. I called her old boss and he was weird about the whole thing. Wouldn't tell me much other than she was the best mechanic he had and he was sorry to see her leave."

"Did he say why she left?"

"Nope. Danced around my questions a lot."

"And Tyler didn't say anything?" she asks, keeping her eyes on the flickering of the television as two people run buck-ass naked through the woods.

"Not really. I've pressed for details a few times but he's not saying much." I shake my head and let it fall in my hands. This isn't the kind of crap I wanted to deal with right now. Yeah, she's helping me out at the shop, but this thing where I care, I told myself I wouldn't and now fucking look at me, trying to figure her out. It's exactly what I wanted to stay away from.

"What are you going to do?"

My hands drop from my face and I flop myself back on the couch.

"There's not a lot I can do. She needs to come to me." In more ways than one. I mean, it's not like I can force her into anything, but it's questionable how she'll react tomorrow. I made it pretty clear what I wanted. Her, right then and there on a dirty bench.

Turning, I pat Raven on the top of the head. "Get some sleep."

"Are you going to move her?" she asks, looking down at Nova who's now sprawled out with her arms and legs like she's making a snow angel.

"Yeah, she hates sleeping on the floor." Kneeling down, I try to gather her up without waking her but it's impossible. The moment I touch the kid, her eyes pop open.

She blinks, rubbing her eyes and then stares at me. "Daddy, where were you?"

"I got stuck at the shop."

"I missed you." She wraps her arms around my shoulder resting her head on my chest. Her hair's in my face but I manage to make it down the hall to her room. "You weren't here to tuck me in."

"I'm sorry, darlin'," I whisper, kissing her forehead when I lay her in the bed.

She snuggles up to her pillow letting her eyes drift shut. "Were you with Lenny?"

My goddamn cheeks flush, the heat rising in my face as I smooth her curls away from her face. "Yes. We had a big job that needed to get done tonight."

Turning my head, Nevaeh's picture on her nightstand catches my eyes. Nova looks so much like her mother. Those wild curls was one of the things I loved most about Nevaeh. She had beautiful curly hair that was as free as she was.

I feel guilty when I see that photograph, and I know I'm doing the best I can for the two of us, but still, it doesn't take the hurt away or make this any easier for me. I'm not sure why there's any guilt, but there is now for kissing Lenny. It's not like I cheated on Nevaeh.

How can I have feelings for someone else when I haven't gotten justice for my wife? That feels like cheating to me.

Needing to be alone in my thoughts and misery, I find myself in the shower late at night. Unfortunately, while my brain is a million miles an hour tonight, my dick is still unsatisfied and thinking about Lenny and her legs wrapped around my waist.

I wrap my hand around my dick and squeeze. Life pumps through it, my needy ache becoming known. I stroke it, thinking about how wrong it is to want Lenny this way, and how strange it is to imagine another woman other than my wife.

Regardless, I just need release. I need to purge these thoughts from my body, like a sickness that won't go away until the fever breaks and the poisons out.

I don't know when it happened, maybe when she walked inside my shop for the first time, but somehow, Lenny has become someone I can't fucking let go of. Hell, I can't go one night without jacking off in the shower thinking of her.

I nod, resting my hands on the edge of the counter in front of me, and I glance around the office. "Yep. Is Raven here yet?"

"No, not yet. She was running late this morning. Should be here any minute."

My eyes wander to the picture on her desk of Nova, and who I think is Lyric, Red's dad. He has to be. Red looks just like him. It's also clear, looking at the photo, Nova is special to a lot of people.

I want to groan at my internal realization. The very last thing I need is to bring this family into my bullshit. My only option right now is Tyler.

"Okay." I wave my hand around. "I'll catch up with her later."

I walk out of the office and look around hoping to spot Tyler. He's standing in his stall with his arms up and hands locked around the back of his neck staring at the car in front of him.

I grab him by the arm and start dragging him toward the parts room.

"What the hell, Lenny?" He yanks his arm out of my grasp.

I don't turn around and keep walking knowing he will follow me.

When we get into the parts room, I close the door and lean again it taking a deep breath. "Ben called." My breath expels with the words, and I want to feel better after telling him that, but it doesn't get easier. The knot in my throat remains, the burning in my stomach bubbling.

"Wait, what? What do you mean he called?" Tyler runs his hand through his hair and looks at me, I can't help but notice something seems off with him.

Tyler places both hands on my shoulders, his eyes dilated more than what I've ever seen before. "You need to go to the sheriff."

"I know I should, and I will but I'm just so damned freaked out right now. He's pissed and saying all kinds of shit like he's going to find me. I'm scared, Tyler. I don't want anyone to get hurt."

He blinks, shaking his head and when he looks at me, I can tell that something is different about him. "No."

"No? What do you mean no?" I'm not understanding what he is trying to say to me.

"No."

Now I'm getting pissed. What the hell is wrong with him?

"Shit, Tyler. This is serious. Could you please try and make some sense? Did you not get any sleep last night? It's like your brain is dragging this morning."

He scratches the side of his head, and then blinks quickly. "No... I just—"

"No what, Tyler?"

"No. I don't think I got any sleep. I woke up in a rush thinking I was late... and I wasn't." I look at him for a minute, giving him some time to get his thoughts together. He and Raven need to take a break so he can get some damn sleep. "Look, Lenny, you're not hurting anyone. We're here for you. Let me talk to Red."

"No," I gasp, horrified at his suggestion. "I *don't* want him involved."

He gives me that look, the one that says "don't be ridiculous." But there's something else. Something that he's either not telling me, or maybe it's my imagination.

The thing is, I know I'm being ridiculous. This whole situation is crazy. Especially the part where I thought I would get away from Ben Snider and not have repercussions.

"I was an idiot to think Ben wouldn't follow me."

"How do you think he found you?"

Running my hand through my hair, I begin to pace the parts room. "Maybe he found out where the restraining order was issued or from the divorce filling... I'm not sure."

He sighs and steadies himself against the shelves. I notice then his hands are shaking. Maybe he's had too much coffee lately. "Okay, well let's think about it. Do you think he'll come after you or is he all talk?"

I try to think about it, the possibility if he'll actually come after me and my answer is yes. Ben would. It's in his nature to see it until... the end.

"Yes. I don't doubt for a minute that he will come after me. Ben sees my leaving as a slap in his face. There is no way he is going to let me go without a fight."

"Okay. Well then, after work today, you and I are going to go to the sheriff's office and report that Ben violated the restraining order."

"Do you think they will do anything? I mean it's not like he broke the order or anything. He just called me."

Tyler rolls his eyes and looks at me with a frustrated glare. "It's a no contact order, Lenny. Yes, he broke it and yes, they will do something about it. Just promise that we will go and report it this afternoon."

"I promise."

"Good. Oh, and I don't want you going anywhere outside of the garage or the house without someone with you. Until we know something about what's going on with Ben, I don't want you alone. Got that?"

Warmth spreads in my chest and I can't help but smile at him. This is what it feels like to be cared for. This is what it having a family is like. "Okay."

We both head back to the shop, which is busy and there is not time to screw around without falling behind.

THE DAY HAS GONE BY SO QUICKLY and before I realize it, it's already afternoon. I know I need to talk to Red and apologize for being late, but I haven't had the time yet today.

When I finally get a minute to grab a quick drink, I see Red for the first time today.

To my left, I can hear Rawley and Daniel talking and then Rawley shoves Daniel. "Fuck off, Daniel. Get out of my face today!"

Daniel stands there for a minute looking at Rawley but makes the decision to turn and walk away. Probably one of the few good decisions Daniel has made in his life.

Well, it's clear everyone is in a bad mood today. Maybe it has something to do with the thunderstorm heading our way; it's got everyone all amped up. I do wonder what went down with Rawley and his harem, and

I can honestly say I think a little differently about him knowing he's so... well, as Raven would put it, slutty.

I decide this time is as good as any to head over and apologize. I need to talk to Red before I chicken out and not say anything at all.

Right when I get to the stall, the crowbar in his hand drops to the ground as it slips off and jams into the engine block.

"Motherfucker!" he curses, jumping back and holding his hand for a brief moment.

Bloody knuckles and bloodshot eyes confirm a couple of things. One, Red has a temper far beyond what I've seen, and two, he didn't get much sleep last night. I want to ask him if everything's okay but I know the answer. He's probably upset about me stopping our kiss last night.

"Hey, sorry I was late this morning."

Red stops what he's doing but doesn't say anything. Doesn't even look at me. He just turns and walks away. Seriously? He's just going to ignore me?

"Reddington!" I call after him.

His body tenses at me calling him Reddington, but he keeps walking away toward the coffee machine inside the office, so I follow him. If I didn't know any better, I would think he's purposely trying to piss me off. And you know, I take the bait because I turn into an idiot around him all of the time.

I look around, making sure Mia and Raven aren't in here before I say, "Look, if you're worried about last night, don't be. I get that it meant nothing." I try to keep my voice from shaking around him. "That's why I left when I did to stop it before we went too far."

"What?" He whirls to face me, outraged, and spits the word out in a hiss.

"That's why I left." Numbly, I turn my gaze to his.

His eyes narrow and I'm reminded of the kiss and the heat from it while I'm under his gaze. "Okay...."

"It's just you know, we got caught up in the moment and I assumed it didn't mean anything to you either."

To you either? That implies I thought it didn't mean anything and that's a crock of shit. It did mean something to me. It meant the world to be kissed like that.

He cuts me off immediately, his finger in my face as he steps closer and anger pulsing in his dark eyes. "Stop thinking you know anything about me," he says, aggravation clear in his tone.

I swallow hard, anger and humiliation washing over me that I'm actually standing here with him trying to act like it meant nothing.

Red doesn't budge, aggression hardening his features as he pours himself a coffee. As beautiful as Red is, this—the angry side—is a sight to behold. Hell, it is damn near fascinating to me.

He narrows his eyes into slits when he turns to me. "So let me get this straight. You think me kissing you last night meant nothing to me, which is okay with you, because it also meant nothing to you?" he repeats with contempt, pressing me to answer him.

No!

I lift a brow, challenging him. "Yes."

He steps right in my face, standing directly in front of me. My breathing spikes, like it always does around him. "Believe what you want, then." His expression clouds with anger. "But know this... I haven't been with a woman since my wife died." He pauses, waiting for me to look at him, as if to let that last bit sink in.

I gasp because it does. It sinks down to my gut and confirms my theory that anything between us is a bad idea. Crossing my arms over my chest defiantly, I stare at the parking lot to see Mia returning to the office. I feel like a complete asshole when I see her coming, like I shouldn't be in here arguing with her son over a kiss that obviously meant something to the both of us.

"Just forget it," Red grumbles, slamming the door behind him as he leaves the office.

Well, that went horribly.

IN THE LATE AFTERNOON, after avoiding Red all day, we're working in a neutral silence when we hear a crash at the end of the shop. I turn my head just as Red takes off toward where Tyler and Colt's stall are at the far left.

My eyes scan the shop landing on Tyler's stall to see him on the ground, blood pouring from the side of his face.

Immediately, I panic, as do Colt, Daniel, and Rawley, as we rush over to him. He shakes violently, his body convulsing in jerked movements. We surround Tyler and I yell to Red, "Should I call 911?"

He shakes his head, all his focus on Tyler. He's completely in control as he tries to keep his head from repeatedly hitting the concrete floor. "No, he has epilepsy. He probably forgot to take his medicine this morning."

It seems like the seizure goes on forever when in reality it's a minute or two. Finally, Tyler goes limp on the ground, blood still flowing from a cut on his head.

"He hit his head on the car," Daniel points out, having seen the whole thing, his voice trembling as he stares down at Tyler with wide eyes. "It was really weird. He was just standing there staring at the car and passed out."

"He suffers from grand mal seizures. He's on medication that controls them but this happens when he forgets to take it." Red reaches beside him for a shop towel and holds it to Tyler's head as he lays limp with his head supported in Red's lap. "He'll be fine. It's nothing to worry about." And then he nods to me. "Can you go get my mom and tell her what happened? We need to get him into the office to lay down for a minute."

Nodding, I take off running, only to run into both Mia and Raven as they're rushing out of the office. "What the hell happened?" Raven asks, trying to appear like she's not worried about Tyler, but the way her eyes widen and her breathing halts, she's panicking seeing her fuck buddy lying on the ground bleeding.

"Apparently he had a seizure," I tell her as we rush back over to Red.

Red takes another towel and wipes the side of Tyler's face where blood from his mouth has trickled down his cheek. "He probably bit his tongue." He looks at his mom next to me. "Can you grab the first-aid kit? He's got a pretty bad gash on his forehead."

Raven leaves to get it. When she returns, she takes over making sure the cut is okay. "Should we take him to the hospital?" Raven asks, kneeling down to their level and touching the side of Tyler's face tenderly as she applies gauze to the cut.

It takes Tyler around ten minutes to come back around, his face pale, his expression one of confusion as Colt teases him lightly while handing him a bottle of water. He drinks it slowly and notices his tongue is bleeding. He spits blood on the floor, away from us.

"Fuck, I'm a mess." Taking a towel beside him, Tyler covers his lap where his jeans are wet. I can't imagine this is easy on him. Here we are all staring at him as he sits propped against his toolbox, urine-soaked jeans and bleeding.

"Why don't you go upstairs?" Red suggests to Tyler, keeping his hand on his shoulder as he sits next to him on the floor. We were going to move him to the office, but decided against it when he began to come around.

Tyler stares blankly at him, and then shakes his head slowly. "No, I'm fine. I gotta...." He looks around and clearly doesn't even remember what he was working on.

"Tyler, I really appreciate what you're trying to do here, but we both know you're not fine." Red waves to the cars. "Besides, I can't have you around all this equipment after you've just had a seizure. Just go upstairs and rest."

"I'll take him upstairs," Raven suggests, stepping forward

Tyler shakes his head immediately. "No."

Red nods to his sister and then helps Tyler up. "Let Raven take you home. Go rest."

Raven steps forward, her arm around Tyler's waist. They exchange a passing glance. The first one in public I've seen yet. He breathes in deeply at her touch, leaning into her side as if he's glad she's here right now. Thankfully, Red doesn't notice the intimacy of it.

It takes them twenty minutes to get him up the stairs. While they're doing that, I pick up the tools that scattered around Tyler's stall when he fell.

"You okay?" Red asks when he returns and sees me trying to make sense of what I just saw.

"I'm fine. That's just... scary." I push Tyler's tool cart out of the way and beside his toolbox. "And I didn't even know he had epilepsy."

Red nods, taking the work order Tyler had and looking it over. "He didn't want anyone to know. The only reason I know is because it happened once when we were younger."

"Why would he hide it though? It's not a big deal."

"To *you* it's not," Red points out and turns his attention toward the car Tyler was in the middle of. He was replacing an engine in an old Chevy Blazer and still hadn't got the engine out. "To him he's vulnerable when he has them. He has absolutely no control over anything. I mean, he pissed himself right there. Do you think any man would feel comfortable with that?"

"Well, no."

Rawley approaches, his hands buried in the pockets of his jeans, his guitar in hand. "I need to take off early. Like now."

I'm in disbelief at the audacity of him to think that would even be an option after what just went down with Tyler's seizure. I look at Red, waiting on his reaction.

Red's jaw flexes, as do the muscles in his forearms as he looks at me, and then Rawley. "Why's that?"

"I got a show in Portland tonight."

Red snorts and takes the tool cart I'd just pushed out of the way and flips it over with a quick flip of his wrist. The sound resonates off the walls, tools crashing to the concrete floor with a loud bang. "If that's more important to you, then go!" he roars back at Rawley, keeping at least five feet between them. I think he's so close to punching his brother the distance is needed.

Rawley narrows his eyes at Red, glowering at his older brother. And then he walks away without saying anything.

Red glares at *me*. "It's like his fucking mission in life is to piss me off."

I'm confused. He said *his*, but he meant me too.

I give Red some time alone, mostly because he walked out back and I remember the time in the parts room and that particular verbal lashing. When he walks away, he needs his space.

"I can stay and help," I say to Red when he returns. My voice is hesitant because I have no idea what his mood will be like after the seizure and then Rawley and him getting into it again.

He stops what he's doing for a second and there's a flash of surprise. A touch of anger... no, actually, it's hurt. He catches himself quickly, smooths the expression out. "Are you sure that's what you want to do? I wouldn't want you to regret it tomorrow."

"Oh, my God." I groan. "Don't be an asshole. It's not the same thing. I tried to be honest with you and you're just throwing it in my face. If you don't want my help, fine, I'll leave, but you don't have to keep being a dick about it."

Where the hell did that all come from?

I even surprised myself with that rant.

When he doesn't say anything, I get visibly flustered as my blood pressure rises. He just stands there and continues to stare at me like I've lost my damn mind. I have.

I decide to try a different approach.

"You definitely know how to make a girl feel special, don't you?" There's a sexiness to my tone that has his attention. Yeah, I'm trying to act that way. I want him to be just as annoyed.

He turns, walks backward a few steps watching me, and then turns back around. His voice is harsher than before, full of a bitterness that I'm beginning to get used to. "I don't know what you're talking about."

I follow him. "Why are you being mean to me today? I'm trying to help here." My voice lowers. "Is it because I stopped us from going any further last night?"

He snorts, picking up a handful of tools from his cart and begins putting them back in his toolbox. "Maybe you should just do your job and stop trying to figure out what my problem is."

Jerk. Asshole. Dickhead. I could go on here. And in my head, I do for a few seconds.

"You don't—" I'm just about to tell him off for being such an asshole when he beats me to it.

"Don't worry about it." He throws down a wrench and slams the drawer closed, beginning to walk away, again, his shoulders tense. His body language is telling me to stay back, but I'm not a very good listener. Clearly.

"I will worry about it because you were being nice to me and now this.... I'm only trying to help."

He turns on his heel and faces me again, irritation lighting his face. "You're trying to help? What exactly are you trying to help me with? You don't know what the hell you're talking about." He stops himself, his brow scrunched. He wants so badly to say more; it's etched in every single emotion flashing in his eyes. But he doesn't.

Suddenly, I blurt out the one question that has been on my mind since last night.

"Why'd you kiss me?" I ask, wanting to know how he can go from hot to cold so fast.

"What are you doing?" He ignores my question searching my eyes for an answer he assumes I have. "Why are you so insistent on making this so much harder for me? You told me it was a mistake and that it meant nothing, but you keep bringing it up."

"Harder for you? You're the one who has been treating me like shit and then kisses me like I'm just supposed to spread my legs for you. Is that why? You're mad because I didn't fuck you?" It's a pretty low blow, but I say it anyway. Apparently, I'm losing my mind because I can't believe I'm saying these things to him.

His lips purse immediately. His face and the way his eyes are stone cold and bleeding with an invisible pain when we make eye contact give him away. I want to know his pain because finally, I'm not the only one experiencing this.

"I cannot believe you would say that to me. Is that really who you think I am because if so, then you don't know *anything*." He's so angry that his confidence and pride waver. He's breaking a little and I can see it's making him uneasy. He wants to show me I don't know what I'm talking about, but his stubbornness gets him too. He's not one that gives up easily. "I told you I hadn't been with a woman since my wife died, let alone kissed one and now you're standing here accusing me of wanting you to fuck me as part of your job description. I can't believe you would even suggest that to me." He turns, leaving me with that verbal chastising but I don't let him and grab his arm.

"Red." I sigh. His name on my lips is something he wants to hear because his face twists when I say it, the words washing over him. "Don't do that."

"Don't do what?" His expression is suddenly livid, as if that one remark sets him off. His eyes search mine, the darkness colliding like waves crashing against a rocky shore.

"Be this way." My eyes dip to his chest, so tense his muscles seem tight and rigid underneath his oil smudged, gray T-shirt.

"What way? This is me." He backs away about a step, dropping his hands to his side. "You're the one fooling yourself."

I blink at his harshness. "You're being an asshole."

"It's not a way. It's me. I *am* an asshole. Took you long enough to figure it out." When I take another step back, he knows I'm angry with the words, but he doesn't stop. "I can't be anything you're hoping I will be. It'd be a goddamn disaster."

I swallow over my irritation. "I'm not looking for anything from you but a job and maybe a little respect," I say.

"You *have* a job," he laughs, but it's condescending. "Respect is earned."

"Stop being a jerk to me then." I'm not about to argue with him about the respect part because I know damn well I'll probably never have that from him.

Annoyance flashes in his eyes, and then he walks away. I watch his back and then my eyes drift lower.

So sexy.

I'm so damn angry at myself because as mad and hurt as Red makes me, the attraction toward him never fades. We stand here and argue to the point where he turns his back and walks away from me and all I can think is he's got the best ass, and I'm jealous of every woman he's ever been with. So jealous.

When Red returns with three bottles of brake cleaner, he notices I'm still there, leaning against his toolbox.

"And you're still here." Red sets the cans on top of his toolbox and stares at me when I don't move. "What do you want from me?"

"You." You can't miss the sadness in my tone, but it also doesn't stop him. Oh God, I said that, didn't I?

He hears me all right, but doesn't let his emotions show on his face. "Everyone else has gone home for the day. You should too. I've got work to do and the last thing I need right now is you standing around. I get you. You didn't want to kiss me. Message received."

He's trying to hurt me. He wants me to leave him alone, but it doesn't hurt me. Well, maybe a little, but he doesn't know my truth and I know he wants to. He does. It's displayed in his eyes. He wants to know why I'm that way. Why I'm denying what is obviously happening between us. I'm not sure I have an answer for him. I'm not even sure I know anymore. Or if I ever did.

When I don't answer, he cocks an eyebrow at me. With a low chuckle, he leans down to pick up the wrench that fell earlier. Tossing it in his tool cart, he waits for a second, giving me another chance to convince him otherwise. I don't. I'm not sure what to say right then. "Are you just hanging around to torture me?"

Looking at him now, I see right through his bloodshot eyes. He wants me to believe that nothing happening today is affecting him. The truth is, he's carrying the weight of the world on his shoulders and it's pretty obvious by his behavior right now he's over it.

I realize I'm being an idiot and say, "I'm not trying to. I'm sorry. I'm just here because I want to help you finish this job. I'll finish the car in my stall and then help you out, if you want. Let's just get this done and I'll get out of your face."

"Do whatever you want, Lenny." And then he turns to walk away.

Glancing outside, I notice the weather has taken a turn for the worse and Red goes over to close the shop doors and then flips the radio on. The rain and wind pick up, blowing gusts of water under the door just as he's closing them. Once they're shut, you can hear them flexing with the wind, creaking, bending and moaning as the metal shifts against the pressure.

A slow country tune flows through the shop and I begin to relax.

Wearing my usual jeans and flannel tied up around my waist, an hour later, I finish up the car in my stall after trying to figure out where the rattle is coming from. People and their goddamn rattles. They sometimes forget these are cars made of metal and plastic and when you're going down the road and all that plastic is flexing, it's going to fucking rattle.

When I'm finished with the Explorer, Red's watching me, his hands on the hoist.

"Help me out here," he says, nodding to the engine he has ready to take out of the car in his stall. "I need an extra hand and you're distracting me." He turns facing the car, and then back to me. "Might as well help out."

My first reaction is to be defensive and say something bitchy in reply, but when I take a second I realize he's teasing which means he's starting to relax. I'm not gonna lie, I breathe a small sigh of relief before crossing my arms over my chest. "So let me get this straight. First you don't want me here, now I'm *distracting* you and you now *want* my help?" I decide to tease right back, trying to make light of everything that we just said an hour ago, but it's slightly entertaining the look that comes over his face.

"You know damn well that you're distracting me." And then he steps closer, his brow scrunched in determination. "Now are you going to help me or what?"

For every part of me that knows pushing Red away is the right thing, there's an equal part of me who can't let him go.

"I don't know. Are you going to ask me nicely?" I step forward, coming to stand in front of him.

What the fuck am I doing?

He stands in front of me now, crossing his arms over his chest, there's the faintest of a grin tugging at his beautiful lips I desperately want on mine again. He leans down to whisper in my ear. "Lennon." Oh God, the way my name rolls off his tongue nearly brings me to my knees. "Would you please do me the pleasure of helping me?" He then pulls away and stares into my eyes.

Warmth creeps up my neck coloring my cheeks. He's read my mind, hasn't he?

He takes a step back, waiting for my answer.

When I don't say anything, his eyes narrow. "Are you going to make me beg?"

I sigh. "All right, no need to beg."

He looks back at me over his shoulder as he steps toward the engine again. "I'm not the kind of man who believes in making a woman beg and I'm definitely not the kind of guy to force a woman to do anything she doesn't want to do."

"I'm sure."

I can't see his face when he says, "It's a good thing you're not wearing those shorts again."

I roll my eyes, following him. "You and those shorts."

He stops and I nearly run into his back when he does this, whirling to face me, his chest pressing into mine. "Stop teasing me."

I hold up my hands in surrender. "Sorry."

I take a seat on the stool near him, waiting for him to tell me what he wants me to help him with.

"I just need help guiding it out to make sure none of the hoses get stuck." He motions to the engine.

It's clear he doesn't need my help and that makes me smile too. He wants me in here with him.

We work in silence for the most part, but it's unbearable as it usually is around him. So I start asking questions.

"Who's watching Nova tonight?"

"She's with my mom tonight." Red stands and reaches inside the fridge not far from his toolbox to remove two beers. He hands me one. "I don't know what I'd do without my mom. Being a single parent isn't exactly easy when you're trying to run your own business."

I take the beer he hands me. "I can't imagine it is. How long have you been a mechanic?" I ask, realizing I don't know much about him and his passion for working on cars.

He looks back at me over his shoulder as he's staring at the engine on the hoist we just pulled out of the car, surprised by the question. "Well I wanted to be a mechanic since I was old enough to turn a wrench." He steps back from the engine and reaches for a shop rag on his toolbox. "I once took an engine apart when my dad was at work. I was ten, maybe."

"So Lyric... was he mad when you took apart the engine or did he help you out?"

"Uh, no, my old man was pissed." Red laughs. "It was the engine out of his truck. And he didn't exactly want it taken apart. There wasn't anything wrong with it. From then on, my dad started bringing me to the shop, teaching me everything from changing the oil to replacing the engine. And putting his back together."

I love that sound of his easy laughter flowing through the shop. God, I wish he'd never stop laughing. "And your dad left the shop to you when he died?"

He takes a seat next to me on the stool beside his toolbox. "Yep." He then looks around the shop. "Sometimes I wonder what the hell he was thinking."

He watches my lips as I speak. "Are you scared it's not going to work?"

"Well yeah, I am." He laughs. The sound makes me smile again because it's so damn captivating. "He spent his entire life making this place work and he's only been gone two months and I'm not sure from Monday to Friday if I can make it work the way he did."

We're quiet, and I think he's going to get up and leave; there's an uneasiness in his posture. The sound of the rain picking up catches his attention as it pops against the metal roof. "Shit... I left my windows down." Squinting at me, he bites down on the corner of his bottom lip, contemplating what he's going to say but still, withholding so much. "I'll be right back."

When he leaves, I sit on the stool staring at my hands wondering what the fuck is wrong with me.

Why did I stop him last night? Truth be told, I know *why* I stopped him. It's because I've made so many bad decisions in my life, I don't even know how to make a good one. It's like my default decision is permanently turned to make the shitty choice.

Given the chance again, I know what my answer will be. There's something deep inside of me, a need, a craving I know won't be cured until I'm with him physically.

16

REDDINGTON

I TRY to fucking ignore her. I do. Especially with everything she said today. If she wants to believe that last night meant nothing, then that's her choice.

Despite that, it's all the same and nothing changes. Nothing in my fixation with Lenny that is.

I'm desperate.

I'm weak.

I can't stay away from her even if I try. She's everywhere. In my thoughts and in my space because her stall is right next to mine. And I insist on punishing myself even more here by allowing her to stay late and then asking for her help with the engine.

I didn't need her damn help. We both knew that. It was my way of getting her to stay late with me.

Still, it's shitty and unfortunate because I'm a goddamn idiot who loves to torment himself.

My bigger problem comes when she starts asking questions and I open up to her and talk about becoming a mechanic and the fear of letting my dad down. She sits there listening like what I'm saying is the most interesting thing she's heard all day and all that does is re-enforce the fact that I'm starting to feel something more for her. At first my attraction to her was purely physical, but now it's... hell, I don't know what it is.

We sit in silence, the sound of the rain picking back up shakes me out of my thoughts. With all that happened today with Tyler, and then Rawley, I totally forgot that I left my window down in the Nova. "Shit... I left my windows down," I tell her and jet out the door into the parking lot through the heavy downpour of rain.

Sure enough, the inside of my car is soaked.

I roll the window up and take a minute standing in the rain, breathing heavily. The restless charcoal sky rumbles, a boom of thunder echoing through the night. I close my eyes, trying to blink away the thoughts of her.

Running my hand through my sopping wet hair, I walk toward the bay doors to finish replacing the engine hoping that keeping busy will help me take my mind off of her.

My problem is as I'm walking back inside it hits me that I know what's going to happen once I'm in there. This almost overwhelming response rushes through my veins, and I know it's not just a matter of wanting Lenny, no, it's a matter of *needing* Lenny.

"You're soaking wet," she says once I'm back. I look down and sure enough, my shirt and pants are soaked, sticking to my body like a second skin.

"Guess so, huh?" As I look back up at her, I would love to take them off, but I'm not sure that's the direction I should go right now.

With water dripping in my eyes, I shake my head, beads of water letting loose from my hair and she laughs and covers herself from the spray. "Were your windows down?"

"Yeah." I exhale a resigned breath, knowing exactly what I'm hoping I'm about to do, though I know I shouldn't.

It's not just the fact that she works for me, even though that should be reason enough. No, I need to know she wants this as much as I do.

Some sort of signal from her that she's caught up in whatever web this is like me. That's all I'm looking for.

As much as I know I need to keep my distance, there's the fact that she's fucking sexy as hell and the temptation that I can't have her, makes me want her even more.

Standing there watching her, I notice there's a tremble to her body and she tenses just for a split second, like she *knows* where this is going. Then she suddenly relaxes, a calm taking over her features like she's made a decision she's been struggling with. A decision that's lifted a weight off her shoulders.

And as if to give me the signal I was hoping for, she walks up to me placing her hand on my chest. "Red.... I'm sorry for the way I was acting earlier. I was just scared... of this. Of you."

My posture weakens. That's it. That's all I need to hear. I know I'm fucked now. She has me. If there were ever a chance of going back after this, it's gone.

I move to stand directly in front of her and cup her cheeks in my hands, my eyes darting from her lips, to her face.

"So I scare you?" I ask, leaning in so my lips graze her ear. My heart races, fire raging through my veins when she intakes a sharp breath.

When I draw back—waiting on a reaction—she looks at me with wonder in those too-big brown eyes. "No," she squeaks. I know she's lying to me. "It's how you make me feel that scares me."

"How about now?" I breathe, and she shivers under my touch when I move even closer, this time her posture weakens. "Does that scare you?"

"Maybe a little," she replies, squirming away from me, drawing her bottom lip in her mouth.

"Just a little?"

Her pouty lips part only a fraction as if she wants to tell me the truth. Only she doesn't say anything. Her eyes shut and she releases a sigh. "Maybe a lot."

I can't take it. I need to kiss her. Leaning in, my tongue sweeps over the seam of her lips, and gently pulls her bottom lip with my teeth. The action sends a wave of chills over my body, gnawing at me.

God, her mouth is driving me insane. I need more of it. I need to be inside her is what I need.

When I think she might pull back, she doesn't. Instead, she grips my shirt and lets me kiss her. Cupping her cheek with my right hand, I deepen the kiss. She tastes sweet and for a second, I want to drop to my knees and taste her pussy.

A resounding growl spreads through the shop followed by a flash of lightning. Lenny startles at the crack of thunder, her hand clutching her chest. "Holy shit," she gasps, parting her lips from mine.

I laugh, my hands on her shoulders. "You okay?"

"Yeah." She looks up at me with those sultry brown eyes. "I'm good."

I swallow, wanting to kiss her again.

As I lean in, there's another loud crack of thunder, the florescent shop lights dimming. The hum of the air compressor fading catching our attention as the power fades. The battery operated lights above my toolbox give me enough light I can still see her. Vaguely.

Slowly, Lenny backs up against the work bench and lifts herself up so that she's sitting on the edge. I step forward, ripping my soaked shirt over my head and letting it fall to the floor. The squeak of my boots against the concrete is barely heard over the rain. Lenny stares at me taking in the sight of my naked chest as I come closer, my heart racing with each move.

Instability paints her face and she beckons me forward with a look that says, come get me, I need you right now. Everything she said earlier about needing distance and regretting the kiss, it's out the fucking window now. I know it.

I *have* to fuck her. That's all there is to it. I can't take it any longer. I'm craving what I've dreamt to be her perfect pussy and her perky tits laid out before me.

Her eyes grow wide at my proximity and I fixate mine on hers, but she doesn't move. No, she won't either because looking at her, and the way her eyes are taking me in, the way she's giving as much as I'm taking with that kiss, I know damn well she's been wanting this as much as I have from the moment she stepped foot inside my shop.

My voice drops to a heavy baritone, as if I'm purposely trying to let her in on a naughty secret. I am. "Do you have any idea how bad I want this?" Making contact with her now, I press my erection against her center, her legs wrapping around my waist as she sits on the edge of the bench.

"Probably as bad as I want it," she tells me, pulling back to look at me. She then she pushes me back, her hands on my chest and slides off the bench in front of me. I don't let her escape and rest my hands on either side of the bench, my lips touching the side of her neck.

As if she needs me to see this, she forces me back. Slowly, she licks her lips and reaches for the hem of her shirt. No bra. Just perfect naked tits.

When I don't say anything, she asks, "What's stopping you?"
What is stopping me?

My morals... my wife... Nova... everything... *her*.

I know I want her body more than breathing, and that's kind of a shitty thing to want.

I'm not sure what's changed from her telling me the kiss was a mistake, to this, but I'll take it. Anything to finally ride this need of wanting her.

"Nothing's stopping me," I tell her, my body in line with hers, no amount of space between us.

She makes me step back again, easing off the bench and turns so that her back is to me. My hands dance over the swell of her ass, her eyes on me over her shoulder. Slowly, she unbuttons her jeans and deliberately bends down to slide both her jeans and panties off giving me a front row view of her perfect ass. Once her jeans are removed, she kicks them to the side and as an unspoken invitation she places both hands on the workbench in front of her.

I step forward, pressing my jean-clad erection into the crack of her ass, causing her to gasp.

"You really want this?" Turning so that her bare breasts are now only inches from my naked chest, she awaits my answer.

"So fucking bad," I growl, letting those questioning eyes bore into mine unabashedly. She can't turn away from me now and I can't fucking tear myself away from the look I'm getting.

Cupping her face with my left hand, I kiss her passionately as I work on getting my jeans undone and kicked to the side as fast as I can before she changes her mind.

This is where I should stop. But I can't.

My hands move up her ribcage and her breaths become deeper as if she's gasping. Christ, she is. My dick is pressed to the curve of her ass and I lose myself in being close to a woman again. But not just any woman, *this* woman.

I kiss her jaw and neck working my way down to her shoulders while my hands start to move as if they have a mind of their own. Kneading her breasts and not so gently rolling her nipples between my fingers, they harden with my touch. I can't concentrate on anything but the way her body reacts to mine, arching almost uncontrollably against me.

She turns her head to look over her shoulder and her breath fans over my face like a whisper and I can't take it. Again, I forcefully turn her so that our mouths can find one another. Her lips submit to mine and our tongues meet, gently at first. But as I expected, what happens next is anything but gentle. It's fucking animalistic as throaty moans and our gasping breaths take over. I keep one hand on her face so I can taste her deeper and she responds by gasping into my mouth and bringing her leg up to grip around my waist. I grasp it, lifting her off the floor and setting her back on the edge of the work bench before I push forward but still, I don't enter her. I don't have a condom on yet, but there's no doubt she knows how badly I want this.

Tools rattle together with my movement, and I'm ready to fuck her against any flat surface, this bench, the wall, floor.... It doesn't make a damn bit of difference to me.

Sure, I should be gentle with her and take my time because I don't know what this could mean, but I'm a starving man. I can't think clearly enough to slow down and I'm racing toward what I know can sedate this unattainable addiction.

"Do you have a condom?" she asks.

I nod. "There's one in my toolbox."

Stepping back, I reach over to my toolbox and grab the condom I've had in there for the last six months. Thanks to a joke between Tyler and Colt.

Lenny takes that moment to lean back and catch her breath. Her hands are out beside her and she spreads her legs a bit wider to give me a sneak peek at her dripping wet pussy.

When I have the condom on, I step toward her again running my finger slowly down her center soaking in her juices. At my touch, she whimpers. Actually fucking whimpers.

"Slide off the bench," I tell her in a slow, commanding voice. She does as I say and as soon as her feet touch the ground, I turn her so that her ass grinds into my cock. My head falls forward, resting against her shoulder as excitement shoots through me with her every movement.

My mouth moves over her shoulder to the base of her neck where I bite down tenderly. "Put your right leg on the table."

She does exactly as I say, her neck arching as I run my tongue over the path my teeth made. I position my cock right at her entrance, guiding my latex-sheathed dick inside what I can only describe as paradise.

I can hardly control myself when I enter her and she clenches around me. My hips automatically move quickly, in jerked motions until I gather my senses and make sure I don't blow my load right away.

"Oh God, Red... you feel so good." Her legs spread wider as we struggle to find proper balance. And then she gasps.

My body shakes as I groan. The way her pussy curves to my dick, the pressure that's already building in my groin with how wet and warm she is, it's too much.

Maybe it's my pent-up frustration for no sex in the last two years, but the visual of Lenny bent over this damn bench has me ready to come the moment I begin to move.

It's her perfect plump ass, the thickness around her hips and the way they look with my greasy fingerprint all over them.

Lenny lets out the smallest moan, her hands shuffling on the bench to find something to grip, letting me know she wanted this just as badly as me. They find leverage on the edge, her fingertips white.

When I begin to move, Lenny's back arches off as she raises her chest off the bench and I want to flip her over so I can see her amazing tits bouncing with every thrust. But I don't. Instead, I keep my right hand on her hip and that amazing fucking ass, threading my left into her hair taking a fist full and pulling back with the slightest bit of pressure.

With each movement, she cries out, begs even. I can barely hear her over the howling wind and rain, let alone see her in the dim lighting but it's enough I have to slow down a few times.

"Oh God, Red. Fuck me. Fuck me hard...," she begs.

Shit. The way she says my name, it's all I can do not to blow my load right now.

I can't rush this. That's the last thing I want.

Squeezing her hip and tightening my hold on her hair, I angle her hips enough that I can go deeper. Thrusting my pelvis upward, she gasps, "Don't stop. Don't ever fucking stop. Please."

As badly as I want to come inside of her right now, I want to make her come on my dick. I *need* to see that.

Gliding my right hand across her stomach, I move it between her legs. Lenny shudders as I drag my thumb over her folds before pressing down on her clit.

"You like that?" My voice is labored. It's been a while.

"Seriously, Red, don't stop," she begs, her voice barely audible over the pounding wind and rain. Every time my name passes between her lips, it sends a jolt of energy to my chest, an almost burning stir I begin to crave.

"I'm just getting started," I tell her. With the way she's moaning and panting out heavy breaths, I know what we're doing. This intensity that's so fucking consuming, it's undeniable. It has me fucking her in the shop because I just can't wait. I have to have her like this. I also know, this isn't the end. Where I once thought if I fuck her, I could rid the need, I know that's a lie now. It will *never* be enough.

Both palms splay out on the bench as if she knows she should brace herself and she arches her back even more trying to take me deeper. That's it. I can't hold back any longer. I move my hand back to her hip and grip tighter, my body repeatedly slamming into hers. With every thrust, my balls slap her pussy causing to her moan louder, the bench shaking and rattling as brake cleaner bottles fall to the concrete with our movements.

Lenny's body stiffens as she cries out, her orgasm rolling through her body, a strangled plea falling from her lips as her pussy contracts around me. "Jesus Christ," I grunt, trying to catch my breath as my breathing spirals out of control.

Moving my hand down to slowly massage her clit, I coax her along, drawing out the sweet sensations for her, whispering how fucking sexy she is when she finally lets go. I kiss her shoulders, marking her skin with my teeth as I suck and gently bite.

"You don't know how fucking badly I wanted to see you come on my dick."

When she looks back at me, her eyes squeeze shut and her mouth opens, but no sound comes out.

Have I rendered her speechless?

As I bend my head forward, I grip her face and so that I can I make her look at me as our lips make contact. Her greedy tongue meets mine and I flip her around and lay her on the bench, her back pressed against the cool metal as she opens her legs to me.

Though I can't see her all that well, the flashes of lightning are enough and the idea that I can't see *everything* is somewhat more of a turn on. It leaves a little to the imagination.

"Christ, you're driving me fuckin' crazy," I curse into her hair, pushing it aside, my hands tangling a fist full before my mouth and teeth find her skin.

With my hands on the edge of the bench, I take a step forward, the bench hits the wall with my thrust inside her. Placing my hands on her hips, I drive her into my every thrust.

Her hands raise up over her shoulders and my left hands slips off her hip and onto the bench before I move it to her neck. There's a moment, a split second when I wonder if I'm being too rough with her.

"Fuck...!" She moans, arching back as her legs raise up and she lays them on my shoulders.

Driven with need, my mouth is all over her beautiful legs that have taunted me for weeks as I slam into her, the bench and tools on it shaking as I do so. I can't take it any longer, my orgasm begins to surface.

I try to keep going, but there's no controlling it this time. Thrusting faster, my body tenses, my orgasm so intense I have to grab onto the edge of the bench so I don't collapse because of its aftershocks, my panting gasping breaths taking over.

Groaning into the side of her calf, my body shudders against her, pushing forward once more, pulsing with my release.

I don't move right away, neither does Lenny as our breathing attempts to even out.

I gasp when I pull out, the heat and intensity immediately replaced by the harshness of my reality. I just fucked Lenny. In the shop.

I set her down on unsteady feet, my heart racing. Attempting a deep steadying breath as I try to collect myself, I step back, but I let my eyes wander to her naked ass on that bench and the ink on her side. I'll certainly never look at my work bench the same.

She stands, a sheen of sweat has formed across her body almost making her glow in the dim light. It's clear by her rapid breaths, she's trying to calm herself down after what just happened. It's also a good sign. I wasn't the only one enjoying what we were doing.

She looks up at me and I wait to allow her to talk first, but instead of saying something, she just starts laughing. *Laughing.* Not exactly reassuring after what I thought was damn good sex. I mean, yeah it was quick, but pretty fucking awesome if I say so myself.

"What are you laughing at?" I ask her, unable to hide the uncertainty in my voice.

She stops and lifts her hand to run through my hair. "I'm sorry. It's just that your hair is a mess. It's standing up in all angles and you look like one of those troll dolls I had when I was a kid. You know the ones that you shake and their hair stands up straight."

Troll dolls, really?

I smile and then reach to her hair mimicking her movements. "Yeah, well yours isn't looking too hot either."

A moment of panic flashes in her eyes, and I can't help but laugh. She brings both of her hands to try and comb through her hair, but seems to realize a hot shower and lots of shampoo are her only options.

I continue to stare at her, noticing her hair isn't the only victim of our impulsive actions. Her face, breasts and hips are covered in greasy hand prints. Her body looks like a road map of our passion. I fucking love the way I look on her. Almost makes me angry she's going to erase any trace of this moment as soon as she gets into the shower tonight.

Watching her, it's clear now there's parts of her that were completely untouched until I got my dirty hands on her, marking her in all the ways she needed.

Another loud crack of thunder and flash of lightning tear me from my trance and I look down realizing that not only are we both standing here naked, but I still have the condom on.

Her gaze travels the length of my body, taking in the sight before her. Clearing my throat, I reach down and toss the condom in the trash next to my toolbox. I need to remember to empty that before Daniel does the trash in the morning. The last thing I need is to come up with a reason why a used condom is in my trash can.

It's not that I'm ashamed or regret a minute of what just happened, but until I figure out what's going on between Lenny and me, I don't need anyone else giving me shit.

After I throw the condom away, I reach down to retrieve my jeans. They're still soaked so pulling them on is a bit of a chore.

Glancing over to Lenny, she's followed my lead by gathering her clothes and getting dressed. I groan internally not ready to give up the sight of her incredibly hot body. Turning away, I reach for my shirt.

Once we both get ourselves together—physically at least—I take a look around the shop. It's obvious that we're not getting anything else done with this engine tonight.

"We should just call it a night. With the power out, we aren't going to be able to get anything else done tonight anyway. The generator only powers the apartment."

Lenny looks at me for a minute, and I can see uncertainty flashing across her face. "Oh, okay. Sounds good." She turns and begins to walk toward the door.

"Hold up. Let me just lock up and I'll walk you around to Tyler's door." I quickly walk over to the office door and then the back doors making sure to lock them both. Heading back over to backdoor where Lenny is standing waiting for me, I stop briefly at my toolbox to grab my keys, wallet and cell phone.

As soon as I get to the door, Lenny steps outside into the rain and heads to the side of the building where the stairs lead to Tyler's apartment. I walk behind her giving her a little distance, trying not to crowd her. I don't know what she is thinking right now, and I have to admit, I really hope whatever is going through her mind isn't regret.

Once we reach the stairs, I grab her by the arm and turn her around so that she is facing me, pressing her against the side of the building. Rain pelts the side of our faces, cool drops against heated skin.

Her eyes are aimed at the ground and I use my index finger to lift her chin so that she has no choice but to look at me. Once she does, I can see the conflict in her eyes. It's obvious her brain is flooded with questions about what just happened. I want to reassure her that everything is fine and we will figure it out, but the truth is I don't know what tomorrow brings, so I decide to say something to calm her in the moment.

I move my hand to cup her face, wiping away a smudge of grease and then place my other hand around her waist. Leaning down, I slowly kiss her neck, my open mouth tasting what I know I'm going to think about all night, and then move to whisper in her ear. "Don't overthink this, Lenny."

Lifting my head, I take a step back. We both stand in the pouring rain, barred in a moment until she smiles, one side higher than the other. "See you Monday, Red."

Sweeping sheets of water from my eyes, I watch as she enters the apartment not turning around as she shuts the door. Letting out a deep breath, I head to my car.

Once inside my car, my mind shifts through the memories of the night.

And I'm hard again.

17

LENNON

"DON'T OVER THINK THIS, LENNY."

Pfft. He doesn't know me very well, does he? That's all I've been doing. Overthinking is my thing lately. Because of that, I slept maybe an hour all night.

Did he regret it?

I literally obsess over every move he made last night afterwards, trying to decipher what his words and touch really meant.

I want to believe being with Red is different, but the truth is, while I know being with Red would be the best thing in my life, it would definitely be the worst thing in his. And not to mention horrible timing.

I knew from the first moment his lips touched mine, I should stop it. Hell, I even tried after he kissed me the night after the Fourth of July party. But damn. When Red looks at me with those dark eyes and took me in like I was the most desirable thing in the world, I couldn't stop. I didn't want to stop. For one moment in my life, I wanted to be with someone who *wanted* me just as much as I wanted him. And for that reason only.

From the time I was a teenager, I had sex for all the *wrong* reasons. I thought being with someone physically was what was expected of me and really had nothing to do with what *I* wanted.

There's not a moment in my life that I can remember what it was like to be desired in that way.

I remember the night in every vivid detail from the way his rain-soaked skin tasted, to the overwhelming sensation of contentment when he entered me, to the way his deep voice tickled my skin as he whispered how much he wanted me. Even the memories are too much and my skin flushes.

I smile, thinking of him. It was just one night, but there's something about him I can't shake.

Rolling over, I contemplate going back to sleep since I've only had a few hours, but I *can't* sleep.

Tyler's door opens, groggy from last night, no shirt on. It's then I remember his seizure.

He looks around the room, then back at me before sitting beside me on the couch. "Did the power go out?"

My cheeks flush as I push my bowl away. I can't eat. My nerves are all over the place. "Yeah."

He quirks an eyebrow at me and rubs his hand over his jaw. "Did you get in a fight with an oil can?"

I start to fidget. Shit. I didn't shower last night. I couldn't. I didn't want to wash away the remnants of last night. "No. Why?"

"You look... like you did."

"Shut up. And *you*, bastard..." I slap him on the shoulder. "Why didn't you tell me?"

He looks confused and stares at me. "Tell you what?"

"That you have epilepsy."

He chuckles, like it's no big deal and reaches for the remote. "Oh, right. I forgot."

"You *forgot* to tell me?"

"No." He waves his hand around. "I mean I was so tired the other day, I forgot to take my medication."

"But why didn't you tell me you had seizures?"

"I pissed my fucking pants for Christ's sake." He shrugs with stiffness, the motion drawing my attention to his shoulder and the back of it that's black and blue from the seizure. "I didn't want anyone to know. It's not a big deal. I've had epilepsy since I was like ten. The only people who know are my parents and Red. Mia knows too, mostly because I had to say something when I was hired."

"So Raven didn't know?"

"No... it's not like Raven and I do a lot of talking." He waggles his eyebrows suggestively.

"Did she say anything when she brought you home?"

His eyes widened. "Not really. But I don't remember a lot about yesterday so if she did, I couldn't tell you what she said."

I relax into the couch beside him. "What's going on with you and Raven?"

He sighs and lays his head back against the couch. "I'm not sure. But the fucking sex is amazing." And then he takes his hands and makes a motion like he's cupping an ass and thrusts his hips up. "Dat ass though."

I snort, slapping his shoulder. "Gross. But seriously, you need a plan."

He winces at my hit. Probably because he's so sore. "Why? It's just sex."

"I don't think it is."

"You're complicating it." He looks back at the television. "We need to call the sheriff today. We didn't do it yesterday. He needs to know Ben has a general idea of where you're at now."

"I know. We will."

I know I should be concerned about Ben, but last night is the only thing on my mind.

Tyler glances at me, again. "You should go shower."

He's right. Sadly I should.

I spend the weekend in Tyler's apartment. I even avoid Raven's request to go to the river and a movie, and then feel badly. I was so scared I'd run into Red if I left that I turned into a hermit. Mostly because if I did see him, I wouldn't know how to act. Monday was going to be hard enough. Especially when I saw that bench.

THE DREADED DAY ARRIVES. Monday morning. The first time I'm seeing Red since the night in the shop.

The moment I enter, I'm reminded again of the night from the way my body reacted to his powerful grasp, to the sound the bench made with every thrust. My eyes land on said bench, the warmth creeping through me at the memories.

I can hear him come inside the shop, and Colt greeting him. My body is aware of how close he is by the way my heart beats faster when his breath hits my neck.

"Here." He hands me a coffee, bumping my shoulder. "Thought you could use this."

"You didn't have to bring me coffee," I say, avoiding his eyes. I'm afraid to look at him.

He dips his head, trying to catch my eyes. "I know. I didn't."

"Oh...."

He winks, bumping my shoulder again. "Relax. Nova made me get it for you."

God, I love that kid.

"How'd everything go the other night with that Chevy truck that was in here?" Colt asks, coming to stand next to Red and me. "Did you get the transmission out okay?"

I smile, eyeing Red. "Power went out. We didn't finish."

But we did.

Red shifts his feet when Colt looks at the ground and then up at Red with a grin.

Quickly, Red kicks something under his toolbox and when I realize what Red kicked under his toolbox, the condom wrapper, what Colt saw, my cheeks pink with embarrassment.

"Looks like Rawley must have been in here...." Colt gives a head nod to Red. "Naughty things happened in here."

Red shakes his head and hands Colt a repair order. "Get to work, old man."

He says something as he's leaving, but neither one of us catch it.

I've never been so happy that Rawley is an irresponsible shit, but I'm not entirely sure Colt believed that was from Rawley, considering it was on the floor in front of *Red's* toolbox. Pretty fucking obvious, right?

"Sorry," Red whispers. "I thought I picked that up."

"It's okay," I whisper back, reaching across him for a repair order. "I'll take care of this one."

His gaze travels from my head to my toes and in a sense, every movement of his eyes is like he's touching me again. It sends a shiver up my spine and rush of excitement through me. Not to mention my fucking panties are wet just thinking about Friday, in this shop, on this bench in front of me.

He continues to watch me for several seconds, as if to tease me maybe, or maybe he's just keeping his distance because he's having the same reaction.

"About the other night... Red... I just... don't want there to be any awkwardness."

He nods once, his jaw flexing as he moves back. Red takes a step forward and speaks softly into my ear, my body trembling in anticipation of his words. "Don't you dare say it was a mistake." I wasn't going to but his expression is pained, a deep line appearing between his brows. "You and I both know it wasn't."

Did he think I was going to say that? Well, I did after the kiss so he'd get that idea, wouldn't he?

His vacant stare holds mine. It takes me a few minutes to rein in my racing heart in order to reply. "You're right, it wasn't a mistake. I think we both needed that."

"Then what were you going to say? What's the problem?"

I scan the shop and notice Daniel's watching so I nod in that direction and whisper, "That's the problem. They see us together. I can't be that girl."

Red shakes his head and then turns again to look at me. "Nobody is asking you to be." He stops and looks away to face the bay doors that are open. His body tenses. "What happens between us is private." I can hear the pain in his voice, I'm upsetting him.

I take a drink of the coffee he handed me. I have no answer. I have nothing. I can't even comprehend where in the hell this conversation went. What exactly did I think this was? I knew it wouldn't be serious. But his expression is telling me something completely different. It's telling me what we both avoided. That one time where we thought this need, this draw to one another would curb the desire. Well, it didn't.

"I'm sorry, I just feel like I'm constantly making bad decisions."

"What do you mean?" There's an undertone of desperation in his voice. "If you think we're a bad decision, then I'll walk away right now and we can both avoid getting hurt. I have a daughter to think about."

I don't say anything, and his eyebrows arch a little, as if he is waiting for me to say something. The shop doors slide open and I'm afraid to look behind me because I know the rest of the guys are starting to arrive and the last thing I want is for them to see this.

When I don't answer, Red's face loses all the emotion he once had. "For the record, *Lenny*, I didn't sleep with you because you were easy. I don't do that. I've never needed to. I don't introduce my daughter to just anyone."

"Why me, then?"

"Why not?" he asks, immediately stepping toward me.

"I'm just not sure I'm someone you should be involved with." And I'm not. "My whole life I've always made bad decision. For once, I'm trying to use my head and not my heart."

He hesitates for a moment, as if maybe he thinks I'm not serious. And then he steps back and looks down, laughing.

"Um, what could you possibly be laughing at? Say something."

"What's there to say? You're basically saying this can't go anywhere between us. When I know damn well you want it to." And then he stares at me. "Would anything I say change your mind?"

When Red asks that, a wave of nausea shoots through me knowing there isn't. "I don't know. I don't know what any of this means. I know I enjoyed the hell out of what we did, and I can't look at this bench the same way, ever again." His voice softens and he blinks slowly, his eyes on the bench. "Then why stop?"

"I'm just scared it's bad timing for us." My voice cracks as I hold back tears. Everywhere I go, trouble finds me. I tell myself to walk away from him right now.

Red turns, beginning to walk inside the office and then suddenly stops, his head bent forward. "Then there's nothing more to say, is there?" I can see him now. His brown eyes bore into mine and there's a sadness lurking in his face.

Tears well up in my eyes. He's waiting for me to say something, only I don't have a response. "Red, I didn't—"

He draws in a heavy breath and notices Daniel approaching him with a broken hose reel in hand. "We'll talk about this later." He picks up a repair order on his toolbox. "Here. See if you can take care of this one for me." He pushes past me, his shoulder knocking lightly into mine as he removes himself from the room, closed off again.

Well, I fucked that all up, didn't I? How did me being scared turn into him thinking I didn't want this. I do want this, so badly, I'm just nervous it's bad timing with Ben. How can I bring someone into my life when mine is so strung out?

Remember when I said I had a shitty decision button stuck on?

It's still on. Apparently.

But I can fix this. I can.

18

REDDINGTON

"I'M GOING to punch you in the fucking face!"

Rawley glares at Raven. "Try it. I dare you. I'm not responsible for what I do next."

Raven looks to me and then points at her desk that Rawley's literally covered with lube. Yes, fucking KY Jelly. Her keyboard, her computer screen, all of it. And if you know Raven and her obsession to detail and keeping her work station clean and orderly, this is a catastrophic event for her. "Red, do something with him!"

I'm still not pleased with Rawley after Friday when he basically ditched us when we needed him. "I can't." I watch the sheriff pull up to the office in his squad car. "Mom won't let me touch his whinny ass."

Rawley stares out the window when the sheriff gets out of his car. "Did you call the sheriff, Raven?"

"No." She takes an entire roll of paper towels in hand. "But I should have. You know it's illegal to fuck a minor, right? I should—"

Rawley punches her in the arm. Hard too. Stepping between them, I grab him by the shirt and slam him into the wall. "Don't hit her. Get to work."

Mom walks into the office just then. "Red, don't hurt him."

Raven lays into her right away about what Rawley did. It's like being around them when they were kids again. Always fighting with one another.

Not wanting in the middle of it, I greet the sheriff outside, keeping one eye on Lenny and knowing I need to pull her aside so we can finish talking. She's bent over a Buick trying to find an emissions leak but all I see is her ass.

"Morning, Sheriff," I say, leaning against the fender of his car.

"Red, we have a situation I need to inform you of," Sheriff Barns mutters for only me to hear.

"Okay." I give a stiff nod. Who knows what the fuck this could be?

"Listen, Red, I'm not telling you this as the sheriff but that little girl in there is in some trouble."

A punch of adrenaline hits my chest. "What?" I look behind me thinking he's talking about Raven because we already know she's been in trouble with the law a time or two. "Raven? What'd she do now?"

He clears his throat and gestures inside the shop. "No, I mean Lennon."

My muscles tense in preparation. "What kind of trouble?" I've had my suspicions that she's running from something, but I don't think I'm as prepared as I need to be by the look on the sheriff's face.

"Well apparently, Lennon filed for divorce as well as a restraining order a few weeks back and her husband isn't taking the news well."

Husband? She's married?

"I received a call from her attorney in Oklahoma letting me know that right after the husband, Ben Snider, received the papers. He started asking around her last job if anyone knew where she may have gone. When no one there had any answers for him, he got pretty heated and started making threats against the owner and his employees. I guess her old boss, Eric, filed a harassment complaint against him and the local sheriff informed her attorney. They sent me over a copy of his file from county." He sniffs, keeping his eyes over my shoulder at the shop. "This guy seems like a loose cannon. He's wanted for a variety of misdemeanors, but the one that interests me the most is a breaking and entering charge about a week ago into the shop she was working at last. He did about a hundred thousand worth of damages and then burned the place to the ground."

Shit. Loose cannon is putting it lightly. This guy seems like a fucking psycho.

I scratch the side of my head trying to make sense of all this. "So did the attorney say whether or not he thinks this Ben knows where Lenny is?"

"He said he wasn't sure what Ben knew, but he got the impression that he wasn't going to stop until he found her. The divorce papers were originated in Oklahoma so there is no way to connect those to her living here, but the restraining order was filed by our office so he could probably do some digging and find out where the paperwork originated from."

Listening to what the sheriff is telling me, my stomach drops. I force myself to unclench my fists in an attempt to stop them from shaking.

One, how could she not tell me she's married? A fucking restraining order? And second, why the hell don't I know about this?

The sheriff continues talking and I try and focus on what he is saying.

"I wanted to let you know the situation so that you and the boys could keep an eye out for any trouble. First sign of anything out of the ordinary, you call me." He stops and looks me straight in the eye with a look of warning. "I mean it Red. You see *any* trouble, you call me, do you understand? I don't want you or anyone else thinking they are going to handle this on their own."

I know what he's thinking. He doesn't want a repeat of what happened to Neveah.

"Yeah, Sheriff, I hear ya. Thanks for coming by and letting me know."

"WHEN WERE you going to tell me about Ben?" I ask Lenny. I'm so worked up I can't even breathe right. Knowing my past and what happened to Nevaeh, how could she have not told me this the moment she found out about my wife?

The look of surprise and horror that flashes across her face is all I need to see to know that this isn't something she *ever* intended to tell me about. "How the hell do you know about Ben?"

"The better question is why didn't you tell me about him? Don't you think this would have been information you should have told me? The fuck, Lenny? The sheriff just came in to tell me to keep my eyes open for trouble because your psycho husband is looking for you."

Lenny opens her mouth to speak, but then stops when she sees Tyler come around the corner.

She turns to walk away, but there is no way we are not going to talk about this so I catch her elbow before she can take another step. She turns to me, a rush of emotions flooding her eyes. "Please Red, just let it go. I don't want you involved." She tries again to walk away.

No. There is no way I can let this go. "Don't walk away from me." With a gentle push forward, I move the two of us into the parts room and away from everyone else.

"I just can't fucking believe after everything I told you about my wife, you wouldn't have said something to me sooner. Before we had sex." My voice is calm and level, but truth be told, my entire body's ready to burst into rage. I'm brought back to that night all over again.

Nevaeh's voice comes to me, asking me what time I'd be leaving, begging me not to work too late and making me promise her I'd be home soon.

"Honestly, Red, I don't see how this is any of your concern. Why should I have said anything? It's my business and I'm handling it."

Because my wife was murdered by her crazy ex. Because I will never again let something like that happen to anyone I care about.

I try so fucking hard to find reason in what she's saying, an understanding in her logic, but I'm so caught off guard by it all, I'm just angry with the entire situation.

"Well, for one I was just informed that Ben is suspected to have trashed your previous employer's shop before burning it to the ground when he didn't get the answers he wanted about your whereabouts."

Her body tenses. I can see the fear in her eyes when she realizes the level her ex has taken this to. "He did what?"

"Burned the shop down when Eric wouldn't tell him where you were."

She gasps. "Oh God, no." Tears surface on her flushed face. "I can't believe he'd do that. Eric's his stepbrother. He's how I even got that job."

I try to remain calm and for that reason, I step back and lean into the shelf in the room, the dim lighting outlining the worried lines on her face as tears silently fall down her cheeks. I fucking hate that she's crying over this, because of him, maybe because of me. "If he were to find you here alone...." I shake the thought away. "Shit, Lenny. What if he came here and Nova was here? Would it be my business then? Huh?"

She's obviously shaken by all this and can barely get the words out. "I'm sorry I didn't tell you about Ben, I just... didn't want to bother anyone else with my problems."

"I get that you didn't want to bother anyone. I do. But knowing what I went through, how could you keep this from me?"

Her shoulders shake with sobs, her face falling into her hands. "I thought I had it under control."

"You know, that's what Nevaeh thought too. She kept telling me not to worry. That his threats were just words. And then I found her dead. Think about how I'd feel or better yet, how *Nova* would feel if something happened to you too."

Her head snaps up. She never took into consideration that I let her into Nova's life too, and how it would affect my daughter if something happened to Lenny? I mean, fuck her for not thinking of us.

"Well, I've got to give you credit for one thing. You proved yourself right."

Her brow creases. "What are you talking about?"

"You do make stupid fucking decisions. No more working late," I say bluntly, wanting the conversation to be over with now. "When the shop closes, you leave. You're not allowed to be here alone." I do realize she lives upstairs with Tyler, but at least she's not alone up there. I'm gonna have to talk to him about that.

"It's not your job to protect me. You don't need the added stress. I'm not your wife."

She might as well have punched me in the face right then because that's a low fucking blow. From the moment I found out about Ben, I knew I was comparing the situations. It's only natural with the similarities and the brutal way my wife was taken from me.

"You're right. You're *not* my wife." I lean forward, my eyes trained on hers. "But that doesn't mean I'm going to stand by and do nothing when some psycho is out there looking for you."

"Tyler helped me get a restraining order against him. There's no need for you to get involved. I *don't* want you involved." She glares, a steely determination settling in her stare.

"Well, tough shit. Because you have a past that you decided not to share... a past that just destroyed a fucking business without a care or concern and is now threatening to come knocking on my door, *I'm* involved."

Her face screws up in disgust. "God, Red, do you honestly think I would allow anything to happen to your shop?" Lenny spits, staring daggers, so still I'm not even sure she's breathing. I hit a nerve for sure. "Why are you really acting this way? Is it that you're truly worried about me or are you determined to help me because you're trying to make up for the fact that you weren't able to protect Nevaeh?"

I peg her with a deadly glare, daring her to continue. Her words hit me hard. Of course, some of my reaction has to do with what happened with Nevaeh. That's only natural, but does she truly believe I'm only trying to help her to make myself feel better? I get that I'm being an ass, but how can she not see that my concern is genuine?

"How could you even ask me that? What happened here the other night that *meant* something to me, Lenny. I care about you, and I don't want anything to happen to you. I've basically put myself out here for you, letting you know I'd be anything you needed me to be."

I let that last part soak in.

She doesn't answer me, her expression one of shock.

I massage the back of my neck and take a leveling breath. I don't want to say anything to hurt her, but I'm so fucking pissed I don't think I can control anything that comes out of my mouth. I can't even stand to look at her, so I turn away from her and walk out.

I stalk outside the shop and into the back parking lot, my patience diminishing with each step.

"Goddamn it!" I shout, throwing up my hands.

I rub the back of my neck in frustration and when that's not enough, my body gives in and hunches forward as I sit on the bed of an old Chevy that hasn't run in years.

Resting my elbows on top of my knees, I run my palms over my face and hold my head in my hands.

"Red? You out here, man?"

Pulling my head away from my hands, I notice Tyler's standing in front of me. "What's going on?"

"You should have told me," I growl, staring him down. "After everything I've been through, you should have fucking told me."

He keeps his face impassive as he shrugs. "It's not my story to tell."

"You're really starting to piss me off with this withholding information."

"I don't know that much about it. Just that he's her soon-to-be ex-husband and he's looking for her. He called my house phone looking for her."

Sliding off the tailgate, I pace the gravel parking lot, trying to reel in my temper and make sense of this. I don't want to see Lenny crying again.

"Look, I get that you're pissed and I'm sorry I didn't tell you about Lenny's ex, but you've been acting strange since she started working here so tell me what's really going on? She's in the parts room crying." Tyler finally asks, knowing there's more to this. He's been my friend for years.

He knows when I'm struggling with more than just him keeping this from me.

"I fucked her." My stare meets his as I wait for him to tell me what an idiot I am. Only he doesn't. "Friday night in the shop. By the way, how are you feeling?"

"I'm fine." And then Tyler's eyes go wide. "Seriously, you fucked her?"

I nod, realizing I probably shouldn't have said anything, but I wasn't sure what to do. I'm in over my head.

He nods. "Okay... so now what?"

"Shit, man. I don't even know." I look over at Tyler who's staring at the Chevy in front of us. "She can't be left alone, Tyler. Ever. When she's not here, I want you with her."

He nods. "Okay."

I'd do it myself but I know exactly where it'd lead. My problem is, no matter how much I try to convince myself of it, having sex with Lenny just once wasn't enough. Twice would just be teasing. I thought if I fucked her, that I could get past the unexplainable need I felt toward her but now that I've been inside her, it's going to be damn near impossible to curb this hunger. Truth is, sex with Lenny everyday still wouldn't be enough.

A WEEK GOES BY. An entire week and we've made it to Friday. I have no idea how either. It's like I've been living in a fog of confusion. One where I'm not sure what's more on my mind, Lenny's ass, or her ex. It's a toss-up.

Lenny's in the middle of diagnosing why a check engine light is on, but one look at the car and I see she doesn't even have the scan tool hooked up. She has the smoke tester hooked up, sure, but she forgot to close the valves.

"You're doing it wrong," I blurt out gruffly.

"What?" She steps back from the car and waves the smoke out of her face.

I still don't look at her. I keep my eyes trained on the engine in front of me.

"I said, you're doing it wrong," I say more sternly, hoping she gets the damn hint she's pissed me off.

"I heard that." Her voice is just as stern, but there's a sadness that I hate. "What am I doing wrong? Can you show me?"

I bite back my initial response, which is to just pick this fucking engine off the cherry picker and hurl it across the shop. "Everything. And no, I can't show you."

It's been like this all damn week, ever since I found out about her husband. The garage is practically a warzone with me barking orders while looking over my shoulder every other minute. I keep expecting that bastard of an ex of hers to show up and start shit. It's made the whole week a fucking nightmare.

"Everything?" I can hear the confusion and hurt in her voice and this is exactly why women don't make good mechanics. They can't take orders without questioning my tone of voice.

"Yes, you're doing *everything* wrong."

Her face contorts as if I've just slapped her, her eyes widening.

I point to the back of the car. "If you're looking for a leak, you gotta hook up the scan tool to close the valves. You have to pressurize it before you can test for leaks."

Lenny looks inside the car where the scan tool is sitting on the seat. She forgot to turn it on.

I turn around. "Like I said, you're doing it wrong."

The thing is, I'm doing it wrong. I shouldn't be treating her like this. She's obviously hurting and I'm not making this any easier on her. When I glance over my shoulder, she's inside the car, swiping away tears and then turning the scan tool on.

Apparently, I'm living up to my reputation of an asshole.

19

LENNON

IT'S BEEN a shit of a week. Foolishly, I'd hoped the weekend would be different. It seems I'm wrong. Tyler won't let me out of his sight and my only option to get any free moments is to run to Raven. Honestly, the only place I want to go is Raven's.

"Where are you going?" Tyler asks when I'm grabbing my keys off the counter Saturday morning.

"To Raven's house."

He stands. "I'll drive you."

"No." I hold up my hand. "I'll go right there. Promise. No stopping anywhere."

I love Tyler, but I need Raven today. She's the first friend I've ever had aside from Tyler.

That's the only reason I can think as to *why* I show up at Raven's house, still in my pajamas looking for ideas as to how to make Red like me again. The week was horrible and I can't take that again. He won't talk to me there, so maybe his sister might give me some advice. Right?

"How can I make it better?" I ask as soon as she answers the door, my tears barely controlled. At some point on the drive here, I started crying and I couldn't stop.

"Oh, honey." She takes me in, wraps her arms around me and pulls me inside the door. "What's wrong?" she asks, watching me walk behind her and into the kitchen where she was eating breakfast.

It's then I notice she's wearing a scarf. And it's the middle of July. "Why are you wearing a scarf?"

She shrugs and passes me a tissue. "No reason. What's going on with you?"

"I slept with your brother."

"Please tell me you're not talking about Rawley..."

"Seriously?" I take the tissue and blow my nose, keeping it in my fist as I flop my hands on the table. "I'm not that desperate."

"Who's desperate?" Rawley asks, coming into the kitchen in just a pair of black shorts hung low on his waist and no shirt. He walks to the fridge, takes a drink of orange juice straight from the carton. "And why are you crying?"

Raven glares at him and points her spoon in his face. "None of your business. Go away."

Smiling, he sits beside me.

"That's not leaving," Raven notes, kicking his chair.

He takes her bowl of cereal and drinks the milk from her bowl. "So what." And then he looks at me. "Why are you crying?"

"I slept with Red," I blurt out, waiting on his reaction.

"Nice." Rawley nods and slides Raven's bowl back to her. She pushes it aside refusing to eat any more of it. "It's about time he got laid. Maybe now he won't be such an asshole."

"Nope," I say, breaking the news to him. "I slept with him last week. He's actually gotten worse."

"Why are you crying then?" Rawley chuckles. "You shouldn't be surprised one bit."

"What are you even doing here?" Raven asks, trying to get him to leave. Rawley's good at annoying Raven and when he knows it's working, he'll keep it up.

"Shush." He waves her off. "I'm helping. Talk to me, Lenny. I'm a man." He has the potential to be adorable right here, but I also know too much about him now to *ever* find him adorable.

Raven sits back in the chair crossing her arms over her chest. "Hardly. You're a whore."

He turns to her, completely straight-faced. "Shut up."

It's pointless to keep this a secret anymore. I can't. I won't go through last week again. It was awful. Anything I said, I was wrong. Anything I did, wrong. All fucking wrong. "He's mad at me because I didn't tell him about my soon-to-be ex-husband who was abusive, so I left him and ran here."

"And he fucked you before he found that out?"

"Yes."

"Shit," Rawley curses, shaking his head in disbelief. "That's rough. That'd piss me off too."

Raven kicks his chair, the jolt causing his body to sway. "What? It'd piss me off. She should have told him."

"You're not helping her. Leave."

His face screws up. "What?" He raises his hands. "I'm trying to. I'm being honest. *She* fucked up."

Great. Even Rawley thinks I'm a horrible person, and he has no morals at all.

"But what do I do now?" I ask, staring at my hands and remembering that night in the shop. I want *that* again because I had never felt more safe and desired.

Rawley taps his index finger to his chin. "Let me think." And then he looks at me. "Why didn't you tell him?"

I sniffle and reach for another tissue. "Because at first... I moved here to start over. I didn't want anyone to know in fear they'd think I was weak. I stayed with a man who was abusive for years because I didn't think I deserved better. I married a man who was a monster, because I thought it was the only option. And then when I left, I realized, I had options and immediately I met Red. Once I found out about Nevaeh, I didn't want to bring back his past. So I didn't say anything."

"Your intentions were good," Raven points out, trying to be the sympathetic friend. "You just need to explain that to him."

"I thought I did..."

Rawley leans forward, his hands resting on the table. "I totally get why he's mad."

"Yes, because you have all the answers." Raven snorts, reaching for a banana to eat since Rawley ruined her cereal. She's very picky and if anyone so much as touches her food in any way, she won't finish it.

He immediately takes the banana from her, peels it and takes a large bit, chewing around his words. "It's because of what happened with Nevaeh that you should have warned him the instant you knew, well before feelings were ever involved."

It's my turn to snort as I relax into the chair, my tears all but dry now. "No one said there were feelings involved."

Rawley twists his head, taking another bite from Raven's banana and then throws the peel at her face. "We all can see there's *feelings involved...* even for him."

"It was just sex," I mumble.

"Red hasn't been with anyone since his wife died," Rawley adds with a mocking tone, like I should have known. "He wouldn't just sleep with someone for the sex. I've seen him at bars and pussy is basically thrown at the bastard, yet he's turned down every opportunity he's had. Until you. Fuck, Tyler even hired a hooker once and he sent the bitch home."

"That's true." Raven points at Rawley, finally agreeing with something he's said.

Leaning back in the chair, I fold my arms across my chest. "Okay, so what do I do now? I feel like the dumbest fuck in the world right now and I can't take him being mad at me. Last week was awful."

Rawley shrugs. "Just fuck him again. Go over to his house and blow him."

My head jerks his direction. "Rawley, I'm serious."

Raven waves him off, leaning forward to rest her elbows on the table, seemingly deep in thought. "Start by apologizing."

Rawley snorts. "There needs to be more than an apology."

"Okay, so what then?"

He thinks for a minute and then smiles. "Feed him. Make his favorite meal, then apologize. If that doesn't work, then fuck him. It'd work for me."

Raven smiles at her brother, and I think it's planned by the devious twinkle to her eyes. "Is that what Sophie did to get you to forgive her?"

His chair screeches against the tile. "Fuck you." And then he leaves. Immediately, Raven leans across the table to high-five me. "Knew that'd get him to leave."

I look at her expectantly. "What do I make?"

"Spaghetti."

"Really?"

"Yep." Raven pushes herself away from the table and to the kitchen drawers near the microwave. She digs through a large cookbook and pulls out a small white notecard. "Make this recipe." And then she reaches for her purse on the edge of the kitchen chair she was sitting at. "Let's go to the store. I'll help you make it."

I look down at the card in my hands and the neat handwriting. There's no name on it, but with the ingredients, I gather this is some kind of special recipe. "Where did you get this?"

"My mom." She shrugs, nodding to the door. "Let's go."

I stand and follow her out the door. "Where'd she get it?"

We're at her car now. "Not sure. It's Red's favorite though."

Her car doors unlock when she clicks the button. A breeze kicks up, fresh cut grass moving through the air. I breathe in deeply, the warm summer air on my back as I get inside the car.

You can do this, Lenny.

When we reach the stop light, Raven stares at me. "So this ex of yours... he's really after you?"

"Yeah, he is. I mean, I knew he'd come eventually. He's always been abusive, just more verbally than anything but then he hit me... so I left that night without telling him." It's weird telling Raven all this because I never open up to anyone in fear they'll think less of me. But then again, talking with Raven came naturally. "I filed for divorce and then a restraining order, and that pissed him off even more."

"That's crazy." Raven gasps as we pull into the parking lot of the grocery store down the street from her house. "What an asshole."

"Pretty much." I pick up the recipe card. "Man, this looks complicated."

I'M RIGHT. It *is* complicated. I mean, the damn thing called for cinnamon. Who puts cinnamon in their spaghetti sauce is beyond me.

I've never thought of myself as a cook, but I can certainly follow a recipe and it usually turns out pretty good. My problem is, deep down, I know who's recipe this is. I know I can't fuck this up.

"I know he's an ass most of the time, but my brother really likes you." Raven tells me as we cook.

I didn't know it, until now, but maybe that was my intention all along coming over here to talk to Raven. Something clicked. I can have this. I just have to be careful, right?

When I have the spaghetti done and placed inside one of Mia's dishes, I wrap the top with foil and take a deep breath. Raven hugs me tightly from behind when I'm at the door, careful not to squeeze too hard that I drop the dish. "It's going to work," she whispers. "Call me later and tell me how it went."

"Thank you for helping me. I've never had a friend like you before, or a friend at all."

She winks and slaps my ass. "Go get him, tiger."

I don't know what he'll say when I show up, but I'm trying this time. I think what scares me the most is falling in love with him, because it's heading there. I know it is.

I don't know how to love. All I've ever been is property: of the state, of Wes, of a tattoo artist using my body as a canvas... of Ben. My strength and weakness at times is my shield. The way I force myself not to love anyone.

Mostly because the purest, most natural aspect of a child's life, unconditional love, I've been denied. That's why it was easy to fall for Ben and his lies because I didn't know any different. I was never given the basic form of love nor did I understand how to accept it when someone showed me they cared.

NOVA MUST HEAR me pull up, because she's the first one out the door and directly followed by Red grabbing the hood of her sweatshirt to pull her back inside the house. When he sees it's me, he lets her come outside and greet me at my car.

"Lenny, it's you."

I open my door leaving the window down. "It is me." I reach across the seat for the spaghetti, my peace offering. "I brought you guys some spaghetti."

Nova's eyes light up. I've missed her smiling face so much this week. Red kept her away from the shop, probably for good reason. "How did you know that's my daddy's favorite food?"

I smile and kneel down to her level tucking one wild curl behind her ear. "Wild guess."

"You must be psycho."

"You mean psychic?"

"Yeah, that." She motions over her shoulder with her finger. "Daddy's inside."

He's not. He's standing on the porch with his hands buried deep in his pockets.

"We're going to the races tonight to watch Daniel."

Crap. I should have known they had plans.

It takes me a minute to meet his eyes. I'm too focused on his appearance in jeans and a T-shirt with a baseball hat on backwards, his arms of steel crossed over his chest.

In his eyes, there's a war. It's the simple lift of his brow that lets him know I'm not welcome. But I stay because it's him and even if he doesn't know it, he needs me here with him.

Well, I've certainly fucked things up, haven't I?

"I'll leave. I just wanted to bring this by." I push the dish forward and he takes it.

His eyes rake over my body, lingering on my shorts. Of course I wore his favorite shorts. His left hand raises and scratches the side of his scruffy jaw, his knuckles cracked and bloody. "What are you doing here?"

I hesitate because he's so intimidating with the way he stands there, eyes boring on mine, waiting for my apology. "I know... I hurt you. I just—"

A sigh rolls off his chest. "I'm *not* hurt," he interrupts.

"Yes, you are."

"He's kinda cranky," Nova remarks from her place beside him, looking up at her dad with wide innocent blue eyes.

A mocking smirk plays at Red's lips. "Nope. Not cranky... or upset." And then he looks down at Nova. "Hey, darlin', go grab your jacket so we can leave."

He turns around too, and takes the spaghetti inside. I stay on the porch, fidgeting with the hem of my jean shorts, afraid to move. I'm such an idiot. I should have called first. Leave it to me to just *assume* I could show up.

Just when I'm thinking of turning around and leaving, Red comes back outside. "So that's it?" he mumbles, pushing himself from the wall he's leaning against, refusing to sit down.

"I don't know." I'm caught off guard by all this, his intensity and the lowness of his voice directed at me.

"Say it then." His head turns to me, his eyes narrow. He stares at me for a second, much longer than I would expect him to before his gaze drops.

"Say what? That I'm sorry? I am."

"Lenny!" Nova comes barreling back out with her coat. "Come with us!"

My gaze cuts to Red to see what he might say about that. He's tight-lipped and quiet, the clench of his jaw the only movement seen.

Yep. I've pissed him off again. Now it's becoming an hourly occurrence.

He looks at Nova. "Go grab your blankie too."

She huffs out a breath. "You're doing this on purpose." And then she steps back in the house.

"Why didn't you tell me about Ben?" he asks when Nova's out of earshot.

I swallow down my embarrassment, ignoring the churning in my gut. I breathe in a deep breath, my eyes on my feet because looking at Red in the eye is hard for me to do after everything that went down in the last week. I hurt him. "I didn't tell you because when I first met you, I didn't think it was any of your business. I wasn't even going to tell Tyler, but I needed a job and I had to explain it to him. I made a huge mistake being with Ben, and it wasn't something I wanted to advertise. Then I found out about Nevaeh and I didn't want you involved more than ever. And then we...." I motion between us. "And then I was scared because I have feelings for you and I didn't exactly go about it the right way. I wanted us to work. I just didn't see how we could with Ben still in the mix."

Nova pops out of the house, curls bouncing all over the place in a wild mess. "Let's go!" And then she grabs my hand. "Come with us!"

Drawing in a deep breath, I know what this means. If I get in this car with them, this is the moment everything changes. It's me saying I'm part of this. I'm committing to the both of them. It's me opening up to Red in ways I've never let someone in before.

I'm ready to do that, for both Red and Nova.

I can't walk away from them. I'm scared, sure, how could I not be?

I look back over my shoulder at Red as Nova pulls me to the car. "Do you mind if I come?"

He shrugs, reaching in his pocket for his keys. "No."

20

REDDINGTON

I GET why she didn't tell me about Ben. I do. She had her reasons, and I understand them, especially given our backgrounds. I have no idea the reasons why she left her husband, and I'm not sure I want to know at this point because I'd probably kill the motherfucker given the chance.

My mind has been in overdrive ever since the sheriff came by the shop. I keep coming back to one thing. I've been at a standstill for two years, never moving forward, just stuck in the past. With Lenny, she makes me want to take a step. I know my feelings for her run deeper than I initially thought, and for that reason, maybe that's why she's sitting next to me. She took a big risk coming to my house, and I'm taking one by forgiving the fact that she was scared.

There's still so much about her I don't know, but the truth is, at this point, I'm willing to look past that. I don't know what I feel exactly, but I know I have to find out. Besides, with the way my daughter looks at her, I don't really have a choice.

As I make my way back to them, two beers and a root beer for Nova, they both smile at me.

"Have you ever been to a race?" I ask handing Lenny a beer. Nova's seated directly in front of us with her mouth full of candy. I set her root beer in front of her and take a seat next to Lenny.

"Nope." She pauses, taking a drink of her beer. "I mean, I've been to drag races and a few motorcycle races."

I nod to Nova. "I bring Nova as much as I can, at least once a month."

Lenny watches Nova for a moment as she stands up and points her finger at a race car that takes the checkered flag, and then flips him off. "She seems to love it."

Lenny had just taken another drink of her beer and spits it out at my daughter's crassness. "She does. She gets a little into it."

Laughing, I scratch the back of my head as Nova turns around and crawls up on my lap. "Lenny, did you know Uncle Colt's nephew works for a race team?"

"Stop calling that crazy bastard your uncle." Nova gives me an exasperated look as if she's offended. "But yes, his nephew Tommy works for that guy Jameson Riley."

"Oh yeah, the NASCAR driver?" I laugh. I'm not surprised Lenny knows him. Everyone, especially women, seem to know who Jameson Riley is.

"Why doesn't it surprise me that you know who he is? Seems like more women started becoming NASCAR fans when he started winning championships."

Lenny turns to me and stares, almost studying me for a minute. "I suppose he's a good-looking guy, but he's not really my type."

I can't help the grin that takes root on my face. "Really?" I raise an eyebrow. "And what exactly is your type?"

"Well, you know. Tall, dark, good with his hands. Oh, and he needs to know the difference between Twilight Sparkle and Pinkie Pie."

The loud laughter that comes pouring out of me takes even me by surprise. I haven't laughed like this in I don't know how long, but the fact that she mentioned some of Nova's favorite ponies, just reinforces the fact that I'm making the right choice. There is no way I can walk away from this girl.

"Well then Lennon...." I lean in, my lips close to her ear and I can't help but notice the reaction she has to it, the quick intake of breath, the wide eyes, all indications she wants me this close. "I guess I just may have a chance with you after all."

As the sun dips, the cooler night air slaps at my face. It's the perfect excuse to justify touching her.

With Nova in front of us again, Lenny leans forward to make sure her jacket is zipped and that she's warm enough. I'm not sure I can even explain how it makes me feel to see Lenny show concern for my daughter. To want to take care of her. This is something I didn't know if I would be able to give Nova again. A positive woman in her life who can fill in the gaps I can't. Someone to tie her hair up since I can't seem to do it right or someone she can turn to when she needs a female perspective. Sure, we've been lucky. We have my mom and Raven, but it would be nice for Nova to have someone else she can count on to take care of her.

Once Lenny straightens back up, my gaze lowers to Lenny's trembling lip as the wind picks up around the track. "You can move closer," I whisper, my breath tempting the skin right below her ear. "I won't bite with the kid around."

"Who said I didn't want you to bite?"

Those words go straight to my dick, and I'm thankful I'm sitting down.

"Well in that case,"—I put my arm around her so my hand is on her ass and move her flush against my side—"careful what you wish for."

She trembles against me, and it brings me serious satisfaction to know that's it's not the chill in the air making her react. No. That's all me.

She turns toward me, her knees bumping my thigh. I move to tuck a tuft of her hair behind her ear just so I can touch her again. "So which one is Daniel?"

"The one constantly hitting shit," Rawley remarks, shaking his head as he comes to sit next to us. "I swear he doesn't understand that you don't have to hit everything on the track. It's like he's playing ping pong off the guardrails tonight."

He takes Nova into his lap, tickling her sides and then smiles up at Lenny. "So spaghetti worked or did you..." He pauses and covers Nova's ears with his hands. "Blow him in the parking lot?"

Blow him? What the hell is he talking about? And how does he know about the spaghetti?

I slap the back of his head pretty hard. "Don't talk like that around my kid. And why are you talking to Lenny about spaghetti and blow jobs?"

"She needed a man's advice." Rawley's hands drop from Nova's ears as he glares at me. "And I'm pretty sure she hears worse from you."

He's probably right about that.

I stare at Rawley, waiting for more of an explanation. When he doesn't answer, I smack the back of his head. Glaring, he rubs the spot I hit. "She came by the house looking. I gave her my idea."

Lenny reaches forward and smacks his ear.

"What the fuck?" he yells, glaring at her.

"You weren't supposed to say anything," she seethes through clenched teeth.

Rawley pauses, his mouth opening and closing, and then he rolls his eyes. "Well you should have said that to begin with. Usually people start with, don't say anything but...."

The two of them argue for a minute but my mind instinctively goes to the mentioned blow job for a good five minutes. Mostly because Lenny's beside me eating nachos and cheese is dripping off her lips. I'd love to see something else dripping off those lips.

They're getting ready to start the main events for the night when Elle walks up with her two kids. Of all the people I wanted to see tonight, she's not on that list.

I do the polite thing and introduce the two of them but honestly, it's the last thing I wanted. "Elle, this is Lenny. Lenny this is Elle. She runs the daycare Nova goes to."

Lenny lifts her hand in a wave. "Hey."

Elle's eyes dart to Nova, and then me, and back to Lenny. She falters a little and then makes a quick recovery, her gaze on mine. "Nice to meet you, Lenny. Wow, Red, I wasn't aware you were dating anyone."

Of course she'd say that.

Nova grins, whipping her head around to look at Lenny and me. "Are you dating?"

"No, darlin'." My gaze moves to Lenny and in a strange way, I don't like that I said no, but I'm not sure how to label us yet. "Lenny's just a friend." Nova seems disappointed by that and frowns. "Yeah, and she's a girl so does that make her your girlfriend? Do friends kiss, too?"

I'm not entirely sure why, but at that moment, Rawley decides to do the smart thing by picking up Nova and throwing her over his shoulder. "Help me out, kiddo. There's a girl over there I want to like me. Pretend you're my kid for an hour so I can get her number."

Nova high-fives him as they walk away. "I got your back, Uncle Rawley."

"Those two are something else," Lenny notes and then nods to Elle walking the other way with her kids. "And she seems nice."

"I guess so. Nova is *not* a huge fan."

"Well, it's obvious she is a member of your fan club. You know, there's nothing sexier than a man who's attentive, whether it's toward his daughter, or his girl."

I snort. "She's married."

"Yeah well, married or not, a woman notices these things."

"Must be why Rawley's currently using said daughter to get a piece of ass." I quirk an eyebrow at her. "But I've never... looked at it that way."

"It's not your looks that get you all the attention."

"Excuse me?"

Her eyes widen before she throws me a relaxed grin. "Don't get me wrong. You're good-looking, but it's the way you look at your daughter is what gets them. Anybody can be a dad, but a single dad who puts his daughter first, shows how good of a person he is. Not a lot of fathers look out for the interest of their children at all times. You do." She glances at Nova in the distance with Rawley. "A daughter needs a dad to look up to. You're the first man she's going to see. You set the standard in where she learns how a woman is supposed to be treated. Not all dads know how to do that."

There's a moment between us as we stare at one another and fuck, do I want to kiss her for saying that. I've only ever had Nova's interest in mind, which is why I hadn't been with anyone since Nevaeh. Not only was the timing not right for me, but it wasn't for her either. I figured, no, I actually assumed I wouldn't be with anyone ever again and I was okay with that if Nova was.

I don't know what to say, for once, and remain staring at her in silence as the engines of twenty-four cars line up on the track.

"Holy shit, it's cold out here!" Lenny says, breaking the silence between us.

I smile, handing her my sweatshirt. "Wear this."

"I can't take that. It's yours. You'll be cold."

"Well then, it will give me an excuse to make you sit on my lap later."

Yep. I'm flirting. For the first time in two years I'm flirting.

And probably doing a horrible job of it by the way Nova eyes me when she returns with Rawley. Her face says, "Get some game, Dad."

Rawley stands and hands her five bucks and pockets the number the girl gave him.

I gotta get this kid friends her own age.

It's obvious Nova's trying to play matchmaker with me too when she squeezes between Lenny and me and takes my right hand and Lenny's left hand and puts them together.

I smile at Nova as does Lenny, and I keep holding her hand because I want to.

It's the first time we've held hands. It's the first time in two years a woman has held my hand. I wait for the panic and guilt to hit me. Wait for pain to hit my chest. After a pause, I exhale out the breath I'm holding. There's nothing but contentment pulsing through me with her hand in mine.

Nova gets up and sits in front of us with Rawley again, smiling back at us.

Lenny's eyes sweep over my lips, my chin, my chest, and then back to my face. "Sorry."

I grin and kiss her forehead. "Relax."

She shivers a little as I get close, and I can see raw vulnerability in her eyes. She's afraid whatever we are starting is only going to end up hurting and that's the last thing I want.

My gaze automatically drops to her chest and the view I now have down her shirt.

Sitting here next to her, the dirtier part of my imagination makes up all kinds of interesting plans for tonight. Especially after the blow job comment.

With the way she watches me, and Nova, there's nowhere else I want to be but with these two, right now. I'm tired of this dance, tired of our doubt and confusion. It's time to take that step forward.

21

LENNON

"JESUS, she's heavy when she's sleeping," Red grumbles, struggling to keep Nova in his arms. Her head's flopped back, arms too as her curls fly around wildly in the wind. Despite her heaviness, he smiles down at her, completely enthralled in her innocence as she sleeps in his arms.

I love the dynamic between Red and Nova and the way he never seems to get annoyed with her incessant chatter. I find it endearing because I was always told I talked too much as a child.

Now I don't talk because I'm afraid I'll be told to stop. Nothing's worse than being five years old and excited to tell someone about your day only for them to look at you and say, "You talk too much."

And now that Nova's asleep, nothing's changed. He still adores her.

I know I'm staring at them, but I can't stop myself.

His face is impassive, but I know his mind is working. It always is. "What?"

"Nothing," I say, keeping step with them as we walk to the car.

When we're at the car, Red opens the passenger door for me despite having to hold Nova with one arm. No one has ever done that for me before. The simple gesture makes my heart beat faster. My cheeks heat when his body leans into me for a second as I slide into the seat and he gets Nova in the back. Drawing in a deep breath, my heart slows, a smile tugging at the corners of my lips.

He climbs into the driver seat and there's a quiet unease between us. "Thanks for coming with us. Nova really likes you."

"I really like her too," I say quietly.

He starts his car. The gentle rumbling and smell of a lean running 427 big block shakes my chest. I love everything about Red's 1974 Nova SS. It's perfect from the rust in some spots to the cracked leather seats and worn carpet. It's a work in progress and a representation of his life in many ways.

Glittery stars paint the blackened sky lighting a path on the road as we're pulling out of the parking lot of the track. Dust kicks up from the cars in front of us creating a cloud in front of his car. The paleness of the night floods the car outlining his face.

"I'm sorry about the things I said," he says when we're driving down his road. "I shouldn't have acted that way last week. It wasn't... me." There's an undisclosed honesty and vulnerability in his every word and I believe him. I know he has a temper, but he never meant to take his frustrations out on me. I'm not trying to make excuses for him. It's a simple truth. It's the purity in his soul.

Some people are dark. They're just bad people and do bad things. That's not Red.

Red waits for me to speak, react to his words, and knowing he is waiting for it drives me back into the bubbling emotions sitting in my chest.

After ten minutes, finally, I have the courage. "Red—"

"Wait. Just let me get this out, okay?" He interrupts, touching my face with his left palm.

I nod, watching as his eyes shift back to the road. "Okay."

"I was a total fuckin' dick last week. And I'm truly sorry for that." He sounds sad, and I know what he's going to say next. The realization that it's coming makes my throat tight.

I give him a nod when we pull up to the house and he parks beside my car, letting him know he can continue. He shuts off the engine and then looks over at me, twisting slightly. "When you first came into that shop, part of me knew exactly what you were looking for. I knew deep down you were looking for an escape. I was ready to be that for you. I wasn't lying when I said I would be anything you wanted." His voice softens as he shakes his head. "And you know, the more I think about it, I was actually upset that you came back after that first day."

"Why?" I keep my voice low, afraid I might wake Nova in the backseat.

"Because I didn't want you to be anything to me."

"That doesn't make any sense, Red." But in reality, it does and I get where he's coming from.

"Listen to what I said." He pauses, my eyes drifting to his. "I told you that I would be anything you *wanted*. Not anything *I* wanted."

Realization slowly feeds its way into my system. He's right. I didn't want Red to mean anything to me either. I wasn't looking for someone to fill the gaps when I came to Lebanon. I was only looking for a job.

"I didn't want *you* to be anything to *me*."

"After one time, I meant something?" I know exactly how that could be; how even the simplest touch between the two of us gave me such a rush I knew there was more to us.

Red nods, his eyes on mine. I don't reply, and he doesn't wait for one.

He's quiet for a moment, just staring at me, before he finally speaks. "Will you come inside?"

I frown. Thoughts of the night in the shop run wild through my mind. It's not that I don't want to because I do, but I want more than sex. I want him. "I don't know if that's a good idea."

An audible sigh leaves his lips. The breath he was holding awaiting my response is enough of a reaction to calm both our nerves. "I'm not expecting anything. I'm just really hungry."

I raise an eyebrow.

He smiles as if he's funny. He makes a clicking sound with his tongue and I watch with rapt attention as he glides it over his lower lip. And then he winks at me. "For that spaghetti. I mean, you did cook for me." His eyes brighten. "Oh, wait, Rawley mentioned something else... maybe—"

"Okay, that's enough." I slap my hand over his mouth. "There's a child back there."

He puts his hand over mine on his mouth and kisses my palm. "Come inside with me, please? Besides, I don't want you driving home by yourself."

He's convincing, isn't he?

He gives me a long stare, searching for my denial. When he doesn't see that, a grin appears. "Please?"

All thought is lost and I follow what my body is telling me. I nod. "Ugh, I can't deny you when you say please."

"That's good to know." He chuckles, opening his door.

He's quiet as he walks ahead of me carrying a sleeping Nova in his arms.

I stare at the ring on his keys, the one attached to his key rings that's clearly a wedding band.

"How can you still live here?" I whisper, my voice unable to reach normal volumes. Not only does it scare me going inside, but I also don't want to wake Nova.

He squints at me as if deciphering the words while his right hand turns the lock and the door cracks open. "It's my house. It's not like I have the money to just buy a new one."

"I know, I just mean with all the memories."

That stops him and it seems he's considering that, until he's not. He shakes his head before he nods inside for me to go in as he adjusts the sleeping child in his arms. "It's the one place Nova knows. I couldn't take that away from her too. Sometimes we make sacrifices for others."

My heart aches at his words. Just fucking aches so badly.

I step inside and peek around the living room we enter into. His house is small and there's not a lot of decoration but what there is, it's clear a child lives with him. Her toys are scattered near the television.

White paper with artwork is pinned up on a framed corkboard display with white trim. It's cute, probably something someone made for him, and Nova's bright soul is all over it. She's a beautiful drawer and seems to love to draw pictures of her daddy and her.

As Red slips down the hall to place Nova in bed, I take a closer look at the drawing. I can see that just past the living room is the kitchen but it's tucked around the corner without a clear view from the front room.

I focus on the drawing in the center. It's one of Red and her, I assume, and then I notice the sky she's drawn and the purple clouds. Above them is an angel. It nearly brings tears to my eyes that she doesn't have her mother around. I don't remember anything about my mother other than a photograph I once saw that a social worker had in my file. I look nothing like her, but that's all I remembered.

"How old was Nova when she died?" I ask when Red comes down the hall.

His breath blows over my ear, a heavy sigh and I can't tell whether I made him mad or not. Twisting my head, I look back at him. "Sorry...I shouldn't have asked that..."

He shakes his head and gives a nod to the kitchen, like he's going in there and I should follow him. "It's okay. She had just turned three in March. Nevaeh died two years ago in May."

Standing in front of the fridge, he reaches in and takes out the spaghetti, placing it in the microwave after stirring it.

Turning back to the fridge, he lifts up a beer in his hand. "Would you like one?"

I nod. "I'm sorry I brought up your wife."

He shrugs. "Don't worry about it." I can tell by the tone of his voice he doesn't want to talk about her. Only he brings up what I don't want to talk about. Ben.

"How long were you married?"

I draw in a heavy breath and take the beer he hands me. The microwave dings and he turns toward it reaching for a plate.

"Do you want some?"

I shake my head and rub my stomach. "No thanks, those nachos are sticking with me."

He chuckles, stirring it. "Okay."

Taking a slow drink of my beer, I contemplate his question and if I should divulge information about Ben. I really don't want to bring him into this, but then again, if I came here, I've already brought him into it. "I was married to him for a year. Stupidest decision I ever made."

He thinks about what I said, his head turning slightly but his body remains twisted to the counter as he takes a spoon out of the drawer beside him and scoops a heaping serving of the spaghetti on the plate. When he's seated next to me at the table—his own beer in hand as well —our eyes meet. "I married Nevaeh because she was pregnant," he admits, as if he's trying to make me feel better.

"You loved her though, right?"

"Yeah." He nods, his eyes dropping. "I loved her very much. But I didn't marry her because I loved her. Seems dumb now to think about it, but loving her never crossed my mind when I proposed to her. Doing right by her did," he tells me this as if it's a confession, one he's never admitted to anyone.

I breathe in deeply after taking a drink of my beer. "You're a great man, Red."

The smallest of smiles grace his lips as though he wants to believe that, and he's not sure he can. "I found her in this kitchen, over there." He points behind him near the dishwasher.

Oh, God... he's opening up to me. What do I do?

"I'm sorry." It's the only thing I can think to say in that moment.

"I didn't tell you that for your apology," he adds, twirling noodles around his fork. He's nearly finished with the plate of food, devouring it completely. "Fuck, this is good."

I cringe. "Raven gave me the recipe. I think it was..." I can't bear to say her name in front of him. Not because I don't want to, but because I'm afraid of hurting him.

There's a pained expression that contorts his face and his eyes tear up just the slightest bit. "Nevaeh's."

"I'm sorry. She knew it was one you liked."

"I do." There's a silence between us when he finishes the spaghetti, the two of us drinking our beer in silence. And then he asks, "So this guy, Ben... do you love him?"

"No." My answer is immediate because I don't think I ever did love Ben. Not in the ways that were healthy at least. "I'm not sure I even know what love is." It's something I've only admitted to him. "I grew up in foster care... pushed from one family to the next, leaving a piece of myself with each one. Not because I wanted to, but because they took them from me. I was a paycheck and property of the state. And then I met Ben and I just sorta fell into giving all my pieces away."

He doesn't say anything to me, for a couple minutes at least as he finishes the spaghetti.

Leaning forward so our faces are close, his breath hits my face, and I'm afraid of what he might say to me. "Dance with me?"

What? Really?

It was certainly asked in the form of a question; he's not demanding anything from me. "What?"

"You said no one has ever *asked* you anything. *I'm* asking *you* to dance."

"Here?" I look around the kitchen, laughing lightly. "Now?"

He stands. "Why not?"

I stand, too, slipping my hand inside of his. "Okay, but there's no music playing."

Once we're in the living room, he takes a remote in his hand and points it toward the stereo under the television mounted on the wall. "Now there is."

I smile at the song, because I know it. It's "Syrup & Honey" by Duffy and I absolutely love this song because of the slow Aretha Franklin vibe to it.

As soon as he touches me, I'm done. My hands are trembling at the simplest of gestures he's so good at: opening doors, dancing.

He leans down to my ear, his warm breath on my skin. "Is this okay?"

The living room is dim, with only the light from the hall filtering into the room. His fingers trace my cheekbone and I know what he's going to ask me. It's in his eyes before his lips let the words pass through.

"If I didn't know any better, I'd think you were trying to seduce me with this dancing in your living room."

"Is it working?" he asks, raising an eyebrow.

I sigh almost pathetically as I sink into him. "Yes."

"Then yeah, I am." He stops moving and cups my cheeks with both hands. It sends a jolt of nerves through me as his body presses into mine.

His hands move to my waist, my arms around his neck. Every hard line is against me, giving me his heat. My skin breaks into a fire, a familiar need surfacing. We begin to sway, his hands on my hips, guiding my body to the beat of the music. I'm completely stiff at first, but when the hard plains of his body press to mine, I give in, nearly sagging against him.

"I can't stop thinking about you." His voice is low as we sway slowly to the gentle sounds, his eyes darting from mine and then to my lips like he wants to kiss me, but he doesn't. He's watching me. Waiting for me to say something. My face burns a brighter shade of red at those words and he notices.

Drawing back, he runs his fingers gently over my cheeks, then stops to cup my cheek again. Naturally, I lean into his warm touch. "I know it's wrong because fuck, we're both in some shitty circumstances but... I can't stop myself." He stares at me, pleading with me to trust him, without asking me to. Without a shadow of a doubt, I do.

"I feel the same way," I say, just before pressing my lips to his. I can't take it anymore.

Breathing uneven breaths, his body reacts, responds, and wants me in all the ways he had before. He groans softly, his lips and tongue searching for more, but then pulls back.

He drags his parted lips down my neck and then over my collarbone and to my shoulder. Growling lightly, he bites at my shoulder. He continues kissing up and down my neck, sending shivers through my entire body, goose bumps form on my shoulders, my nipples hardening against his chest. That kiss was nothing like I've ever experienced in my life. The way his mouth moves against mine, his calloused, cut-up, hard-working hands, his breathing, all of it. It's slow and it's meant to be as he kisses over my sun-kissed skin, heating it to degrees the sun could never reach.

His mouth trails up my neck to my lips, giving me what I need as his mouth moves over mine, what he wants but knows he shouldn't have. It's tentative at first, gently parted lips and a slow, gradual build before his tongue sweeps over the seam of my lips.

And then he kisses me deeper, humming when our tongues meet from open-mouth kisses. When that's too much that we can't breathe without heavy, gasping breaths, his mouth moves to my neck. I release a needy sigh because they're the most desperate sound with each pass of his mouth over my skin, like it's not enough for him. Like it will never be enough. I'm right there with him.

It's definitely not enough for me.

Climbing his body, he gives me a lift, hands low, holding me there against the wall. My mind doesn't bother trying to make sense of any of it.

He doesn't say anything, but he does draw me closer, his arms so strong, so right. Gazing down at me, watching, I run my hands up the tight straining muscles of his back flexing under my fingers.

Between my legs, I burn for him. Though our encounter a week ago was quick, my body remembers his touch and the pleasure of him inside me. It's telling me, *Jump his bones damn it.*

He runs his hands from my hips to my ass. I shiver and press myself closer to him. Breathing heavily, he sets me down when the song comes to an end.

Pulling my hair to the side, he uses his teeth against my neck, barely brushing but enough to make me moan, his lips hovering over my ear. His hand envelopes mine and pulls it to his side. "Come with me." His voice is low and seductive as he draws me near again.

My body certainly wants to go with him, my pulse throbbing in my temples at the heat of his stare as I follow him. His hand comes to rest against my lower back, just above my ass as we enter his room. I turn around, never looking at my surroundings, when the click of his lock draws my attention.

Wordlessly as he pulls his shirt off and lets it fall to the floor. In the shop, I didn't have a good view of him. It was too dark in there, but now, with the light coming in from his porch, it illuminates his body in a soft orange glow. The solid lines of his chest are marked with detailed ink. I notice the tattoo on his chest again that spreads over his heart. It's the words "Heaven" in a fancy script surrounded by three sparrows.

My eyes move to his and he looks at me as if I'm important to him, already. As if he's stopping his life to look at me, because he has to in that moment. Something's making him.

"Lenny." My name is an exhale. I love when he says my name, and I hang on the conviction it gives me. He immediately takes my face in his hands. "Fuck, I want you so bad." He breathes the words against my lips and the groan he lets out races up my spine. I moan into his embrace, melting around him, giving myself to him.

His grin gets a little higher at my response. He certainly likes the effect he has on me.

I kiss his shoulder, and then his neck softly, as though I'm unsure what to do.

"I haven't stopped thinking about you all week," he whispers, his voice becoming gruff. He then moves his hand down my hip before he eagerly slips his large hand in the front of my shorts. Okay, he's getting impatient. I get it. I'm just as excited for this to happen and he's about to find out as he slips his finger inside me.

"Fuck... you're so wet for me." He moves his finger in and out, and then adds another, pushing them in slowly. I can't help but gasp.

"You like that?"

"Yes."

Helping him out, I lift my shirt over my head.

He reaches for the buckle of his jeans. "Are you nervous?"

My chest tightens as I sit down on the edge of his bed. "I just... yeah, a little."

Yep. A lie. I'm a whole lot of nervous. This is different from the shop. When we fucked before, it was purely need. This isn't. This has the potential to be more, and I know that.

That shit is what's scary.

His warm hands cup my face and brings his mouth to mine as he lays me down on the mattress, climbing up my body. "Don't be. I would *never* hurt you or do anything you weren't comfortable with."

A low groan from the back of his throat vibrates through me as his chest presses against my breasts, pushing me deeper into the mattress. His mouth is hot and wet, devouring mine, his tongue circling the inside almost desperately. This is far more intense than the night in the shop and I realize at the time, he must have been holding back. Only now, he isn't. It's in the sturdiness of his touch, the pressure of his fingertips when he angles my face to kiss me and the groan of pleasure he lets out when I arch my back into him and let my hips meet his again.

He stops kissing me for a moment, his hands sliding from my face down the length of my body and to the button of my jean shorts, his disheveled hair falling into his eyes.

I lift up my hips and allow him to remove them and he lets them fall to the floor beside his jeans. We're both naked and I think he's going to go for it when he slides down my body.

"Shhh," he says against my neck. "We have to be quiet."

Crap, his daughter is in the next room.

And then his face is between my legs and breathing isn't something I can do. I've never had anyone go down on me. Ben was too selfish for that and the other guys I slept with only wanted one thing from me.

Red is different.

As he makes his way down my body, his hands splay over my hips. He looks up at me and waits for my reaction. I have no reaction but a stunned look on my face.

He settles on the mattress, his head between my legs. "Has anyone ever done this to you, Lennon?"

Oh God, the way he says Lennon just sends my nerves sailing.

He must have sensed by my look that I had never trusted someone to. "No."

He smiles, his hands moving to my thighs as he lowers his face. With one last look, he licks his lips and then kisses my inner thigh, softly.

The moment his kiss touches my center, it's like nothing I've ever experienced. The pleasure, the sensations, the rush of losing control with someone in this way makes me glad I never let anyone do that before. I'd never want to be this vulnerable.

Because that's what I am right now.

Completely vulnerable for him.

Maybe because it's Red, I'm not entirely sure. It's just that I've never felt anything like this before and I never ever want it to end.

With each pass of his tongue, I'm left weak. With every groan he gives me and the way he grips my thighs so tightly, I know he's just as helpless.

He doesn't spare anything while doing this, his fingers and tongue working together so every touch and caress pulls me closer to spiraling into bliss. My hips rock into him, the muscles of my thighs tightening as he takes his thumb and presses down on my clit, his other finger curled inside of me as he laps at my juices.

My desperate pleas for him to never stop are greeted with his equally needy grunts and growls.

"Jesus, you're so fuckin' wet for me."

I throw my hands over my head, arching my back as the wave hits me all at once. When I'm moving around too much, he puts his hands on my hips, pinning me to the mattress. I look down at him, his shoulders flexing as he grips me so tightly I think I'll have bruises.

When I'm finished shaking, he moves up my body, and reaches in his nightstand to retrieve a condom, ripping it open with his teeth.

He flips me over onto my stomach and kneels behind me so he's straddling my backside. His left hand moves up my spine for a fist full of my hair as he bends my neck back. Sucking on the base of my spine before kissing his way back up and sighing into my mouth as he angles it toward him. "I can't wait any longer."

He's not waiting any longer, his patience gone as he enters me with a low growl from deep within.

We both gasp when he's in, breathing escaping me entirely, but all I can do is inhale a much-needed breath.

Red doesn't move right away, when he does, it's slow as if he's wanting this to last.

He lowers his lips to the back of my neck when he begins to move a little faster, but still, he's not rushing. It may be torture, but it's the sweetest agony.

Within in a minute, I realize he has a way that he moves, much like he did in the shop that night. It's a swagger that only he can pull off.

One of his hands is in my hair, but his other hand snakes around my front between me and the mattress and begins to caress me again.

Instantly heat begins to build within and I'm gasping and whimpering at what he's giving me, something no one else has cared to give. He's not just fucking me. Red could never do that. It's not in his heart to do so. This is in his heart.

His mouth nips at my skin, his hands on my ass forcing me into every move he's making with each thrust inside of me

"Come for me, baby. Just one more... come for me," he begs in a low raspy voice that makes me shiver, rattles my bones. He pleads for more, "Give me one more."

He's begging for me to *give* in and *give* him what I've never given anyone else.

It's not his movements that do it—though they're enough—it's that voice and those words. Oh, and his hand between my legs that I'm desperately grinding against. Until Red, I've never had an orgasm during sex.

Wanting to give all of myself to him, my body arches off the mattress an inch, curving around him, my hips angling just enough that nothing remains of my control. I'm gone completely.

His groan is low as if this sight is too much for him to bare. "That's it, fuck... so good."

His weight settles into me more and he grunts with each thrust, touching his forehead to my shoulder blade. Words fall from his lips, but I can't hear them, all I focus on is pleasure that shoots through me and blinds me.

Red slams his hips into mine even harder while I rock myself into his hand, his bed creaking with our steady movements.

Twisting my head, I watch as his head drops forward, his teeth sinking into his lower lips. The sight too much to bare. I squeeze my eyes shut, my orgasm surfacing, my legs shaking as the warm burst of waves rush throughout my body as I come for him a second time.

Just as I don't want it to end, his thrusts come a little faster and I know what's coming. He's breathing hard, chest heaving, every muscle tensed as he hovers above me. He looks at me, a quick glance, then his eyes dip low. He slams into me two more times, his eyes squeezing shut. I angle my ass so that he can plunge deeper inside me. "That's it, baby. Come for me," I whisper, when I know he's about to release.

His orgasm stretches long and delicious. When he moans, it vibrates through my entire body. His cock pulses, swelling and pumping as he fills me with his release.

"Holy shit!" He pants, slumping forward but still supported by his shaking arms.

Well, fuck. That was amazing.

Red draws in a deep breath, still panting as he rolls to the side. I almost whimper at not being connected any longer.

An influx of emotions, contentment, love, fear, they all flood through me when it's over and I turn toward the window, unable to look at him.

We lay in silence, and I want to look over and stare at him all creepily like an obsessive teenage crush, but I don't.

Red doesn't seem too interested in moving either. His touch is slow and tentative at first, mirroring his slow breathing. A gentle kiss follows before he wraps his arms around me, pulling me close. His hold becomes a little tighter when a soft sigh escapes him, tickling my skin. It's exactly what I want.

I lay awake for what seems like hours afterwards. I listen to him softly breathing in my ear and holding me close to his chest.

There is no sound in the house. Nothing. It's as if the world has stopped and it's just us.

22

REDDINGTON

MY BEDROOM IS PAINTED in dim blue light. Beside me, Lenny's sleeping. With her back turned to me, I'm gifted with a pretty good view of her naked ass. My hands slowly glide over milky white skin I want to bite. It's been a long time since I've felt the softness of a woman beside me as she sleeps.

Touching my forefinger to the black ink over her hip, she stirs, her breathing accelerating.

I have no idea what it is Lenny's doing to me.

I know I want her here. I know I can make her happy. I know she fills a void in my life.

"Again?" she asks, laughing lightly.

"Shhhh," I say, moving between her legs.

Lenny gasps at my weight on her, my lips trailing over her collarbone.

She reaches up, her arms around my shoulders as her body arches around me, her eyes squeezed shut. "I should get going...."

"Did you like my cock buried deep in your pussy?" I ask in the space between her neck and shoulder.

"Y-y-yes," she barely whispers, a pleased, erotic fucking whisper as she arches into me.

I move my hand from the mattress to the heat between her legs. "Then stay... so I can do it again."

"Fuck me," she says firmly, gripping my hair with both hands and fisting strands between her fingers. Needing no more invitation, I part momentarily to put on a condom and then I move her right leg up and then slip inside her dripping wet pussy. She grabs on to my back tightly, wrapping a leg up around my hip as I move to position.

That position seems to be what she wants, her leg falling away as her hands once again go to my hair. I'm beginning to understand she's a hair puller and I fucking love it.

"Oh God." She moans, tossing her head against the pillow.

"You like that, don't you?" I ask between thrusts.

"Yes, so much."

The early morning breeze through the open window moves through the room capturing her small pleas for me to go deeper, harder, faster, thrusting into her with a ravenous intensity I know she wants from me.

I need to see her body, but I can't in this position so I pull out completely, sitting back on my heels and then slap the side of her ass. "Get on your knees."

With a wicked smile, she does as I say. I put her hands on my headboard. "Hold on."

Lenny lets go and looks at me over her shoulder, ready to say something. I put my hand on her cheek and turn her head back to the headboard. "I said hold on."

Her tiny body shakes with laughter. "You're so bossy. Next thing I know you're going to ask me to find the rattle in your headboard."

"You're the one who demanded I fuck you harder. Don't complain when I leave you sore."

I press my palm between her shoulders, her face in the pillow. The position gives me a nice view of her full hips and the ink spread across her left side.

Goddamn, she's beautiful.

Pressing forward, my erection slides between her ass cheeks. Both my hands go to her ass, spreading her cheeks.

As I'm watching this beautiful sight, Lenny mumbles, "What are you waiting for?"

My hand moves from her ass to her head, pushing her face into the pillow. "Shut up." My other hand goes to my erection, guiding myself inside her warm, wet center.

Lenny laughs, but I quickly wipe that grin away, along with any talking when I start pounding into her. The harder I slam into her, the more she reacts, the tighter her pussy clenches around me, the louder the moans rip from her throat. So I fuck her like she wants.

Needing a better angle, I raise my right leg up so my foot is flat on the bed, my knee bent. With my left hand squeezing her hip, my right splays out over the small of her back. Her body starts to unravel. A tremble rushes through her body as she attempts to control her movements. All the while, her moaning pleas for me never to stop fill the room.

I don't stop, not until we we're both letting go and my body explodes with pleasure as I release inside of her.

"So fucking good," I whisper, slumping against her back.

"Now that's a wake-up call I could get used to," Lenny sighs in pleasure, falling back asleep in my arms.

SHE FEELS SO GOOD, touching me, exploring my body. Her hands trail over my ribs and she stops to look at the artwork and word imprinted there. Moving them lower, she reaches my stomach, lower... lower....
Ah, yes.

Grasping my dick with her hand, she moans into my neck, kissing me. "Ready for more?"

Three times in the last seven hours would be a bit much for a man nearing thirty, though stopping her seems ridiculous and my dick definitely wants to go again.

And then Nova knocks on the door. "Why is the door locked, Daddy? I want to come in there."

Lenny jerks her hand up, her leg that was draped over my thighs comes up and knees me right in the balls.

"Fuck!" I groan, cupping my balls with both hands as I turn away from Lenny immediately.

"What's wrong, Daddy?" Nova asks, her voice elevated in concern.

"Nothing. I'll be out in a minute."

Lenny's eyes are wide, her hand cupped over her mouth as she stares at me. "I'm so sorry."

I shake my head and stand, well, try to. It takes me a second. When I can move without pain, I kiss Lenny's temple. "Get dressed. I make a mean waffle."

No way I'm letting Lenny leave today. She's staying here tonight.

Dressed only in a pair of shorts, I pad out to the kitchen to make breakfast with Nova behind me.

Lenny emerges a minute later wearing a pair of my sweat pants and her tank top from last night, a messy bun on top of her head. "I have so much dirt in my hair from last night and I'm pretty sure my ass is exfoliated from all the dirt on your sheets." And then she looks at Nova and slaps her hand over her mouth.

I smile, crossing my arms over my chest to watch her sit down at the table. "You're welcome to take a shower if you want."

Her eyes immediately go to my bare chest, a blush painting her cheeks, and then at Nova who's staring at her iPad.

"Did you have a sleepover?" Nova asks, eyeing me and then Lenny.

"Uh...." Lenny panics, looking to me for an answer.

I set a waffle in front of Nova and kiss the top of her head. "Yes, she had a sleepover."

Nova scowls at me as I lean over her chair, my hands resting on the table in front of her. "Daddy." Her arms cross over her chest. "No fair. I wanted to have a sleep over with you guys."

"Sorry, darlin'." I laugh, moving away from the table to check on Lenny's waffle.

My back is turned to the grill when Nova asks Lenny, "Did you get laid last night?"

Yes, actually. Twice.

I turn and wait to see what Lenny's going to say.

"What?" Lenny stammers, clutching her chest in horror and looks at me for an answer.

"She slept great," I tell Nova, moving around the kitchen as I remove the waffle from the iron and place it in front of Lenny. "She said the bed was a little hard." Lenny's eyes snap to mine, her cheeks heating with crimson as she lets out a nervous chuckle when I wink.

"Daddy's bed is really hard," Nova agrees, just before stuffing a large bite of waffle in her mouth, a drop of syrup dripping from her chin.

Lenny turns her attention to her plate and the remains of her waffle. "It is pretty hard."

23

LENNON

IF THERE WAS a moment in time I'd want to capture and hold forever, it'd be right now. I'd keep it deep within the spaces of my mind so I could go back to it anytime I wanted to. I'd live in the pause, in the space between his breaths as my name fell from his lips.

I know last night shouldn't be such a highlight, but for me it was. And this right now is, in his arms just as the sun lights his room and bathes the two of us in summer sweet rays.

For me, this is as close to perfect as it can get.

Red Walker is a lot of things I'm not. Complicated. Okay, we have that in common. But he doesn't fear losing control like I do. I don't think he fears love like I do either.

In some ways, he lives his life on the edge of control and while that terrifies me, I find it insanely hot because there's something devastatingly beautiful about him.

It seems we're balancing each other out. And that's what's so foreign and difficult for me to understand because I've never connected with anyone like this. I've had to balance myself most of my life.

I never knew what it was like to have someone touch me like his. A strong, addicting grip I could easily beg for, something I needed to breathe.

And for the first time in a week, I haven't thought about Ben and my situation all morning. Not because I've forgotten, but because Red has a way of keeping my thoughts from him.

If the wounds my heart has were on the outside, I'd be a rusted bare metal car with a blown motor. It's such a shitty thing to say, but I've been hurt in so many ways over the past twenty-three years, it's hard to know how to react when someone begins to treat you the way you should be.

I constantly forgave my mother, and Wes, and eventually Ben for the things they put me through. I told my heart to forgive because it was easier than hurting.

It's not until I walked away from that life, those lies, that I finally have a choice not to forgive and remember that I deserve better than the life I lived back then. I deserve to be loved with wild passion. I deserve to be appreciated and that's something Red can provide for me. I'm sure of it.

"Are you mad at me?" I ask Red as we sit in his backyard drinking beer as Nova plays with her horses in the sandbox.

"What would I be mad at you about?"

"For not telling you about Ben."

"No, I'm certainly not mad at you." He draws in a breath. "But you and I both know it's only a matter of time before he finds you."

"I know."

"So what's his deal anyway? Why's he so hell bent on finding you?"

I realize then I haven't given Red much information about me at all. "I met Ben at a really shitty time in my life, kinda similar to meeting you." I snort and he lifts his lips as if he wants to smile, but can't. "I met him at a bar and went home with him that night. Just a couple of months later, he asked me to marry him. I was so enthralled with the idea that someone loved me enough to marry me that I said yes. It was never that he loved me. It was that he wanted to control me."

"And what made you leave and run here?"

I have to force myself to breathe, long calming breaths and clear my head. I'm afraid I won't make much sense if I don't. "One night I came home from work and he hit me in the face. And some other things... anyway, something snapped inside of me and I knew I needed to get out then or I might not."

Red's jaw clenches in anger. He's quiet for so long I'm afraid I've freaked him out. I put everything out there. All of it because he deserves to know the truth. "What about this Wes guy? Your foster dad?"

"I haven't seen or spoke to him since the day I left his house when I turned eighteen."

He nods and smiles at Nova who comes up to him with a dirty sticky face. "Can we have s'mores for dinner?"

"No, but you can have s'mores for dessert. How about hot dogs and hamburgers for dinner?"

Nova's eyes light up and she glances at me as she hands me a hair tie. "Okay. Lenny, are you gonna stay today?"

I take the hair tie and put her hair in a ponytail out of her face. "If you want me to."

"I do!" Feeling her ponytail, she seems satisfied and takes off running back to her sandbox.

Red reaches for my empty beer in my hand and tosses it in the garbage can. "Want another?"

"Sure."

For hours, we sit outside and talk while Nova plays and never once do I get the idea there's anywhere else he'd rather be. He listens to me talk about the various foster homes I was in, the way I was shuffled around and left to take care of myself.

"It says a lot about you as a person to look past how others have treated you."

I flip those words around in my head for a while, grasping their meaning and why he said them to me.

Nova squeals with delight beside us, clapping her hands and pointing to the grass beside the sandbox. "Look, a snake!" She then picks up the red and black garter snake as it curls and coils, attempting to get away from her tiny dirty hands. "Daddy, you want it?"

The look on Red's face takes me completely by surprise. I can't tell if it's more fear or disgust. He starts to shift in his chair as if he's trying to put more space between him and Nova without it being obvious.

"Nova, go put the snake back where you found it." I can tell he's trying to sound authoritative, but honestly, he just sounds nervous. Needless to say, his plan doesn't work and to his horror, she tosses it in our direction and throws the snake directly at Red. It literally lands on his lap.

In a jerked motion, he jumps up knocking his beer and chair to the ground and flings the snake out of his lap. "THE FUCK!"

It hits the concrete with a slap and slithers to the edge of the grass between the fence and the patio.

I can't help the look of surprise that has to be so obvious on my face. "Are you afraid of snakes?" I ask, barely able to keep from bursting out in laughter. The thought that Reddington Walker is afraid of snakes is one of the funniest damn things I can think of. He's easily six two some 200 pounds of tattooed bad boy and here he is looking like he wants to climb on the roof to escape a snake.

"What? No," he says not at all convincingly, keeping his eyes on the snake as if to make sure it doesn't turn around and attack.

"He's lying." Nova puts her hand on her hip. Sassy little thing.

Red glares down at his daughter, stepping sideways away from the snake another step. "I am not."

"Okay, well then, pick it up," I challenge, quirking an eyebrow at him.

Nova giggles, jumping up and down. "Yeah, Daddy, pick it up."

His gaze falls from mine, and to the snake. "Nope." And then he walks into the house.

FOR THE ENTIRE DAY, I stay at Red's house with him and Nova. We don't do much of anything aside from lay out in the sun while Red cuts fire wood. When the sun begins to dip down, clouds roll in, peppering the sky with gray, some dark, some lighter as a mist of rain falls.

"It's about to pour on us," Red notes, looking up at the sky. "Nova's gonna be pissed if she doesn't get her s'mores."

"Yeah, she seemed hell-bent on them," I say, smiling up at him as he places another chunk of wood in their fire pit.

He reaches for my hand again and I smile. "And there's nothing better than a gooey marshmallow between graham crackers with chocolate oozing from it," I say, trying to tease him a little.

He draws in a whistled breath watching me, shaking his head with his eyebrows raised, as if to say, I'm screwed. "You shouldn't say those things to me."

"Why?" I ask, letting out a chuckle.

"Because I have no control when it comes to you." His hand goes to my bare thigh and higher until it reaches the edge of my jean shorts. "I can't deny you no matter how hard I try and I've only known you a month. I don't see how that's possible."

"Don't believe in love at first sight I take it," I blurt out, wanting to slap my hand over my mouth. I feel completely stupid for saying that and immediately realize I said love in that sentence and want to take it back. Only I don't.

I wait.

I want to see what he's going to say next.

He turns his head and he stares at the house where Nova is changing her clothes. "I don't believe in love at first sight," Red says almost in a conversational manner. "That's just a fairy tale for romance novels and movies." He waits, and then asks, "Do you?"

"Do I what?" I'm stalling because I'm not entirely sure how I'm going to answer that. Do I? When I said it to him, I was teasing, making light of the situation. I really meant it when I'd told him don't think I know what love is. I've only ever known what I was told I should feel.

When I don't say anything, he reminds me of the question. "Believe in love at first sight?"

"No." My nerves jump a little that I'm talking about this with him. "I guess maybe I don't. People throw the word around too easily these days. They wanna say it as soon as they lay eyes on someone and it doesn't work that way."

He nods, taking in my confession.

"The only reason you've never been in love is because no one has ever given you a choice in the matter," he says and then his eyes find mine again, wanting to see my reaction.

"There's probably some truth in the matter, but couldn't you say the same thing about your situation? I mean you said yourself you married Nevaeh because she was pregnant."

He presses his lips together, weighing his response. "I married her because she was pregnant, yes, but it didn't mean I didn't love her and that I didn't want Nova. She was definitely something I never saw myself doing, the whole baby thing, but once I saw Nova, that all changed."

Before he can say anymore, I ask, "And you certainly never saw yourself being a single dad, huh?"

"No... never. I don't know what the fuck I'm doing." His eyes move from the fire he gets going to Nova in the kitchen with an armful of stuffed animals trying to drag them out of the house with her. When she has them on the porch, one by one, she brings them to sit around the fire with us.

"You're doing great with her." I turn in the seat to face him now. "She's a good kid."

Red breathes in deeply and then slowly lets it out. His right hand moves from the ax he had been holding and lays it on the ground before sitting next to me on the log in front of the fire. "I'm not gonna lie to you. I loved Nevaeh with all my heart. It wasn't easy on me. For a while, I thought I'd never move on and then one day, it got a little easier. Didn't hurt as bad. And then the next... same thing. It's been two years now and it's gotten easier."

"But you're not over it?"

He shifts slightly, maybe uncomfortable with my question. Though there's no sun, he squints and I think maybe it's painful for him. "I don't think you ever get over that."

"Do you ever see yourself getting married again?"

"For a long time I would have told you no." He smiles over at me. "I think about it more now than I did when she died. I told myself she was it for me. I would never love again, but I'm slowly coming around to the idea of maybe."

I smile, realizing I know him a little better now. Like somehow that confession gives me what I'm looking for from him. A little truth. Not that he was keeping anything from me, but I can tell he's reluctant to say anything to me. Maybe from fear, I'm not sure. "Are you worried about what Nova thinks?"

Nova steps back from her animals, completely oblivious to Red and me talking, and runs inside the house. "I used to be, but I kinda let her take the lead on that. She seems to like you though." He laughs with a nervous edge and then leans forward to rest his elbows on his knees. "What about you?"

"I don't even know where I'm sleeping next month, let alone what I'm going to do." I laugh, thinking about the fact that I don't know what I'm doing with my life.

Red laughs too, raising his hand to scratch the underside of his jaw. "Yeah, well, you at least have a job." And then he looks at me. "And you have a place to sleep." I know he's not referring to Tyler's couch. By the look on his face, he's talking about his bed.

"Thank you, I appreciate that."

He smiles at the song that comes on the radio, giving my shoulder a nudge and when my eyes catch his, I want to drown in their depths. "Wanna dance?"

"What?" I laugh, looking around but thankful for the subject change nonetheless. "It's raining."

It's only a sprinkle and hasn't stopped Nova in bringing out her entire bedroom.

"Oh, please. When has the weather ever stopped a girl like you?" He stands and extends his hand to me, nodding to the yard. "Come on, get up before I change my mind."

I let him help me up from the chair. We walk to the middle of the yard where he takes my hand in his.

His hands wrap around my waist drawing my body near. "Thanks for staying today," he whispers in my ear. "Even though she's in her own world right now, Nova loved having you here."

I pull back and shake my head. "You just enjoyed staring at me in the yard with my bra and underwear on." I didn't exactly have a bathing suit with me. Hell, I was still wearing last night's dusty clothes. But when a five-year-old asks if you want to go swimming in her kiddie pool, you strip down and go swimming.

Red raises his eyebrows in amusement. "Well, any chance I get to see you half naked is worth it." He forces me to lay my head against his chest, his body slowly moving in circles.

"Except in the shop?"

"Yeah, I'm not too comfortable seeing the guys staring at you." His arms tighten around me, holding me a little closer as I wrap myself around him. It's good to be with him like this, my head against his chest hearing the gentle rhythm of his heart.

Inhaling, the fresh smells of rain and wet dirt invade my senses. I'll remember this moment right here, too. I will because while he's slow dancing with me, the rain starts again and it's something I've never experienced before. As if my heart is telling me to remember this, cherish it because it's going to be a memory I keep, a sliver of light in a darkness that surrounds me at times.

A slow creeping smile overtakes me, though, formed by visions of what it would be like to fall for him. I imagine it's similar to this, slow dancing, a gentle breeze, and raindrops like the night's kisses.

"What do you want, Lennon?"

I take a deep breath. I want a lot of things, but then again, all I really want is what I've never had before. True boundless love. "You. I want you, and though it scares the ever living shit out of me, I want to be part of your lives."

He moves closer, bringing his arms up and cupping my face. "Then what are you afraid of?"

I stare into his beautiful brown eyes. "I'm scared that all of this will come crashing down. I've spent my life believing I couldn't be happy. I'm scared to need you."

He shakes his head, keeping his eyes locked on mine and then leans forward to rest his forehead against mine. "Don't be scared." He pulls his face back and looks down at me. "I'll keep you safe."

I smile. "As long as I'm not being attacked by a snake, right?"

He glares. "You just ruined that moment."

"I told you. I've got horrible timing."

His hand slides to my ass. "I know a guy who might be able to adjust that for you."

"Daddy, why are you touching Lenny's butt?"

We both freeze at that moment. Looking at each other with surprise at being caught. Suddenly, Red slaps my ass, and I yelp not expecting it.

"She just had a bug on her butt, darlin' and I was getting it for her." I put one hand on my ass rubbing the spot where he just slapped the hell out of me while giving him a look of promise for revenge.

Nova's brow pinches in thought. "Oh. Well, make sure you hit it hard."

Red looks down at me and smiles. "Will do."

He convinces me to stay with him again that night, not that it's all that hard, but he says something when we're inside his room.

"I kept my head down for a long time," he tells me. "But with you, I looked up."

"I'm glad you did," I say, leaning in to kiss him, just once.

"I'm not going to let him hurt you anymore, Lenny." He places his hand on my cheek. "I won't let him anywhere near you."

For the first time in my life, the promise of his words resonate and settle themselves in my soul. I'm safe here, with him.

24

REDDINGTON

LENNY ENDED up staying the weekend with me, and I can honestly say it was the best weekend I'd had in a long time.

"Daddy, can we go to Mommy's grave before you take me to preschool?"

I didn't take her yesterday so I knew this was coming. I let her tell me when she wants to go. I never force her. Sometimes we miss a week.

"Yeah, real quick." I kneel down to her level trying to calm her frizzy hair. She immediately shakes my hands away and hands a hair tie to Lenny as she walks by into the kitchen. "Do you mind if we make a stop?" As soon as I say it, I realize the awkwardness of taking her to Nevaeh's grave. That's probably a bit strange for her, right?

Lenny bends down and ties Nova's hair up for her. It seems I've been replaced in the hair department. Not that I was any good at it anyhow. "I have my own car here, Red. I can drive myself to work."

"Yeah, you can," I agree, "but I'd like to follow you. Just in case."

I know she wants to protest, but doesn't. "I don't mind if you want to stop. I can just wait in my car."

Nova reaches for my hand. "I think Mommy wants to meet her."

Nova once made me take a stray cat to her grave to see if Mommy would approve. I'm guessing she didn't because the cat ran away the next day. Nova didn't seem too upset by it either. She simply shrugged and said, "I don't think Mommy liked him."

So what's gonna happen when we take Lenny?

I hope she doesn't run away.

THE MORNING IS QUIET, a cool breeze from the south picking up. The smell of rain in the distance dances around us as we walk toward Nevaeh's grave. There's a heaviness in my gut, weighing me down. Guilt.

I let Nova talk to her alone, like I always do and then she takes off to drag Lenny out of her Bronco.

"I met a girl," I say into the wind as I kneel beside Nevaeh's grave. "I don't know what it means right now, but I can see she really cares for our daughter." My eyes move to Nova and Lenny in the distance, hand in hand looking for the perfect flower and giving me some time alone. "Maybe that's all that matters right now." I draw in a deep breath and look down at her headstone. "I told myself for a long time I couldn't move on, but then again, is that a life I should be living? I don't know, but for the first time since we lost you, Nova is wanting to be around a woman other than my mom and Raven. Lenny is the first girl Nova's liked in a long time. Maybe she's trying to tell me something here."

Nova comes running up, Lenny walking a little slower behind her as though she's unsure of where her place is in this moment.

Nova grabs her hand tighter and stares up at her with innocence. "My mommy would have liked you."

Tears well up in Lenny's eyes. "I'm sure I would have liked her too."

Looking up at her, seeing the concern in her eyes, I can't help but know bringing her into our lives is the right thing. Though everything's happening fast, it's not a mistake for the three of us to take this next step together.

I understand the life she's running from and I want to be the one who takes her away from it. I know how situations like this end and I don't want that to happen to Lenny. Not if I can help it.

She'd said to me last night, "I wish I'd met you first." I thought about it a lot this morning, and what those words meant to me. At first, I didn't know how I felt about it because of everything she's been through. That's putting a lot of pressure on me to be perfect for her.

AFTER WE LEAVE the cemetery and drop a disgruntled Nova off at daycare, Lenny and I head into the shop. We're already running late, and I don't want to think about how much shit I need to get done today. Most importantly, I needed to talk to Tyler about Ben. I need a plan in case he shows up at the shop.

First thing when I walk into the shop, I look around to see where Tyler is. I spot him walking out of the parts room.

"Hey, man, got a minute?"

Tyler stops and looks at me, his brow pinches together as his eyes dart to the office and back to me. "Yeah sure. What's up?"

"I wanted to talk to you about the situation with Lenny and her crazy-ass ex."

He nods, seeming to relax. "What do you know?"

"Is this guy someone we need to really be worried about?"

"Honestly, Red, I don't know." Tyler shakes his head, scratching the back of his neck. "Lenny hasn't told me much about him, but I do know she's scared of him. Considering her fear, I think that gives us enough reason to worry."

"Yeah, when the sheriff stopped by last week, he told me Ben was making it clear that he wasn't giving up until he found her. Even burned down her last employer's garage when he couldn't get any answers out of them."

Tyler looks shocked by this information. "Seriously? Shit. That is totally fucked-up, man. Ben sounds like he's losing it. What do you think we should do?"

"We need to make sure she's safe. No leaving her alone. When she's not here at the shop, she needs to either be upstairs with you or at my place with me." I level him a grave look. "I mean it, Tyler. Not even a quick trip to the grocery store. There's no telling what this guy is capable of, and I don't want us letting our guard down for a second until he's caught."

"Absolutely, Red. I agree. She and I already talked about making sure she was with someone at all times after she filed the restraining order."

I give a quick glance around the shop, my stare landing on Lenny. She's at my toolbox grabbing something and turns around and heads back to her stall. I watch as she returns to whatever she's working on.

Tyler must follow what I'm looking at because a grin suddenly appears on his face. "Hey, so I heard you and Nova had some company at the races the other night."

I turn to look at him wondering where he is going to go with this information. "We did. Lenny stopped by to drop something off when we were getting ready to leave and Nova asked if she could come along."

"Ah. Nova wanted her to come along." He waggles his eyebrows suggestively. "Well, it was nice of you to let Nova invite a friend." Rolling my eyes, he continues. "I also heard that Elle was there and got the impression you and Lenny were dating. Heard it a got a little awkward."

What the hell. Rawley and his big fucking mouth. Since when did he become a gossiping little bitch?

"I can't help what Elle thinks she sees, and no, there was no awkwardness. Lenny and I are just friends."

"Just friends?" His brow raises. He's sees right through my bullshit lie. "It's obvious you both have feelings for each other. Just be careful man. You've both been through a lot and I don't want to see either of you get hurt."

I hand him a work order. "I know."

I do know. I know I'm positive this woman came into my life for a reason. If that means protecting her, then I will. My dad used to tell me it doesn't matter what's in front of you. It matters what's behind you. As in, who's got your back when you need it.

Lenny's never had anyone look out for her and that's changing.

25

LENNON

"THERE YOU GO." Red smiles and bumps my shoulder with his. "Four new tires."

"Thanks, but I could have done this myself, you know." I give him my own smile. The late afternoon sun giving way to gray clouds in the distance illuminating his face and the sense of pride it holds that he was able to do something for me.

I hadn't realized it, but after the long drive I made here from Oklahoma, I was in desperate need of some tires.

"I do know that, but..." He moves closer and cups my cheek with his hand. He smells like oil and gas, my two favorite scents. "...don't you think it's nice to have a man around every once in a while to change your tires?"

I wink, pressing my lips to his palm once... twice. "It *is* nice. So how much do I owe you for this tire replacement?"

His expression darkens with lust, blinking slowly. "Oh, I'm sure I can think of some way for you to repay me."

Internally, I'm debating inside because though I know I needed tires, it's still foreign to have him helping this way because he wants to. Do I really deserve all this?

"Why is hard for you to believe I wanted to do something nice for you?"

"Because no one ever has."

Red's beginning to be able to read my moods and facial expressions easily and tips his head. "Come with me." And then he grabs my hand, a jack handle, and takes me behind the shop to the old 1950 Mercury Coupe. He then touches the hood with the jack handle. "What kind of car is this?"

"1950 Mercury Coupe."

He grins, winking at me. "First of all, I can't tell you how fucking sexy it is to me that you know that." Raising the jack handle up over his head, he brings it down on the hood with a grunt. The rusted metal buckles under the force, the violent bang against the hood is deafening and I flinch, my eyes fluttering as he continues to hit the car. After the hood is dented, the windows smashed out of it and the headlight, he looks at me, panting and drops the jack handle to the ground.

"What kind of car is this?"

At the sound of his voice, I lift my eyes from the car to his. "It's still a Mercury."

"Exactly." He steps forward, his hands on my hips as he dips his head to catch my eyesight. "Nothing I do to this car will ever change the fact that it's a 1950 Mercury. It might be a beat-to-shit, rustic pile of junk, but it's still a 1950 Mercury Coupe." Realization hits me when he touches his hand to my cheek, his calloused skin from a hard-working man moving over me. "Nothing that's happened to you, defines you. It will never change who you are inside. A good person. A deserving person."

Running my hands up his chest, I fist the fabric between my fingers, knuckles turning white. I'm so freaking turned-on by all this and the fact that he's all sweaty now I have to show him how much I appreciate this. Because he's absolutely right. Nothing will ever change who I am inside. "Do you have to go get Nova?"

"She's with my mom tonight. I have to go get her after this."

"Can you be a little late?"

He nods.

"Then come with me."

THE GRAVEL SHIFTS under my tires as we hit the dirt country road, my Bronco shaking from side to side with each worn out rut. The grass lining the road is tall, overgrown and hugging the edges, swaying with the warm summer breeze.

"Does anyone live down this road?" I ask Red when he looks at me like I'm crazy for turning down this road.

"I don't think so, but do you know where you're going?"

"Not a clue." The sky rumbles and I know I should have put the top up, but it's all part of my plan. "Is this a dead end?"

His eyes don't meet mine. He's watching where we're going, probably trying to figure out if I'm taking him out here for a reason. "Yeah...."

About a mile down the road, it opens to a clearing with a cul-de-sac between trees. Perfect private spot.

When I come to a stop, his eyes shine as the awareness hits him. "You want to have sex with me out here, don't you?"

I give a nod to the backseat. "Yep. Now get your ass in the back."

It's about then the sky opens up and lets out a pattern of fat rain drops that make a pop as they hit the leather seats in my bronco. It's not pouring, but it's enough we're gonna get wet out here.

Beads of water drip from Red's chin and then his eyes sparkle play-fully as a smile tugs at his lips. His breathing turns heavy as he reaches for my hand to help me in the back. "Did you drive me out here for sex in the rain?" Red asks, his smirk sexy as hell.

"Yep."

He laughs at my enthusiasm when I straddle him. "Are you sure?"

Over his shoulder, the clouds roll in low, like fog blanketing the country road we're parked down. "Shut up and take your clothes off. I've always wanted to do this."

His hand rises and wipes down the side of my face, freeing it of the rain. "Sexy. Yet so demanding."

"Damn right."

He removes his shirt, my knees pressing into the leather seat, his eyes holding mine like heavy weights as I rock against his jean-clad erection. I don't even care that my bronco is getting wet. All I care about is this, him, the moment we're in and the way his eyes are intent on mine.

My lashes sprinkle water on my cheeks when I blink, soft wet kisses from the sky. I settle my weight on him, molding to every hard, defined line of his sculpted body. The cool rain on my back gives me a jolt, adding to the spike in my adrenaline that he's this close again, something I swear I'll never get used to.

His hands rise, sweeping water from my cheek. "You're beautiful, even when soaking wet." The words are caught against the space between my neck and shoulder.

The rain picks up and I smile, closing my eyes at Red's heavy, hot breath warming my skin immediately. Arching my back, I rock into him, his hands on my waist and dipping inside my jeans to palm my bare ass. "But you'd look even better naked and wet."

Impatient, greedy hands work my wet shirt over my head and then palm my breasts, rolling my wet nipple between his thumb and forefinger. "I agree. Sex in the rain is worth it."

"We haven't even gotten to the best part yet." I moan at his touch, consumed by him and wanting everything and anything he's going to give.

His lips make a path up my shoulder slower than I care for and I'm eagerly tugging at him, writhing against him. He seems hell-bent on taking his time and it's both frustrating and endearing that he's wanting this to last. It seems anytime we're together, he's trying to stop time, slow it down and worship me. And though I completely appreciate that, I can't slow down when it comes to Red. I don't want to because I've waited so long for this with him, the feeling of wanting to stop time.

The rain picks up and my body slides against his as I tip my head back, his hands cradling my head, his mouth moving over my chest to my nipples and then back up again with a growl of frustration as he drags my hips back and forth of his rock-hard erection. I nearly come with just that, such a delicious rhythm of movements.

Pulling my hair to the side, he gently nips my wet overheated skin, barely brushing but enough that it sends my nerves over the edge and my thighs clenching in anticipation at what's to come next.

Moving my hands lower to the buckle of his jeans, I get the leather worked apart enough to unbutton them. Without breaking the kiss, I unzip them and reach for the button of my shorts. I have to get these clothes off. I desperately need him inside me.

Raising his hips, he nods for me to get up so he can get his jeans off. Standing in the back of the Bronco, rain pelting my face, I look up at the sky as his hands slide up my thighs and grasp the edge of my jean shorts. If you've never taken wet jeans off, it's surprisingly difficult.

With a lot of effort on both parts and nearly falling out of the back of the Bronco, Red gets them off. When I look down at him, my hands thread in the wet strands of his hair, fisting the darkness between my fingers.

He groans against my center, licking me once and then I'm being yanked back down onto his lap. Apparently, he's done waiting now.

Before he enters me, he reaches over and gets the condom from his wallet, quickly putting it on.

My legs part, allowing him better access. His muscles flex when he pushes up, the movement of his hips causing me to shudder. Right now, in this position, I'm in complete control here and we both know it. I stretch to accommodate his thickness. A rush of shivers vibrate through my entire body.

"Fuck me," he whispers, coaxing me along with his hands gripping and slipping on my ass cheeks.

As I rock my hips back and forth, I hit the right spot, so deep, so right. Closing my eyes, I hold him as tightly as I can, riding him in a slow, steady rhythm. My hands slip over his rain-soaked shoulders and up in my own hair as I twist and grind into him.

"Jesus Christ, you're sexy...." He grunts the words, his eager hands gripping my hips.

When I look down at him, wet strands of hair sticking to my face, he gives me a look. I close my eyes and breathe in deeply. He knows what's happening. I'm falling for him and it's evident in times like this.

"You're so beautiful like this, Lennon," he pants, briefly closing his eyes and swallowing hard. "Naked, wet, vulnerable...."

I've always imagined that when I fell for someone, it would happen, or could, in a moment. Not over time, but an actual moment where I can look back and say, yep, it was right then.

I've just never had it happen to know what it looks like. A "forever" moment. The kind that demands I be in it, and understand it. I guess in some ways, I'll know when because from then on, nothing's the same, right? I'd think differently and I know, should I leave this to chance, this might possibly hurt.

It'd be like jumping into muddy water off a dock on the hottest summer day. The heat, it's too much to take and I know there's relief in jumping. Only, I can't see the bottom. I have no idea how deep it is, or what's lurking under the surface, I just know the water's muddy. Despite the mud, I'd dip my toes in and it's cool. It's a relief from the sweltering heat blistering my skin.

Forgetting the hesitation, I'm jumping in.

In the back of my Bronco when the sun dips down over the trees and rain kisses my cheeks, I jump into that muddy water with Red.

"IT'S TUESDAY. Nova wants to go see Tony tonight. Would you like to come to dinner with us?" Red asks, watching Nova sit quietly on his toolbox staring at his phone after all the guys left for the night. Mia had just dropped her off.

I'm beginning to understand Nova likes a schedule. I guess that might be normal for kids. Sunday's she wants to see her mom. Tuesday's she wants Italian food and to see Grandpa Tony. I assume this schedule thing is because it gives her a sense of security to know what to expect. I know I would have loved that as a child.

I smile, relaxing in the relief I found these two. In Oklahoma, or any other place I'd been, all I saw was darkness in my future. A path that had no beginning or end. Now, though it holds uncertainty, I have something to look forward to.

"I'd like that," I tell Red, my smile a little brighter. "I've been craving that lasagna."

He winks, hip checking me reaching for his keys on his toolbox. "And then later... in my bed...." His voice trails off when I scrunch my nose. "What?"

"Sorry, but it's you know, that time of the month. I started this morning."

"Man, really?" Red hangs his head. "Damn it."

"Sorry."

His eyes light up. "We can—"

I cut him off immediately when he squeezes my ass with one hand. "Nope."

He pouts, his bottom lip out. I laugh because I know where Nova gets that look from now. "Blow job then?" You can't miss the eagerness in his proposition.

"I think that can be arranged."

He pulls back and hits the button to close the bay doors for the night. Everyone else went home hours ago, but here we are, taking our time leaving. "I'll be right back. Let me just go lock the back doors. Rawley left the damn keys in the forklift out back. It'll take me a minute and then we can go grab some dinner." With a quick kiss on my cheek, he leaves.

Nova watches him walk by her. "Where are you going, Daddy? I'm hungry."

"Gotta lock up. Stay with Lenny." And then, he's out the back door.

Making my way down to Nova, I stop in front of Red's toolbox and smile up at her as she sets her dad's phone down and lunges herself into my arms. "Hey, pretty girl. Did you miss me last night?" Last night I decided to stay with Tyler. It was tough. After the rain last night, I needed to wash clothes so being at the apartment was easier.

I hated being away from Red and Nova, but I also thought it was important they have some time just the two of them. Look at me, already forming an attachment after one weekend. In all honesty, I formed an attachment the moment I saw them at that pizza restaurant together. If not then, it was the Fourth-of-July party.

"I always miss you, Lenny." Her arms tighten around my neck. "Can we have a sleep over tonight?"

"Maybe." I tickle her ribs, her laughter flowing through the air.

You know those times where everything just seems to fall into place and it appears that maybe you will finally be able to relax? I'm pretty sure those don't exist for me. And might never.

"Who's that?" Nova asks, pointing behind me, her brow scrunching.

I don't have to turn to know who it is. My heart pounds vigorously in my chest, a reminder of the graveness that's before me.

I'd let my guard down. I jumped into that muddy water and got mud in my eyes.

"Lenny...." He breathes the words from behind, the hair on the back of my neck standing on end.

Everything good instantly disappears, leaving me with a steady, yet painful thump in my chest.

Ben found me.

The air compressor kicks on, the belt squealing in the distance as Ben approaches behind me, his boots scraping against the concrete as he drags his feet. I don't turn around. My fixed gaze is trained on Nova, hoping she'll listen to me. "I want you to run." Nova's eyes widen, her tiny body tensing as I set her on the ground. A wave of apprehension sweeps over me as I whisper, "Go now."

She tries to run, but Ben blocks her from the door and points a gun at the two of us. "Nope. She's staying."

Oh my God! He has a gun!

Maybe Nova understands the danger we're in because she says nothing. Absolutely nothing and grabs my hand.

"You look different," Ben says, pointing a gun at me, waving to my body. He takes another step toward me and Nova, his walk slow and sure, filled with arrogance. He looks different. His usual clean-shaven face now has a two-week beard and he reeks like tequila.

Icy fear twists my heart, pulls at my chest. "I am different." My jaw clenches, my blood rushing in pulsing waves through my body. "What are you doing here, Ben?" My body is fully aware of how close he is, and my instinct is to run, but I also know that there is no escaping this now. Not with Nova here. Instead, I tuck her behind me, blocking her from Ben.

"I told you, Lenny. I told you that you wouldn't get away from me." He pushes the words through his teeth and the barrel of his gun aimed solidly at my head. "You didn't listen." His tone borders on mockery and I know there's something very different about him. "You *never* fucking listen. So now I had to come all the way here to bring you home."

"I am home."

Dark and sardonic laughter spills from him as he waves the gun around the shop like a lunatic, his actions jerked and sudden, as if he has no control over them.

I begin to shake as the fearful images build in my mind at what he's going to do with that gun. "What... here? You gonna play mommy to that little shit?" His angry lit eyes land on mine. "You must be fucking kidding yourself if you think these people are going to let you into their family. It's only a matter of time before they realize what a piece of shit you are and then what? Huh?" His eyes blaze as he takes another step toward me and jets his chin up at an odd angle. He's on something. He has to be. "What are you going to do then, Lenny? I'll tell you what you're going to do. You're going to do the same goddamn thing you've always done. Come crawling back to me. Well, guess what? I'm not going to just sit around waiting for you to beg your way back into my bed. No. I'm here to take back what's mine!"

As sweat pours from his brow, wide black eyes pin me. It's glaringly obvious Ben is more than drunk. He's high on something. Probably cocaine. It was always his drug of choice. If his eyes don't give him away, his jittery movements do. He's volatile, and there's no reasoning with him.

"I'm not going anywhere with you, Ben. Just go." I step back. I'm trapped now between Red's toolbox and the welder next to it, my skin prickling with the threat of him moving closer. I can't back up anymore, and I already have Nova squished. Darting my eyes to the back door, I try to breathe normally, try to see this situation for what it is and remain calm for Nova.

Ben dips his head forward, another exaggerated motion, trying to catch my blurry stare. "You want me to walk away?"

"Yes, I do. I want you to leave." My words and body tremble, the thump in my chest making me painfully aware of the danger, and how it can potentially end. It's in his staggered step, the low voice, the black eyes; all reminders he's unstable and could react at any second.

He lowers his gun for a moment, looking at me with a mix of confusion and anger. "I gave you *everything* and this is how you repay me?" He suddenly throws his arms to the side knocking over a tool cart. The loud crash and his sudden burst of anger sends a tremble through my body.

Then he moves his unsteady stare to Nova as she peeks out from behind my leg.

He blinks, focusing on her, his labored breathing faltering as if his heart is beating out of control. "What's your name, sweet girl?" His voice is softer when he steps to the right to see her. He wants her to trust him. I know the voice because it's how he got me into his life in the first place.

Nova's eyes flicker to him as she wraps her arms around my legs. "Nova."

"Where's your daddy?"

"Not here," Nova tells him, scowling. She's lying to protect him.

"Are you lying to me?"

She's seemingly unaffected by him and says, "No."

"Hmm...." Ben laughs, straightening his posture stiffly and pointing the gun at my head now. "She must be hanging around you too much. Has that lying thing down good."

"I never lied to you... Ben."

"Yes, you did," he spits, his words laced with accusation as he waves the gun around. "You lied and you know it."

A warning voice whispers in my head, telling me to choose my words carefully. "The only thing I ever lied about was loving you."

That wasn't chosen carefully.

His eyes narrow, blinking rapidly. "You know what? I've changed my mind." He begins pacing the space between us. "I'm not gonna take you back with me after all, no, it's better we just end this *here*."

Here? Oh God, no, please no. Not here.

"It doesn't matter now, does it?" His voice remains cold and lashing to the point, I flinch away from him. "Whether you loved me or not doesn't matter because after today, you'll *never* get the chance to love anyone." He suddenly stops pacing and cocks the gun loading a bullet into the chamber.

Every muscle tightens, locks in place, and I can't physically move. All the fear and shame for what I brought into their lives comes crashing over me. I think about a lot of things in that moment: fear, regret, blame, guilt.

All of that leads back to this moment.

I led Ben here.

He's here for me.

He's holding a gun, pointed at my head, because of my choices.

I put them in danger.

With death staring me in the face, I know I have no choice but to stand here, and I also know any second Red is going to come walking in behind me and Ben will see him. I even count the seconds from the time I hear the latch of the backdoor to the ten seconds it takes for him to appear.

I turn slightly, stiffness marring my movements as my gaze shifts to

Red as he takes the first step inside, met with Ben holding a gun.

His steps are hesitant. He knows he needs to be careful the moment he sees the gun pointed at my head.

Ben notices him and turns to aim the gun at him. "Ah, yes, welcome to the party, Red. So nice of you to join us."

Slowly, Red looks at me, all emotion gone from his face as he swallows, his jaw flexing.

There's a moment when he stares at me, his expression darkening with an unreadable emotion. I swallow hard, trying to manage a feeble answer as to why I've put his daughter in danger. "Oh God, I'm so sorry, Red."

His furious stare sweeps to Ben. "Lenny, where's Nova?"

Ben smirks and tilts his head in my direction. "Oh, don't worry, Red. Your precious little girl is right here. Safe and sound... for now."

At that moment, Nova takes a deep breath and moves from behind me stepping to my side so that she is in clear view of not only Red but Ben.

Red spots her, and I can see a small flicker of relief flash across his face, but his relief is short lived as he turns his gaze back to Ben. "Get the fuck out of here before I shove that gun up your ass." Each word is a growl, a distinct warning, but he doesn't move from his place by the door.

Ben gestures to Nova with a sharp nod. "I wouldn't be so tough acting there, *Reddington*. I can bring you to your fucking knees right now and you know it. You may not even care what I do to Lenny, but we both know what you do care about, what you are afraid of." And then he points the gun at Nova's head and snatches her by the hair to his side.

I gasp in horror, my hand flying to my mouth, a sensation of intense sickness and despair sweeping over me. "Don't hurt her!" I scream, grasping in thin air attempting to catch her. I'm not quick enough.

"Daddy...," Nova whispers, her word shaking as she winces in pain, her lips imprisoning a sob from letting go.

Ben kicks my knee, buckling my stance immediately. "Shut the fuck up! Stay back!"

I want to kill him for touching her, and it's everything I can do to stay still. Standing up, I refuse to show any pain.

Red takes a step toward Ben, unable to stand there. There's fire in his eyes. It courses through him, burning steadily until he is engulfed completely. "Let her go, you piece of shit." He shakes his head when he speaks, every muscle rigid.

"No. I don't think so. So tell me, Red, how long have you been fucking my wife?" Ben asks him, keeping a tight grip on Nova's hair.

My heart hammers erratically as a hint of arrogance touches the corners of Red's mouth. I can tell he wants to say some smartass comment that's guaranteed to piss Ben off, but he has enough sense to know the danger we're in and the fact that his daughter has a gun pointed at her head. In his eyes, I can see his struggle to remain impassive, refusing to give him the satisfaction of an answer.

"What's the matter, Red?" Ben's eyes narrow, rigid, hard, cold, black eyes that hold no repercussions of his impulsive actions. He begins to pace again, dragging Nova with him. "Cat got your tongue or is it that you don't want your little girl knowing how her daddy is fucking a lying whore?" Red has his arms by his side, but I can see them twitching, his body's natural reaction to protect his daughter. He wants to run to her, but it's taking all of his strength to hold his ground.

"Daddy!" Nova screams again, tears running down her face as she tries to break free to run to Red.

Ben is quicker and grabs her hair, yanking her to the ground and away from Red. "Where do you think you're going, you little shit?"

"Nova!" I scream, watching him throw her like a ragdoll.

"Let. Her. Go!" Red growls.

Ben quickly grabs Nova off the ground and grabs a hand full of her curls to keep her at his side.

"Why should I, huh? I mean, you're the one sleeping with my wife." Ben's eyes glaze over. It's the drugs. They make him emotional. "Where I come from, there's consequences for that."

"You fucking son of a bitch!" Red's control is fading. "Let her go!"

"Daddy!" Nova cries, sobbing now. "He's hurting me!"

Ben shakes her. "Shut the fuck up!" And then he slaps his hand across her mouth, letting go of her hair to keep her silent. She's going to bite him. I just know it. Silently, I beg her not to. If she does, it's over. He'll shoot her in the head. I can tell by the fitful expression on his face, he would pull the trigger on her without a second thought.

Tears forming in Red's eyes, he knows it too. "I'm going to kill you!" he vows, his body convulsing in anger. "Let go of my daughter! I'm going to kill you... *I'm fucking*...." He can't finish, he can't even catch his breath when Nova begins to scream hysterically, fighting against the hold Ben has on her.

I pray right then Tyler can hear this from upstairs. I want her to cry louder so maybe she has a chance at surviving this.

"Ben, let her go!" I scream. "She's a little girl and has nothing to do with this."

He turns to me, eyes wide and crazy with anger. "This is your fault." He holds the gun tighter to Nova's temple, the metal of the barrel making an indentation against her skin. "She's going to die because of you." He shakes his head erratically, his voice somewhat quiet, yet holds a coldness I can't shake. "That's on *you*. Everything's fucking on you, Lenny."

"Shut the fuck up!" Red roars, his face blazing with wrath as he steps forward once more. "Let my daughter go!"

"Now, now. No need to yell." Ben's voice is suddenly calm and relaxed as he eyes Red. "What did you think was going to happen, Red? Do you think I'm going to just let you take what's mine? Fuck you. Touch what's mine and there will be hell to pay."

"I'm going to say it one more time, you take that fucking gun away from my daughter's head or I'm going to kill you. Lenny's not your goddamn property. She left you. Get that through your thick skull. It's over. You're never getting her back."

"You're right, but not because you said so. No. It's because *this* is where it ends." Ben lifts his chin, giving Red a nod. "Let me ask you, does this feel familiar to you? I read about you, you know. Amazing what you can find on the internet these days. Didn't your wife die because you weren't man enough to save her, am I right?"

Red reacts in one swift movement twisting around to the tool cart beside him and sends it crashing to the ground.

Please, God, let Tyler hear this!

"Ah, look at that. What's the matter? The truth hurts, don't it? You're losing control now. I'm getting to you, aren't I?" Ben glances at me and smiles. "Even the toughest of them fall."

"You got nothing on me, you fucking son of a bitch." Red never moves his belligerent focus from Ben. "You think you're a man? You come in here with a gun threatening a child. You're nothing! I can promise you one thing, you're not walking out of here."

I reach over and try to pull Nova away from Ben's grasp, but all my attempt does is piss him off more. He takes the butt of the gun and slams it into the side of my face. "I told you to stay there. You never fucking listen!"

Stunned, I blink rapidly to regain my vision.

With the force of Ben's movements, Nova stumbles to the ground, her knees hitting the concrete as she falls from his hold.

She scowls at Ben and stomps on his foot. "Leave her alone!" she screams at Ben and grabs onto me.

Holding her to my side, I use my other hand to feel the side of my face. It's wet as blood rushes from a gash on my cheek. My eyes instinctively go to Red as he picks up a jack handle and takes a step toward Ben.

A wicked smile curves Ben's lips as he leans in to whisper harshly in my ear, his eyes on Nova. "Looks like he's ready for a fight now."

When Red takes another step, Ben reacts and fires the gun.

The bullet just misses Red's left foot and ricochets off the lift and into the wall. "I said stay the fuck there! Stay back! Don't move!"

Red stops immediately as Nova lets out a cry of horror, her hands over her ears as her wailing cry pierces my ears.

I have to do something. I can't stand by any longer and let this happen. "Enough, Ben! Okay? You win. I'll leave with you! I will. Just leave them alone." I reach for Nova, scrambling with lies, anything to get him to lose focus on Red and Nova. "Please!" I scream, a suffocating sensation threatening to swallow me whole.

"No! Too little too late, Lenny. You had your fucking chance for that." He glances at me, wild eyes and quick breaths. "I don't want *you* anymore." His voice stings my face like a blast of cold water. "And because you're such a fucking pain in my ass, I'm going to kill them both while you watch."

There's no doubt in his words as he loads another bullet in the chamber. Nothing unsure about his actions. He wants to destroy my future, a future I deserve without him in it. There's a brief second when I look into his volatile scowl, beg him to think about what he's doing. He can't. His head has long since spun and made sense of anything he's doing.

My gaze shifts to Red. He's fixated on Ben, never moving. He looks at the gun and I see the severity of what's happening reflected in his eyes. The realization Ben is not just making empty threats, but there's also no way in hell Red's going down without a fight.

Ben shifts so that he's facing Nova and aims the barrel of the gun straight at her temple. Red takes a step toward him, his fist clenching, his jaw tight as his mouth clamps shut.

"Daddy! Please!" Nova screams again.

"Everything is going to be fine, Nova. Just stay calm and trust me, okay?" Red urges her, his grip tightening on the crowbar in his hand.

"If I were you, I'd stay out of this," Ben says, not bothering to even look at Red, his eyes locked on me, the one who's betrayed him. "I won't miss the next time."

"No. Fuck you." Red moves forward another step, not caring. "Put the gun down now!" His voice is sharp, a menacing growl that makes me flinch as he defensively blocks Ben from Nova and me. He doesn't touch him, but he's close enough, aware of the weapon in his hand. "Get away from Lenny and my daughter or I promise you you're going to leave here in a fucking body bag."

"I doubt that." Ben aims the gun at Red now, agitation in his jerked movements. "You see, Red, you're forgetting something very important right now. I hold the power."

Red's shoulders tense, his eyes cold and detached. "The only reason you're not dead right now is because you're holding a fucking gun like a pussy because you can't fight like a real man." I shift slightly, hoping to block Nova from Ben's sight. I'm not sure if it's from shock, or what, but she's not saying anything now. Her eyes are sharply focused on what is happening in front of her. Her face red, blotchy marks color her cheeks and neck, the only indication of her fear.

Please don't let this ruin her. Please don't let her remember it.

Ben looks to me, his eyes intent, darkness and drugs restricting his mind. "How's it feel, Red?" His focus shifts back to him, his anger abated somewhat under the warm glow of his patronizing smile. "Here you are again. It's like déjà vu. Another situation where you can't protect the woman you love. Well, who's it gonna be, your kid, or my wife?"

Red swallows hard, trying not to reveal his anger. "Neither, you stupid son of a bitch. It's going to be you if you don't put that gun down."

"Leave us alone!" Nova yells out of nowhere as she lunges and slams Ben's knee with a wrench.

"Fuck!" Ben yells as his body jerks in pain. His reaction gives Red the opening he's been waiting for to lunge and knock the gun out of his hands.

They collide with a grunt against the lift. Red gets the first swing in and knocks the gun to the floor. The next hit is a heavy blow that connects with Ben's jaw and attests to Red's strength and power.

The intensity of the next few moments has me forgetting how to breathe. They collide and fall to the concrete floor, wrestling around, taking swings. Red's punches are quick and with a force I never imagined he was capable of. Sure, he's a big guy, but this is something else entirely. It's fueled by pure rage and pent-up emotion.

There's something more here than him protecting his daughter. Each blow confirms it. His intention is to take back what was taken from him two years ago, a situation so similar but he's determined to make sure it ends. He wasn't going to let Ben walk away without getting the vengeance that was rightfully his to recover.

Red's hits come with relentless force and for the briefest of moments, I stare in disbelief at what I'm seeing. I've witnessed the harshness his temper could release, but this is entirely different. It's almost animalistic. A lion protecting his territory. The problem is, Ben is high and doesn't feel the same pain. Nothing can stop him and that's against Red.

They part for a split second as Red wipes the back of his hand over his mouth and lunges for Ben again. They slam into a car, Ben's head snapping back with the force of Red's body plowing into him.

Red's wild eyes, mixed between fury and fear, land on mine. He knows this can twist at any second allowing Ben to get the gun at their feet. "Lenny, GO! Get Nova the fuck out of here!"

Ben thrashes around, struggling against Red's grip as he tries to free himself as blood pours from his mouth and right eye. It's then with Red's attention on us, Ben gets a solid hit in on Red. He staggers back against the lift, trying to find his footing.

As they fight to gain control over one another, I rush Nova across the shop, our feet scrambling against the concrete to the exit. Once we're outside, I turn to Nova, my hands shaking as I wipe away her tears. "Nova, baby, listen to me. I want you to run upstairs and get Tyler!" I rush her toward the stairs. "Tell him to call 911!"

She turns and starts to run up the stairs. I wait for her to get to the top before rushing to get back inside. I'm hoping that I can somehow distract Ben so that Red can take him down until the police get here. But before I can get one foot through the door the sound of a bullet exiting the chamber cuts through the blood whooshing in my ears. It's like a crack of thunder, but it's Nova's scream that makes my heart stop. I look up and she's standing at the top of the stairs, her hands fly to her ears, her wide eyes fixated on mine.

I inhale a quick, sharp breath and run into the shop just in time to see Red fall to his knees.

26

LENNON

HAVE you heard of Newton's third law of motion? Every action has an equal and opposite reaction? It all goes back to one saying. You're able to choose, but you're never free from the consequences of your actions. There's no reset, there's no takeback, there's an action, and an outcome.

My consequence is this. Red, lying motionless before me, the front of his shirt soaked in blood.

It's the distant howl of sirens that brings me back and Nova reacting to the scene before us. She cries, nearly uncontrollable begging for her daddy to wake up.

"Red, please hold on!" I scream when his head lulls to the side, but between the rush of my blood and my pounding heart, it sounds like a whisper.

His head turns at the sound of my voice, his bloody face causing me to gasp at the sight. I hadn't realized he'd been hit that much. His face is swollen, his chest, mouth, and hands bleeding and I know he's in trouble. I have to find where he's been shot.

Just as I'm searching, lifting up his shirt as gently as I can, Tyler comes barreling through the door. "Holy shit! What...?" His voice fades when he sees Red on the ground and Nova screaming. "Oh my God."

I have his shirt open and then wad it up to make a ball to put pressure on the reddened hole in his chest that's oozing with dark congealing blood. The moment pressure is applied to his chest, he moans weakly, trying to lift his hand to mine. It's breaking my heart to cause him more pain, but I have to stop the bleeding. A sob rips from my throat. "I'm so sorry. I'm so so sorry!"

Tyler stops and stares down at Ben, ten feet from Red where he lays unconscious in a pool of blood with a torque wrench beside him. Red must have hit him with it.

"911 is on their way."

"Is he dead? Get the gun away from him!" I bark orders at Tyler, and he checks his pulse after kicking the gun away.

"He's alive... I think." Tyler whispers and then rushes to Red's side.

As I sit here trying like hell to stop the blood pouring out of Red's chest, to save his life, all I can think of is ending Ben. I can see the gun. It would be easy. He deserves to die, but I can't, not from some moral obligation, but because finishing Ben would mean leaving Red and I can't leave Red right now. So I remind myself that with the bastard alive, at least he will have to pay for what he's done.

I don't focus on Ben. I can't because seeing Red on the concrete is more than I can take. Hatred and sadness rush through me. I brought this here to him. A scream dies inside my throat as I cry next to him, not just any cry, it's the kind of cry that might never stop. It's the cry of someone who is undeserving, but dared to take anyway. It's the cry of someone witnessing the worst possible pain and knowing I've put this family in this position.

It hurts to look at him, burns even worse when I look at Nova kneeling beside him, Tyler's arms wrapped around her. I ache so badly that tears sting my eyes, burning like drops of acid. My chest tightens with each breath as I watch him dying in front of us.

"Daddy... no. Please no!" Nova shakes her head, screams bursting from deep within. "You can't leave me!"

Red's eyes flutter open at the sound of her voice, his breathing short and ragged. Looking at me with so much pain and fear, he tries to lift his head, but it's clear he has some broken ribs from the bullet and by his rattled breathing. His left hands grasps mine on the floor beside him. "Keep her with you, please." His voice wheezes as he coughs up blood. He turns his head to look at Nova. His hand shaking as he tries to reach for her, his eyes brim with tears, red and puffy. "I love you... Nova.... Don't... l-l-let her... go," he whispers, his eyes closing.

"Red! Red, please don't close your eyes. Stay with us, please. Help will be here soon and then everything will be okay. Just please don't close your eyes."

He doesn't respond. His body's still except for the sound of his labored breathing, the only evidence that his body is fighting to stay alive. I press harder on his wound hoping that the pain will cause him to open his eyes. But he doesn't react.

My tears fall uncontrollably as I lean down and whisper in his ear, "I won't leave her," I vow. "I promise. I'll take care of her until you come back to us." I'm fading, my tears constricting my vision.

Suddenly the world comes back into focus, and I can hear the sirens out in front of the shop. Before I know it, the paramedics rush inside and I'm told to move so they have room to work.

It's the last thing I want to do. To let go. I don't want this to be the last time I ever feel his warm skin under my hand. I stay there knowing I need to get out of the way, but afraid to leave. Tyler comes up behind me and reminds me of what I have to do. "Lenny, let them do their job. You have to let go. Nova needs you."

THEY AIRLIFT Red to Portland on a LifeFlight, and he'll be heading immediately into surgery as the bullet punctured his right lung.

The moment they load Red in the helicopter, Tyler and I take Nova and begin the hour drive to the hospital. The last thing I want is to bring

Nova with us, but the most important thing is getting to Red. And because I'm too scared, Tyler calls Mia on the way there to let her know.

When we finally get to the hospital, Tyler runs to the emergency room registration to find out where we need to go. They inform us that Red was brought directly into surgery and directed us to the family waiting room. So we do as we're told and begin the long wait, hoping every time the door opens it will be someone who can give us information as to what's going on.

When we're seated, Tyler looks at me. "Do you want some ice for your face?"

I had completely forgotten about my eye where the gun hit me. It's numb and swollen, but it's the last of my worries. "No, I'm fine."

I wish my heart were as numb as my face.

As I wait for Red's family to arrive, cradling Nova in my lap, fear takes a firm grip of my heart and squeezes. I could lose everything. Not only the man and child who have found a space in my bruised heart, but his loving family too. While logic tells me Ben is responsible, I still brought him here. He chased me to Red's shop. That's on me.

When the door swings open and Mia and Raven rush into the waiting room, I think for those briefest moments, they will hate me. Finally see me for what I am. Cursed. Trouble. Underserving. I'm afraid they'll take Nova from my arms and hate me forever.

As they rush over to where Tyler and I are sitting, Nova stirs slightly in my lap. She fell into a fitful sleep about a half hour ago, her wild curls draped over my bloody jeans as I stare at Red's mother.

"Oh my God, Lenny! What happened?" she asks, her voice a low whisper, careful not to wake Nova.

"I'm so sorry," I tell her, swiping away tears that won't stop. My face burns with the action.

"Lenny, look at me." She kneels down, tears flooding her eyes at the sight of the blood on me. "What happened? Where's Red?

"I'm so sorry!" It's all I can say as the shock of the situation begins to take over.

"Was it Ben?" Raven asks, looking at Tyler.

Tyler nods and puts his hand on my back in attempt to comfort me. "He showed up... waving his gun around making threats. He shot Red in the chest."

"No! Is he okay?" Raven gasps, drawing in several calming breaths and sits next to Tyler. He reaches for her hand and holds it tightly. "We don't know anything yet. They rushed him into surgery as soon as he got here, and no one has come out to talk to us yet."

Mia falls to her knees and Nova wakes up, pushing her curls from her face as she looks around.

I wait for it, the reality to come crashing around her. And when it does, she stares at me, her arms around my neck. "Lenny, where's daddy?"

I kiss her temple, never wanting to let go of her. "He's with the doctors, darlin'." I use Red's nickname for her, wanting to comfort her.

Tyler clears his throat and looks at Mia. "Ben is here somewhere too. Red nailed him with a torque wrench to the side of the head. Sheriff Barns said he's under arrest, if he makes it."

Rawley storms through the doors with Jude and Hendrix close behind him. His eyes dart around the room and land on mine. "What happened? Where's Red?"

Mia immediately reaches for Rawley, pulling him to her side, her sobs captured by his chest.

"I don't even know how it happened," I say to them when Raven takes Nova to the bathroom. "They were arguing and Ben shoved Nova and Red lost it. He lunged for Ben and they began fighting. Ben had a gun and shot Red in the chest. The only thing anyone will tell me is that he was taken into surgery. They said any personal information is only given to family. I don't know if he's okay."

Mia stands from her chair, suddenly calm, or attempting to be. "Okay, well I'm going to see if I can find out anything." She walks out to the nurses' station and speaks with one of the women behind the desk.

When she gets back to our seats, her expression tells me she wasn't able to find out anything more than we already know, which is nothing. So we do the only thing we can. We wait.

Raven comes back from the bathroom with Nova, and she immediately climbs onto my lap and wraps her arms around my neck. I grasp her tightly, trying to give her as much love and protection as I can. I know I should get her out of here. That this is no place for a little girl, but I can't leave until I know that Red is going to be okay.

IT TAKES five hours before someone comes out to talk to us. Both Rawley and Nova are asleep by this point, but not once did I close my eyes. I couldn't.

A doctor walks in wearing scrubs and carrying a clipboard. "Family of Reddington Walker?"

"Yes." Mia jumps up from her seat. "I'm Mia Walker, Red's mother." The doctor approaches and motions for Mia to have a seat. He then kneels next to us and removes his scrub cap. "Reddington is stable now and in the ICU. As I'm sure you know, he was brought in with a GSW to the chest. He's very fortunate the bullet hit more on the right side than the left. We took him into surgery immediately as the bullet pierced his right lung and it collapsed. We had to crack his chest because his ribs splintered and wanted to make sure none of the fragments damaged his organs. You can see him in a couple hours when we get him settled in the ICU." The doctor reaches out and touches Mia's shoulder. "Be prepared when you do see him. There's a tube in his mouth helping him breathe along with a chest tube. It's a flexible tube we inserted into the space between his chest wall and the lung. It's attached to a suction device and used to evacuate air and any residual blood or body fluids from the chest cavity to help keep the lung inflated. Once his lung heals and can stay inflated on its own, we'll take the tube out. It could be a couple days. He's going to be here for a couple weeks at least and total recovery time depends on him.

Anywhere from a month to two. He needs to take it easy and it will take time for him to heal."

"Do you have any questions for me?"

We stare at him.

"How long will it take for him to be awake?" Mia asks.

The doctor draws in a deep breath. "Once he shows us signs of being able to breathe on his own, we'll remove the breathing tube and ease him off the medications. It could be a few days. He's strong though, so it could be within the next twenty-four hours. He has a long road ahead of him, and there are still some risks of complication and infection. He's in good hands, though."

I didn't want to hear that. I know Red's a strong man but can he pull through this?

WITH RED IN THE ICU, there's nothing we can do at the hospital, so I leave with Nova, Raven, Rawley and Tyler, and head to Red's house so Nova can sleep in her own bed. Mia stays with her son.

It's around three in the morning by the time we get to the house and I put Nova in bed. Rawley, Raven, and Tyler sleep in the living room, but I imagine there won't be much sleeping tonight.

Just as I'm in Red's bed, there's a soft knock on the bedroom door and it creeks open. Nova stands in the doorway with tear-filled eyes. "I'm scared. Can I sleep with you?"

I can imagine she's horrified.

"Of course you can, honey." I nod, patting the side of the bed. I knew she wouldn't stay asleep and I'm kinda glad she didn't. The thought of sleeping alone after all of this scares me, mostly for her.

"I'm so sorry for what you saw today." I tuck the blankets up around her and pull her into my chest.

She worms herself closer and sighs a shaking breath. "I'm scared. What if he comes back here and takes me?"

"He's not going to hurt you. I promise. He's going to jail for a long time."

I hate that I just promised her something I can't guarantee.

Lying here in his bed, beside his daughter, my tears spill over. All my life I've only dreamed of a world where I would have the kind of love and acceptance I've gotten from Red, Nova, and the Walker family, and now, as I lay here holding onto Nova with every shred of love I have in me, all I can do is sob. For the first time, I have everything to lose. Not knowing if Red will make it, not knowing what tomorrow will truly bring, I'm sobbing so hard I can barely breathe.

If and when he wakes up, there's little chance he'll forgive me for endangering his daughter.

I cry for my stupidity.

I cry for Nova.

I cry for Red.

And I cry for what he told me the day before this happened.

"I won't let anything happen to you. He'll have to go through me to do it."

Because of me, Red's words came true.

27

REDDINGTON

PAIN RADIATES through my body in waves. The intensity of it comes and it goes, a constant aching in my bones, my chest, pretty much everywhere, but it's distinctly centered in my chest. Every time it gets to where I think I can't handle the pain any more, a moan coming from deep in my throat I can't control, warmth travels up my arm followed by periods of nothingness.

I sleep, for long periods of time, but at least the pain is gone.

Then I awake again, the dim lights of the room comforting. Movements and sounds around me are unfamiliar.

Something stirs me from my sleep, dim lights filtering through the blinds in the room. I might be in my room, but as I lay here staring at an unfamiliar ceiling, I allow myself to take in my surroundings. Searching for something familiar, something I recognize to assure myself of where I am, all I find is disappointment. This isn't my room.

Where the hell am I?

There's a machine beside me, a low whoosh sound that flattens every few seconds and three additional monitors surrounding me. It's then it hits me.

It's a hospital room.

Swallowing, afraid to move, I notice my throat burns, like hot lava was poured down it. The simplest of motions from blinking to moving my head come back slowly, as though I'm waking from a deep sleep.

My head feels like it's full of cotton balls as I try to recall why I'm here. I continue to stare at the white ceiling, blinking several times. Everything begins to come back to me in waves, unclear and clouded waves, but I remember what I need to.

Ben showing up, him grabbing Nova, the fight.... I was shot in the chest.

Looking to the nurse beside me messing with my IV, a wave of panic invades my thoughts immediately. Nova. If I'm in the hospital, where is she? The last thing I remember is being in the shop and Lenny holding her.

I swallow, again, struggling to speak. "Where the fuck is my daughter?" I barely recognize my voice, gruff with sleep and aggravation.

"Oh, you're awake." She smiles at me, like I should be happy to see her. "I'm your nu—"

I don't have time for her fucking introductions. I need to know where Nova is, that she's safe. I try to sit up, but I'm immediately reminded of why I'm here. Pain shoots through every nerve, causing my body to spasm like it's on fire "I don't care who the fuck you are. I just want to know where my daughter is."

The nurse is trying to calm me, telling me I need to relax and not move because I could cause more damage to my already battered body, but she doesn't understand that I don't give a damn about myself. I have to know where my daughter is.

Quickly rushing to the door, the nurse calls for help, but my struggle doesn't last long. Whatever my injuries are, they root me in place. "Mr. Walker, we need you to stay calm and not move. You've suffered a severe gunshot wound and sudden movement could cause more damage to your chest."

Suddenly, my door bursts open and my mom is the first person to rush in that I recognize, her hand clamps over her mouth and tears roll down her cheeks. "Oh my God, Red...." She breathes in relief. "You're awake."

Looking at her, I can see a mix of relief and exhaustion in her face. I don't know how long I've been out or how badly I'm hurt, but I'm guessing things were bad. Our eyes locked on one another. Hers looking for reassurance that I'm okay and mine taking in the reality of my situation. I don't say anything to her. I'm not sure what to say and then the nurse asks me if I know where I'm at.

"Hell?" I ask, glaring at her. "Where's Nova?"

"Can you tell me what you remember?" The nurse presses, like I should be answering her and not concerned with my daughter.

"Enough." I grunt at the onset of pain moving through me, my eyes follow my mother as she sits next to the bed taking my hand. "I don't want to talk about it right now, but that motherfucker better be in jail or dead. Now where the hell is my daughter?"

"He's gonna pay, Red. Don't you worry about that," Mom assures me. "As soon as he's released from the hospital, he's going straight to jail."

I blink, my focus fading as my eyes drift closed momentarily. "Released from the hospital? Why?" I try to recall if he was injured during our fight, but I can't. It all seems so foggy and pieced together.

"From what we can tell, after you were shot, you managed to hit him in the head with a torque wrench and cracked his skull."

I don't say anything as I begin to try and process that night. It comes back to me in flashes of memories, mostly of my daughter crying. A flood of emotions overtakes me. My heart pounds erratically in my chest. The monitor next to me begins to beep faster and it's all I can do to not hyperventilate.

I look at my mom, careful not to move by body in any way. "Where's Nova? Is she okay?" There's panic in my voice as fear threatens to swallow me whole.

Mom moves from her chair beside me to sit carefully on the edge of my bed. Gently, she places her hand on my face, cupping my cheek. "Oh,

Red. She's fine. A little scared but fine." Tears well up in her eyes. "You did good. You protected them and kept them safe."

"Where is she, Mom? Who's been taking care of her? I need to see her."

She smiles reassuringly. "She's with Lenny. We thought it best that Nova be back home sleeping in her own bed. Lenny didn't want to leave you, but Nova was clinging to her so hard that she didn't have much of a choice. She hasn't left her side since you were brought in. They should be here any minute."

The idea of Lenny taking care of her brings me relief. I remember asking her to watch over her but maybe I was thinking it and didn't say it before I passed out.

"How is Lenny? Is she okay?" I suddenly remember Ben hitting her with the butt of his gun. "That bastard hit her pretty hard."

"Relax. She's fine. There's a bruise under her left eye, a small cut near it where Ben hit her. But she's okay." She draws in a deep breath, her fingers moving slowly over my torn-up hands. "Lenny.... She's worried about you, Red. She kept apologizing over and over saying it was her fault all this happened."

I'm careful, but I shake my head, my eyes squeezing shut at the onset of pain. "She can't think that way. It's not her fault. I knew he could show up. I knew and we still had our guard down. She had no way of knowing things would get this bad."

Mom nods and then reaches up to brush tears away. "I know, but I don't think she's going to believe us until she hears it from you."

There's no way I'm letting Lenny take the blame for this, or go on letting her think it's her fault. It wasn't.

Just then, the door cracks open and curls bounce inside. The relief is overwhelming as my eyes flood with tears and I gasp. "Nova...." My breath comes out in a sigh as I struggle to breathe.

"Daddy!" she squeals in delight, rushing toward the bed in a run. Internally, I cringe thinking how bad this is going to hurt when she jumps on me.

My mom leaps up from her place next to me to catch her, holding her back before she can reach me. "Careful with, Daddy, Nova. He's in a lot of pain and shouldn't be moving around."

Nova frowns, the disappointment marring her happiness at seeing me. She stops beside the bed, tentatively reaching for my hand. "Daddy... you're okay, right? Are you much better?"

"I'm fine," I whisper, touching the side of her face. Tears roll down my cheeks as I try to control the blast of emotions coursing through me, but I can't. I'm so fucking happy to see she's unharmed. I don't give a shit who sees me crying. "It's so good to see you, darlin'. Are you okay? You're not hurt, are you?"

"No, I'm not hurt." She comes closer, just another step and squeezes my hand. I can't imagine what she's been going through because of what she witnessed that night, and I'm almost afraid to ask right now. So I don't.

"How long have I been out?" I ask my mom, refusing to let go of Nova, but the fading begins with each blink as the pain medication begins to kick in.

"Three days."

I focus on Nova again. "Are you being good for Lenny?"

"You don't need to worry, Daddy. Lenny's got this. We went and had our toes painted this morning so they would look pretty for when you woke up. They do a better job than you." I try to look at her toes but there's no way I can.

I almost smirk. "Is that so, darlin'?"

There's a noise beside me, feet sliding against tile, and I turn my head to see Lenny leaning against the doorjamb. She smiles at me, tears forming in her sad, brown eyes and a sensation bursts in my chest before sinking into the pit of my stomach. I'm so fucking happy to see her alive and unharmed. I'd gladly take a bullet for her. Am I mad? Sure. I'm fucking pissed my daughter was in danger because of this crazy bastard. But I also know it wasn't Lenny's fault. She was doing everything she could to escape that douche bag. I know she would never have knowingly put us in that kind of danger. You can't blame her for Ben's delusional mind. She was trying to move on. I blame him for taking that chance from her.

"Nova, sweetie." Mom stands and reaches for her hand. "Let's give Daddy and Lenny a minute. Wanna go pick out a treat?"

"Yes!" Nova looks at me. "Is it okay, Daddy?"

I wink at her. "Definitely."

When they're out of the room and we're alone, Lenny turns toward me, her tears of apology streaming down her face. "Red, I'm just so sorry. I never meant to put Nova in danger," she says immediately, as if I need to know that first before she says anything else.

Thinking back to the night, and how it could have ended, had I not walked in... I don't have a response, at least not one I can voice. I reach for her hand when she steps near me. "I know you didn't. None of this is your fault," I say, hoping she believes me. "Come over here."

After she cautiously approaches my bed, carefully sitting beside me, Lenny cups my cheek. Instinctively, I lean into her hand despite the obvious bruising to my cheek. "You don't look so good. Are you in pain?"

I almost laugh, but I don't because I know the pain that will come if breathing hurts this bad. "Nah, I'm tough."

"I know, but you look pretty banged up."

"Oh, please." I attempt to roll my eyes, and even that hurts. "We both know I look hot in this hospital gown."

Lenny eyes my body, her eyes dragging slowly over me. They flood with tears again. "I just can't tell you how sorry I am. I knew that Ben was becoming more unstable, but I never thought he would show up and do this. To threaten Nova and shoot you. I swear I never thought he would come after anyone but me...." She sighs, the dejection in her voice somewhat suffocating.

"Hey, listen. I know you're feeling a lot of guilt right now, but we're not going back to that. We're not going to blame or accuse."

She nods, brushing away tears as she sits gingerly on the edge of my bed. A nurse walks in and then smiles. "Mr. Walker, I paged the doctor and informed him that you're awake. He's going to stop by soon." And then she closes the door, giving us some privacy once again. I know I only have a few minutes before Nova's back, or I fall asleep, but I need to ask her this. I have to know where we stand.

I clear my throat, but it's gravelly. "Look, Lenny. You need to know that what happened doesn't change anything. The way I feel about you hasn't changed."

"Red...." She shakes her head and I sense denial. She's afraid of bringing me unwanted drama and I get that, but I'm not letting go after this. If anything, taking that bullet and having her take care of my daughter as if she's her own cements that for me... I'm not letting this woman out of my life.

"Listen." My voice is drawn out now, slow and lethargic. "I'm in this, kinda deep with you. I don't care what happened. I just want to know when I leave this fucking place, you'll be with me."

"I will." She's quick to say, her eyes snapping to mine. "I'm not going anywhere."

My mom walks in and Lenny stands, distancing herself from me. She can tell I'm about to fall asleep when Nova kisses my cheek and then grabs her hand to stand beside her.

"I think Daddy needs a nap," Mom suggests.

Lenny kneels beside her. "I think he does. Should we let him sleep?"

Nova nods. "We should. We'll come back soon, Daddy."

I smile at Nova and wink at Lenny, mouthing "Thank you" to her as they exit the room.

Just after they leave, the doctor comes in and explains to me the extent of my injury. He lets me know I'll be in the hospital for a few weeks and then it'll be at least two months before I'm able to lift anything heavy.

Once he leaves, I ask my mom, "Shit, Mom. What am I going to do about the shop?"

She smiles, touching my hand. "Don't you worry, Red. We got everything covered. Tyler and Lenny are amazing and believe it or not, Rawley has been helping out. Even Jude came up and was doing odd jobs to help. We ended up closing the shop this week because of the police investigation, but it's all good. Everyone understands."

She knows me and gets how hard this is for me. All my life I've taken care of things that needed to be done by myself. I never relied on anyone. This will be the hardest part. I have no choice but to rely on them.

"You're an incredibly strong man, Red. Being a dad isn't a job. It's a life and one you've managed to do well for two years, by yourself. And now with the business, it's a lot for anyone. It's okay to ask for help. It's okay to need help. It's not a dirty word or a sign of weakness to lean on anyone else."

I know what she's saying makes sense, but that doesn't mean it's gonna be easy. It seems like my life has been a series of unplanned circumstance. From Nevaeh's unplanned pregnancy and then her being taken from us so brutally, forcing me to raise our daughter alone, to my dad suddenly dying, leaving me with a business I wasn't ready to run. But through it all, I've kept my head up and tried my hardest to keep moving forward, taking care of what needed to be done.

I never wanted to ask for help.

28

LENNON

PEOPLE CAN TELL you everything will be fine, but it's hard to believe them until you know for sure, it will be.

In the days following Red's surgery and the three days that pass when he's taken off the ventilator and allowed to breathe on his own, it's like that for me.

I thought for sure that first time I saw him he would be upset with me. Blame me for endangering his daughter. Blame me for bringing this poison into his and Nova's life.

But from the moment I entered his hospital room that morning and I locked eyes with him, all I saw was relief. He wasn't angry or disgusted because he's Red, and just like his mother said, he loves unconditionally.

I remember back to when I was five. I was staying with this lady and her twelve kids. There weren't really twelve kids, but most days it felt like there were. Anyway, for some reason I would pee the bed, like all the time. I don't know why. I just went through a phase where I did.

The first couple of times it happened, she acted like it was no big deal. Everybody makes a mistake, but by the tenth and eleventh time, she got pretty fed up. Eventually, she ended up taking me back to the group home. Said the monthly check wasn't worth the hassle of having to put up with me and piss.

That moment set the tone for my life. Growing up, it was never about caring for me or what was best for me. No. It was all about the monthly check and what *I* could do for them. The only time I felt some sort of affection or caring was with Tyler's Aunt Maggie. But when she passed and Wes moved us away, the pattern resumed of giving me the bare minimum. Keeping me fed and clothed so he received his check every month.

I can't help but think at some point, Red's going to decide I'm too much work. That my negatives out way my positives. There is only so much being a good mechanic is going to get you. I mean, the guy was shot dealing with my ex-husband.

Then, I remember how I stood in the doorway of his hospital room expecting hate and only saw relief. I'm so grateful this is Red and he's completely different from anyone else I've ever known. He's warm and caring, even with the harshness of his bitter words at times. In a matter of weeks, he changed everything I thought I knew about love and life, and certainly not to take it for granted.

By Friday, a week after he was shot, it was time to make some decisions at the shop. Mia had closed it for the week given the police investigation, but we still needed a plan for when we opened on Monday. Without Red as the lead mechanic, there would be no way we would be able to manage the turnaround needed.

One thing was for sure, even though I didn't want to, I was going to have to take Nova to daycare with the promise we would go to Portland tonight to see Red. I didn't want her at the shop just yet. We'd been inseparable in the week following the accident. And I do mean inseparable. She'd been sleeping in Red's bed with me ever since.

She didn't want to go and cried more than I thought my heart could take. I had no idea how Red did this every day.

"Look, Nova. I really have to go into the shop today and sort some things out and then we open on Monday. We've been closed since Daddy got hurt and we really need to get back to work. It's going to be really busy and I don't want you to get bored. If you don't go to Elle's, then I'm going to have to take you with me and I don't want to do that."

Nova stares at me in the backseat of Red's car. I'd been driving his around since the accident because my Bronco wasn't exactly kid friendly with the missing seatbelt in the back. "Please, Lenny! Don't make me go. I don't want to be away from you," she cries, brushing tears away. "I don't care if I'm bored. Please just take me to the shop. I'll be super good."

How can I deny her? I can't and that's the problem.

When I walk into the shop, Nova in hand, I knew being back was going to be different. It was the first time I'd stepped foot in here since that night and I was sure the memories of what happened were going to come flooding back.

I didn't have time to think about it because not only were we closed for the week, the guys had broken out a case of beer while cleaning up the shop. There, sitting on stools were Tyler, Colt, Rawley, Jude and Daniel. Drinking. At ten in the morning.

"This is why I shouldn't have brought you here," I whisper to Nova as we enter.

She smiles and watches them closely. "I like it when they drink. They're funny."

"It's too quiet without him here yelling at us," Daniel says almost conversationally, looking around as I approach them while shaking my head. "I keep waiting for him to yell at us for sitting around."

Colt spots Nova and she immediately crawls on his lap with her arms around his shoulders. He offers her his beer but she shakes her head like this is a regular occurrence.

Just then, Tyler sways on the stool, nearly falling off and then catches himself with a laugh. It's clear the drinking started way before we got here. Shit, did they not sleep last night? "He saves that for Rawley."

Rawley snorts, a trace of laughter in his response. "Don't worry. I was at the hospital last night. He yelled at me for ten minutes about something I don't even know."

Watching them, I wish I could join them, but I don't. Instead, I lean against Red's toolbox. The last thing I want is to numb my pain. I don't deserve that, but they're slightly entertaining and taking my mind off the scene before me and the fact that I'm standing in the exact spot he was shot. The concrete is discolored from where it was cleaned.

"We're probably going to fuck this place up," Colt says, raising his beer in the air.

"We'll be fine," Tyler defends, but then looks around at the shop full of cars and the mess left by the police during their investigation. "Okay... maybe we have some work to do."

The side door opens drawing our attention. It's Raven.

"What the hell are you guys doing? Get up." Raven kicks Rawley in the shin after staring at Tyler for a minute.

"We're stressed out," he tells her. "So we're taking a break and drinking."

"Why do you care?" Tyler asks, trying to hand her a beer. She denies it and swats his hand away. "It's not like we're open for business." And then he eyes her body suggestively.

Her eyes shift around the shop attempting to ignore him. "Well, dumbass, I came to answer the phones and let customers know there's going to be a delay. Someone's gotta work around here. Doesn't seem like you guys are."

Her stare locks on mine and I shrug, shaking my head at them. "I'm sorry. I was going to take the beer away but they're kinda entertaining."

"Aw, come on, Raven, don't be mad at us." Tyler grabs at Raven's ass when she walks by him and she slaps his hand away.

"Knock it off, Tyler."

For someone who's trying to maintain no contact, he's suddenly grabby with her. "Well, can you at least get us some donuts or something? We're hungry."

"Nope." Raven smiles and reaches for my hand to pull me toward the office. "Nova, come with us."

Nova gives Colt a shrug. "I have to go."

"Raven!" Colt calls out when we're at the office door.

"What?" She glances over her shoulder trying to hide her amusement. She thinks they're funny too.

"Can you get me another beer?"

"Screw you, Colt. Get it yourself!"

The door slams behind us and she looks at me with wide eyes. "Did Tyler seriously just try to grab my ass in front of everyone?"

I nod with a smile.

As the morning passes, Raven and I are answering messages and contacting customers when a white car pulls up and Berkley walks in. She struts right past Rawley and straight to hug Tyler.

Rawley shakes his head and makes his way to the office. "Are you okay with that?" I ask Rawley, even though I'm more curious what Raven thinks of this.

Nova looks up from her coloring to see who we're talking about and then stands up on the counter so she can see. "Is that Berkley?"

Rawley shrugs, clearly not caring one bit. He grabs Nova off the counter and begins tickling her side. "I don't own her."

Raven's reaction is a tad different as she watches Tyler pull back from Berkley and smile, his hand on her hip. He's drunk, I have to remind myself of that.

"She's a bitch," Raven grumbles, sorting through papers and organizing her desk. "I can't believe she'd come in here like this."

"She said she wanted to make sure Tyler was okay," Rawley adds.

Nova rolls her eyes struggling to get away from her uncle tickling her. "I say we punch her in the tit."

Raven, Rawley, and I stare at Nova. "Nova, you can't say that."

"Okay." She puts her hand on her hip. "Let's slap her in the tit."

I frown. "That's not what I meant."

Rawley smiles. "Sweetheart, you're making me proud." And then he high-fives her and turns to Raven. "Why do you care if Berkley's here talking to Tyler anyways?"

Raven begins to fidget and adjusts her stapler about a million times.

"Why are you even here? Since Dad died, you've done nothing but show up late and piss off Red. It's not like you care."

He leans forward and knocks her stapler off her desk with a swipe of his hand. "I'm not heartless, Raven. Just because I don't want to make this my life, doesn't mean I don't care. Red's my brother too and I want to be here to help him out. Since Dad died, everything fucked up, and now Red's been shot and in the ICU. You're not the only one affected by it." And then he squints at her and leans into the wall, his arms crossed casually over his chest. "Wait a minute... you never answered my question. Why are you so pissed off about Berkley being here?"

Raven leans down and picks up her stapler. "I don't know what you're talking about."

Rawley's smile is so wide it looks unnatural as Raven's cheeks heat with embarrassment. "You're fucking him, aren't you?"

"What's fucking?" Nova asks, popping a handful of candy in her mouth from Raven's desk.

Shit! I should have taken her out of here or at least ear-muffed her.

"You can't repeat anything you heard in here," Raven begs of Nova when Rawley leaves.

After brushing her curls from her face, Nova holds out her hand expecting to be paid.

Raven groans as she places a dollar in her hand only to have Nova shake her head. "Five bucks to keep quiet."

"It always used to be a dollar."

"This seems important. Make it five."

"You're such a little hustler." Raven sets her purse down and throws herself back in her chair. "What a mess."

Once the drama of Berkley visiting Tyler at the shop dies down, we go back to work. With what seems to be the norm in a small town, everyone's heard about what had happened to Red and were very understanding about their repairs taking a bit longer to get done. It was so overwhelming to hear all of the concern that folks had for Red and his wellbeing. All I could think is once everyone gets the full story, they will start to blame me for endangering one of their beloved residents.

Around four o'clock we decide to call it a day. Nova's running out of things to keep her busy and I'm worried she's going to decide taking Colt up on his offer for a beer is good idea.

Looking over at where Raven is doing some last minute filing. "So I was thinking of heading over to Portland to visit Red tonight, wanna come with us?"

She reaches for her bag. "Why not? That way he can see I'm lying about sleeping with his best friend and I can feel even worse."

I can't tell if she's joking or not. "Are you being serious right now?"

Raven shrugs. "No, not really. Let's go."

29

REDDINGTON

I'VE NEVER BEEN one to take time off. It's just not my thing, I've been going like hell since the moment I started walking.

Now it seems time is all I have and it's passing by unbearably slowly.

I need to heal.

They tell me I have months of healing ahead of me.

They tell me I'll also be out of work for months. It's certainly not something I am prepared for. I have to make money and who's going to run the shop?

There are days where I feel like I'm locked into some kind of continuous loop with no way out and no hope for moving forward. I am simply here, dependent on others.

The pain fades with each day, but it's never gone completely. It hurts to breathe, speak or to even be touched. It hurts to think.

Physical pain is fading as the days go by and in its place, a stiffness takes over.

There's more to it. Though I don't want to admit it. I'm sad and confused, frustrated at the very thought of most things.

Here I am, holed up in a hospital bed while Lenny is taking care of my kid, yet I can't get my mind right because the very thing I swore I could protect Nova from, happened right before her eyes. And the fact I hadn't protected Lenny is there too, gnawing at me, a painful reminder of Nevaeh.

If I didn't have the reminder then, I certainly do when Tony comes to visit me. I've been in the hospital for an entire week and believe me, I'm ready to fucking leave.

"You'll never forget that shit, kid," he says slowly, understanding my feelings when it comes to my wife. "There are memories that will forever be with you and unfortunately, this, even Nevaeh dying, that's one of them."

The mention of her name makes me sick to my stomach. The emotion, the fear, the devastation creeps up and the lump in my throat rises again. My reaction for so long with Nevaeh dying has been withdrawn, ignore it. I don't talk about it in fear the emotions will drown me. Escaping it all together isn't happening. I lost my wife, an amazing woman, but it didn't define the rest of my life. It's then Tony offers me some insight. I had forgotten he too had lost his wife.

"You can miss her and you can wish she were here with you now, but that's just being selfish. You can't focus on the life that's gone because you need to be thankful for what you do have, in front of you. Nova... Lenny. It's okay to move on. Nevaeh would have wanted you to. Believe me."

Tony was absolutely right. She would have wanted me to for Nova's sake and my own. And when I think about it, I would have wanted her to as well.

IT SEEMS I have endless visitors while I'm in the hospital. Nova and Lenny come and see me every day, along with my mom to have me sign some insurance forms and ask me how I feel about the changes they're going to make at the shop.

"Raven leaves for college soon, doesn't she?"

Mom takes the forms I signed and puts them back in the envelope. "Yeah, but we should be fine. Jude is gonna help out."

Pushing out a deep breath, I stare at the pen in my hand. "Mom, I can't afford this. I know my insurance will cover most of it, but how am I going to pay for my house if I can't work and fuck... Nova starts school in the fall. This couldn't have come at a worse time."

"When I set up the insurance policies for you, we added supplemental plans. It will pay out based on the critical care policy. It will be enough for you to pay your doctor bills and pay your mortgage. It takes care of all that for you so you can heal. You also have accidental insurance that pays your salary when you can't work."

I'm taken back by her words for a moment. "You did that?"

"Yes, Red. It's important to have coverage. If it weren't for your dad and I having it, I would be screwed right now. When he died, his policy paid off our house and the construction loan we still had on the addition to the shop."

I knew my parents were smart with their money, but I can't tell you the relief I have knowing they had helped me with this and made sure Nova and I were taken care of.

"Thank you." I glance out the window unsure of what to say next as a flood of emotions hit me.

"Sometimes it hurts to look at you." She swallows, the action forced as she blinks slowly and then finds my eyes again.

"Why?"

"Because you look just like Lyric and this... nothing slowing you down was him."

"You haven't lost me, Ma."

"I know, but you're just like your father... and you're a spitting image of him when he was younger." She swallows again, her tears no longer hidden. "We put too much pressure on you. I told Lyric when he shared his plan for the shop that it was a bad idea. I didn't want the added pressure on you."

"It wasn't too much."

"I know it wasn't... because you're a strong man."

Most of the customers I used to get would come in with an oil light on. And I'd ask them when it came on. Some knew when, others didn't. They'd shrug and tell me a few days.

Most were lying.

It'd been on for months judging by the oil leak under their car.

Anyway, my point is they saw the warning light, the leaking oil and the smoking, but they chose to ignore it. Eventually, if you ignore that oil leak long enough, the engine begins to break down the oil and contaminates the engine. Sooner or later, it starts knocking and you can throw a rod. You'll be buying a new engine after that. Word of advice here, don't ever ignore an oil leak.

30

LENNON

AFTER NEARLY THREE weeks in the hospital, Red's coming home this afternoon. It's such a relief to know he's well enough to leave the hospital. I know there's a long road to full recovery, but coming home signifies so much.

With Mia and Tyler heading up to Portland to get him, my plan is to make something he'll love considering he's been eating nothing but hospital food.

Raven's supposed to be here any minute to go with me to the grocery store so I can restock the house and also get the ingredients to make Red's favorite dinner, spaghetti.

I'm so freaking excited to have him coming home and not stuck in a hospital bed an hour away. I spent most of the morning jittery and chugging coffee, which is *why* I'm jittery.

Raven shows up, with a very tired looking Rawley, around nine that morning. "You ready to go?" she asks, once her and Rawley walk through the door.

I nod reaching for my purse on the table. "Rawley, can you keep an eye on her?"

He nods, staring at his cell phone as he takes a seat at the table. "Yeah, sure."

Raven smacks his phone out of his hand knocking it to the floor. "No, dumbass. *Actually* watch her."

Glaring at her, he reaches down and snatches his phone. "I am, and you know, I'm getting the impression you think I'm an irresponsible turd."

"No, we don't think you're an irresponsible turd, we *know* you are."

Nova comes walking down the hall, still in her pajamas, eyes Rawley, and then me. "You're leaving me with him?"

I lift her up on the counter in front of me. "I'll be back in an hour. We have to get some things at the store for dinner."

Nova considers my words for a moment, and then sighs. "You promise you're coming back, right?"

It breaks my heart that she worries. She's been through so much and I can understand how she needs to be reassured. "Why don't you play with uncle Rawley for a little while? Maybe ride your bike?"

"Fine." With the heaviest of sighs, Nova slides off the counter. "But don't blame me for any trouble he gets into. Come on Uncle... let's go play in my room." And just like that, she leaves and heads back down the hall to her room. No hug goodbye. Nothing.

I look at Raven. "Is she mad at me?"

"No, she does this to Red whenever he leaves her and she doesn't want him to."

Wow. I'm not exactly sure how to process this. She's never been mad at me before, other than the one time I attempted to take her to Elle's house.

Once we arrive at the grocery store, it becomes clear that it's going to take longer than originally planned. *Any* kind of shopping with Raven seems to take longer than necessary. I'm a list girl. I know what I need and I try and make any shopping trip quick and painless.

Not Raven. No, even at the grocery store she has to walk down every isle and I swear she's read every damn label. She even took the cart from me so I had to follow her. Damn alpha shopping bitch.

"Hey, so when do you head back to school?" I ask knowing her summer is coming to an end and she'll be heading back to Eugene.

"Classes don't start until after Labor Day, but I'm probably going to head back about a week early just to get settled in."

"So are you and Tyler going to try the long distance thing?" I'm asking because since Red was shot, Raven and Tyler haven't been together as much. I suppose it could be blamed on Tyler taking on so much responsibility with the shop and Raven helping me with Nova.

"No. Well, I don't know." She puts about five tomatoes in the cart, never looking at me. "We haven't actually talked about anything. This whole thing started out as a no strings attached friends that fuck, but now I'm not sure how either one of us feels. I kept thinking he would bring it up the longer it went on, but then with Red getting shot everything has kind of taken a backseat."

I know she doesn't mean to, but hearing her say that Red getting shot has put everyone's lives on hold makes me feel worse. My shitty choices have affected so many people. I know everyone keeps telling me it's not my fault, but I don't know if I will ever be able to truly believe them.

"Do you think you want more?" I ask, walking along with her. "Could you see Tyler being more than just a fuck buddy?"

Raven turns to look at me and I can see by her expression she wants more with Tyler. "Yeah, I think I do, but I'm not so sure he feels the same way. It's not like I fit his usual type when it comes to relationships."

I know what she's referring to. Tyler's last girlfriend, Berkley, is built like a bikini model with a face to match. Raven is beautiful but she's curvy with a larger chest and not as tall. She has an edgier look to her, but that doesn't make her any less attractive. In her eyes, she'll never amount to what Berkley is.

"Well, I don't think you should be jumping to any conclusions. I see the way Tyler acts when you're around," I tell her. "He *definitely* feels something. Things are settling down now. Red is coming home and the shop is taken care of. No more excuses."

She smiles at me, relief in her eyes. "Yeah, you're right. I'll talk to him soon. I mean Eugene is only two hours away. It's not like it would be impossible to keep seeing each other. I could come home on weekends or he could visit me at school. It could work."

I can't help but smile at her enthusiasm. Her perkiness can be contagious.

Finally getting to the aisles I need, I begin grabbing the flour, baking powder and shortening.

Raven's standing by the cart with a look of total confusion. "What the hell are you doing?"

"What do you mean what am I doing?" I look at her, and then the cart. "I told you I was going to make strawberry shortcake for dessert tonight. I wanted to make the biscuits from scratch. You know, add a personal touch."

She laughs in my face. "Okay, but you do realize that Red isn't going to give a shit if your biscuits are homemade or not. The only thing he's gonna care about is whether you're naked when you serve them." I can't help the laugh that comes flying out of my mouth. I love Raven and the shit she says. "Which reminds me, are you going to wear the shirt I got you?"

Noticing that people are starting to stare at us, I take a deep breath and shake my head at her. "Seriously, your brother is coming home from the hospital after being shot. He had his chest cracked open. I don't think having sex is on his mind. And no, I'm not wearing a shirt that says, 'Stay well lubricated. Sleep with a mechanic' while your mother is around."

"Your first day at the shop you wore one that said 'Get off my dick'. How is that any different?"

"It just is. I had nothing else to wear that day."

Raven giggles and then starts pushing the cart toward the next aisle. "Anyways, you go ahead and tell yourself he won't be thinking about sex, but my money's on the horn dog. Gun shot or not, Red's a man and men think with their dicks. Plain and simple. And I'm thinking of getting one of those shirts for me."

"The mechanic one?"

"Yeah...."

"What if people think you're talking about your brothers?"

Her eyes widen. "Good point."

WE FINALLY GET BACK to Red's house after what seems like the world's longest grocery run. In reality, it's been two hours, but seriously, it's a damn grocery store.

As I'm unpacking everything, Raven comes barreling into the house making a beeline to the living room. She's dragging a very pissed off looking five-year-old behind her and I notice Nova's wearing a bike helmet and has a pillow strapped to her chest and back.

What the fuck were they doing?

Raven storms up to Rawley coming down the hallway and stops inches from his face. "I told you to watch her!"

"I am. I watched her getting in the wagon with the olive tree kid."

"His name is Oliver. And what were you going to do, just sit here while he went barreling down the road with your niece being dragged behind him?"

"Whatever." He blows her off, rolling his eyes. "I made sure she had a helmet. I thought it would be fun to see where it goes."

It's then we both realize what he's wearing. He's wearing a prom dress.

"What the fuck are you wearing?" Raven asks, gawking at him.

Rawley looks at his dress, confused as to what the big deal is. "We were watching Frozen before this little shit ditched me."

Nova slaps his thigh. "Don't blame that on me!"

Raven slaps his shoulder from the other side. "That still doesn't explain why you're wearing *my* prom dress, asshole."

Stepping out of the line of fire, he holds up his hands in defense. "If a five-year-old asks you to wear a dress, you put the fucking dress on. Don't be a jerk."

Raven eyes him up and down. "You look ridiculous."

"Bitch please," he talks in a casual jesting way. "I look good."

Rolling her eyes, Raven walks away.

I on the other hand can't stop looking at Rawley. Not because he looks good in a dress, but because it looks uncomfortable. Touching the shiny material with my hand, I ask, "Is that itchy?"

He lets out a deep breath, his eyes widening. "So much. I can't believe she wore this thing all night."

"I only wore it for like ten minutes to get my picture taken." Raven says from the living room. "The rest of the night was spent in the back-seat of Holden's car."

Rawley tenses, his nose scrunched up. "Please tell me you dry cleaned it. And another thing, why the hell was your prom dress at Red's house?"

Before Raven can answer, Nova walks up and flops herself dramatically on the floor. After all, she's wearing a pillow and a helmet. Why not flop yourself around the house.

She stares curiously at Raven and asks, "Why did you spend the rest of the night in the back of some boy's car?"

Her eyes go wide as she looks to me for help. "Nova, why don't you go to your room and unstrap your pillow and put them away. Daddy could be home soon."

I think Nova realizes she's not going to get an answer from Raven because she turns and heads down the hall.

Raven breathes a sigh of relief, body relaxing and immediately returns her glare to Rawley, "The dress is here because I wasn't going to wear it again and Nova liked it so I gave it to her."

Rawley shrugs reaching for the zipper on the back of the dress to finally take it off. "I don't know why you thought it was a good idea to give this to her." Raven and I both laugh as he literally strips down to his underwear in the living room and throws the dress at Raven's face. "It's not a dress it's a torture device."

THE MOMENT I've been waiting for arrives. Mia and Tyler finally make it home with Red around four that afternoon and it seems so surreal that he's here, home and safe. For the first time in weeks, I take a deep breath.

From the moment Ben walked into the shop, it was if every breath I took was thick with guilt and worry. Seeing Red now slowly making his way through the door brings me so much relief.

As soon as he comes inside, he pauses and looks around. It's as if he's memorizing this moment. Like he needs to remember this exact place in time.

When he came home.

When he survived.

Turning his stare to me, we both stand and soak in the sight of each other, my heart in my throat. There's so much I want to say to him. So many things I've already said, but feel as though I need to say them again and again. To make him understand how sorry I am and how happy it makes me that he's forgiven me for the hell I had brought to his life.

We continue to stare as he cautiously approaches me and places a warm palm on my cheek, looking into my eyes. All I can see is acceptance and adoration. "Hey," he whispers.

Oh God, that whisper.

Sighing, I nearly sinking to my knees. "Hi."

Leaning down, he kisses my cheek, brushing his beard against my face. He decided not to shave in the hospital and he rocks the beard thing so well, I might have to ask him to keep it for a while.

Feeling him this close, the warmth of his skin, the way his whiskers tickle my cheek, I can't help the chill that shivers down my spine.

Too soon, before we have a chance to say anymore, Tyler comes over and helps Red get settled on the couch. "Come on, bud. You should sit."

It's cute seeing Tyler so attentive to his best friend. I think in some ways he feels a little guilty too.

Nova must hear everyone's voices because she comes barreling down the hallway.

She stops just short of Red and cautiously looks him over. Slowly examining him from head to toe. "Are you okay daddy?" she asks in a voice so small.

His smile is wide, his eyes wrinkling at the corners. "Yes darling, I'm okay. Daddy's just sore and needs a little more time to get better."

Nova still doesn't move, rooted an arm's reach from where Red stands with Tyler by his side.

"Okay, well do you think you could come outside with me and watch me play?"

Mia looks as if she is going to step forward to maybe tell Nova to give Red some time to get settled, but Red raises his hand slightly as if to signal her that he can do this. "Sure, darlin'. I'll just sit on the porch and you can play while I watch, okay?"

A huge smile comes across Nova's face. "Yay! Come on, Daddy!"

Once Red is settled in a chair outside, Nova gets to work explaining every single thing she's done since he's been gone. You would think he was gone for three months instead of three weeks, but then again, to a five-year-old, having her father shot in front of her and then to be away from him for so long, it probably feels like a lifetime.

I stand at the backdoor watching Red as he talks with Tyler and Rawley while Nova entertains them, looking for any signs that he's in pain or needs something. I'm so engrossed in my stalking I don't even notice when Mia walks up beside me.

"How's everything going?" I jump at the sound of her voice, turning around to face her.

"Okay, I guess." I shrug, trying to remain nonchalant around his mother. "I left her with Rawley for an hour and Raven and I came back to her inside of a wagon, ready to go down a half pipe with a pillow strapped to her chest and a helmet to her head."

She laughs, as though she's not surprised by this at all. "With who?"

"The little boy across the street. Oliver. He said he wanted to make her fly." I keep my voice low because the last thing I want is for Red to know his daughter was up to no good today.

"Nova's been talking about him lately. I think she calls him Ollie, right?"

I nod. "Yeah that's him. Nova's mentioned him like five times this week and for her to do that, he must be pretty special."

Laughter in the backyard catches my attention and I turn to look for Red.

Mia follows my line of sight and I can see absolute love she has in her eyes for her son. "It's okay to be in love with him you know?" Mia tells me.

Sighing, the pressure building in my chest at the conversation twist. Leaning back against the door frame, I smile. "I know it is and I am, very much so," I tell her. "It's the last thing he needs though. I've brought nothing but trouble to his life, and even though I know it's incredibly selfish of me, I still can't help that I'm in love with him."

"None of what happened was your fault Lenny," Mia assures me. "You didn't do anything. It wasn't within your control."

"How can you say that?" My voice is timid, even though I try for it not to be. "Ben was here, for me. How is that not my fault?"

Mia looks at me intently, as if by her stare she wants to convince me of one thing. I know where Red got that stare from now. "Just because Ben came after you, doesn't mean you're responsible for his actions. Nothing that happened means you don't deserve to fall in love with my son. It doesn't mean he doesn't deserve to love you back, and it certainly doesn't mean you can't be there for Nova, because that little girl out there, she's fallen for you Lenny and that doesn't come easily for her."

I think about her words, flip them around in my head before I say, "Nova told me her mommy sent me to them."

Mia smiles tenderly, her stare moving back to Nova and her wild curls. "They've been waiting for you for a while. You all deserve to be happy. Let yourself have this." And then she reaches over to hug me whispering in my ear. "He needs someone to help him love again."

As we part, I scrutinize Red's pain level looking for any sign of discomfort. While I know he wants to stay outside all night and watch Nova, it's clear by the way he's so stiff, he's starting to feel the effects of sitting upright in a hard chair. Tyler notices too and we decide to move everyone inside where Red can be more comfortable.

"Can I help you with the spaghetti?" Nova asks, wiping dirt from her face as she walks into the kitchen.

"Of course." I help her up onto the stool beside the stove and tie her apron on her.

"I think my daddy loves you," Nova whispers, stirring the sauce with me, our hands over one another.

I kiss the side of her temple breathing in her rich honey scent. "Why would you say that?" My heart beats faster at the words, wondering how she can tell something like that. She's a child.

"Because I know," she says, keeping her eyes on the pan. "Auntie says love scares Daddy."

It scares me too.

"Now that daddy's home, are you gonna leave?"

"I'm not sure. It's up to daddy."

She smiles. "I think he wants you to stay."

Glancing over my shoulder, I catch Red's stare and he winks at me.

I hope he wants me to stay because the idea of leaving the two of them isn't something I ever want to think about.

HOURS LATER, everyone is sitting around Red's kitchen table, laughing and enjoying each other, and it's easy to believe everything's going to be okay. The spaghetti was a big hit and Nova was so excited about the strawberry shortcake that I thought she was going to bounce right out of her seat. Red even remarked about how good the biscuits were and asked if I baked them from scratch. This of course gave me justification to stick my tongue out and throw an "*I told you* so" look Raven's way.

The warmth it brings to my heart, looking around and seeing the happiness in this room, it's like nothing I've ever felt. The sense of family and togetherness is something I never even dared to dream about in the past. Now I can.

After dinner's finished and the table is cleared, everyone begins to say their goodbyes, as if they know Red needs to rest.

Mia claims she's tired from a long day, while Raven and Tyler say they're heading over to Murphy's to watch Rawley's band play.

And just like that, I'm alone with Red.

Poor Nova had been so excited for him to come home, she fell asleep right after dinner on floor underneath the coffee table.

"I would carry her to bed, but I might just fall over," he teases, attempting to stand up, and then gives up. "I'm just gonna sit here for a few more minutes." It's then he notices a drawing on the table.

"Nova drew this for you today." I push the drawing toward him. It's one of the three of us walking in a park and her mom in the clouds.

Red eyes glaze over with what looks like tears threatening as he tears his eyes from the drawing. His lips part and he heaves in a long-winded breath, then blows it out slowly.

Seeing him emotional, I can feel the tears threatening, but I swallow, attempting to push them down. "I don't know that I can ever truly make you understand how sorry I am about all of this. I never meant to hurt you, or Nova. I swear I never meant to bring you into this."

My statement seems to bring him out of his thoughts as he looks at me like he's confused. "I can't tell you the thoughts I had when I walked into the shop and saw him holding a gun to your head, and my daughter at your feet. I thought...." He breathes out, slowly, shaking his head. "I thought that was the end, again. The idea of losing you, too, wasn't something I was going to accept. I couldn't. With Nevaeh, I had no control.

Finally I was in a position to do something. I was so amped on adrenaline I don't even know what was happening around me in those minutes. All I knew was I had to get that gun away from him."

The night flashes in my head, the images that haunt my dreams surfacing. Ben grabbing Nova by the hair and her screaming.

"I know." I swallow, tears stinging my eyes. As much as I want to move on from that night, this conversation is one we need to have.

"Hey, listen," he reaches out and touches my hand. "I didn't mean to upset you." But then he asks, "Remember when I said I'd be anything you needed me to be?"

"Yes."

"I need to revise what I said."

"Okay." My heart beats erratically. I'm not sure where he's going with this.

"I'll be anything *we* need. I can't save you. Hell, I don't even know if I can save myself. But I might be able to make this work between us. I think that maybe we can save each other."

The truth of what he's saying and the love I see in his stare give me the strength I need. "I think we can."

A huge smile lights his face and I can't help but smile back because that smile is for me. "Can I start by kissing you?"

"I'd like that."

As I move closer so my face is only inches from his, Red leans in carefully, his lips pressing to the pulsing hollow at the base of my throat, leaving my mouth burning with a fire I desperately want him to put out.

I need his lips on me. Everywhere.

He's slow, taking his time as he sears a path up my neck and over my jaw claiming my lips. His tongue traces the soft fullness of my lips covering mine hungrily. We kissed in the hospital, a few times. But it was nothing like this.

I return his kiss with reckless abandonment, probably a little too eager. Just the touch of his lips on mine sends a shock wave through my entire body.

Careful of his injuries, I pull him tighter against my chest. He winces, jerking away from me an inch and then I'm afraid I've hurt him so I draw back suddenly and stand in front of him. "I'm sorry. Did I hurt you?"

As I stand there, he stares at me for what seems like the longest minute ever. Thinking I've hurt him more than he's leading on, I reach over to his bag from the hospital on the chair to retrieve his pain pills. "Here, maybe you should take one of these."

He swallows, snapping himself from his trance. His voice is quiet, shattering the silence between us. "I'm okay." Reaching for the two pills, he then takes the glass of water I hand him. "You don't need to baby me."

"I'm happy to help." I shrug, trying to appear calm and collected as I sit down in the chair next to him. "Nova was a lot of fun these last couple of weeks. That kid is something else. I mean, she's just so strong."

Red nods and looks at the floor. His eyes seem darker, vulnerable, but alive when he sees me, in his house, caring for his daughter. Or maybe the kiss got to him too. I'd like to think so. The few kisses we shared in the hospital were nothing short of amazing, but still, being here in his house is different. "Thank you for all your help this week."

"It was the least I could do," I joke, attempting to make fun of myself.

He nods again, and we both stare at the million drawings Nova made for him. The one in front of him matches the ones on the walls, but instead of drawing just her dad and herself in them, I'm in each one, her angel mommy looking over the three of us. It's enough to bring tears to my eyes.

"We got a little carried away with the coloring the other night," I say, unsure how he's going to take it.

Red nods again, blinking a few times as if he was trying to figure out what was happening. "Again, I really can't thank you enough for watching over her. She's so happy with you here."

I'm happy here too, and I know he can see that. It's in my smile. But even with that happiness, I still need to be honest with him and tell him more than what I told him in the hospital.

"Red." I lower my lashes and stare at my hands. "I have some things I need to say to you... things I didn't feel comfortable saying in the hospital, and it's important that you listen to me. Because I can't keep them in any longer."

A sudden flash of uneasiness comes over him. "Okay...."

Taking a deep breath, I decide not to wait any longer, and start spilling everything I wanted to say over the last few weeks. "When I was younger, I used to tell myself, don't get attached to anyone. It's not worth it. That's why I'd never fallen in love. I didn't let myself in fear it would turn out badly. And it did. My mom gave me up for adoption, Maggie died, Wes was a bastard, and Ben, you know how that ended. I could blame a lot of my insecurities and fucked-up shit in life on that alone, but I won't because I strongly believe you are what you make of a situation.

"When I came to Lebanon, it was a fresh start for me, or at least I thought it was. I just never saw myself falling in love for the first time, and falling in love with your daughter too. I thought I understood how love worked. To love someone the way you need to, there's a certain amount of dependence there. You're trusting them with a part of yourself that you don't give to just anyone. For me, I never gave it. You're trusting them with your heart. It took me a while to realize that because I've never trusted my heart."

His expression relaxes as he lets out a long breath. "You should."

"Let me finish," I say, slapping at him but careful not to actually hit him.

Red licks his lips, leaning away from me, a smirk playing at bay. "Fine. Finish."

"Well," I smile, too, "I actually was done. I know that you don't just meet your match and say I love you and everything works out perfectly. It doesn't happen that way for people like me. I know that."

"It happens like that sometimes," he points out.

"True. And I also believe it's harder to love someone and then to walk away. Love is messy. It's messy and scary and... well, I want that with you." When I finish my speech, a huge weight lifts from my shoulders.

Even if he rejects me now, at least he knows how I feel. How I've felt all along.

As I raise my eyes to his, he's smiling. But there's a certain sadness to his eyes. I remember it from the first time I met him. It's still there. A sadness he's not sure he can let go of. A hole he may never mend and that's okay. He shouldn't be forced to mend.

"How long did you rehearse that for?" he asks, his voice cracking, and then he looks up at me like he needs me to breathe, but I also know he doesn't. Maybe it's relief? He's a strong man. Although, I've come to realize even the strongest can be brought to their knees.

"I rehearsed it for weeks. You terrify me. You fucking terrify me because I don't know how to make this work and I'm afraid of loving you, and her," I cry, gasping. "I've never felt something like that before."

Red's arms wrap around me immediately, tighter than before, and I let my head fall to his shoulder as I sit on his lap.

"I know it terrifies you," he agrees, turning his head into my hair, then sighs. He speaks softly, trying to make me see. He then pulls me flush against him, so close his heart beats against mine.

I know it terrifies him, too. It has to considering how he let this woman into his life and then she puts him and his daughter in danger. And not only that, but it's a reminder of exactly how his wife was taken from him.

Red opens his mouth several times to speak and then finally asks, "Do you trust me, Lenny?"

"Should I trust you?" I ask teasing, and he arches an eyebrow in surprise, making me look in his eyes, hating the heartache at the expression on his face. "I'm teasing. I do trust you. Completely."

"Then tell me you mean it. Tell me you want this as much as I do." There's an easiness about Red in times like this I love. Just when you think he's always going to be a hardass, he shows you a softer side.

"I mean it. I want this with you." And then my eyes dart to the drawing. "And her."

He looks at me and shakes his head. "We may end up deciding we made a huge fuckin' mistake. But...what if it's not? What if it's the best years of our lives? We have to try, right?"

He is absolutely right. "We should try."

It could end in tears. It could. And heartache. But then again, it might not. It might be the chance of a lifetime. A chance at finding happiness together after a lifetime of nevers.

I want to tell him I love him, let the words fall out, so natural, so true that they have depths I can barely understand. I can understand three very simple ones. The ones he is looking for me to say to him.

Cautiously, my eyes find his as I lean in, my hands resting on his thighs. "I mean it," I say, pressing my lips to his.

With a jerked motion, his fingers dive into my hair, winding in the strands around his hands as he inhales deeply. It's everything I'd been waiting for since I left him in the hospital. Our lips part and he slides one hand around my waist pushing me to the edge of my chair. He wants me on his lap so I willingly come forward to sit on his lap again. This time I straddle him.

Red seems all for the kissing. In fact, he practically attacks me once we're in this position. His tongue excitedly exploring my mouth giving into the passion but there's a certain amount of himself he's forced to hold back. The parts of him that are still injured.

Needing to breathe, we part, gasping, and stare at each other. "Jesus," he murmurs, running his nose along my jaw, attempting to catch his breath. "I don't see how I'm going to wait." His eyes scan over me, lingering on my breasts before dipping lower. A slight smirk touches his lips, his eyes blazing with desire. "I missed you."

When he raises his mouth to mine, again, my eyes flutter closed. I fight back a shiver, wanting to melt into him right then. As he fists my hair in his hands, his groans become lost against my lips.

Our kiss is slow but promising, and then it turns into something else entirely. Impatient. And I know where this is going by the hardness he attempts to rock my hips against his. I should probably stop it given he was freaking shot in the chest, but it's really hard to do that with him kissing me like this.

He moves his mouth over mine, firm and demanding, groaning low in his throat. Fuck, he tastes so good and my hormones run rampant. I don't want to stop.

Our kisses slow, and our breathing evens out. His hands travel over my curves, taking their time before he finds my face again. Sweeping my hair from my cheeks, the other one fists my shorts as he groans.

My hands are on his chest, his rapid breathing evident by the rise and fall when he suggests, "Let's go to my room."

I giggle. "Nope. Not happening, buddy. Your doctor said to take it easy. And I believe he specifically said sex shouldn't even be tried."

He shakes his head, his hooded eyes barely open as his gaze never leaves my chest. "Fuck the doctor."

"That doctor saved your life, dude."

"And now I need some tender loving care." His hungry lips search my neck attempting to lure me in. "It's been weeks."

"You went two years without sex. No strenuous activity until your checkup in a month."

His hands palm my breasts hastily. "Because *I* went two years without it... I *shouldn't* have to go two weeks. Besides, you can just be gentle with me."

"You're going to overdo it." I moan in response to his touch when his hand comes between my legs dancing over the nerve endings clad by denim. Drawing myself closer, letting him know it's definitely more than okay. It's perfect. I never want him to stop, but I need him to. "It will start out gentle and then you'll get caught up in the moment and get all demanding and start ordering me around. Before you know it, I'll be on my knees and you'll be pulling my hair."

His fingers tangle in my hair, tipping my head back to expose my skin for him. His stubble scratches against me, leaving shivers in its path and I bury my face in his neck, breathing in his rich scent. God, I missed him.

Letting out a breath, he chuckles lightly. "You know me so well." His breathing increases when my lips are on his neck, his head falling back, his hips raising up as he groans at the contact our hips make with one another.

Well fuck, now I'm dry humping him on the kitchen chair.

I can't help it. I'm drowning in him, his scent, his kisses, his touch. My hands slip off his shoulders to his chest.

It's then I have another reminder of that night. The bandage over the right side of his chest where he was shot. "I know I keep saying it, and I'm becoming redundant now, but I'm so sorry," I say, gently running my fingers over the white gauze.

Red shakes his head. "Don't be. I'm not. I saved you and now," he whispers in my ear, "now you can make it up to me."

"We can't have sex, Red. It's out of the question."

Drawing in a deep breath, I go back to my chair, attempting to calm my breathing.

Red's suddenly serious and stares at me. "Look at me, Lenny. Because I need to make sure you're okay with this." I look over at him and he watches me as he talks. "You said some things a few minutes ago and I think it's time I do." I nod because I knew this was coming. Naturally, he'd have more of a reaction once he thought about what I said. He searches my eyes for several seconds. Rubbing his fingertips along my neck, he moves them slowly and then releases a long, deep breath. "Back when Nevaeh died, I didn't value my life very much," Red tells me, tracing circles on my skin. "But things have changed. I don't know how to handle it. Since I was shot, it's been a rush of emotions even I don't understand because I've had to depend on others for the first time in my life. You've had a hard life and it doesn't just go away. You can't fix everything that's been done to you. Sometimes, just like an engine, there's unrepairable damage. It doesn't mean you can't move on though, but I know this isn't going to be perfect overnight. Like you said, it's messy."

"You're right, it won't be but I don't want to be her replacement," I tell him.

"You're not," he says immediately. "You know, when all this started with us, guilt consumed me for wanting you. Part of the guilt still exists. I was upset with myself for wanting someone other than the mother of my child. When I buried Nevaeh, I assumed I buried my heart with her. I convinced myself I wouldn't love like that again." I close my eyes at his words and when I open them, tears fall freely. "I can't and won't compare you to her or my love for either of you because it's different. It has to be." His brow pulls together as our eyes lock on one another. "I love you."

As the significance of what he's said to me sinks in, it takes me a moment to decipher my emotions. I can't put into words what it is. My heart beats faster and slower at the same time, as if that's possible.

Closing my eyes, his words warm my heart beyond belief. Red came to me, or maybe I found him at a time when I'd just poured myself a drink. A glass of Scotch if you will, the kind that burns so badly when you take a drink, but I knew there'd be relief in it. Red... he was a couple of ice cubes I stuck in there. Taking the edge off, he took me into a heady trance, letting the love course through me with each sip.

Looking at him now, emotions flood me. I'd rather die than let go of this with him. His love, bravery, passion for anything he does, I can't live without that.

"I love you," I tell him, meaning those three words more than anything I've ever said to him.

Taking my hand in his, he places a kiss in my palm, his smile widening before saying, "Now can we have sex?"

"Nope."

MY NO POLICY on sex doesn't last long. In fact, it's like a ticking time bomb. I'm not sure the pain pills Red is on, but he is constantly having to put a pillow on his lap to conceal his erection. Probably doesn't help I wear shorts a lot but hello, it's still kinda sorta summer.

It's now the middle of September and I'm still living out of my bag, shuffling from Red's house to Tyler's. I don't want to move myself in, and Red hasn't asked so I'm still waiting, though I sleep at his house nearly every night.

Last night was the first night Red slept in his bed in two months. He's been sleeping in a recliner in the living room since he came home.

His first night in the bed, he was all hands on all night. I can't blame him. It has been a long time since we've done anything, aside from me giving him blow jobs.

After I've taken Nova to school, I head straight back to the house because Red said he needed something. I walk through the front door and down the hall to see him sitting on his bed, naked.

"Come over here." His voice is low, like a whisper of a dirty secret I desperately need to hear.

"You called and said you needed something." I place my hands on my hips, knowing where this is going, a cold shiver spreading through me at the sight of him completely naked. "What do you need?"

"You," he breathes as if he's recalling the smoldering passion between the two of us, his eyes raking slowly up my body.

I step toward him and he wraps his arms around my waist. "I'm going to be late, Red," I tell him as he's kissing up my shoulder. I know where this is heading.

"It's a good thing you know the boss." His teeth drag over the sensitive skin of my lips as he kisses me, heat rippling under my skin.

"But do you think you're ready for this?"

He nods and gently pulls me on the bed with him.

We glide together as his hands snake around my back, his mouth eagerly seeking out mine once again.

He lays me out before him, his large hardworking hands roaming over me.

His eyes close, his need growing stronger when his weight sinks into mine. My legs open without hesitation, reacting to the high of being held against his strong body.

"Way too many clothes in the way here." Drawing back, he takes my shirt and bra off, letting them fall to the floor next to the bed. "Don't you dare try to stop me or say I'm not ready for this. I *can't* stop any longer," he practically growls. His hands go lower, resting on my hips, and then hooks the edges of my panties, each fingertip grazing me with just the slightest touch and then some pressure. "I'm tired of blow jobs." I raise an eyebrow and he's quick to say, "They're amazing, but I need to be inside you. I can't take this any longer."

Bending down, his lips brush over my right breast and then my nipple, giving me a slow, deliberate kiss, then flicking his tongue over that same path of pebbled hardness.

"And you need this just as badly."

I nod. "I do, I'm just—"

His fingertips silence me. Slowly, his hands move downward, skimming the length of my body. His fingertips brush my center, the touch exactly what I need. My lashes droop in sweet bliss.

Just before I think I might drown in his touch alone, the low gravel of his voice brings me back. "Did you miss me this way?" His eyes hold mine, waiting for my answer. He wants reassurance I want this too.

"So much," I tell him, watching his face.

Once he has my panties off, his hands explore my thighs and then back to my hips.

A lurch of excitement courses through me knowing where this is going. His eagerness for it, the hungry rushed touches, the tender sounds from his heavy breathing, it thrills me even more, sends my heart and breathing soaring in anticipation.

He presses forward again, his hips rolling and I gasp at the contact of my bare center meeting his erection. My back arches, my hands gripping his sheets. "Jesus, Red...."

His weight presses into mine again. His movements are slow and deliberate, our lips moving together at a sensual pace. Guiding my hands to his back, I pull him close to me, savoring the mass of his hard, tight body forcing me further into the mattress. I thought I was doing okay with the no sex thing but now my body is telling me something else entirely. I fucking need him so badly.

The way he moves, his attention to my every curve, it's different. All of it. He's making love to me, or attempting to. It's been so long since we've been together this way, I'm not sure how long we can keep this up. He's giving me a piece of himself, but most of all, he's giving me the chance to see the difference between letting someone take something, and giving it to them.

His breath dances over my shoulder, my name on his lips like some kind of prayer, and my heart soars so high it might never come back down. My eyes close and I arch my neck back into the pillow, giving him more of my skin, more of me in any way.

His hips jerk at my touch, his erection sliding eagerly between my folds and I want him inside, right now. My other hand grips his arm as he holds himself above me, his head bends forward so all I can see are the sharply defined edges of his shoulders.

"You want me, Lenny?"

My eyes open, and I stare into the darkness of his captivating brown eyes.

"Yes."

He continues to glide between my wet center, the head of his cock hitting the most sensitive bundle of nerves and I'm ready to come.

"I do," I practically beg, lifting my hips and chasing the need rising from deep within.

"No... that's not what I want to hear." He kisses me slowly and thoroughly, grinding into me, knowing he's getting me off by his motions. "I want you to *say* you want me."

"Make love to me," I moan, threading my hand through his thick tousled hair and pulling his lips back to my neck. Those open-mouth kisses are exactly what I need, and the idea of him stopping sends my heart pounding. "But don't stop this just yet. I missed your kisses."

His answer is a groan against the sensitive skin, nipping with his teeth. He knows what I want, angling his hips at just the right motion, his cock pushing against my clit in the most delicious way.

He knows how to get me off. He's gifted in that way, or maybe it's just that it's been so long since I felt anything but his hand between my legs. Now it's his hardness, so warm and smooth as he grinds his hips into mine.

It's only seconds maybe, because it's been that long and my vision dims, until a scream rips through my throat as my orgasm crashes over me.

When I finish shaking, Red draws back, an arrogant smile touching the corners of his mouth as he reaches to our left for a condom. Without pulling away, he brings the foil to my lips. I bite the edge of the wrapper, and he twists it the opposite direction.

Reaching between us, he moves my legs farther apart, watching my face the entire time as he slips the condom on and enters me.

Shuddering at the sensation of him filling me, I bring my hands up around his neck, my breath expelling in a needy sigh.

So right.

His tormented grunt and the way his body shudders reminds me he wants this just as badly as me. I think he wants to go slowly, but those first few moments after he enters me were nothing like that.

"Fuck me," I beg, only to have his hand raise from my shoulder to clasp over my mouth, his head shaking against my skin.

"Don't talk dirty." He moans as he flexes his hips, a shudder ripping through his body. "I can't take that. Being buried deep inside your pussy is all I've thought about in the last fifty three days. It's been so fucking long. *So long*... and I'm trying to slow down."

I'm not surprised he knows exactly how many days it's been, but I'm caught up with his enthusiasm, moving with him in any way I can, curving to his strong body. The way his hips rub and drag in all the right places, I'm close to my second orgasm. It's amazing to me how easy it is in the hands of the right man.

"Goddamn it..." he pants, heavy words captured against my burning skin. "I missed you." He's grunting with each movement but his wince is enough to tell me he's overexerting himself. "I missed you *so* fucking much," he repeats, his hands curling around my shoulders, pulling me into his movements. "You're so fucking tight I can't take it."

"Don't talk dirty," I remind him, smiling as our lips meet.

His hips move languidly for a while as I caress the length of his back and the tautness of his muscles. His body tenses at my touch, each movement slower than the next for fear that at any moment, this will be over. I never want it to end. I'll be perfectly content having him right here in this bed, forever.

He keeps his eyes level with mine, and the pressure begins to build, a slow and sweet ecstasy swirling inside my lower stomach and I know I can get there again. Goose bumps shiver across my skin, the scorching heat of his kiss leaves me weak, rubbery, and sedated as the waves wash over me. I stare up at the ceiling as he rocks himself back and forth, him holding on as I'm letting go.

My fingertips tear into his concrete shoulders as I arch helplessly against him, moaning out his name in a desperate plea. "Reddington...."

He curses against my skin in response to my throaty call of his name, his body jerking in time with his release. I thread my fingers through his hair as we lay there.

"*So* good." I kiss his neck.

"Kiss me," he whispers, long lashes lowered, gasping for breath as his body continues to shake. "Just please fucking kiss me."

When the tip of his tongue glides over the seam of mine, I open to him. His lips part over mine and I kiss him deeper, giving myself to him. I will *always* give myself to him. I have to. Now more than ever.

Handling me with care as our breathing slows, he blows out a long breath and eases his body from mine. "Was that worth being late?"

I laugh, shaking my head as I look over at him. "I don't know. Boss Man can be a real dick sometimes."

31

LENNON

RED ONCE TOLD me that I expect him to be the perfect guy. It was last week.

For days I contemplated what he meant by that. I was almost sorta pissed at him. Like he was accusing me of wanting something unattainable. How could someone like me, after everything I've been through, expect someone to be perfect?

I mean, fuck, look at Ben, and then take a look at Red. Clearly, I'm not one to be asking for greatness here, right?

Although, when I look back on my life, I can see the pattern of destruction that's led me to this. The part where Red said I need perfection. It's not his fault.

Growing up, there were times when I wished I had a different life and told myself that when I found it, it would be perfect. I'd dream about it even, having a family and a husband, all that.

See where I'm going with this?

I wanted perfect, whether I knew it or not.

I desperately need a happily ever after. Or my version of it. And that version includes a man built from steel and a girl with wild curls and the brightest blues.

I need to know there's something in life that's not evil. To know what it feels like to be touched by a man who is honest and loves me for me, not for what I can provide for him, or do for him.

Sometimes you need people on your side. You need friends, family, and people who care about you.

I have that now.

I was granted my divorce from Ben, about two days before he was sentenced for attempted murder and aggravated assault. Because of his head injury, his sentences was delayed for a while. I wasn't happy when the verdict came out because really, twelve years in prison was a fucking slap in Red's face for the pain we've all been through.

Nonetheless, he'd be behind bars and I'm no longer married to that monster.

"WHERE'S NOVA?" I ask when I come through the door Friday night. Red's been back at work a week now and I'm still technically living with Tyler but sleeping in Red's bed every night. I keep thinking he's going to ask me to move in with him, but he hasn't.

Red smiles, it's adorable and so unlike the man I first met. His grin sparks my own. "She's with my mom tonight."

"Oh." I set my phone on the counter, watching him place two containers in a bag along with a blanket on top. "What's all that?"

"I'm taking you on a date."

"What if I don't want to go on a date?" He has to know I like to play hard to get, tease him a little for my own enjoyment at times.

He stops and stares at me. "You don't want to go out with me?"

"I'm still deciding," I tease. "Where are we going?"

"Can't tell you."

"Then I'm not going."

He sighs and watches me carefully, his hands resting on the table.

Dark eyes hold mine until he knows I'm gonna crack. "You're missing out then."

There's a moment of silence between us and I can't deny him. "Fine." I groan. "I'll go with you."

He's quiet for a minute. I feel bad for teasing him. "Wow." He laughs. "Don't do me any favors."

I snort. "Oh, shush." I wait a few seconds, chewing on my lip. Then I say, "I'm only teasing you."

Red turns to look at me. "Lennon?"

"Yeah?" I look over at him.

"Will you go on a date with me?"

I don't intend to laugh in his face, but I do because he's so cute, and Red and cute are never words I imagined in the same sentence. I reserve those for Nova.

When he levels me a glare, I clear my throat. "Yes, yes I will." I peek inside the bag. "What's in there?"

He knocks my hand away gently. "Stop that. It's a surprise."

I raise my hands in surrender and take a step back. "You're grouchy today."

Leaning in, he kisses my cheek. "Let's go."

Okay, so a date.

THE DRIVE from his house isn't far and soon we find ourselves at the river sitting in front of a jet boat. "What, are we searching for, gators or something?"

"We don't have gators here." He chuckles, reaching for the bag of food beside him. "And it's a surprise."

I point to the man approaching the car. "Who's that guy?"

"That's Sheldon. Remember him? He owns that Plymouth GTX. I fixed his tractor a while back so he agreed to take us somewhere."

"Where?"

Red nods outside. "Just get out and see."

"So he's going on a date with us?"

He rubs the back of his neck. "Damn, you're impatient."

I throw my hands up. "Well, you could be taking me out here to ditch me."

He stops and laughs, once. And then his face his completely serious as his eyes narrow. "Yeah cause taking a bullet for you did me in. Now I wanna get rid of you so I can get on with my life."

"Hey, *you* said it."

He looks down, eyes squinting. Trying to decode my words. For all his overconfidence that he was strong and recovered so quickly, there's a part of him that's haunted by the fact that I saw him weak and he did depend on me in a lot of ways. "Lenny?"

"Yeah."

Red shrugs, and his tone turns neutral. "Shut up and let me be nice to you."

"You're being dramatic now."

His eyes narrow but he says nothing more.

Trying hard not to laugh, I purse my lips together and we follow Sheldon to the boat. I don't say anything as we get out and into the boat. I also don't say anything as we speed through the river and to a place he tells me is called Fry Creek.

And then I see it. His date. Straight ahead on the cover where the sand and rock wash up the rivers bank is a small table covered with a white linen tablecloth. It's complete with a mason jar candle and two plates. He planned this. For me he planned a special night.

I'm speechless for a moment, before saying, "Red.... Wow."

"You were saying about me being dramatic?"

"Nothing. I was saying nothing."

He leans over and kisses my temple, his rough chin scraping against my cheek. "That's what I thought." And then he points to the raft. "Even comes with a bed."

"Did you bring that out here?"

"You never know when you might need a bed."

I could say something snarky. I could, but seeing this romantic side to Red, I'm nearly in tears. No one has ever done something like this for me.

His expression softens when he notices my sad expression. "Are you crying?"

I clamp my lips together as if that will stop the rush of tears. "No."

He wraps his arm around me, bringing me to his side as the boat stops. "It's okay to cry sometimes."

I know it is. Still doesn't mean I want to.

Sheldon leaves and Red takes out the food he brought for us. We're a few minutes into dinner when I ask him, "Why does an engine knock?"

Red's brow scrunches, trying to understand what I'm talking about. "Usually the engine timing is off but it can be for a variety of reasons."

"Let's go with ignition timing being too far advanced." He nods. "Causes spark knock, right? So the fuel is lit on fire too soon before that exact moment it needs to during the pistons stroke." He nods again. "Everything in my life has been bad timing. Spark knock. *Until you*. And I thought you were bad timing too. I met you at a time when I had no business falling in love, but I did because you were bad timing. You were the mechanic I needed to fix my knocking engine."

He can't keep a straight face for long because he's fucking dirty like that and bursts out laughing.

I glare. "See... this is why we can't have mature conversations like adults."

"You turned it dirty, *not me*."

"Still, I was trying to make a point."

"You did make a point." He winks, relaxing into the chair.

"What's that noise?"

Red looks around. "I'm not sure... but I hear something." And then his face pales as he watches behind me. "Oh fuck!"

I panic and turn around, falling out of the chair. "Holy shit, that's a big dog."

"In what world, would that be a dog?" Red asks, helping me up.

I stare at the black spot in the distance moving toward us with a slow stride. It's definitely *not* a dog.

In my state of sheer panic, I blame Red, naturally. "Who the hell brings salmon to a river where black bears live?"

He glares, a scowl I never want to see again. I've offended him.

"I'm sorry," I'm quick to say, not wanting him to be upset with me because this was clearly a well thought-out plan. He just hadn't invited the bear. "That was mean of me."

"Fucking right it was mean. Be nice."

I breathe in a shaky breath. "Remember that fear you have of snakes?"

"No." He still refuses to admit it.

"Well, I have that same fear... with bears."

"Let's use the raft," Red suggests when the bear moves closer.

We do and end up getting soaked in the process but distance ourselves a good hundred feet from the bear. "Bears can swim, can't they?"

Red eyes the bear with fear. "Yeah, they can."

Just when I think our lives might be over, the bear stops on the edge of the water and stares at us and then decides our half-eaten dinner is what he really wanted, not us.

Red's head drops to his forearm when he sees we're not in danger at the moment. "See, he wants salmon. Not us."

Shivering at the chill of my wet clothes, I stare at him. "Why did you really bring me out here?"

He sighs, the tense lines of his face relaxing. "I was going to ask you to move in."

Our foreheads press together, the smudged sky making his eyes look even darker. I push his hair back from his forehead. "Tell me you love me."

He doesn't say it often. He doesn't need to. But I need to hear it sometimes.

Holding my face in his hands, his thumbs moving back and forth over my cheeks, his eyes darting from my lips, to my eyes. "I love you, Lennon."

I smile, softly, looking into his eyes. "Good. Because I kinda love you. And I'll move in with you."

Have you ever watched a sunset from start to finish?

The colors change with each layer, dark grays, purples, fading into pale blues and then the richest golds, orange, pink and red. If I had to compare it to anything, I'd compare it to the last few months. What started out dark, colors seeping into my blackened soul was changing now. This guy beside me, the one intently watching a bear finish our dinner with a scowl on his face, he saturated my heart with his love. He's proof that even the darkest of times can end beautifully if you look up.

He's proof that you can be loved for reasons you thought you didn't deserve and with more love than you can possibly imagine. In a lot of ways, he's restored my faith in not only love, but men in general. He taught me that being with someone didn't mean you belonged to them.

If someone were to ask me, how do you move on after everything I've been through?

I'd say love, even after you've been disappointed.

I might even go as far to say, believe, even after you've been betrayed.

Or maybe I'd just say find a guy like Reddington Walker and never let him go. He's one of a kind.

For a long time, and even now, I've wondered when it would be my time to be happy?

Finally I know when that is. It's now. Fuck everything else that's happened.

Fuck my mom for giving me up with no explanation.

Fuck everyone who gave up on me and said they couldn't take care of me.

Fuck Wes and his dirty lies and neglect.

Fuck Ben and everything he took from me.

Fuck not feeling good enough for someone like Red, because I am.

32

REDDINGTON

SO I ASKED Lenny to move in with me. Surprised the hell out of me even. She'd been basically staying at my place since I was shot, so it just seemed almost normal for her to live there.

What's difficult for me is the morning before when I had a key made and noticed I still had my wedding ring on my key chain.

I had to remove it, right?

They say you have one true love, one soulmate and when that comes along, and leaves, that chance is over.

Do I believe that?

Six months ago, I would have said yes. I did believe that.

But that's like saying an old rustic car can't be restored. It goes back to my theory of beating the crap out of that car in front of Lenny to prove my point. Even if you're damaged, it still doesn't take away who you are inside.

I don't think we get to choose who and when people come into and out of our lives. There's something bigger in the works as far as that goes. Like my wife sending us Lenny. I could never imagine moving on from Nevaeh. It just didn't seem possible. And then it wasn't so impossible.

But I also think Nevaeh knew Lenny needed us.

Lenny... she's different than she was when she first stepped foot inside my shop.

I'm sure I'm different too. No, I *know* I'm not the same. Life has a way of doing that to you whether you want it to or not.

Being here, now, in front of Nevaeh's grave, seems I don't know, different. A place where I once felt her presence is now just a grave, nothing more. A headstone marked with a life that was taken from me.

What changed and why? Part of me is angry I don't feel the same way. Had I forgotten her?

No. It wasn't that.

Kneeling next to her grave, I remove my wedding ring from my keychain and take the ring in my hand, staring at the black metal. "I don't want you to think I didn't love you or don't anymore because that's not the case. It never will be. I loved you... *God* did I fucking love you, Nevaeh." My voice breaks with the words, emotion swelling up in my chest. "I still love you even now." I sigh, hanging my head as I let out a shaking breath, tears streaming down my cheeks. "But that love has changed since you've been gone. I will *always* love you. You're the mother of my child, but for me... I have to let you go. For Nova, I have to let you go." Taking the ring between my thumb and index finger, I set it on the headstone knowing someone will steal it. "This is yours. I think maybe I should have given it to you when you passed away, but I held on to it self- ishly. I never wanted to move on. I didn't. And I'm still not sure how I did so suddenly, but you know, you had something to do with it. Nova thinks you chose Lenny for us... and I think she's right. I will always hold you in my heart." I stand, brushing away the tears and bury my hands in my pockets. I'm about a foot away when I turn and smile. "And thank you... for *her*."

I LEAVE the cemetery and meet Lenny at my house before we're going to swing by the apartment to grab the rest of her clothes. That's when I notice Nova has taken Lenny's blanket and pillow and put them in her room on her bed.

It hasn't been easy on Nova since I was shot. She saw and heard a lot of fucked-up shit that night, and it's been a huge battle trying to get her to sleep in her own room again without someone in her bed with her.

It took me a long time to talk to Nova about that night in the shop where I nearly died in front of her. Weeks actually. Finally I did and asked her if she wanted to talk about it. There's a certain amount of innocence in her I'm thankful for, because despite her remembering that night vividly, she talks about it as if I was her own personal super hero.

Super hero, or just plain old dad, I will always struggle with how to protect Nova. I think all parents do because there's only so much you can protect them from and some things are out of your control.

I lean into the doorframe and watch her arranging her stuffed animals to make room for Lenny. "Nova, darlin', Lenny's not sleeping in your room."

Nova rolls her eyes and stands in front of me with her hands on her hips. "Don't be shellfish, Daddy."

"You mean selfish?"

She taps her finger to her chin, contemplating what she said. "Yes."

"Still... she's not sleeping in here with you."

"And why not?"

I kneel down and take her hands in mine. "Because Lenny.... she's going to sleep in my bed."

A look crosses her face, one I've never seen before. I can't help but think it might be realization maybe?

"Is she like my mommy now?"

Anxiety rushes through me. "Well, no. Nevaeh will always be mommy. Lenny's going to live with us and she's my girlfriend. I don't know where this will take us next but I know I want her here with us, and I love her."

There's a smile on her face, so cute and adorable. "I love her, too, but why does she get to sleep with you?"

And we're back to that.

"Because I get cold at night." More like my dick gets lonely.

Don't say that to her.

"Are you cold every night?"

"Yeah?" Yep. That's presented as a question.

"Maybe you need more blankets."

Fuck. How do I explain this?

"I have blankets. Lenny." Wrong fucking answer.

Nova stares at me, her face blank. "Can she sleep with me at least two days a week? You can have the other three."

She's negotiating a sleeping schedule already.

"We'll talk about it later."

With a heavy breath, she steps away and walks past Lenny in the hall. "You ready to go?" Lenny asks me. "Your mom's here to watch Nova so we can get my stuff and then you have your follow up with the doctor."

"Right... yes." I reach over, turn the light off to Nova's room, and then make my way out to the living room to see Nova sitting on the couch, arms crossed over her chest and refusing to look at me.

"What's wrong with Nova?" Lenny asks when we're in the car.

"She's upset you're sleeping in my room."

"Oh, poor girl." She can't control the burst of laughter that leaves her lips as we pull out of the driveway.

"No. Poor me. Think of *me* in this situation."

She laughs.

AS WE PULL up to the shop, I park behind Raven's car as a rush of emotions hit me because so many times my life has changed here, inside that building. It's just a building surrounded by four walls but when you think about it, Nevaeh told me she was pregnant in there. I asked her to marry me in the parts room and Nova took her first step inside there. My dad died on the floor in front of me, I fucked Lenny against a workbench in there, and finally, I was shot and nearly died in almost the exact same spot my dad died.

So yeah, this place holds a lot of memories for me. It's different now. I still own the business and run it, but I'm a little more laid back then I have been in the past. Mostly because I've come to realize I have a family who's there to support me when life's unsteady. You can't always be strong on two feet. Sometimes you need others to give you a little balance. I have that now.

Lenny stares at my keys as I give her the key to my house when we're just about ready to leave the apartment with the last of her things. "Where'd your ring go?"

"I gave it to Nevaeh this morning," I say smoothly, no expression on my face. "I think it's best she has it."

"You did what?" She eyes me with a calculating expression. "Someone's going to steal that, Red."

I shrug. "Probably." I knew someone would, but it was more about me moving on than it was about someone stealing it.

"Just tell me what you want from me?" Tyler shouts behind the closed door of his room. I hadn't even realized he was here.

Both Lenny and I stop what we're doing and look at each other.

"You know, I've been putting on a show in front of my brother, your friends, work, all that, but I'm tired of pretending. I'm leaving in two days. Tell me where we stand," the girl yells back.

I chuckle, shaking my head. "Sounds like Berkley and Tyler are at it again."

Lenny's eyes widen. "We have to go, *now*."

That voice... it sounds strangely familiar. It's not Berkley's. I'd know Berkley's soft voice anywhere.

"What the fuck is *she* doing in there?" I ask Lenny, knowing by the look of surprise on her face, she knows that's Raven in Tyler's room.

Raven. As in *my* little sister.

There's an imperceptible note of pleading in her face. "Calm down."

"I won't calm down." Lenny physically blocks me from going into the room. "Did you know about them?"

Her eyes widen. "Yes, *but* it wasn't my place to say anything."

I throw my arms up backing away from her. "What the fuck is wrong with people thinking they know what's best for me?"

She glares at me, never backing down. She's incapable of it. "What's your problem with them being together if they're happy?"

"There's six years between them!" I practically shout as she pushes me out the door and down the stairs.

There's a smile creeping across her face and I don't like it. Mostly because it's making me weak. "There's four between us."

"So."

"Is this our first fight?" she asks, walking backwards until her back hits the side of my car.

My expression softens. My anger is immediately replaced by something else when she bites down on her bottom lip. I want to be mad, I do, but she has a way with me. "You know what that means, right?"

"Make-up sex?"

I nod, leaning in to kiss her, realizing this is a distraction, but I'm okay with it. "Should we try out the workbench again?"

"You read my mind."

I could stay mad, and I'll probably have some words with Tyler about him and my sister but this, Lenny moaning my name as I fuck her against the bench in the shop, there's nowhere else I'd rather be.

My dad once told me your life is like an internal combustion engine. Essentially an engine goes through four stages. The suck-squeeze-bang-blow theory.

For a while, I wondered why he compared life to an engine.

I guess, in some ways, I understand now. Every step you take, every breath, every choice, it all leads to another change, another cycle in the process. An endless cycle of change. While an engine has one set cycle, life does too.

Everything leads back to the start, the suck, the give and take.

"I love you," she whispers against my neck, her breathing heavy and strained as she arches into me.

I press my lips to the sensitive skin above her collarbone, the spot I know she loves. "I'll never let you forget it either."

ALSO BY SHEY STAHL

RACING ON THE EDGE

Happy Hour

Black Flag

Trading Paint

The Champion

The Legend

Hot Laps

The Rookie

Fast Time

Open Wheel

Pace Laps

Dirt Driven

Behind the Wheel – Series outtakes (TBA)

STAND ALONES

All I Have Left

Awakened

Everlasting Light

Bad Blood

Heavy Soul

Bad Husband

Burn

Love Complicated

Untamed

How to Deal

Promise Not to Fall

Blindsided

Revel

Sex. Love. Marriage.

Saving Barrette

Redemption

Room 4 Rent

When We Met

Paper Hearts

Between the Stars - Coming Soon

THE FMX SERIES

Shade

Tiller

Roan

Camden

CROSSING THE LINE

Delayed Penalty

Delayed Offsides

Delayed Roughing (TBA)

THE TORQUED TRILOGY

Unsteady

Unbearable

Unbound

ANCHORED LOVE

The Sea of Light

The Sea of Lies (TBA)

The Sea of Love (TBA)

AUTHOR ACKNOWLEDGMENTS

I write so many of these lately I never know what to say anymore, or if anyone actually reads this part of the book. I hope they do!

The idea for Unsteady came to me because as most know, my husbands a mechanic. I grew up around cars and racing so naturally everything I hold passion in, writing included, will steer that way. There's two more books to this series and I can't wait to complete the story.

Thank you to Becky with Hot Tree Editing. I learn so much from you.

Tracy Steeg, you're a beautiful person and always design the best cover designs, I adore you sweets!

Sara Eirew, thank you for the amazing photo. It's perfect for Red and Lenny.

Lauren, I'm so glad you responded to my need for a BETA reader, you wordy bitch, lol. Not only do you get invested in the characters with me, you believe in what I'm doing and that says a lot about you as a person. Love you girl! #heavysouls #wordybitch #tinyframes

Janet, Barb, Marisa, Shanna, Ashley's, Jill and Rachel, thanks for always being there for me.

To my girls in my groups and my readers, thank you so much for everything you do for me and our late night talks about nothing at all.

And finally, thank you to my family for always supporting me and this dream. Oh and my own personal mechanic for inspiring Red and all the other characters in this trilogy.

ABOUT THE AUTHOR

Shey Stahl is a USA Today and Amazon best-selling author. Rom-coms and sports romances with a unique writing style are her lady jam.

Her books have been translated into several languages, and if you haven't laughed, cried, and cursed in the same book, you're reading the wrong author. Shey lives in Washington State with her adrenaline-addicted husband, a moody preteen daughter, and their asshole cat.

In her spare time, she enjoys pretending to be Joanna Gaines while remodeling her house, iced coffee (only the good nugget ice), hiking in the mountains of the PNW, and hanging out at the local dirt tracks.

Made in the USA
Middletown, DE
08 October 2023